Seduced

Irresistible attraction—seduction guaranteed!

Praise for three best-selling authors –
Emma Darcy, Miranda Lee and Sophie Weston

About MARRIAGE MELTDOWN

'Fan-favourite Emma Darcy delivers a spicy love
story…a fiery conflict and a hot sensuality.'
—*Romantic Times*

About THE MILLIONAIRE'S MISTRESS

'Miranda Lee's latest book sizzles with
passionate characters, sensual scenes and
an enticing premise.'
—*Romantic Times*

About Sophie Weston

'Sophie Weston has wonderful character
and story development.'
—*Romantic Times*

Seduced

MARRIAGE MELTDOWN
by
Emma Darcy

THE MILLIONAIRE'S MISTRESS
by
Miranda Lee

THE INNOCENT AND
THE PLAYBOY
by
Sophie Weston

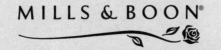

MILLS & BOON®

*MILLS & BOON and MILLS & BOON with the Rose Device
are registered trademarks of the publisher.*
Harlequin Mills & Boon Limited,
Eton House, 18-24 Paradise Road, Richmond, Surrey, TW9 1SR

SEDUCED © by Harlequin Enterprises II B.V., 2002

Marriage Meltdown, The Millionaire's Mistress and
The Innocent and the Playboy
were first published in Great Britain by Harlequin Mills & Boon Limited
in separate, single volumes.

Marriage Meltdown © Emma Darcy 1997
The Millionaire's Mistress © Miranda Lee 1998
The Innocent and the Playboy © Sophie Weston 1997

ISBN 0 263 83156 6

05-0502

*Printed and bound in Spain
by Litografía Rosés S.A., Barcelona*

Initially a French/English teacher, **Emma Darcy** changed careers to computer programming before marriage and motherhood settled her into a community life. Creative urges were channelled into oil-painting, pottery, designing and overseeing the construction and decorating of two homes, all in the midst of keeping up with three lively sons and the very social life of her businessman husband, Frank. Very much a people person, and always interested in relationships, she finds the world of romance fiction a happy one and the challenge of creating her own cast of characters very addictive.

Emma Darcy is the author of more than 75 novels including the international bestseller, THE SECRETS WITHIN, published by MIRA® Books.

She enjoys travelling and often her experiences find their way into her books. Emma Darcy lives on a country property in New South Wales, Australia.

Look out for Emma's latest passion-filled stories in her *Kings of Australia* trilogy, in Modern Romance™

THE ARRANGED MARRIAGE – June
THE BRIDAL BARGAIN – July
THE HONEYMOON CONTRACT – August

MARRIAGE MELTDOWN
by
Emma Darcy

CHAPTER ONE

FROM an outsider's point of view, Gina Tyson had the perfect marriage. Some days Gina could actually pretend it was. After all, she had a beautiful home right on the shoreline at Bondi, Sydney's most famous and picturesque beach. She had three lovely children, two boys and a girl. She had a husband any woman would envy…on the surface. Not only was Reid tall, dark and dynamically handsome, he was wealthy enough to deal with life on his terms.

Nevertheless, *surface* was the key word. Her marriage was wonderfully smooth and shiny up-front. Underneath, Gina was going slowly mad with frustration. And behind the frustration was the gnawing fear that this was all she could ever expect with Reid—house, family and a token man at her side. Her husband lived his own life, which Gina felt was one step removed from her, even when he was with her. As now.

She had cooked his favourite dinner tonight—escallops of veal in white wine. He was enjoying it, too, at the other end of the table, not sharing his enjoyment with her. The intimate eye contact and appreciative comments she craved were not forthcoming. Indeed, none of the special effort she'd made was

having the desired effect. Which was hardly a recommendation for the advice in the magazine articles
on how to revitalise your marriage.

Her personal re-imaging was a miserable failure. If
Reid had noticed any difference in her appearance, it
was obviously irrelevant to him. He certainly hadn't
been sparked into seeing her as a newly desirable
woman. Gina wondered if she should have been more
daring.

She'd flirted with the idea of having her hair dra-
matically cut, but it had always been long, and in the
end she couldn't bear the thought of the lustrous mass
of rich brown locks dropping in limp, dead chunks
onto the salon floor. She had compromised. The thick
waves were now cleverly layered to her shoulders,
giving her hair more bounce and curl.

The beautician had given her amber eyes a deeper,
almost mysterious look with artfully applied make-
up. Her eyebrows were more neatly arched. She was
assured that the russet red of the lipstick and nail polish was a power colour. It was all wasted on Reid,
even the new clothes over which she'd spent hours
making up her mind.

To her, the black satin lounging trousers and the
tiger print silk chiffon tunic with the gold chain belt
had seemed a sexy outfit, elegant and sensually alluring. It hadn't raised so much as a flicker of interest
from Reid. Maybe if she'd made a bolder choice,
been bolder about everything…but it wasn't in her
nature to be bold.

Her Italian mother had drummed ladylike principles into her precious little Gianetta from birth. A good Italian girl—never mind that Gina's father was fourth-generation Australian—did not flaunt her body in an immodest fashion. Clothes should grace women, not expose them. Perhaps because she had only been seventeen when her mother had died, Gina couldn't feel comfortable betraying her advice, yet sometimes she wished she could be like the women who had no shame at all in what they wore, or didn't wear.

On the other hand, maybe it simply wasn't possible to jolt Reid into re-appraising her and her place in his life. Any change she made he would view as purely superficial, like a change of decor in the house. If it pleased her, that was fine by him. It wouldn't affect what he thought or felt or did.

Like her futile attempt at evoking a romantic mood with the table setting tonight. Reid had remarked on the centrepiece of exotic tiger lilies and golden candles, inquiring if she was experimenting for some future dinner party. An innovative change from roses, he'd said. It didn't occur to him it might be especially for the two of them. Gina had felt too deflated to tell him.

There was no obvious romance in the dinner service. Reid didn't believe in keeping the best for visitors or putting it aside for good, as her mother used to. They dined in the dining room every night, using silver cutlery, Royal Doulton or Spode crockery, the very finest crystal glasses—Lalique tonight. It's not for show, it's for use, Reid insisted, when Gina worried about breaking something. Nothing was irreplaceable, he invariably said, but Gina didn't entirely agree with that sentiment.

She toyed with the food on her plate, unable to muster up an appetite. The dearth of emotional rapport with Reid was deeply troubling. It hadn't been so obvious when they'd been involved with having babies. Both of them loved their children. But had Reid ever really loved her? Gina was beginning to doubt it. Worse, she was beginning to wonder if some other woman supplied what he didn't look for in her.

'Is there anything that requires my personal attention before I fly off on Sunday?'

Reid's bland inquiry scraped over a string of raw nerves. Gina wanted to scream, *I do!* but when her gaze flashed up to meet his, the look of impersonal weighing in his eyes shrivelled the hotly impulsive response. He meant possible problems relating to the house, car or children. He wasn't anticipating any. Just checking.

Gina swallowed her private angst and played the checking game, too. 'The trip is only for a fortnight, isn't it? One week in London? One in Paris?'

'Yes. The business meetings are all lined up. I don't expect any hitches.'

'Neither do I. If needs must, I'll get in touch with you.'

He nodded, returning his attention to his plate as he said, 'I'll be staying at Durley House in London.

It's in Knightsbridge. Quite close to Harrod's if there's something you fancy my picking up for you there. I'll give you the contact numbers before I go.'

Reid Tyson went on eating his dinner as though he had said nothing to concern his wife in any way whatsoever. Maybe he hadn't, Gina argued, clinging to the craven desire not to confront. She didn't want to look foolish, yet every female instinct she had was aquiver, twanging a warning. This business trip to Europe was not the same as previous ones. Deep in her gut, Gina knew it. And Reid had just given her the first tangible evidence of it.

'Why the change?' she asked, her tone as light as she could make it, pretending ordinary wifely interest, pretending she had nothing to worry about, pretending everything in her personal garden was still rosy.

Reid gave her a blank look, his mind obviously having moved on from the delivery of a piece of information she had to know should an emergency arise at home. Gina felt stupid for pursuing something that seemed to be of no consequence to him. He raised an eyebrow, trapping her into explaining her question.

'You've always stayed at Le Meridien in London. Why not this time? I thought you were happy with it,' she said, shrugging to deny any suggestion of concern on her part, projecting idle curiosity with almost painful intensity.

'Familiarity has advantages. It can also become boring. I felt like a change.'

Familiarity…boring…change… Was she hopelessly neurotic applying those words to his feelings about her? Acutely sensitive to the distance between them, the lack of true intimacy, Gina watched Reid return his attention to the veal on his plate, watched him carve the meat with expert precision and fork it into his mouth in a steady rhythm that denied any perturbation of spirit.

Sometimes Gina found his self-sufficiency chilling. She did now. It spurred her to engage his attention further, whether he liked it or not.

'I've never heard of Durley House. Does it belong to some European chain of hotels?'

He shook his head, his expression dismissive as he chewed on.

'How did it attract your interest?' Gina persisted. 'A business brochure?'

'Does it matter? I'm booked there now—' a sardonic twist of his lips '—for better or for worse. I'll leave you the contact numbers. I promise it won't be any problem to you.'

The flippant use of words from their marriage vows and the note of condescension in his promise goaded Gina into a mutinous stance. 'Is it too much trouble for you to answer some perfectly natural inquiries from me, Reid?'

His look of surprise evoked a self-conscious flush. It was highly uncharacteristic of her to challenge him in any shape or form. He was eleven years older, almost forty to her relatively youthful twenty-eight, and very much a mature, sophisticated and successful man of the world. He specialised in electronics, becoming a high flyer in that field in his mid-twenties, running an international business long before he'd swept Gina off her feet and into marriage. He was a man of incisive decisions, totally self-assured and confident of carrying off any task he set himself.

For the past six years Gina had been happy to go along with whatever he directed. After all, it was rather overwhelming to be provided with everything she wanted, and Reid had been doing that from the first day they'd met. It wasn't that she was submissive. Raising questions simply hadn't seemed appropriate. Until now.

It was more than six years, almost seven, she corrected herself. The seven-year itch was not a cliché without good reason. Gina didn't want to acknowledge it but she felt Reid was losing—had lost—interest in her as a woman. Making love had become an occasional perfunctory act since the birth of their daughter, their third child and the much-wanted girl to complete their planned family. It was as though Gina had now served her purpose for him and she was relegated to the role of mother of his children.

The miserable, hollow feeling she'd been doing her best to repress for months swallowed her up again. She stared at Reid's surprised look, a rebellious demand in her eyes, uncaring what he thought of her reproof, needing answers. She didn't want to live out the rest of her life with him like this. She was only twenty-eight. The rest of her life comprised a lot of years. It wasn't that she wanted more from him. She wanted more *of* him.

His eyes narrowed thoughtfully, riveting blue eyes, dynamic in their impact when they focused on a problem. 'What are you upset about?' he asked, adopting an air of patience as he set what was left of his meal aside and picked up his glass of wine. He relaxed in his chair and waited for her to enlighten him. His mouth softened into an encouraging little smile.

It made Gina feel like a fractious child. He was prepared to indulge her with his attention for as long as it took to sort out her troubles. He listened. He always listened. Yet somehow there was never really any two-way communication. He focused entirely on her, drawing out her thoughts and dealing with them constructively without ever really revealing his.

She used to find this immensely flattering—such single-minded concentration on her needs and desires. It demonstrated a depth of caring that cocooned her in emotional security. But she'd come to recognise it as the kind of security one gave to a child who wasn't expected to comprehend anything beyond her own self-absorbed world. Gina now found the attitude intensely frustrating. It was like a blind, behind which Reid kept his private thoughts, his inner life, totally hidden.

'Do you realise we don't talk about anything except what's happened with the children?' she blurted, her hands lifting in agitation as she took the bull of contention by the horns. 'Or what I've bought for the house or garden or myself or… It's all domestic stuff. Trivial bits of home life.'

His eyebrows momentarily drew together. They smoothed as he delivered a calmly considered reply. 'I don't find them trivial. Why should you? I clearly recall you telling me your main ambition in life was to be a home-maker for the family you wanted to have.'

It was true. It was still true. And Gina suspected it was why Reid had married her—a young, fertile woman who was eagerly prepared to give him the family denied him by his first wife. The reminder of her personally favoured and chosen life path was delivered in a reasonable tone that somehow suggested Gina was being unreasonable in her criticism of its inevitable outcome. She floundered, trying to find words to express what she meant.

'Is it suddenly less satisfying than you expected it to be?'

There was a hard edge to Reid's question.

'Stop turning this back onto me,' she flared. 'It's you I want to know more about. Why can't you answer my questions instead of dismissing them out of hand?'

He made an apologetic gesture. 'Tell me where and how I've offended.' His voice relaxed into a dryly amused tone. 'I didn't realise I was cutting off some burning point of curiosity.'

Gina burned, all right, but not with curiosity. He was making her sound ridiculously pettish, and she saw nothing at all petty about her concerns. They were important, critical to filling in what was missing in their relationship. Missing for her, anyway. She took a deep breath and spoke with slow deliberation, determined not to have her questions brushed aside as irrelevant.

'I was asking you about Durley House.'

'So you were,' he replied, hardly forthcoming.

Gina gritted her teeth. She would not be deterred. 'What does it have to recommend it to you?'

'I told you. It'll be a change.'

'How much of a change?'

'It's a small place in comparison, away from the big hotel scene, less impersonal, more geared to making people feel at home.' He rattled out the information in a matter-of-fact tone.

'Sounds cosy.'

'One would hope so.' Said with a finality that suggested her curiosity should now be satisfied.

Gina didn't care for the idea of Reid being cosy with his personal assistant, who was accompanying him on this trip. Paige Calder might be a career-oriented woman, but the sleekly groomed, thirty-something blonde certainly wasn't sexless. She wasn't married or living with a partner, either, and she could hardly fail to find Reid attractive.

Not only did he have the aura of power that all women found fascinating, he was a strikingly handsome man who seemed to get even better-looking as he grew older, more impressive, more distinguished, more everything, and still not a thread of grey in his glossy black hair or an inch of flab on his superbly muscled body.

Paige had been with Reid for six months now, having come to him with such an amazing list of credits in her career résumé only a fool would have failed to employ her. On the other hand, personal assistant to Reid Tyson was a plum job that had drawn many highly qualified people. Gina had a niggling wish that the successful applicant had not been quite so svelte in her fashion sense or so perfectly polished in her manner.

Was it coincidence that Gina had grown more and more aware of the distance between herself and Reid over the past six months? Was Paige Calder providing cause and effect? Had *she* suggested they would be more comfortably accommodated at Durley House while in London?

'How small do you mean?' Gina felt impelled to ask, hoping it wasn't too intimate. 'Is it a boutique hotel with only a few rooms?'

With an air of finishing the subject once and for all, Reid gave what he probably considered a comprehensive rundown on the place. 'It doesn't have rooms in the hotel sense. Durley House specialises in suites, and there are only eleven of them. They provide full secretarial and office facilities with fax machines, twenty-four-hour room service, private parties organised if required. A nice touch to doing business over there.'

And Paige would brilliantly fulfil the role of hostess for him, Gina thought jealously. 'Well, I hope it will prove a good move for you,' she said, trying to be fair-minded. 'With you and Paige taking up two of the suites, you're sure to get every attention from the staff.'

Reid's gaze dropped to the glass in his hand. He swirled the wine as though examining it for colour. Gina smothered an exasperated sigh over his shuttered expression. She couldn't force him to open up to her. Suspecting Paige Calder of encouraging infidelity was probably rather ridiculous. Reid wouldn't be inveigled into doing anything he didn't want to do. He chose. All the same, Gina felt there was more behind the choice of Durley House than Reid was revealing.

'One suite,' came the firm correction. 'It's a two-bedroom apartment with its own drawing room, kitchen, bathroom…like a home away from home.' He flicked her a derisive look. 'There's no point in having two suites.'

Gina's stomach contracted as though it had been punched. She sucked in a quick breath and didn't pause to monitor the words that buzzed through her mind like a chainsaw. 'You're sharing this home away from home with your personal assistant?' Her voice sounded high and brittle.

'It's the most convenient arrangement,' he casually affirmed.

'Very convenient.' Her voice got more full-bodied

as her blood heated up. 'Did it occur to you that I might object?'

He looked at her weighingly. 'Why should you?'

'I don't care to have you living with another woman, Reid.'

'This is a business trip, Gina. I live here. With you. I'm going away on business. I'll be returning to live here. With you. What possible objection can you have to Paige being on hand while I'm doing business?'

Oh, the measured condescension of that little speech! Gina churned. He might—*might*—be innocent of ulterior motives, but what thoughts were thriving in the mind of his oh-so-personal personal assistant? And had Reid given her cause to think them, flirting with the possibility and opportunity for sex on the side?

'Did Paige Calder suggest this Durley House to you?' Gina probed, determined now on having that point satisfied.

'Yes, she did.' No hesitation. No flicker of guilt. 'One of her former employers used it. She thought I would benefit from it.'

'Not to mention herself.' The words steamed out.

Reid put on his stony face, the one that stopped an excess of rowdy nonsense from his sons. 'That's an unbecoming remark, Gina. Paige will be working as hard, if not harder than I will on this trip, keeping on top of the paperwork.'

If that's all she keeps on top of, Gina thought savagely, her fevered imagination seeing the long-legged blonde taking every advantage of the situation. She picked up her glass of wine and took a deliberate sip, trying to cool down, trying to match Reid's crushing control.

She didn't like being accused of unbecoming behaviour. Maybe she had an old-fashioned mentality, but she found it unbecoming for her husband to be sharing an apartment with another woman, business or not. She could hardly demand that he not go, but there was a resolution to her heartburn.

'I'd like to be with you on this trip, Reid. It's not too late to arrange, is it? Even if I have to take a different flight.'

'Why on earth—' He grimaced and rolled his head as though she had come up with the ultimate absurdity. 'If you'd like a trip to Europe, Gina, I'll give you one. Properly planned and organised so you can tour with pleasure and comfort, seeing and doing all you want to see and do. It needs thought and—'

'I want to be with you on this trip. Just to be with you,' she insisted with stubborn determination not to be put off.

Reid heaved an impatient sigh. He held her gaze with intimidating steadiness as he spoke, measuring his words slowly to make sure they sank in. 'I'll be working day in, day out. It's totally impractical, your accompanying me. I won't have time to entertain you.'

She measured her words right back at him, bristling at the intimation that she couldn't handle herself independently of him. 'I don't need you to entertain me, Reid. I can entertain myself. I've been doing it for long enough while you work. I can do it in London and in Paris, too. And when you've finished work for the day, I can make sure the apartment *is* a home away from home for you.'

'I'm paying for that already.' He put down his glass, pushed back his chair and stood up, tall and formidable and forbidding. 'This is a ridiculous idea, Gina. Give it away, there's a good girl.'

'I'm not a child!' she hurled after him as he turned away from the table.

He paused, looking over his shoulder, ice to her fire. 'Then act responsibly. Give some thought to our children. You've never left them before. To go flying off to Europe at a moment's notice doesn't exactly prepare them for the absence of their mother. If you want to spread your wings, at least do it with some reasonable forethought and not on a blindly possessive impulse.'

On that note of chilly condemnation he walked out on her, heading, no doubt, for his private den where he played endlessly on his computers or fiddled with his sound system to find some extra tonal quality.

Possessive...

Why did Reid make it sound mean-hearted?

Didn't she have the right to be possessive?

He was *her* husband.

Her hand was trembling as she set her glass on the table. She withdrew it to her lap and sat with both hands clenched there, struggling to contain the turbulence tearing through her, the hurt, the fear, the dreadful uncertainties, the sickening sense of emptiness.

She was a good mother.

She wanted to be a good wife.

One did not preclude the other, did it?

She wouldn't desert the children with people they didn't know. It was only for two weeks. They would miss her, but it wouldn't do them any harm. Maybe it was hopelessly wrong of her to hang so much on this trip, but she couldn't shake it off. Somehow, it portended the course of her marriage. She had to go. She had to change the ground between herself and Reid and make him see her as a person, as a woman, as a wife.

She had to be more than the mother of his children!

CHAPTER TWO

GINA stilled her hairbrush in midair. Her heart took an agitated leap and catapulted around her chest. Reid was coming up the stairs, his footfalls slow, heavy…tired? It was almost midnight. What if he was too tired? It could be embarrassing, humiliating.

The thought blew her mind into frantic activity. She didn't have to go through with this tonight. Tomorrow might be better. Tomorrow she could work at putting him into a more mellow mood over dinner and then she would feel more comfortable about making an approach.

Her gaze flew to the king-size bed, where the decorative cushions in navy and gold satin had already been removed and the deep cream top sheet was turned down ready for occupation. She had time to dive under the covers. The bed was so wide—a mistake, Gina often thought—they rarely touched in it by accident. Reid wouldn't know what she was wearing.

Giving in to last-minute panic, Gina leapt to her feet, almost tipping over the stool in her haste to move away from the dressing table. She was halfway to the bed before she realised she still held the hairbrush, having wielded it mindlessly for the past hour.

Swinging around to replace it on the table, she

caught sight of herself in the winged mirror—three images of a woman in frightened flight. It jolted her into a defiant stance. What was she afraid of, for heaven's sake?

There was nothing wrong with a wife showing her husband she was willing, interested, wanting him. Even if he was too tired, the promise was extended for when he did feel like it. The blatant invitation of the wickedly designed nightgown had to leave him in no doubt intimacy was desired. If she couldn't carry this off with aplomb, she was a hopeless case.

Besides, his response should indicate whether her marriage was in serious trouble or not. It had to be faced, before he went off on this trip with Paige Calder. Hiding her head in the sand—or the pillows—was not going to help resolve anything or make the problem go away.

Cowardly cover-ups were out.

Naked truth was the way to go.

Well, not quite naked. An ironic smile flitted over her lips. The nightie allowed her some dignity if Reid ignored or dismissed its purpose.

She ran the brush through her hair again, trying to act naturally as the door she'd left ajar was pushed open and Reid stepped inside their bedroom. She always left his bedside lamp on for him, so the soft light in the room did not initially alert him to any difference in the normal routine.

For the moment before he realised she was not in bed asleep, he looked weary and dispirited, as though the world he inhabited was not a good place. His shirt sleeves were rolled up his forearms, his vest unbuttoned, tie hanging loose, suitcoat slung over one shoulder, hooked on the thumb of his right hand. Then awareness snapped through him, straightening the slump of his body, tightening his face, sharpening his eyes.

He looked at her, stared at her, tension beating from him and striking her with a force that squeezed her heart. Something almost violent flashed across his face. A muscle spasmed in his cheek. His chin jerked up slightly. Then he stepped back, closed the door behind him and with the air of a man casually surveying the talent, propped himself against the doorjamb and ran his gaze over the points of interest drawn by exotic lace patterns on the soft lustre of red satin.

It wasn't flattering. It wasn't exciting. It was shaming. It made her feel like a street girl with her wares on show. Her nipples peaked in an agony of self-consciousness. Her stomach cramped into knots. A painful flush clung to her skin.

It didn't matter that she told herself the nightie was more tantalisingly suggestive than revealing. Reid's penetrating perusal stripped her of any sense of allure or protection. It blasted her confidence and left her helplessly tongue-tied, knowing with devastating certainty she had somehow made a dreadful mistake.

'So it's finally occurred to you I'm a man,' Reid drawled. 'I daresay it's difficult for you to move me out of the habitual slot of prime provider…with sperm bank attached.'

Gina's jaw dropped. His words fell like beads of acid on her brain, burning through the initial shock of them and forcing her to seek some mitigation from their painful impact. 'I don't think of you like that!' she sputtered.

'Too crude and down-to-earth for you? I guess you have me more nicely pigeonholed as *father of my children.* Same thing.'

The stunning turnaround of what she believed was how *he* thought of *her* left Gina speechless.

'You must have been screwing yourself up to offering me the use of your body since dinner,' he went on, waving dismissively at her supposedly seductive gown as he moved away from the door and strolled over to the valet chair on his side of the room. He grimaced an apology. 'Sorry I'm not appreciating the effort. It probably cost you a lot in personal turmoil. But I'd rather you didn't…suffer me—' eyes piercingly cold '—out of some mistaken notion of saving our marriage.'

Gina felt as though all the air had been sucked out of her body. She seemed to hang in some sort of suspended animation, her gaze fixed on him as his appalling perspective pummelled her mind. She'd wanted him to open up, wanted the truth of where she stood with him, but the bitter feelings he seemed to be nursing… Surely this was a distortion.

Had he been drinking in his den? He sometimes

had a glass or two of port. Yet if alcohol had loosened his usual control, maybe this was what he truly felt.

He draped his coat on the back of the chair, undid his tie, slid it out from under his collar, dropped it over the coat, each action performed with calm deliberation. There was no obvious evidence of barely repressed volcanic anger, yet the sense of electric vibrations that could connect at any moment hummed through the room.

'You can relax, Gina,' he assured her with a mocking little smile. 'Our marriage is not under threat. Just as you need me to support the children, I need you to keep my family with me. So you don't have to do anything. Your position as my wife is unassailable.'

His bitter logic goaded her into pained protest. 'I don't *suffer* you. How can you use such a word? What possible cause have I given you to even think it?'

'Too strong for you?' he retorted flippantly, tossing his vest on the seat of the chair. His fingers worked down the buttons of his shirt as he weighed her protest, eyeing her consideringly. 'Well, maybe it just feels that way to me,' he conceded. 'You probably think of it as *letting him do it.*'

She lifted her hands in agitated supplication. 'Reid, I'm happy for you to—to…'

'Sate my male urges with you when I need to?'

'I meant for us to make love.'

He laughed mirthlessly. 'When have you ever made love to me, Gina? You taking some active initiative apart from wearing tonight's bit of lingerie? And that's only a signal, isn't it? You didn't mean to actually do anything yourself.'

Gina was thrown into helpless confusion. It was plain enough that Reid saw her as a totally inadequate sexual partner, yet she didn't understand what she had done wrong. Her mother had always told her it was sluttish to be forward. A gentleman led. A lady followed. Men did the chasing. Women had the right of saying yes or no. Her upbringing had been steeped in such dictums.

But surely Reid knew she responded to his kisses and caresses, and took intense pleasure in the act of intimacy. Sometimes the feelings were so overwhelming she quite shamefully lost control of herself, hardly knowing what was happening to her. Had Reid interpreted her cries at such times as suffering?

'What would you like me to do?' she asked, bewildered, needing instruction, struggling to come to terms with his accusation.

He was already bending to remove his shoes and socks and didn't bother looking at her. 'Forget it, Gina,' he said in a fed-up tone. 'One can't manufacture desire. It's either there or it's not.'

Did he mean him or her?

He was wrong if he thought she didn't want him. With his shirt off and his torso bare, the golden sheen of his skin in the lamplight was enticing. He was a beautifully made man and a wonderfully masterful lover. This past month she had lain awake many nights, willing him to reach out for her. Would it help now if she reached out to him? Initiated action?

He dragged off his trousers and underpants. It was immediately obvious Reid was feeling no desire. Afraid of making even more of a fool of herself in his eyes, Gina stifled the fluttering impulse to close the distance between them. He shot her a look of steely pride as he straightened up, moody and magnificent in flaunting his nakedness in front of her.

It made Gina feel crippled with inhibitions that she couldn't do the same, that she needed some dressing on her body to cover a multitude of sins, her mother would have said. Yet in her mind and heart Gina knew there shouldn't be any sins if a couple truly loved each other. Why couldn't she put that into practice?

'I'm sorry for…for not being what you want,' she blurted in deep anguish of spirit.

'Don't look so stricken. It's not the end of the world. Just the end of pretence.'

'No.' She shook her head vehemently. 'You've got that wrong, Reid.'

'Try some honesty, Gina.' His eyes glittered with derision as he spelled out his interpretation of honesty for her. 'You don't want me, but you don't want anyone else to have me. That's what this is about, isn't it? I have to give him this or he might have it with Paige Calder.'

He had things half right, making them all the more difficult to refute. She desperately didn't want him going to some other woman, but she hadn't thought of using her body as a bargaining chip to stop him. It was her need to feel closer to him that had motivated her action tonight.

'Let me tell you something, Gina,' he went on, his eyes searing her with contempt from head to foot. 'Sexiness is not an erotic arrangement of satin and lace. It's not a lush female body. It's a state of mind.' He tapped his forehead. 'It's what's buzzing through your brain cells.' He turned his hand out to her in emphatic demonstration. 'It's an intense focus on another person.' He stabbed a finger of accusation. 'And you don't do that. You're always focused on yourself.'

'No, that's not true,' Gina cried, desperate to turn this awful debacle around. It was so crushingly negative.

Reid waved in disgust at her denial. 'Even what you chose to wear—supposedly for my pleasure—is designed to focus attention on you.'

'I meant you to see that I do want you, Reid,' she pleaded.

'Sure you do.' Disbelief slicing her contention into tatters. 'Like so urgently you wait up here for hours, titivating yourself up, brushing your hair.' He moved towards the ensuite bathroom, tossing scorn at her as he went. 'Something wrong with your legs, Gina, that you couldn't come to me? Something wrong with your mouth that you couldn't use it to communicate your burning desire, one way or another?'

'I waited because I didn't want to interrupt you—' and risk rejection '—if you were doing something important.'

'Something more important than my wife actively wanting me?' he mocked, anger edging his voice, biting out at her. 'Well, clearly, we have a different set of priorities. Now if you'd sashayed down the stairs in that nightie, wriggled onto my lap, hung your arms around my neck and told me, with the punctuation of a few hungry kisses, that you were tired of waiting and you wanted me right now...' He snapped his fingers like a magician producing a conjuring trick.

Gina fiercely wished she'd had the courage and confidence to have done precisely that.

Reid reached the bathroom door and paused, giving her a deadly little smile to herald his final indictment of her behaviour. 'But we both know you don't want me that much. Easier to wait and let Reid do the work if he feels in the mood. Then you can simply lie back and think of Durley House and England.'

The anger seething through his words shut off all avenues for any open-minded listening. Gina shook her head over his twisted reasoning, and even that action seemed to incense him. His eyes blazed blue fury, denying her any defence.

'I'm sure you won't mind excusing me from this increasingly distasteful scene. I need a *hot* shower.'

Oh, the scathing emphasis on that blistering piece of irony as he thrust the bathroom door open. He topped it off with a final bitter blast.

'Your goddamned nightie, your goddamned selfishness and your goddamned assumptions leave me
bloody cold.'

He used the door to shut her off and shut her out.

Gina wasn't feeling so hot herself. For several
minutes her body was racked with convulsive shivers.
The horrifying revelations of how Reid saw their relationship held her paralysed, staring at the bathroom
door as though it was the door to hell.

An intensely strong and tormenting survival instinct told her she had to go through that door.
Somehow she had to make herself do it. Because Reid
was wrong about her, and if she didn't show him he
was wrong—right now—she'd never be able to. So
she had to go and open that door and... Her mind
couldn't come to grips with what should happen next
but something would, something that had to be better
than the nothing Reid had left her with.

CHAPTER THREE

IF SHE let herself think, Gina knew she would lose her nerve. *Just take one step at a time,* she instructed herself, *and don't dwell on what you're doing or what he'll do.* The ensuite bathroom was her bathroom, too, and she had every right to step into it. Which she did. Then, mercifully, sounds and sights filled her thinking space.

Water splashing against the tiles—beautiful Italian tiles that shimmered with a mother-of-pearl sheen, running from floor to ceiling, a gleaming cascade of subtle colour. Steam swirling from the shower stall, making misty patterns on the glass, inviting magically disappearing finger drawing.

Lots of glass, a luxuriously spacious shower big enough for two, though she'd never shared it with Reid. Timing was always wrong. No, that was an excuse, an evasion, rising out of an excruciating self-consciousness that manufactured excuses and evasions… A natural shyness made worse from having babies—bulging belly, stretch marks, breasts bursting with milk, veins showing blue on her thighs. So many years of shrinking from letting Reid see her naked.

Yet she was in good shape now. No distortions. And the marks had faded. There was no reason not

31

to share his nakedness, every reason to, if she could only make herself do it, like on their honeymoon. Reid had coaxed her into feeling natural about it then, before she got pregnant. Why not again now? Why not?

Reid never minded being naked. She stared at him through the glass, admiring how perfect he still was...her husband. He stood with his back to the spray, the water beating on his head and shoulders, bouncing off his muscles, streaming down the curve of his spine, matting his hair. His eyes were closed, his lips thinned, his jawline tight and aggressive as though his teeth were clenched. His hands were curled into fists. However hot the water was, it was not ridding him of tension.

Explosive energy trapped inside him—that was how he looked. Terrible, turbulent energy trapped and being silently, grimly processed into something more manageable. Reid was so good at control. His loss of it tonight was a frightening measure of his dissatisfaction with her.

Fear swirled again in paralysing waves, fraying her courage, attacking her innermost soul, shaking her with a cyclone of devastating doubts. What if she didn't have it in her to give what would satisfy him? He was special. Everyone recognised and acknowledged that. While she...what had she ever done to be any kind of match for him? He'd chosen her to be the mother of his children. That was it. Fresh out of university, she hadn't even held down a proper job when Reid took over her life and gave it the purpose she'd wanted.

But now she felt hopelessly lost. *It wasn't supposed to turn out like this*, she cried in silent anguish. *I love him. I always have. And he feels cheated, too.* So he had expected more, wanted more from her, apart from the children. Tonight, with the stripping of pretence— however hurtful and shocking—there was the chance to do something. She had to try, had to, though how and with what God only knew.

Reid's head tipped back. His chest expanded as he drew in a deep breath. Then he was shifting position, turning, blowing out his pent-up feelings, opening his eyes…and he saw her standing there, staring at him. He stopped and stiffened, anger at her invasion of his privacy showing clearly on his face.

Gina felt like a rabbit caught in the glare of head-lights, death and destruction zooming at her far too fast for her to energise her shaky limbs even if she'd had a reaction planned. Which she hadn't. She had come to be with him because the emptiness was un-bearable. She hadn't meant to behave like a peeping Tom—was a woman called a Tom?

Reid leaned over and flung open the shower door. Suddenly he wasn't inside a glass enclosure, one step removed from her. He was hot, immediate reality, steaming flesh and muscle reaching for her, teeth gnashing, eyes blazing with fiercely challenging intent.

'You want me, Gina?'

His voice was hard, terse, savage, reflecting the expression on his face and the viselike grip of his fingers around her wrist. He yanked her into the shower stall with him, not waiting for a reply, uncaring. She had come after him. His whole body bristled as if to say, *Then come after me all the way.*

He caught her other wrist and pulled her under the spray, his eyes wildly exulting as her carefully coiffeured hair flattened under the beating water and the scorned nightie got an unceremonious drenching. 'Want to run back to safety now?' he taunted, releasing her in an exaggerated gesture of freedom granted.

Her heart quailed. There was not a gram of receptivity in Reid. It was torn out of him, and he was all primed to tear her apart. Yet what was safe? There was nowhere to run to even if it was possible to get her jelly-like legs to work. If she wanted a life with Reid she had to stay and hold her ground, no matter that she was scared stiff and teetering on collapsing in a heap.

'No,' she managed to croak. 'I'm staying here until you listen to me.' Maybe it was stubborn madness but she didn't care, was beyond caring. Somehow she had reached and passed the point of no return.

'Dangerous to tempt the devil you've raised,' he warned.

'I want you. I do. You've got it wrong, Reid,' she cried, lifting her hands to sweep the wet hair from her face so he could see she meant it, uncaring how she looked, driven to do whatever was necessary to convince him he was mistaken in what he thought of her.

In his eyes she saw cynical disbelief. 'Well, let's see how desperate you feel about it.' He took hold of the lace edging her cleavage and tore the centre seam open, ripping it down past her waist. His eyes gloated over the wreckage of the offensive nightie. 'That should help you show me how serious you are about wanting me.'

Gina was dazed by the unexpected act of violence, yet nervously encouraged by it, too. Reid wasn't turning away from her. He was confronting her assertion, giving her the chance to act on her words. It was shatteringly clear words alone would not touch him.

She didn't look down. She knew the wet satin was clinging to her hips and torn lace was flapping down the underside of her bared breasts. Her stomach was heaving, her thighs quivering, but with all the mental force she could muster, she quelled the panicky feelings of inadequacy. Her hands gathered purchase on the slippery fabric. With a sense of wild recklessness and total commitment, Gina ripped the seam completely asunder.

It startled Reid. It even sucked the breath out of him. His eyes widened in awed wonder, and Gina felt a dizzy rush of triumph. She'd done it! Stunned him out of his prejudiced mood. Only a momentary stunning wasn't enough. She had to overturn the cold, selfish image he held of her in his mind.

A sense of power zinged into her fingertips, dispelling the crippling fear and lending a somewhat tremulous confidence in what she was about to do. She kept her chin tilted high. So long as she didn't look down, she could pretend her body belonged to someone else, a bold, brazen woman who liked showing it off. It was easy then to hook the shoestring straps off her shoulders, thrusting her breasts out in proud nakedness as she wriggled out of the remnants of her nightie.

He looked down. He seemed fixated on the pulped pool of fabric at her feet. Acutely aware of its negative impact on Reid, Gina stepped out of it and kicked it aside. The nightie was finished with. Moving on from it was critical to establishing something different.

Strange how her mind had suddenly snapped into a supercharged state, working above the chaos of feeling that would normally confuse and torment and put her into a hopelessly dysfunctional state. Her nerves were thrumming and jumping, her insides were mush, her heart was booming all over the place—in her temples, her ears, her throat, her chest—yet her mind was floating, crystal-clear, ready to seize on Reid's reactions and find a positive response. Did shock do that? Or was it intense need?

All she really knew was her whole consciousness was filled with a sense of absolute crisis. Her life was turning on what happened now. Trivial actions were not trivial. They carried enormous meaning, levels and levels of meaning that stretched beyond her active comprehension and into the darker realms of instinct—deep and primal instinct.

Like getting rid of the nightie, shedding its connotations of rejection, because that was what this rift was about—perceptions of rejection, feelings of rejection, tunnelling deep and hurting to the point of spontaneous eruption.

It was gone now, the nightie, discarded, repulsed by both of them. The surprise on Reid's face was also gone. His expression hardened, giving nothing away as his gaze travelled up her nakedness and ruthlessly challenged her intent.

'So you've unwrapped the gift. Am I now expected to play with it?'

His eyes said nothing had changed if she wanted him to take over the action. His eyes said no way in the world was he going to do any touching or caressing or kissing tonight, just for her to fall back into a passive state and accept it all as her due or duty. His eyes said, *Your move, lady, and it had better be good.*

Inspiration or desperation, Gina didn't know which. She reached for the soap. 'Your muscles look so tight.' Her voice purred, probably the effect of being half-strangled with nervousness, but it came out huskily caring, which was good, because it was what she genuinely felt. She quickly laved her hands with creamy foam. 'I thought I could give your neck and shoulders a rub.' Fingers and thumbs sliding up the taut chords of his throat and down to work his flesh, digging and soothing. 'It might help you loosen up and relax.'

He wasn't sure. His eyes seared hers with questions. His chest contracted, recoiling from the brush of her breasts as she leaned forward to work on him. But it was only an initial, instinctive reaction to a touch he didn't trust. He remained still after that, a stillness that screamed of waiting, waiting to see how far she would go, how long she would or could sustain this role.

Manipulation for self-interest? Or a genuine wanting, a genuine giving?

True or false?

Focus on him, entirely on him, Gina fiercely instructed herself, and it made it easy to forget herself. The inhibitions that so frequently choked her impulses didn't get any room to play their usual havoc. She blocked them with blind determination to channel every bit of her energy into giving Reid the kind of pleasure he gave her when he made love. Because he was not wrong about that. He was the one who had always generated the pleasure, not her. She had not appreciated that abysmal failure on her part until tonight.

She massaged his shoulders with gentle pressures, then slid her hands over his chest, soft, soapy, slippery, sensually caressing, palms fanning his nipples, teasing them as he sometimes did hers, not knowing if it gave him similar sensations but hoping it did, wanting him to feel tingly and excited, wondering if he would be aroused if she ran her tongue over them. She bent her head to try it.

'No!' The word exploded from his lips. His hands flew up to snatch hers away from him. 'You don't have to make yourself do this, Gina. It's not necessary!' A strained, passionate denial of giving he couldn't accept, couldn't bear. He didn't believe in it. 'Don't you see?' His eyes were sick, tortured. 'It's too damned late!'

'But I can do it. I want to,' she insisted, pleading for the chance, needing to show him it pleased her to pleasure him.

'Why? Because you don't want to face the truth about yourself?' he mocked savagely. 'Because you're frightened of what it might mean to your future?' His face twisted in anger. 'Damn it! I told you it was safe.'

'I don't want your *safe*!' she exploded at him. 'I want to know what it takes to satisfy you.'

'What? So you can build up some secure little equation in your mind? If I give it to him three times a week—'

'No, no, no.' She shook her head in anguished frustration. 'I care about now. About how you're feeling.'

'And *you'll* feel better if you can think of me as having been fixed up. Satisfied.' He grasped her upper arms and shook her, his eyes wild with fury at her persistence. 'That's it, isn't it?'

'Yes,' she screamed, driven beyond any reasoning with him. 'Yes, I want you satisfied.'

'Right! Then we can scale down the seduction program and get to meltdown quite fast if it's only me
you want to satisfy.' He hoisted one of her arms over
his shoulder to hang around his neck, then guided her
other hand to his groin. 'It doesn't take much to
arouse a man. A little skilful manipulation. A few
kisses for encouragement. Show me how willing and
eager you are, Gina. Start kissing me.'

It was a command, ruthless in testing her claim and
its staying power when the going got rough. Shocked
by the ferocity of their interchange, she hooked her
arm more firmly around his neck, bringing his head
down so she could press her mouth to his, but the
distraction of his hand forcefully teaching hers how
to fire his manhood with desire made her lose all concentration on the kiss. It didn't exactly miss its mark,
but the delivery was haphazard.

'That kiss is about as exciting as a wet rag,' Reid
hissed.

She attacked with more vigour, shutting him up by
invading his mouth and shooting her tongue over his.
Then in some weirdly primitive way, the pumping of
their hands—tangling so intimately and excitingly
with their private parts—and the pumping of her heart
put a pumping rhythm into the kiss that Gina found
intensely erotic. And feeling Reid grow in her grasp
was even more erotic, the power of fast and furious
stroking inspiring her mouth to move in a wilder ex-
ploration of active sensation.

Just when they were attaining a stunningly new

level of togetherness, it was blown apart. Gina cried out in dismay as Reid wrenched his mouth from hers, took his hand away and hoisted her up against the shower wall, her feet dangling above the floor, her arms flailing against the abrupt detachment.

'Why? What?' she sputtered, floundering in confusion.

'Legs around my waist. Come on, Gina. Move it,' came the harshly urged instructions.

Dazed, she obeyed. He scooped an arm under her buttocks as she grabbed his shoulders for support and leverage. She almost levitated with shock as the hard, thick bolt of his shaft tunneled straight into her, so fast and deep her every nerve end sizzled and every inner muscle clenched at the invasion. The air whooshed out of her lungs. Her fingers curled into claws, nails biting into Reid's shoulder-blades.

'You wanted it,' he accused, as though excusing his roughness.

It was such an incredible feeling, his hotly throbbing fullness triggering a warm, convulsive creaming inside her. 'Yes,' she said fervently, then with newly enlightened curiosity sparking through her, she breathlessly asked, 'is this better for you?'

His laugh had a reckless edge to it, and he proceeded to give her a demonstration of piston-like action that raised more steam than the hot shower. Reid's energy was amazing. Gina figured he needed release from a lot of things and secretly exulted in having pushed him to this extraordinary encounter in their bathroom.

Incredulity kept billowing through her mind. To be doing it like this, standing up against the wall with water spraying over them! And it felt so wild and wonderful! Bed was far more comfortable, but... Gina suddenly comprehended completely how familiarity could be thought boring. This was certainly an exhilarating change. Bold and brazen, too. And she didn't mind a bit. Not one little bit!

She closed her eyes, revelling in the sheer wanton carelessness of it all, the freedom from any ritual, the totally uncivilised sense of flesh crashing into flesh and igniting explosions of sensations, one burst after another spreading through her.

She felt Reid push even faster, his hands clutching her bottom convulsively as his whole body tensed towards climax. Yes, she thought with sweet elation, squeezing him with her thighs, wanting him to feel her wanting him, welcoming him, relishing his pleasure and satisfaction. He came in fierce spasms, as though he couldn't wait to have done with it. Then he rested them both against the wall, hauling in breath, waiting for the heaving of their bodies to subside.

'Well, that's a start,' he rasped, tilting his head back and giving her a devilish smile that taunted any complacency she might feel with this outcome.

'A start?' she echoed foolishly, not understanding that it wasn't a finish.

'It's called a quickie, Gina. All it does is take the

edge off.' His eyes mocked her ignorance of male sexuality. 'Ready to go on? Or have you had enough?'

'Go on where? To what?' The unknown sent a shiver of apprehension through her, yet she would be inviting his scorn if she couldn't cope with whatever he had in mind.

'Oh, I think some riding lessons could top it off. Not to mention other little services you might do if so inclined. But I don't want to push you too far on your wifely mission to give satisfaction. By all means call a halt now, and I'll quite understand.'

The anger, the cynicism, the acid challenge to her sexuality hadn't been washed away. They hadn't even been diluted. They glittered from his eyes, simmered in his voice and slashed the value of any reassessment she might think she'd earned so far.

He meant to make it an endurance trial. He meant to show her up as insincere or incapable of delivering on her promise. He wanted her to face it and back down and prove him right.

Her heart rebelled against accepting any defeat in this arena. Her mind swore it could encompass anything Reid threw at her. Her body actually tingled with anticipation. Her blood was well and truly up.

From some deep, primitive well of female human nature came the age-old sense of contest with male aggression. She laughed at his suggestion that she call off now and flung down the fateful words that would carry her through the night.

'It won't be me who says enough!'

CHAPTER FOUR

IT WAS late when Gina awoke. She knew it instantly. The quality of light in the room was not early morning. It was brighter, more settled into the day. There were no sounds coming from anywhere upstairs. It felt very late. It also felt very different.

Full consciousness brought a prickly confusion of thoughts and feelings. Had she really done all those things with Reid last night? Amazing that she'd not only had the nerve, but actually held it in the face of such unexpected—undreamed of—variations of sexual activities. Although the rewards had been almost instantaneous. And still stirring her to marvel over them. She'd had no idea bodies possessed so many pleasure points.

Memories swirled through her mind, images that made her blush at the incredible boldness of her own behaviour. Though at the time it had seemed a natural progression from what had happened and what was happening. Somehow she had blocked off fearful thinking, knowing it would flood her with the inhibitions that chewed up natural instincts. She had concentrated fiercely on going with the flow.

A mad little giggle erupted from her throat. Flow

was right. She'd felt like a raft on a white-water ride, tossed into chaos, afloat on a wild and unpredictable current that was carrying her hell-bent through all sorts of confrontations with nature. The muscles around her groin suddenly clenched in exquisite recollection of sensations that had burst upon her like shooting rapids.

She took a deep breath to settle herself, firmly resolving not to start feeling squirmish or squeamish about things. This was good. Better than good. Apart from the sheer, mind-jamming, physical bombardment of pleasure, anything so intensely intimate between a husband and wife had to bring them closer together. In every sense.

Finding herself a little bit achy in places, Gina eased herself onto her side. Reid was gone. Probably long gone if he left for work on time. What was he feeling this morning? As amazed as she was? Satisfied? Looking forward to entering a different stage of their marriage now that it had opened up to him? Excited at the prospect? Most especially, did he feel more loving towards her?

His side of the room only told her it was empty of his presence. His pillows were tossed against the bedhead, obviously having been collected from the floor. The top sheet was slewed across the bottom of the bed. Gina realised she didn't have any of it over her, only the quilt, which was also in disarray, dragged onto the bed diagonally as a makeshift cover when nothing else could be easily grabbed. Total exhaustion, she reflected, blurred choices.

She'd fallen asleep naked, something she couldn't usually do, accustomed to always wearing something to bed. She was still naked, which meant she hadn't stirred from the moment she'd sunk into oblivion. It was a strange feeling, being bare all over. It had the downside of feeling unprotected and the upside of feeling free.

Get used to it, Gina told herself. She didn't want Reid to ever be in any doubt that she *was* willingly accessible to the desires he had been suppressing for most of their marriage. An irrepressible grin spread across her face. Far from being turned off, as Reid had cynically anticipated, she was well and truly turned on to experiencing all she could with her husband. What they needed to do, she decided, was share their thoughts and feelings far more openly.

Her gaze drifted to the digital clock on his bedside table. Ten twenty-three. Shocked to find it was that late, Gina scrambled out of bed in a rush. Reid must have told everyone she wasn't to be disturbed.

She took a quick shower, noting the ripped nightie was gone and wondering what Reid had done with it. Dressing didn't take long. She pulled on her new pumpkin-coloured cord jeans and the lovely dark blue and pumpkin voile shirt that felt so good to wear. Her hair was somewhat chaotic, having been left to find its own shape last night. Rather than spend time on it, Gina tied it back with a scarf.

Before going downstairs she stripped the bed and shoved the linen down the laundry chute. She wanted everything fresh again for tonight.

Feeling happy and hopeful about the future, she went in search of her children and found them in the kitchen, being catered to by their nanny, Tracy Donahue, and generally supervised by the house-keeper, Shirley Hendricks.

Jessica was in her highchair, making a chewy mess of a biscuit in between sips of milk. At fifteen months, she didn't yet have all her teeth. Despite the crumbly smears around her beautiful rosebud mouth she looked adorable, her big brown eyes so alive with interest in everything and her copious brown curls tied into a topknot with a pink ribbon.

Bobby, the irrepressible little hellion of the family, was sitting on the table, a mixing bowl between his thighs as his fingers made short work of licking out what was left of the chocolate icing that had been made for a fresh batch of brownies.

With his fair hair—it would go dark like Reid's, his grandmother declared—and his father's blue eyes and the chubby cherubic face of the very young, Bobby still looked like an angel at almost four years old. He was, however, unbelievably precocious, dreadfully mischievous, hyperactive and needed an adult eye on him every minute he wasn't asleep.

Apparently no disaster had yet occurred this morning, but the mixing bowl did look somewhat precarious. Tracy was busy slicing up the tray of brownies. Shirley had her back turned, standing beside the appliance bench, waiting for the electric jug to boil. Gina decided avoidance action was a wise move.

Calling out good morning to everyone, she swooped on the bowl while Bobby was distracted by her arrival.

'Aw, Mum! There's still some there,' he protested. 'And what are you down here for? You're supposed to be in bed.'

'Mumma, Mumma!' Jessica crowed with joy, lifting her arms to be picked up for a cuddle.

Would it be irresponsible to leave her children for two weeks? Gina fretted, recalling Reid's criticism of her impulse to accompany him to London.

'It's only a plastic bowl, Mrs. Tyson,' Tracy assured her.

Gina looked at the thick white plastic in her hand and laughed at herself. 'So it is. Sorry, Tracy. Habit, I guess.'

'Well, you can't be too careful with that one.'

The comment was accompanied by a nod at Bobby and a wise look that belied the young woman's youth. Although Tracy was only twenty, she had worked as a nanny since she was sixteen, and having come from a family of thirteen children, she was no greenhorn when it came to looking after little ones. A country girl, born and bred on a farm and imbued with practical common sense, she'd been with them since Jessica's birth. Gina *did* trust her with the children, even Bobby. Reid's remark had made her hypersensitive. That was all.

She handed the bowl to her holy little terror, gave him a quick kiss and hug, then lifted Jessica out of her chair for a cuddle. 'Did Patrick get off to school all right?' she asked Tracy.

At five, Patrick was very conscious of his status, the oldest child, firstborn son and, more important, a schoolboy who knew a lot more than the other two and was learning every day.

'Yes. His dad took him this morning,' Tracy answered, her eyes lively with curiosity as she added, 'Mr. Tyson said not to disturb you.'

'I was just making a pot of tea,' Shirley Hendricks chimed in. 'Thought I'd take it up to you with some biscuits. In case you were feeling queasy.' This with a knowing look at Gina's stomach.

Clearly Shirley had figured it was time for Gina to be pregnant again, going by the spacing between the children. Having virtually come with the house—she had cleaned for its previous owners, remained as caretaker when they had left and considered the granny flat at the back of the garage her residence by right of occupation—the sprightly, take-everything-in-her-stride housekeeper had been through three long bouts of morning sickness with Gina. To her, Reid's stricture to let his wife lie in, in peace, signalled another baby on the way.

Gina laughed and shook her head. 'I'm not pregnant, Shirley, but I would like a cup of tea. Reid and I had a very late night.' Warmth seeped into her cheeks as some of the highly erotic memories flitted through her mind. 'He must have thought I needed the sleep.'

'Ah!' said Shirley with a knowing nod.

At forty-something, a mother of two grown-up daughters whom, she breezily declared, were better off for having their no-good father desert them, Shirley led a highly active social life at various local clubs. She'd kept her curvy figure trim, and her hair was regularly dyed a chestnut red with gold tints and styled by a hairdresser friend who shared her interest in looking good.

Men featured highly on their list of interesting hobbies, but being mature now, Shirley was very selective over whom she allowed into her life, which was very much organised to suit herself. Nevertheless, she'd informed Gina on many occasions that she could still go around the block whenever she had the inclination. And around the clock, too.

Gina had always smiled rather vaguely at the latter comment, not quite sure what to make of it. Suddenly, looking at the merry twinkle in Shirley's eyes, Gina had a lightning flash of comprehension. She had entered the world of women who knew, women who'd been there, done that, and were perfectly comfortable with the experience.

'Well, it's a pity Mr. Tyson had to go to work,' Tracy remarked. Her mouth twitched as she gave Gina an arch look. 'He looked a bit peaky this morning. I reckon he could have done with more sleep himself.'

Yes, he must have been tired, Gina thought, barely catching a feline little smile. He hadn't called a halt, either. It had to have been almost dawn before they'd slid into sleep during a breather between lessons.

Despite his fatigue this morning, she hoped Reid was feeling the time had been well spent. He was surely feeling softer towards her. It showed caring consideration that he'd instructed she not be disturbed.

'Oh!' Tracy's attention swung to the kitchen window. 'There's Steve!' she said in a swoony voice.

Shirley rolled her eyes at Gina. 'Amazing coincidence how Tracy makes brownies the day the pool cleaner comes.'

Gina grinned. Steve had taken over from the previous cleaner a month ago, and he was a sight to behold. He had a glorious mane of sun-bleached blond locks that rippled to his shoulder-blades in careless disarray and a body that bulged with gym muscles, all of them on stunning display.

Steve wore tight short shorts, making sure no-one missed what Tracy breathlessly declared 'the cutest bum in the world.' His T-shirts, emblazoned with the company slogan Whistle for the Experts on the front and The Whistle Pool Cleaning Company on the back, were definitely two sizes too small for him. Nevertheless, they stretched valiantly around his magnificently developed torso. The general effect evoked a terrible temptation to whistle.

On top of all that, if his satiny-smooth glowing skin could be bottled and sold by some tanning-lotion manufacturer, the company would make an instant fortune. Only the sandshoes on his feet—no socks—indicated he was, indeed, human. They were of the battered, well-worn variety, beloved of surfies who actually surfed instead of adopting the cult image.

As a fantasy figure for a golden god of Bondi Beach, Steve fitted admirably. He was, in a word, gorgeous. He also had a peacock strut that knew it. Tracy drooled over him, and he accepted her worship as his due with a lazy smile and kindly condescension.

'Better make the most of what time you've got him here, Tracy,' Gina advised. 'He only comes once a week.'

She flushed to the roots of her hair. 'He sort of talks to Bobby when I go out. Not me. Let's face it. I'm not pretty enough for a guy like that to take an interest.'

'That might not be true,' Gina mused, eyeing Tracy consideringly.

The young nanny was not conventionally pretty, but she had almost a magnetically attractive face when her dancing hazel eyes lit up with happiness. Her dark hair was cut in a gamine style that suited her cute face with its sprinkle of freckles across her cheeks and retroussé nose, and her smile was truly infectious. It was Gina's private opinion that a warm personality generated a powerful attraction by itself. Certainly her three children were sold on their nanny.

Steve might work hard on his surface looks because he wasn't so sure of himself inside. A woman like Tracy had a lot of positive things to give, never mind that she was long and lean and her father had told her she was built like a greyhound.

'You won't know if you don't try,' Gina went on, thinking of herself with Reid last night. If everyone held back, no meeting ground could ever be established. 'I'll keep Bobby here with me and Jessica. Go on out to the pool by yourself and strike up a conversation. You've got a captive audience while he's doing his job.'

'But what will I talk about?' Tracy cried in anguished self-consciousness.

'Food,' Gina suggested. 'Take a plate of brownies. Ask him if he follows some health diet. Tell him he's in such great shape you wondered if he could give you some advice. There's no point in hanging back, Tracy. If you want something in this world, you have to take some initiative.'

And therein lay the real lesson from last night, Gina thought with satisfaction.

'You're always bemoaning how thin you are,' Shirley pointed out. 'Ask him if he thinks women should build up their muscles. He might offer to teach you how.'

'Go on, Tracy,' Gina urged. 'What harm can it do to give it a try?'

'Okay!' She expelled a chest-loosening breath and quickly piled some brownies onto a plate. 'Food and muscles,' she recited on her way out.

Shirley placed the tea things on the table for Gina then eyed Steve through the kitchen window. 'Actually, I rather fancy him myself. Every woman should have one of those.'

Gina laughed. 'You mean like a toy boy?'

'Why not?' Shirley gave her an arch look. 'A guy who'd perform on cue and not talk back could go a long way with me.'

Gina shook her head bemusedly. It wasn't her idea of bliss. More than anything she wanted a sharing relationship, not one where roles were handed out and kept restricted.

'Well, each to their own,' Shirley said with a worldly shrug, moving away from the window and starting around the table. 'Now that you're down, I'll go and do the upstairs.'

'I, uh, stripped the bed in our room. I meant to remake it with fresh linen.'

'I'll save you the trouble,' Shirley tossed at her as she reached the door, not the least embarrassed by Gina's embarrassment. 'Bobby's into the brownies.'

'Oh!' She turned her slightly flustered face to her wayward little son. 'You should ask first, Bobby.'

He looked at her with belligerent righteousness. 'Steve didn't ask. And I live here. He doesn't.' He bit into the chocolate slice to thwart any removal from his grasp.

'Steve is a visitor.'

'Is not. He's doing a job, cleaning the pool. If he can have Tracy's brownies, so can I.'

This superior piece of logic was delivered while feeding his face, a point Jessica didn't miss. 'Chockie, chockie, me!' she cried, copying Bobby's belligerent tone. Jessica had a highly developed sense of fairness where her siblings were concerned.

'Pass the tray over, Bobby,' Gina ordered, not prepared to get into one of his elongated arguments. Her second son would drive a judge crazy if he ever got into a law court.

'She'll only make a mess of one,' he grumbled, grudgingly doing as he was told.

'I'll help her eat it,' Gina said, choosing one of the thinner slices.

'It'll make you sick again,' he warned.

'I haven't been sick.'

'Yes, you have. Daddy said so.'

'When did Daddy say so?'

'This morning. I heard him tell Patrick.'

'Then you must have heard him wrong, Bobby.'

'Did not. 'Sides, he asked us to keep quiet and stay downstairs until you got up.'

'That's not saying I'm sick.'

'Patrick asked if you were. It was when Tracy was fixing Jessica and he and Daddy were leaving for school. I followed them to the door to say goodbye and Patrick asked Daddy straight out, Is Mummy sick?'

The little devil mimicked Patrick's seriously important tone. Gina could not doubt this conversation had taken place.

'Then Daddy said—' Bobby arranged his face to mimic his father, whose expression had obviously been one of irritable impatience. 'Sick and sore and sorry for herself, most likely. But not to worry, Patrick. Your mother will be back to her normal self in no time flat.'

Bobby reproduced the cynical mutter with an innocent accuracy that stamped it as a true rendition of what was said and how it was said.

And the bottom fell out of Gina's bright new world.

Tears burned her eyes. She struggled to hold them back, not wanting to cry in front of the children. But her heart and mind were crying. How could he? How could he?

Apart from the slighting way he had spoken of her to Patrick—and overheard by Bobby—for Reid to so grossly undervalue what had transpired between them last night, to dismiss it as an aberration she would quickly recover from—it was so dreadfully unfair, untrue.

She shook her head, sickened by his rejection of what she had seen as a major breakthrough in bringing a new intimacy to their marriage. Nothing had been gained. Nothing resolved. Nothing at all.

Unless she could change his mind about it, make him see it differently.

Initiative. That was what she'd preached to Tracy.

Reid had castigated her for holding back on positive action. If she was to show him he was wrong, she had to give him positive action, and a lot of it. Quickly! So he could see he was wrong. Very, very wrong!

CHAPTER FIVE

A BASKET of roses?

For him?

Reid shot a frowning look of inquiry at Paige Calder, who stood holding the door she had opened to allow the delivery woman to enter his office. The latter had charged in like a tank, bearing what was obviously an expensive and extravagant florist's arrangement.

Apparently his personal assistant saw no reason to offer an enlightening comment. There was a tight look about her mouth that spelled disapproval or displeasure. Her eyes were a study in cool assessment, watching his response to what had to be a misdirected gift.

Her stand-off attitude added another pinch of vexation to what had already been a wretchedly unproductive morning. Why on earth had Paige let this nonsense past her? It was part of her job to protect him from uninvited intruders.

'There you are!' the delivery woman stated with satisfaction, planting the basket smack in the middle of Reid's desk, regardless of what papers it sat on or disarranged.

Directly confronted with this big, bustling bully of a woman, the kind who refused to be awed by anyone or anything and liked to say her piece, Reid pushed back his chair and rose to his feet, intending to be firm and succinct in dealing with the situation.

The delivery woman gave him an up-and-down look as though sizing him for the type of man who was sent roses. The profusion of heavily scented blooms had to number at least three dozen. Whatever statement it was sending to someone, it was over the top, in Reid's somewhat jaundiced opinion.

'I'm afraid you've made a mistake,' he said flatly. 'These can't be for me.'

'No. No mistake. I've got the order right here in my hand.' She held out the slip of paper with an air of triumph. 'See for yourself. Mr. Reid Tyson. Administration block of Tyson Electronics at Bondi Junction. That's here, and that's you, all right. No mistake at all.'

'So it would seem,' he conceded, having no choice.

'Personal delivery. That was the customer's instruction. Most insistent, she was. Don't give it to anyone but Mr. Reid Tyson. So I came myself to make sure.' She smirked at Paige as though she had avoided that trap with flying colours, then set the piece of paper on the desk and offered him a pen. 'I'd appreciate it if you'd put your signature on the order form, Mr. Tyson. That proves the point, doesn't it?'

'Who—' He bit back the inquiry, not wanting to

engage this woman in further conversation. The customer had to be someone playing a joke. A remarkably tasteless one.

'Message for you in the envelope.' The female equivalent of a Sherman tank twirled the basket around to point out the square of white tied to the handle with scrolls of green ribbon.

'Thank you,' he said, and swiftly scrawled his signature on the order form. He handed it back with a dismissive little smile. 'Your proof that you've delivered.'

'Ta. Bit of interest in a dull day.' She had sharp, gossipy eyes. 'Not many men get sent roses. Matter of fact, you're the first on my books.'

'Well, I'm glad I've given you a new experience. Now, if you don't mind...'

She laughed. It was a big belly laugh. Unbelievably, her gaze dropped to his crotch then twinkled. 'I reckon you must be real good at that, Mr. Tyson... giving new experiences. All those red roses.' She shook her head and laughed her way out, fairly splitting her sides.

Huge joke!

Paige did not move to see her off. She maintained her station by the door. It was glaringly obvious she was no more amused than he was.

Was she waiting to gauge what was happening in his private life? Waiting to see who had felt prompted to send him roses? Reid had to acknowledge Paige probably felt she had reason to consider herself the front-running candidate for a new experience with him, and the roses would seem to make a hash of that expectation.

Not that he'd made Paige any promises. He still wasn't certain he wanted what she was subtly but undoubtedly offering. But going along with her Durley House suggestion was, well, if not a green light, an indication that he was in an amber zone.

Nevertheless, she didn't own him. And she needn't think she did. Or ever would. He looked her straight in the eye and deliberately asked, 'Anything else, Paige?'

She looked at the roses, then at him. 'I thought you might like to pass them on. To a hospital or nursing home.'

'I'll let you know.'

It was an unmistakable dismissal. Paige inclined her head and departed. One of her major talents was knowing when to retreat after putting in the push. Paige Calder was a very smooth operator. Reid appreciated her expertise at making everything easy. Too easy? he wondered.

He was plagued with uncertainties this morning. And now this ridiculous basket of roses arriving, giving him more aggravation. Who the devil was having fun at his expense?

He pricked his finger with the pin in his irritable haste to get the envelope off the basket. He ripped it open with glowering impatience, pulled out the note-paper, and wanting only to be done with it, cast his gaze over the words typed on the small embossed page. *Just to say I love you and thank you for a fantastic night—Gina.*

CHAPTER SIX

GINA headed up the stairs to Reid's office, the receptionist's compliment still ringing in her ears. 'Love that orange on you, Mrs. Tyson!' It gave her courage a boost.

Yesterday she had dithered over buying the figure-hugging orange coat dress. Today she had walked into the boutique, put the dress on, paid for it and walked out in it. Bright and bold, she'd told herself. And very positive.

Having reached the executive floor, she took a deep breath and marched on, head up, shoulders back, tummy in, no butterflies allowed. A glance at her watch showed it was just on noon. Perfect timing for lunch.

The roses should have prepared the path. The florist had assured her Reid had been personally presented with them. No problem. So he knew very positively that she was not sick and sore and sorry for herself. Absolutely not!

She had moved like a whirlwind since Bobby had repeated those words. Her mind was more focused than it had probably ever been in her life. Her aims were very clear. She was also gripped with a sense of urgency. Whether that was instinctive or intuitive, realistic or not simply didn't matter. She felt it and she was acting on it.

Paige Calder was at her desk in the outer office looking very classic. Her neutral blond hair was tucked into a smooth French pleat. Her make-up was an artful blend of pale colours. A dusky pink blouse added a touch of feminine allure to the elegant simplicity of her long-line suit in a fashionable shade of oyster.

Gina had a moment of terrible self-doubt. Paige looked like a beautiful, soft English rose. Was that image more to Reid's taste than a vibrant wild poppy?

She shook her head at her dithering. There could be no retreating now. She pushed her feet forward, resolved on following through regardless of consequences. At least Reid couldn't fail to take notice of her.

'So, how's everything for you, Paige?' she asked brightly. The other woman's head snapped up from her work. Gina gave her a dazzling smile and prattled on, not wanting a conversation. 'You look great. But then you always do. I've never seen you ever not perfectly put together. You look positively glowing today. Like a pearl.'

By this time Gina had reached the door to Reid's office and Paige had risen to her feet, one hand extended as though wanting to pull Gina back.

'Mrs. Tyson—'

'Oh, do call me Gina. I'm sure you call my husband Reid. I'd like you to be just as familiar with me. And please go on with whatever you're doing. I'm just dropping in on him.'

She'd turned the handle while speaking and forestalled any preventive action on Paige's part by simply pushing the door open, stepping inside and closing it quickly behind her. She swung around to confront Reid and smiled a bold smile.

Her heart was fluttering like mad, and she desperately needed reassurance that she was embarked on the right path. Her stomach also needed calming. In fact, only her mind was in trustworthy working order. *Bold*, it said. *Keep thinking bold.*

Reid had been tilted back in his super-duper executive chair, feet on the desk, chin on his chest, his face set in a ferocious scowl, his gaze trained narrowly on the splendid basket of roses adorning the corner of his desk in front of his feet.

Her abrupt entrance startled him. His feet fell off the desk, his chair jerked forward and he spilled onto his legs, towering quickly to his full height. His face ran through a gamut of expressions—shock, disbelief, guilt, anger, bitterness, irony—swiftly settling into a watchful wariness with a strong undercurrent of tension.

He did not return her smile. He looked as though he didn't know what to do with her smile or the roses or her unexpected presence in his office. For some unfathomable reason this gave Gina a boost in confidence, enough to get her moving, anyway. Initiative was what he wanted. Initiative was what she had to deliver.

She pushed forward, still smiling, working a melodious lilt into her voice. 'I felt so happy this morning I wanted you to know it.' She waved to the basket of roses. 'I wanted to surprise you, too.'

'You certainly did that,' he said, waiting on his side of the desk, not coming to meet her.

It goaded her on, his taunt of last night echoing in her ears. *Something wrong with your legs, Gina, that you couldn't come to me?* He couldn't accuse her of not coming to him today, though his waiting, watching stillness made her extremely conscious of every step she took, conscious of what she was wearing—and not wearing—under her dress, the garter belt and stockings leaving the tops of her thighs bare, her flesh heating there as her legs rubbed together. She kept talking to quell what could easily become a debilitating rush of nervousness.

'I thought over what you said about me expecting you to be the active lover all the time. And I remembered the pleasure it gave me when you sent me roses. I wanted to give you the warm thrill of feeling loved and valued and very much in the other's thoughts.'

Slashes of burning red seared his cheekbones. 'It's not quite the same with men,' he muttered tersely. Embarrassment? Guilt that he hadn't thought to send her roses? He hadn't done that in a long time, not since the day after Jessica was born.

She skirted the desk, refusing to be put off. 'Why isn't it the same? It's a message of love either way.'

'Is it?' Hard, suspicious, turning towards her but more in challenge than welcome.

'What else could it be?' she asked, feeling her throat start to tighten. She needed some encouragement to carry this off.

'A game people play,' he answered flatly, his eyes boring into hers. 'A manipulative game.'

'That is so cynical, Reid.' She set her handbag on his desk and reached up to curl her arms around his neck, her eyes chiding him for taking such a viewpoint. 'I love you. I wanted to show it. I want to show you now, too.'

Something wrong with your mouth that you couldn't use it to communicate your burning desire, one way or another?

She went up on tiptoe to kiss him.

His body was stiff, unyielding, his eyes cold and hard.

'Let's have lunch together, make love in the afternoon,' she murmured, trying to soften him. 'I booked a room for us—'

'Oh, for pity's sake, stop it!' he growled, his eyes blazing a savage rejection as he snatched her arms away from his neck and held them forcibly at her sides. 'Nobody changes their nature overnight. I'm not a fool, Gina. Don't make me lose what respect I have for you.'

'Respect?' she echoed blankly, her heart hammering so hard she wasn't sure she heard him correctly.

He winced and released her, stepping back so quickly there was no stopping him from wheeling away from her. He paced around the desk, putting space between them before he spoke to her again, his hand slicing the air in deep agitation.

'Look! I'm sorry about last night. Okay? I'm sorry.' He shot the words at her in short explosive bursts, as though he hated them but was forced to say them.

I'm not sorry, she thought, but couldn't get her mouth to work. How was it when she tried to seduce her husband, she ended up driving him away from her? Even when she was following his instructions? It seemed she was damned if she did and damned if she didn't. How did one get a win-win situation?

'It shouldn't have happened,' he went on. 'I wish it hadn't. You didn't deserve what I did, and I sure as hell don't like myself this morning. There's no need for you to—' he sucked in a deep breath and let it hiss out between his teeth '—to rub it in,' he finished grimly, his hands clenching into angry fists.

Gina shook her head over his tortured reasoning. 'So that's why you organised for me to sleep late this morning. You didn't want to face me. Because you felt bad about yourself.'

'I didn't want you to feel pressured.'

'Would you mind telling me why you should feel bad about letting me know what you want?'

'Damn it, Gina! I virtually assaulted you last night. I completely lost it. Then to go on for so long…' He shook his head, deeply disturbed, unable to explain or excuse himself. His eyes looked sick with self-recrimination.

'Don't you think it was a release for both of us?' she asked softly, wanting to reach out to him, to soothe his anguish and wipe away the guilt.

'God knows!' he muttered, grimacing at memories he didn't want to share, didn't want to even look at again. 'What I'm trying to say is, don't think you have to service me or indulge me.' His face was a study of revulsion. 'I'd hate it. I know it would be false, and I'd hate the thought of you forcing yourself to—' his mouth curled in distaste '—*please* me.'

Bewilderment coursed through her. Didn't he understand about loving, that to give was to receive, as well? 'But…it pleases me to please you,' she offered tentatively.

'Oh, come on, Gina!' He threw his hands up in disgust. 'I'm not a child to be pampered and cossetted and told I'm a good boy, no matter what!'

Gina bit down on her tongue, frightened of riling him further. His eyes were blue bolts of lightning-fierce resentment, stabbing at her in violent flashes. It seemed whatever she said he latched onto and turned against her.

'You don't suddenly have to send me roses,' he thundered at her. 'You don't suddenly have to make yourself look sexy and available.' His eyes raked down the line of buttons on her dress. 'What were you thinking of? Offering me a quickie on the desk?' He laughed abrasively. 'No. Not quite that far. You went for something more genteel, booking us a room.'

A hot tide of blood scorched up her neck and sizzled her cheeks.

'Oh, God! Strike that!' he pleaded gruffly, shutting his eyes to close out her mortified look, rubbing at his eyelids with finger and thumb as though trying to erase the image of her stricken face. 'It's not you I'm lashing out at, Gina. It's me. Because of what I did, this is what you feel you have to do. And I hate having hurt you like that.'

'You didn't hurt me, Reid,' she insisted quietly, appalled that he had been torturing himself by seeing his loss of control as an abusive crime that shamed him and drove her into paths she would not normally choose.

He shook his head, dropped his hand and lifted a bleak gaze to her. 'If you want to play pretend, Gina, I'd prefer we pretend last night was a bad dream. Then no action has to be taken. We can go on as before.'

'You weren't happy with before,' she pointed out.

'I can live with it.'

'You think repressing your needs is a good way to live, Reid?'

'It's not your problem, Gina.' It was an evasive answer. 'And I won't make it your problem.' He avoided looking her in the eye, too.

Gina suddenly had a very bad feeling, a shut-out feeling, a feeling like he'd be moving on and leaving her behind, sealed up in her box labelled *mother of his children*. She took a deep breath and laid the terrible suspicion on the line.

'Maybe you intend to find another outlet for them. Is that your answer?'

'Don't nag at it,' he sliced at her, obviously discomforted by the question. 'You've got nothing to worry about. It won't affect your life.'

Oh, my God! He *was* considering another outlet! Gina suddenly found it hard to breathe. Her mind recoiled from the thought of Reid going to another woman for sexual fulfilment. Her whole body recoiled from it. And he had the incredible blindness to regard such an act as not affecting her life!

Gina seethed over that presumption. As though he knew everything there was to know about her! And he hadn't even taken in what she'd been saying, dismissing it because he thought he knew better.

She worked hard at recovering her breath. She needed it. She had to turn this around right now, set him straight before… Or had he already… No, she couldn't even approach that thought, let alone give it standing room in her mind.

'What makes you think I'm happy with the life you've allotted to me, Reid?' she fired at him.

He frowned, unsure where this was leading.

Her chin went up, and her voice lifted with it. 'What makes you assume I was happy before last night?'

He jerked his head as though she was talking nonsense.

Her eyes flared in defiant challenge of his know-all attitude. 'What makes you think last night was all your doing? Do you recall my begging you to stop? Do you?'

'No.' He looked shamefaced. 'I think you submitted to it as some kind of endurance test.'

'Think rites of passage, and you'd be closer to the mark,' she retorted vehemently. 'I had no idea what was possible between a man and woman until last night. Now I do know. The clock can't be set back, Reid. And what's more, I don't want it set back!'

There! That was the truth, and Gina wasn't about to let him ignore it. At least he was looking at her with some uncertainty now, which was a step in the right direction. If he would just get off his judgment seat and give them both a chance to feel good things about each other, he would very quickly realise he didn't need another woman at all. Not for anything!

There was a knock on the door.

It opened before either of them could say yea or nay. Paige Calder hung onto it, half in, half out, showing reluctance to interrupt but doing it. She cast an apologetic look from one to the other, tactfully including Gina before settling on Reid, who had instantly pulled on his authority mask.

'Please excuse me. I'd just like to know if lunch is off, Reid. We were going to leave at twelve-fifteen.'

It prompted both of them to check their watches. Paige was being a stickler for punctuality, Gina thought, frowning in frustration over the untimely intrusion. It was only twelve-eighteen. Surely a little more leeway could have been taken before she broke in on them.

'Make it twelve-thirty,' Reid said decisively. 'If you'll wait in your office…'

Gina couldn't believe her ears. He was going off to lunch? Leaving her flat in the middle of one of the most critical conversations in their lives?

Paige flashed him a warm smile. 'Of course,' she said and withdrew.

The smile got under Gina's skin. Disappointment was already under her skin, burrowing into the confidence she'd had in her marriage, but there was something very twosome about that smile that added nasty little claws to her disappointment. It wasn't exactly intimate, but it definitely smacked of a private, mutual understanding. With *her* husband.

'A change of priorities?' she sliced at Reid, too agitated to let the matter pass.

'Pardon?' He frowned at her, not at ease with a wife who suddenly wasn't behaving according to pattern.

'You said last night there would be nothing more important to you than your wife actively wanting you,' she reminded him. 'It seems you have a lunch that is more important than being with me. And you made up your mind without so much as a hesitation over the invitation I gave you.'

'I thought I'd dealt with that, Gina,' he said quietly.

'So you don't want to have lunch with me.'

He looked pained. 'Another day...'

'And you don't want to make love with me.' She could hear herself getting snippish, but she couldn't help it.

He expelled a long breath. 'I think this conversation is better deferred until this evening.'

Dismissed! Just summarily dismissed. No reward for her efforts to make a step up in their marriage. He wasn't even trying to meet her halfway.

'I take it business comes first, then.' The words spouted from her mouth in an angry burst. 'Perhaps, in the few minutes we have left together, you'd like to tell me what the big deal is with today's lunch.'

His face tightened. 'It's a matter of keeping my word.'

'Well, integrity is always admirable. To whom are

you keeping your word, Reid? Someone critical to your future success and happiness?'

A muscle in his cheek contracted. 'Just let it go, Gina. We'll talk tonight.'

She could not, would not let it go. Her heart was ravaged by his insensitivity. 'Give me a name,' she demanded. 'A name so I can think, yes, that's perfectly understandable. I can appreciate Reid not wanting to miss a lunch with him. Or is it a her?'

'I'm taking Paige out to lunch, Gina.'

It skewered her heart.

'It's her birthday today.'

'Her birthday,' she repeated numbly.

Never mind the wife who gave birth to your three children! Never mind the marriage that could have been reborn last night!

'I promised this lunch to her some weeks ago,' he went on matter-of-factly. 'Some other day won't do. Birthdays are birthdays.'

'And that has priority.' Her voice sounded shrill. She felt she was cracking open, unable to hold anything together.

He grimaced at the implied criticism. 'I see no reason to disappoint her.'

She laughed, a wild trill of mad amusement at the irony of that sentiment. 'Well, that certainly marks the value you place on the women in your life, Reid.'

'Don't blow this out of proportion, Gina.'

Her eyes scythed him as she picked up her handbag

from his desk and started for the door. 'Her birthday,' she mocked. 'Makes her another year closer to you in experience and expertise. You probably don't have to teach Paige anything. And so very convenient for you, isn't she?'

He moved to intercept her. 'Now, look—'

She swung on him, her voice shaking with a burst of violent fury. 'You look, Reid! And get this straight from me. Go and enjoy your lunch with your other woman. But I'd better not smell her on you when you come home tonight, because you made promises to me on our wedding day, and God help you if you ever forget them!'

The passionate tirade stopped him in his tracks. He looked absolutely stunned. Never before had she blazed at him in such a forthright fashion, and certainly never with such a sexual connotation. It shocked Gina, too. She hadn't known she was capable of it. But she wasn't about to take any of it back.

She tossed her head, strode to the door, wrenched it open—and was faced with Paige Calder waiting at her desk for Reid to take her to lunch.

No way in the world would Gina allow *her* to see she was upset or leaving defeated.

A smile, a diversion…

Please help me, God!

Her brain went clickety-click and spewed out Durley House, London.

The path ahead was lit.

'Sorry to hold you up another minute, Paige,' she said sweetly, adding an apologetic twist to her smile. 'I'm sure Reid's travel agent must have given you a business card. Could I trouble you for it?'

'No problem.' She opened a card folder on her desk and deftly extracted the one requested.

Gina swept over and took it. 'Thank you.' She felt she might choke on the words but she forced herself to add, 'Have a nice lunch, and happy birthday.'

'Why do you want the card, Gina?'

Reid's voice cut in before Paige could say a word in reply or comment. It came from his doorway, hard and strong and tense. Apparently he'd recovered from his shock enough to come after her. In her hyped-up state, Gina decided he could do with another shock to really lay things on the line.

She constructed an absolutely brilliant smile as she turned to face him. 'Don't you remember, Reid? You told me last night if I wanted a trip to Europe I should plan it properly. How better to do it than with your travel agent?'

It was her exit line.

She hoped it would stick in Reid's mind and rob him of more than one appetite over his lunch with Paige Calder.

CHAPTER SEVEN

THE telephone on his desk buzzed, dragging Reid's mind to the business he should be dealing with. He'd thought he had his personal life more or less settled. Now there seemed to be a whole bunch of new elements running around and not in his control.

'Reid Tyson,' he said into the mouthpiece. It came out like an announcement of credentials, an affirmation of who he was, what he was, a man who'd made his world and was a success by anyone's measure.

'It's Liz Copeland from World-Finder Travel.'

Alarm shot through him. Gina on a rampage through Europe? She wouldn't go that far, would she?

No. Much more likely the call was about the business trip to London and Paris. Paige was handling the details with Liz, but Paige wasn't here. He'd left her in the city, giving her the rest of the afternoon off after their lunch in the Chifley Tower. For all the use he'd been in the office since his return, he might as well have taken the afternoon off, too. Except he wasn't ready to go home yet. Not until he had Gina figured out better than he did at the moment.

'How are you, Liz?' he rolled out. 'What can I help you with?'

She was a highly competent and efficient agent who'd always provided precisely what he wanted and covered every contingency. Like that train strike in Italy last year. It would have messed up his Milan trip if Liz hadn't had plan B ready.

'No problem, Reid,' she assured him. 'I simply haven't been able to make contact with your wife, and it's almost five. I'm about to leave the office. So I thought I'd let you know that everything's on track. The bookings have been made and confirmed.'

A chill ran down his spine. 'What bookings?'

The only sound at the other end of the line was the hiss of a sharply indrawn breath. Then slowly, tensely, 'You didn't know your wife was coming to see me about joining you on your trip?'

His jaw clenched. It took an act of will to unclench it and produce a calm, rational explanation for the ignorance that made him look a fool. 'I knew she was coming to see you about a trip to Europe. But not this one.' A hesitation for natural pondering. 'She must be thinking of surprising me.'

'Oh! And now I've gone and spoilt it. I'm sorry, Reid.'

She might be, but she still sounded wary and worried. Reid knew the travel business was very tricky when it came to men travelling with wives—and women other than their wives. Sometimes it took very discreet handling. Liz had had no warning brief about his wife. She might have blown an account if she'd made a wrong assumption.

'Gina probably would have told me tonight anyway,' he soothed, hating the thought of anyone imagining disharmony in his marriage. That was intensely private and personal. 'Do I understand you've managed to get my wife a seat on the same flights booked for me and Miss Calder?'

'Yes, I have. Though I'm afraid I couldn't get her a window seat on the flight from Sydney to London. The only seat available in first class was one in the centre row, a bit back from where the other two are booked on the side. Perhaps Miss Calder won't mind exchanging seats with your wife so you can sit together and she can watch whatever view there is?'

'I'm sure we'll be able to organise something appropriate. Thank you, Liz.'

'Oh, and please remind your wife I need her passport tomorrow. There's the visa for France and other matters to attend to, and time is short.'

It was Wednesday. They were flying out on Sunday. Time to sort this out was very short, indeed.

'I'll tell her,' he assured Liz.

'Great! It's lovely that you'll have this time together. Your wife explained she's been so busy with your children over the years she's never had the chance to accompany you to Europe until now. She said it'll be like a second honeymoon for you.'

'Yes. It's a nice idea,' Reid managed to bite out. 'Thank you, Liz.'

'Well, anything I can do to make it more romantic for you, let me know. Bye now!'

First the roses. Now the second honeymoon!

And bypassing him without so much as a do you mind.

He put the receiver on its telephone stand and stood up. He was ready to go home. He was not into game playing, and Gina had better find that out before she went any further.

CHAPTER EIGHT

GINA'S heart skittered as she heard the deep thrum of
Reid's Jaguar moving into the garage. Her fingers
fumbled over the ice-cubes as she picked four from
the tray Shirley passed to her from the refrigerator.
The lemon on the kitchen bench beside the long
glasses of gin and tonic still had to be sliced. Gina
wondered if her suddenly tremulous hands could do
it without cutting herself.

'That sounds like Mr. Tyson's car,' Tracy remarked, between tasting and stirring the bolognaise
sauce for the children's dinner.

'He's home earlier than usual,' Shirley commented,
hunting in the pantry for water crackers to accompany
the pâté Gina had bought.

Much earlier than usual, Gina thought apprehen-
sively.

Which could mean a lot of things.

Gina wasn't sure any of them would be good.

Her stomach started to tighten. Her whole body
started crawling with tension. She stood at the servery
bench between the kitchen and the family room,
watching her children at play with their grandmother,
knowing she herself was playing with dynamite.

Lorna Tyson was a lovely woman, a gracious lady and the kindest mother-in-law any wife could hope to have. She was a widow in her sixties and made an art form of keeping her life busy, belonging to a bridge club, a garden club and a choir, as well as being a volunteer worker for several community services. Her blue eyes twinkled with vitality, a tendency to plumpness kept wrinkles away, and her softly styled blond hair helped take ten years off her age.

Gina had had no compunction about roping Lorna in to help, knowing Reid would give his mother anything. It was a matter of stacking the cards on her side as much as possible. Nevertheless, the happy domestic scene currently being played out here could well be brought to an abrupt halt once Reid was informed of the new developments in their situation.

For the past half hour, ever since she'd called the World-Finder office and Liz Copeland's assistant had assured her the bookings were confirmed, fear had been gnawing at her. Was she taking this too far? Reid wasn't going to like her leaping over his head, intruding on arrangements he'd already made.

Rebellion kicked in. If nothing was going on with Paige Calder, then why shouldn't it suit him to have his wife accompany him to Europe? She'd fixed his objection about preparing the children for her absence, as he'd soon find out. There was no valid reason he should oppose her tripping off with him.

She forced herself to saw slices off the lemon, feeling sicker and sicker as she waited for Reid to come through the door linking the garage to the gallery that overlooked the family room. For most of her marriage she had basked in Reid's approval. He'd always been kind and considerate to her. In the warmth of his regard she'd felt safe within the family nest.

But that had broken down last night. Maybe they'd both been role-playing for too long, pretending everything was perfect. The good wife. The good husband. The good parents. The good marriage. The guts of it had spilled out now and there was no papering over them. They had to deal with the truth, not hide from it or pretend it wasn't there. It was the only way to go forward. Surely Reid must see that.

Gina set the knife down and dropped slices of lemon into the long glasses. The drinks were ready, but she was wound up so tight, she couldn't bring herself to move. Let Reid make the first move this time, she thought fiercely, fearfully. Her heart beat like a mad metronome as she waited, her gaze trained on the door he would be coming through any moment now.

It opened.

Then he was there on the gallery, looking down at her, and it was as though the rest of the family receded into some other dimension. She could hear them, see them on the fringe of her vision, yet they were outside the tunnel of intensity that ran between her and Reid, pulsing with a larger-than-life reality.

She had the weird sense of being intimately linked to him yet at the same time removed from him, seeing him as a stranger.

She knew instinctively he was seeing her the same way. And it made him angry, the loss of what was familiar. He was smouldering with anger, as though he had been deceived.

Maybe he had been. Maybe she was, too, deceived in the man she thought she'd married. Had they both fallen in love with images that were now shattering? The awful thought filled her with a hollowness she couldn't bear. She would not allow they did not know each other at all. It was only a matter of matching up again on new, more honest levels. Otherwise…

No, she couldn't—wouldn't—look at otherwise.

That was too frightening.

'Daddy!' Bobby yelled, breaking through their private thrall, his arms outflung as he soared and dove like an aeroplane, flying towards the steps from the family room to the gallery, determined to reach his father first.

'Dad-Dad-Dad!' Jessica crowed, waving and clapping from her grandmother's lap.

'Grandma's here, Daddy,' Patrick announced importantly, though he couldn't keep a bubble of excitement out of his voice. 'And she's going to stay with us while you and Mummy are away.'

'I'm so pleased you're taking Gina with you on your trip, Reid,' Lorna Tyson chimed in. 'Even though you'll be working, it will be lovely for her to explore London and Paris.'

Reid's gaze swept instantly from Gina to where his mother sat on the sofa facing the television set. Lorna beamed at her son, delighted to find herself of use to him for once. While she adored her grandchildren and indulged them, taking joy in seeing them happy, it was Reid's pleasure she really sought.

She'd confided to Gina that her two daughters were always asking her to do things for them but Reid never did, and he'd been such a tower of strength to her after his father died, she didn't know how to repay his goodness. Not that he expected her to, but it was nice, really nice to be asked to do something for him. Well, for all of them, of course. It was just that Reid was so super-organised, she didn't feel needed by him, and a mother liked to feel needed. At least a bit.

Gina held her breath. A wife liked to feel needed, too. Needed and wanted and loved! Reid could blow it all apart right now, demanding explanations, throwing her plan out in a storm of rebuttals that would leave no-one in any doubt Gina had acted against his will and desires. She could feel the sword of wrath swinging like a pendulum. Then suddenly, incredibly, it was sheathed.

'It's very kind of you to take over for us here at home, Mum,' Reid said with a smile, a slightly stiff smile but a smile nonetheless.

'Oh, the children and I are going to have tremendous fun together. I'm really looking forward to it,' Lorna enthused.

Bobby landed against his father's legs, and Reid bent to haul him up to shoulder height, shushing him to cut off the aeroplane drone. 'Sure it won't be too much for you?' Reid asked his mother, raising his eyebrows at his superactive younger son.

'Now don't be worrying about the HT, Mr. T.,' Shirley called from the kitchen, her penchant for initials reducing Holy Terror to its barest minimum. 'Between the three of us, we'll have the problem pegged, won't we, Tracy?'

'We'll do the job, no worries, Mr. Tyson,' came the swift and cheerful back-up from the trusty nanny.

'Really, Reid,' his mother chided. 'As if I'm not experienced! I might remind you that you were more than a handful at a certain age.'

'Well, I can see the women's club is swinging into affirmative action,' he drawled with every appearance of good humour as he carried Bobby down to the family room. 'On your heads be it!' he added cheerfully.

Women's conspiracy, Gina interpreted, not missing the glitter in Reid's eyes before he hooded it. He was holding his fire, scouting the situation, bottling his anger for later. Pride wouldn't let him explode in front of his mother or his staff. Most especially his mother. The good-marriage-show went on, at least in front of others. No rocks anywhere in sight.

'It's so exciting,' Tracy bubbled. 'Mrs. Tyson flying off to Europe with you on Sunday. Paris in the spring...'

'Mummy said she'll bring us back lots of pictures,' Patrick declared, seeing the advantages for himself in show-and-tell at school.

He was more like her than Reid, Gina thought, not only in looks, with his wavy brown hair, olive skin and amber eyes, but also in nature. He wanted approval too much. Approval and reassurance. His younger brother never looked for either. Bobby moved to his own beat.

'Dad-Dad, me-me!' Jessica demanded, scrambling off Lorna's lap, jealous of Bobby getting first nurse with their father.

'Wait with Grandma, Jess,' Reid directed her. 'Down you go, Bobby. Looks like Mummy's made some drinks here, and I'm a man with a thirst.'

'I'm a jet plane,' Bobby cried, and was off and running the moment his feet hit the floor.

Jessica hung around Lorna's knees, pouting to be picked up.

'They're G and Ts,' Patrick informed his father as Reid strolled towards the servery bench where Gina was still stationed. 'That means gin and tonic, Daddy. Mummy made one for Grandma 'cause she likes a G and T.'

'So do I, Patrick. It's lucky Mummy has made two of them.' Reid's gaze swung to Gina, a full blast of dangerous derision as he added, 'Though perhaps she's in dire need of one of these herself. Are you, darling?'

Her throat seized up. She shook her head and pushed the two glasses across the bench to him, silently pressing him to take the second drink to his mother and keep the happy family charade going.

He picked them up but he didn't move away. Gina's head swam from the tension of all that was being left unsaid. It seemed to hang between them, brooding, gathering force.

'You've been very busy this afternoon,' he remarked in a casual tone, belying the dark turbulence she sensed in him.

Gina swallowed hard. She was not going to be intimidated. To her mind there was justification for what she'd done. A surge of defiance brought a flush to her cheeks and a challenging fire to her eyes, turning the amber to molten gold.

'I would have preferred to be busy with you,' she said, then dropped her tone low enough to keep the words private. 'But that plan fell through since you chose to spend your personal time with your personal assistant.'

A blaze of blue flashed savage intent. 'I'm sure we can make up for that later tonight.'

'Not worn out then?' she shot back at him, still smarting over his choice to be with Paige Calder.

'I've suddenly found huge stores of energy. Must

be the prospect of this second honeymoon you talked about to Liz Copeland.'

Gina's heart skipped a beat. He'd known what she'd done before he came home. It was probably what had brought him home early, only to be faced with more of a fait accompli. He was pumped up, but not with desire to make love with her. It was barely repressed fury fuelling the energy burn inside him.

'Dad-Dad!' Jessica shrilled, impatient for his attention. She pushed away from Lorna and set off tottering towards him.

Seeing his daughter's single-minded charge, Reid called to Patrick. 'Take Grandma's drink to her, will you, son? I've got to pass on a few messages to your mother.'

Gina waited tensely for the messages, aware that Reid was setting up some uninterrupted space for them to converse without appearing rude to his mother or anyone else.

Patrick raced to do his bidding. Reid deftly handed him one glass, set the other on the bench and bent to scoop Jessica up with perfect timing. He swung straight back to Gina, holding Jessica so she could coo her triumph to her brothers over his shoulder.

'Liz said to remind you to bring in your passport first thing tomorrow morning,' he went on silkily, taking a primitive satisfaction in dancing around the target before going for the kill.

'When were you talking to her?' For some reason it seemed important to pin down the timing.

'Oh, about forty minutes ago.'

Not long. He'd probably set off for home straight after the call. 'Does Paige Calder know?'

The fury flared at that question, and Gina realised in a flash how much Reid would hate being made to look a fool, especially by his wife. 'No, she doesn't,' he answered, then leaning forward over the bench to shut everyone else out, he very deliberately elaborated, his voice dropping to a low throb that beat only at her.

'I gave Paige the rest of the afternoon off after her birthday lunch. She wasn't in the office when the call came in from Liz. For which I am grateful, since in the normal course of events, Paige would have taken it and heard how my wife had gone behind my back—'

'While *you* were lunching with her,' Gina fiercely interposed.

'On her birthday,' he retorted.

Gina glared. 'Well, the birthday girl will be getting a surprise tomorrow, won't she? Her trip with you will have a wife in tow.' Gina's chin jutted with stubborn and defiant determination. 'I'm not going to change my mind, Reid.'

He rocked back from the bench, steely pride on his face. 'And I'm not going to change my plans, Gina.'

'Well, at least I'll know who's sharing your bedroom.'

'I see your point.' His smile promised she'd know, all right. He'd hammer the knowledge to an absolute surfeit of knowing. 'The question is, can you live up to it?'

'I'm ready to answer that question any time, Reid. It was you who evaded it today.'

'Not evaded. Postponed. Let's see how you feel in the morning. Maybe you'll have changed your mind by then.'

With that parting shot he lifted his gin and tonic in a mocking toast to her, sipped it, then left her to go to the sofa and converse with his mother. There he learnt that Lorna was staying overnight in the guest suite so she could observe the usual morning routine with the children tomorrow. Gina silently promised her husband that none of the plans she'd made today were about to be changed.

He proceeded to play the good son brilliantly, the good father until Tracy took the children upstairs to bed, the good husband and host during the dinner party with his mother. There was an edge of exhilaration to his performance, higher spirits than usual. Excitement about the trip, his mother would think.

Gina knew better.

It was anticipation, all right, but not about the trip. He was secretly planning, envisaging what he would do and say when he finally had Gina alone with him in the privacy of their bedroom. It was in his eyes every time he looked at her. And he wasn't seeing her as the mother of his children!

Lorna Tyson would think Gina was excited, too. She was right. Excited, exhilarated and exultant. Because Reid was taking notice of her. Reid was more intensely focused on her than he'd been in years. And that meant she was winning. He certainly wasn't thinking of Paige Calder.

The contrast to last night's cool distance across the dinner table was huge. The air fairly sizzled between them with challenge and counterchallenge being silently, intimately exchanged. The fear that had gnawed at Gina earlier was gone. She wasn't defeated. She had room to move, and move she would. She was looking forward to proving a point.

CHAPTER NINE

REID had her hand locked in his, no possible escape from him, as they bade his mother good-night at the top of the stairs and parted from her to retire for the night. He set a strolling pace along the wide hall to their suite, apparently in no hurry, perhaps wanting to relish the sense of being alone together—no walking away, no turning aside, no bolting anywhere, no ringing in anyone else—and having the power to direct the moment of reckoning at his leisure.

Asserting control, Gina thought, but if he thought he was going to control her, he could think again. The sense of mutiny that had been driving her all afternoon was as strong as when it had first erupted. She was not going to occupy the compartment Reid seemed to have assigned her to.

'I had no idea you were so passionate about sharing a bedroom with me, Gina,' he remarked sardonically. 'I thought you considered it more the done thing in a marriage than your heart's desire.'

'What gave you that idea?' she asked, wondering what she had done to cause him to form this false assumption about her. She couldn't deny she had been at fault in not making him feel desired, but she had never once indicated separate rooms might be more desirable, not even when she was heavily pregnant.

He slanted her a derisive look. 'Well, for a start, you chose a bed for us that you could get lost in,' he drawled. 'We might as well have been sleeping apart, for all the intimacy it promoted.'

Judged by the bed she disliked! Gina huffed her annoyance at the absurd irony. 'The interior decorator chose the bed. She said a room that large needed a king-size. It was a matter of space and proportion. It wasn't my choice at all.'

'Then why go along with it?' He sounded totally unconvinced.

'I didn't know any better at the time.'

'You've had almost seven years to know better, Gina. Most nights you could have driven a truck down the centre of that bed without it touching either of us. Don't tell me you hadn't noticed.'

His sarcasm stung. 'I didn't like it any more than you did,' she retorted.

They'd reached their bedroom door. His hand was on the knob. He paused, turning to look at her face on, his eyes raking hers. 'What do you think lying to me will win in the long run?'

'I'm not lying!' Gina protested.

The riveting blue eyes bored into hers as he laid out a line of relentless logic. 'At any time during the past seven years you could have got rid of that bed. You've changed plenty of other furniture you decided you didn't fancy any more. You've had absolutely free rein with expenditure on this house, inside and out.' He raised one taunting eyebrow as he delivered the punch line. 'If you didn't like the bed, Gina, why didn't you change it?'

Her stomach contracted. The unanswerable question. 'I don't know,' she murmured miserably.

He opened the door and scooped her into their bedroom ahead of him. Faced with the monster bed, Gina suddenly did know why she hadn't changed it.

A smaller bed wouldn't have looked as good, and because of that, it would have invited questions from anyone who had seen the much more impressive and stylish big bed. It would have been embarrassing to explain she needed to minimise the size to make snuggling up to her husband seem normal.

Even if no one had asked about it, such a change would have been an obvious move towards a more intimate situation—strikingly obvious—and a lady was never obvious.

Gina mentally writhed over all the strictures that had circumscribed her behaviour in regard to sex and sexuality and the marriage bed. It wasn't her fault, she wanted to cry. Her mother, the nuns at school, the sheltered life of being an only child who wasn't encouraged to mix much, the ignorance of still being a virgin when she married…she hadn't really known how to behave.

The door clicked shut behind her, sealing their privacy. She and Reid together in a room that was his as well as hers.

'*You* could have said something about the bed, Reid,' she burst out, swinging to face him. 'Why didn't you?' she demanded. It was a reasonable question. She wasn't alone in this marriage, and he was older and more experienced.

'A man's a fool if he doesn't learn from his mistakes,' he said tersely.

'What mistakes?' Gina cried in bewilderment.

He sketched a mocking bow. 'Intruding on my wife's space.'

She shook her head, sure she had never designated personal space where he wouldn't be welcomed.

Seeing her lack of comprehension, he elaborated as he strolled around her to his side of the bed. 'I'm well acquainted with all the husbandly sins. Expecting my wife to give more than she wants to. Encroaching on her rights as an individual. Interfering with her decisions. And, heaven forbid, asking her to be accountable to me for what she chooses to do.'

Gina was stunned by the underlying bitterness.

He gave a derisive snort. 'Never mind the broken promises on her side! A woman has the right to change her mind.'

'I have never accused you of any of these things,' she declared vehemently. 'Or complained—'

He laughed. 'I've never given you reason to.' His

eyes were savage as he added, 'I didn't want my second marriage to go the way of the first.'

His first? The relationship he'd determinedly buried behind him as totally irrelevant to what he felt and had with Gina? He'd never made any comment on his ex-wife, not even when they saw her reporting a story on television news.

Reid had dismissed their break-up and divorce as the natural outcome of irreconcilable differences, he being a family-oriented man, she being single-mindedly dedicated to her career. But suddenly the spectre of that relationship had a dark overhang on theirs. Words Reid had thrown at her took on shadows from his past. *A manipulative game people play... Self-absorbed selfishness...*

'I have always listened to what you want, Gina,' he went on, anger beginning to edge his voice again. 'I did my best to either make it happen for you or give you the means to make it happen for yourself.'

'I'm not your first wife, Reid. I'm nothing like her,' Gina pleaded.

'That's what I thought,' he said self-mockingly. 'And it was a big part of your attraction. We actually had some harmony going between us in both wanting the same things.'

It sounded as though he thought she had deceived him. Gina frowned, unsure how to defend herself.

He picked one of the decorative cushions off the bed and crushed it between his hands. 'Have I ever let you down with support for what you wanted within your chosen domain, Gina?'

'No, you've always been very good to me,' she said quietly, keeping still, wanting him to spew out all the pent-up feelings he'd never revealed to her.

'In fact, you've had a smooth run in this marriage up until last night, wouldn't you say?'

'Yes. Shiny-smooth,' she agreed with a touch of irony.

The simmering anger suddenly exploded into furious fire. 'Then just because something doesn't go all your way for once, what the hell makes you think you can not only intrude on *my* space, but tramp all over it any way you like?'

He slung the cushion he held onto the armchair where they were usually piled at night. 'Interfering with *my* decisions,' he shot at her as he picked up another. 'Demanding accountability from me.' The cushion was hurled onto the chair so he was free to jab a finger at her. 'Even after I'd assured you your position was absolutely secure. And I do not lie, Gina.'

No, he did not lie. That was true. She'd never even heard him tell a white lie to anyone.

He dragged another cushion off the bed and punched it. 'I hate dishonesty,' he said with vehement passion. 'I especially hate it when it screws other people up, playing them for fools to get some perceived personal gain. It all has to do with me, me, me, me!'

He held the cushion like a punching bag and belted it onto the chair.

His hand chopped the air as he went on. 'I am telling you right now, Gina, you don't have to do *anything* you don't want to do—'

'But I—'

'Hear me out! You have every right to be the way you are, and I have no right to want to change you. So you can back off and just be yourself, and I'll respect that. I will respect it,' he repeated, as though stamping it into his mind. And hers. 'You won't hear another word of criticism from me. We're married and we stay married.'

'Oh, that's wonderfully fair of you!' Gina slung at him, pumped up from having to take in so much.

'Yes,' he retorted. 'I have this fixation about being fair. And keeping my word. Even to giving a birthday lunch to a valued employee.'

'And just when did you decide marriage was about a bill of rights?' she demanded. 'This is the first I've heard of it. I always thought marriage was about bonding and loving.'

'Sure! If you believe in fairytales,' he scoffed. 'You're lucky if you get a partnership where you can both agree I do this—' he grabbed another cushion '—and you do that—' and another '—and these bits we do together.' He banged the two cushions into each other then tossed them onto the pile.

Before she could say anything he threw out his

hands, closed them into fists and weighed them as he delivered his beliefs. 'Now we happen to have a reasonably amenable partnership going, Gina, and I won't mess with it. I sincerely hope you won't mess with it, either. Because there aren't any fairy stories in this world. It's about making the best of what you've got!'

His cynicism and his acceptance of less than what there could be between them were fighting words to Gina. 'I will not have you making rules and judgments for me, Reid. This is my life, too. I came to you today—'

He flung out a dismissive arm. 'You came because you thought your cosy little world was at risk and you'd better put some effort in.'

That was true, but it wasn't the whole truth.

'I'm telling you you don't have to, Gina,' he went on, his tone losing its vehemence and fading into a deep, bitter irony. 'You're fine as you are. As for bonding and loving, we have our children.' His mouth curled in a travesty of smiling appreciation. 'You gave me my children, and I guess that's about as much as a man can ask of a woman.'

Gina's heart sank. How did one fight through such a deadly wall of disillusionment?

Reid expelled a long breath and twitched a hand at her. 'Just let today and last night go as mad heat-of-the-moment reactions.'

I can't, she thought.

'I'm sure we can come up with some excuse to postpone your urge to see Europe this time around. My mother won't carry on about it, so it's no big deal.'

He was giving up on their marriage. Gina was so appalled, all she could do was shake her head as he spelled out his view of their future.

'We just keep on occupying our separate sides of the bed—' he tossed the last of the decorative cushions and placed one of the pillows down the centre. '—then, by the time I come home from my trip, this little contretemps will be smoothly tucked away in the past and you won't have to do anything.'

'No,' Gina said firmly. Her only recourse was to take positive action now, if it wasn't already too late. *I won't believe it's too late. And I won't let Reid believe it, either.* 'That bed is going tomorrow,' she stated decisively. 'Which would you prefer, a double or a queen-size?'

He shook his head as though she'd totally lost the plot. 'For God's sake! It's not the size of a bed that counts. It's how you use it. Why are you persisting with this?' he cried in exasperation.

'Because you're wrong! You're terribly, terribly wrong!'

'Wrong, am I?'

It was exploding the anger in him again, but Gina couldn't back down. 'Yes, you are. I came to you today to show you I want to be close to you. I want to give—'

'Give!' he yelled at her. His eyes blazed fury at her apparent refusal to take the deal he was offering— his honest, fair deal. His chest heaved as he worked up another head of steam. 'You call that a display of *giving*?'

'Yes, I do. I thought of everything I could to give you pleasure,' she defended hotly. 'To make you feel good about us instead of how you felt last night.'

'So you put in all this grade-A effort—' his chest heaved as though he needed to pull in enormous amounts of oxygen to keep his brain from exploding '—and when you didn't get the response you wanted when you wanted it, you went behind my back in a jealous fit of pique and pursued your own self-interest, regardless of how it affected me.' Then with pure acid dripping from his tongue, 'That's truly great giving, Gina.'

She wasn't going to wear that. He might have cause for anger, but he was not blameless in what had tran-spired today. 'You weren't listening to me, Reid. At least I've made you stop and listen. Maybe you'll even hear what I'm saying.'

The gasket he'd been holding down in his mind blew. He glared blue bolts of lightning at her then turned and hurled the quilt off the bed. 'Words are cheap,' he jeered, removing the barrier he'd set with a pillow. 'Even roses are cheap where there's no shortage of money. And promises are very, very cheap when there's no delivery.'

He straightened up and faced her, hands hooked on his hips, eyes taunting. 'If I'm so terribly wrong, prove it! Give me a taste of the second honeymoon you sold to Liz Copeland behind my back. Show me what I supposedly missed out on with your offer of love in the afternoon. What I'm now paying for!'

The boiling resentment colouring his voice and priming his aggressive stance had a choking effect on Gina. Her mind screamed, *Here's your chance! Be bold! Show him!* Her body reacted like a petrified piece of wood. It was as though her legs didn't know how to move. She needed warmth, encouragement, approval…the sense of being loved.

'Come on, Gina.' He applied a silky whip with a sting that burned. 'Don't you want to check if Paige Calder left her smell on me?'

It unfroze her. It ignited a fire that would have melted steel. Anger blazed, flooding her with strength of purpose. She could have faced a raging bull. 'You're running a risk if she did, husband mine!' she hissed, taking off her shoes and advancing on him with unshakeable intent.

He laughed softly, goading her.

She stopped his laughter.

She grabbed his shirt and tore it open, buttons popping off and flying everywhere. She insinuated a knee between his thighs, meaning to apply some provocative friction to his private parts while she undid his pants. But he misread her intention.

'Oh, no, you don't,' he rumbled, hooking his hands under her arms, and the next moment she was flying, hurled onto the bed. Then he had a knee between her legs, and his body was looming over hers. 'You want to play the bitch, I'll oblige,' he threatened.

Wild at being thwarted, she punched at his shoulders, dislodging his arms. In a furious twist, she pulled him down, rolled to put him underneath her and heaved herself up to straddle him, slapping her hands on his chest to hold him still. 'Let be!' she yelled at him, needing two breaths to get the words out.

His hands curled around her wrists, ready to exert his strength. 'Maiming is not my idea of sexual pleasure,' he growled.

'Nor mine. Will you just stop putting me in the wrong all the time? And thinking the worst?'

'A knee in the groin…'

'I haven't got three hands. How was I supposed to excite you and undress you at the same time?' she fiercely demanded.

A long expulsion of breath from him. Then a slow, wicked grin. 'Well, just you shimmy up to my chest now, and I'll take care of my undressing for you,' he drawled. 'And sitting right there across my rib cage you could unbutton that in-my-face orange dress and

excite me some with what you've got underneath it.'
His eyes glittered. '*If* you have a mind to.'

The devil was in him.

The thought excited her. The urge to be wicked
flowed over her anger. She had permission. She had
approval. She could do anything she wanted to. She
had nothing to lose and so much to gain, the prospect
blew away any reservations.

'Then let go my hands, Reid,' she said silkily, smiling with satisfaction in the situation. She was on top.
And in control.

He surrendered his hold on her, but she could feel
the tension in him, the coiled readiness to seize the
initiative from her if she played him false. There was
no trust in him yet. Gina was acutely aware of being
on trial. Nevertheless, the chance was being granted,
and the confidence from what she had learnt last night
started tingling through her.

Definitely not a convent girl tonight, she promised
herself. There was no place for prim modesty. The
kind of things strippers did flitted through her mind,
bold, brazen and blatantly focused on sexuality. Such
openly lusty actions would certainly deny any hesitation or shrinking from the challenge, not to mention
rubbing Reid's cynical disbelief right in his face.

An extra burst of adrenaline increased the tingle in
her blood as she knelt and manoeuvred forward, her
eyes taunting him as she began unbuttoning her

dress—her bold, out-of-character dress that had succeeded in catching his attention.

'Do you like this colour on me, Reid?' she asked. 'Do you think it looks hot and sexy?' She could hardly believe the words tripping off her tongue, but she'd secretly wanted to say stuff like that. It felt deliciously naughty.

'It clicks a positive switch. Truth or tease?' he rasped, lifting his lower body to slide his pants down.

'Both,' she declared, flashing the dress open. 'It leads to this, which is supposed to be a turn-on. True or not?'

His gaze ran over the black lace bra, designed to push a cleavage to maximum dimensions, the strappy garter belt circling her hips and holding up her stockings, and the V of black lace and silk that could be more accurately described as scanties, not panties.

'It adds allure to the female body,' he dryly acknowledged, his legs very active, the thud of shoes hitting the floor testifying to their agility. 'On the other hand, let's not mistake window-dressing for anything other than it is. Anyone can play dress up.'

'No one in their right minds would bother donning this gear for dress up. It's too uncomfortable,' she informed him airily, snapping one of the suspenders. 'It only has one purpose, and that's getting people horny. That's what the saleswoman told me.'

'Does it make *you* feel horny?' Reid asked sardonically, his legs pumping his trousers off.

'Mmmm.' She hauled the dress from her arms and threw it on the floor, not to be outdone in the un-dressing stakes. 'It makes me very aware of myself physically. The bra seems to compress my breasts, yet gives me the sense of spilling out of it. Actually it's good to get it off.'

She suited action to words and another garment hit the carpet. She smiled at him as she ran her hands up and around her breasts, soothing away the sense of constriction. She'd seen erotic dancers in a recent movie do it. Reid could be as sardonic and cynical as he liked. It wasn't going to affect her. Proving him wrong was the name of the game, and she was rev-elling in every wickedly outrageous moment of it.

'You want a man's point of view?' he asked, eye-ing the free and voluptuous swish of unfettered flesh above him.

'I want yours,' she said, making it strictly personal.

'Sexy is not confining your breasts at all. The jiggle of the female anatomy is what's sexy. Breasts, bottom and—if we're getting personal—you do have a superb arrangement to jiggle.'

It was his first—albeit grudging—concession to what was really happening here. It gave a huge charge of confidence to Gina, not to mention a rush of warm pleasure through the admired anatomy. The envy she invariably felt towards tall, slim women—like Paige Calder—was instantly squashed. Reid liked her curvy.

Her smile shone with an inner delight he could not

possibly turn sour, and there crept into his eyes a questioning he hadn't given room to before. Gina quite revelled in some hip swaying and poking her bottom out this way and that as she undid the suspenders holding up her stockings and whipped off the garter belt. It made her feel sexier and sexier.

She was eager to work her body over his, sensually sliding and stroking. When she lowered herself on top of his groin she exulted in the strength of his arousal, the tension in his thigh muscles. It was intensely exciting to caress him with the silk crotch of her panties before moving the panties aside and using the soft, slippery heat of her own sex to drive anticipation to screaming need.

'Does that feel good?' she asked.

'Yes,' he answered gruffly.

Bit by bit she was leeching out his cynical disbelief.

'Be better inside,' he added, definitely into eager cooperation now.

So she worked him inside, playing every erotic game with their flesh that she could think of, varying contact points and pressure. It was incredibly arousing to watch his face, to see his appraisal of her changing, softening, the glitter of fierce approval in his eyes, the fraying of control, the sudden feral look at climax, and all the time, every sweet moment of it, *she* was doing it to *him*.

There was a wild ecstasy in bringing it off, showing him, driving the point home. And swirling underneath the ecstasy was the deep, primitive beat of possession—my husband, my man, my partner, mine!

CHAPTER TEN

SHE watched him dress. Reid knew she was waiting for him to say something. He let her wait. The feeling of being manipulated was strong, and he hated it.

If it was jealousy driving Gina, it was amazing what jealousy could inspire a woman to do. Last night she had shed inhibitions as though they had never existed. She'd given him fantastic sex. What he'd put her through the previous night certainly hadn't been lost on her, a fact he found intensely disturbing.

What was real and what wasn't? The change in her was too abrupt, too extreme for him to believe in it. He wondered how long the act would last. Until she felt the danger of Paige was over and done with?

Strange how she had zeroed in on Durley House. It was obvious that nothing he said was going to divert her suspicions about it. Which meant falling in with her plan to accompany him on the trip if he wanted to keep their marriage intact. He no longer had a choice. He wasn't about to risk a divorce action.

'Have you tried a waterbed, Reid?'

He finished tying his shoelaces and stood up. She was lying on his side of the bed he had criticised, completely naked, hugging a pillow as though she

111

was missing him to curl up against. It put a tightness in his chest and an ache in his groin that he could well do without.

His first wife had used sex as a weapon. Did all women use it to get what they wanted? He would never have thought it of Gina. For her to go on with it, even after he'd given her an out… Was it pride, loss of face, disbelief that he'd keep his word about marriage security if he had sex with another woman, or something more primal? Possessiveness was an insidious instinct, demanding far more than it should.

'Forget the bed,' he said. 'If you're coming to Europe with me, you'll have more than enough to do in the next few days.'

Her face lit with relief. 'You don't mind my coming?'

He gave her a hard look. 'Don't expect me to change my plans, Gina, because I won't. You've forced this on me. Just don't mess me up while we're over there.'

'I won't.' She grinned with delight in having won. 'I'll make it good for you, I promise.'

He nodded and left her, unable to quell a fierce hope that the change would prove real and lasting. Their marriage would be almost perfect if it did.

Take one night at a time, he advised himself. *The truth will reveal itself soon enough.*

CHAPTER ELEVEN

GINA was intensely relieved to finally arrive at the Silver Kris Lounge. The long walk through the international terminal—Singapore Airlines' first-class lounge was at the far end of it—had left her burning with embarrassment. She'd been stared at by so many men, heads swivelling to follow her. Never in her life had she felt so painfully self-conscious.

'Don't wear anything tight or restrictive,' Reid had advised. 'Being in the air for over twenty hours will make you very conscious of any little discomfort.'

Her black stretch slacks had seemed like a good idea, since they readily gave with every movement. They didn't crush, either. They did hug her figure, but she'd never felt spotlighted by them before. No, it was the lime green jersey jacket drawing attention. To be more accurate it was the bra she wasn't wearing that was the real problem.

Her bras could feel tight after a while. Besides, Reid had said it was sexy for breasts to jiggle freely. Taking these two factors into consideration, and wanting especially to show Reid she was listening to what he liked, the decision to go braless had seemed right. She hadn't realised it would be so obvious to everyone, or that she'd feel like dying of mortification.

Reid guided them to an unoccupied corner of the lounge. Gina quickly chose the armchair with its back turned to the rest of the room and barely stopped herself from huddling into it. With Paige Calder sitting opposite her, pride wouldn't allow her to show any discomfort.

'Would you like a drink, Gina?' Reid asked, still standing. His tone was kindly, though there was a strained look in his eyes.

'Coffee would be lovely,' she answered gratefully. 'Paige?'

'I'll come with you. Help you carry.'

The personal assistant personally assisting, Gina thought ruefully, but she was glad to be left alone to regain some composure. Relaxing was nigh on impossible. She desperately wished she'd packed a bra in her carry-on luggage. It was all very well to be sexy for Reid in private. That's where it should stay, Gina decided. *In private.*

She could actually enjoy being naked now. In private. Even being bold was getting easier. Reid definitely liked it. The anger was gone, but he was still keeping her at an emotional distance, wary of the sudden turnaround in attitude and behaviour. Gina knew he wasn't won over yet. It was as though he was waiting for her to regress, not trusting what she offered, though accepting it readily enough, revelling in it when he let himself go.

She had the feeling if she put a foot wrong on this

trip, the heat between them would suddenly turn into the snow of Mount Kosciusko. Despite Reid's surface compliance to her tagging along, Gina suspected a brooding resentment to having had his hand forced.

She had been sneaky. There was no denying it. Nevertheless, on this one occasion she felt the end justified the means. It would show Paige Calder that Reid's bed was well and truly occupied. It would also show Reid a second honeymoon was not a bad idea. They did need to focus more on each other to build something better out of their marriage.

Paige was brightly discussing some business with Reid as they returned, bearing cups of coffee and a plate of dainty gourmet sandwiches. She broke off to address Gina, presenting a face full of indulgent understanding that somehow made Gina feel like a spoilt brat.

'Liz Copeland said you'd like to take my seat once we're on board.'

'No, I didn't say that,' Gina instantly protested. It had been the travel agent's suggestion.

Paige shrugged prettily. 'Whatever. It won't matter to me, as I've viewed all there is to see many times. And I daresay it's no trouble for Reid to lean across the aisle to speak to me if he has any further thoughts on the business meetings tomorrow. I'll tell the crew.'

'No, please.' Gina was horror-struck.

Reid frowned at her.

Paige raised her eyebrows as though Gina was being tiresomely capricious.

'I wouldn't dream of taking your seat or interfering with any of the plans you've made,' Gina expostulated, her heart squeezing tight as she remembered Reid laying down that law.

'It's no big deal, Gina,' he said testily.

'I don't mind being shifted,' Paige said with sweet reasonableness.

'But I never meant to encroach on time that should be spent on preparing for important meetings.' No way was she going to lay herself open to blame on that score. She was here under sufferance. 'I don't want to be moved,' she rushed on. 'I've got my own seat, and I'm perfectly happy with it.'

'But don't you want to be with Reid?' Paige pressed.

Gina decided then and there that she hated the woman. Of course she wanted to be with Reid. But she wanted even more not to be put in the wrong on this trip. She turned to Reid, appealing directly to him, anxious for him to believe her.

'I told you I'd look after myself. I'd feel really intrusive if I took Paige's seat, Reid. I promised you I wouldn't get in the way or mess anything up and I won't. I'd prefer to leave everything as it is. Okay?'

'As you wish,' he agreed, but he didn't look happy about it.

Gina felt hopelessly confused.

Hadn't she just passed the test? Done the right thing? She wished Reid would make his mind up one way or the other, because she really needed some good positive signals from him.

Reid sat in his first-class seat on the Singapore Airlines flight to London, pampered by the ever-attentive steward and stewardesses, his every whim and comfort being served. He was hating every second of it. He could hear Gina chatting to the person sitting next to her in the centre row and inwardly railed at his impotence to change a situation he'd brought upon himself.

She'd done precisely what he'd asked of her—not interfering with set plans, not intruding on time that could be fruitfully used on discussing the business to be done in Europe, keeping right out of the way. *Don't mess me up,* he'd said. So here he sat, sipping superb champagne as though it were acid and feeling more messed up than he'd ever been in his life.

He wanted her beside him. He'd been looking forward to having her beside him on the long flight to London. It was a new experience for her. He would have enjoyed her joy in it. That was one thing he'd always loved about Gina, her capacity for joy. She was great with the children. Their kids couldn't have a better mother. He'd tried to get it across to her he valued that far more than the sex he could get anywhere if he so chose.

Not that he wanted it anywhere. He certainly couldn't get it better than what Gina had been giving him the past four nights, and that was confusing the hell out of him. He'd come to terms with what was possible and not possible from his marriage. Gina was throwing his conclusions into chaos.

It was almost as though she was possessed by a different personality to the one he'd been accustomed to living with. If she'd been imprisoned in a cocoon of uptight repression all these years, the butterfly was emerging with a vengeance.

The clothes she was wearing today had him simmering. Her black trousers outlined every roll of her curvy hips and the delectable cheekiness of her bottom. Even more eye-catching and distracting was the lime green jersey wrap jacket.

Although it was loosely fitting, the soft fabric clearly revealed there was nothing between it and Gina's breasts. It also had a tantalisingly accessible look about it. No buttons to stop a hand sliding inside the long, dipping opening. He'd been thinking of what he might do when they lowered their seats for sleeping and the lights were out.

Now… He glanced at Paige, sitting serenely beside him, gazing out the window, keeping her thoughts to herself, probably aware he was distracted, disturbed and in a diabolical mood. God only knew what she thought about the situation. Not that he particularly cared at this point, but he would have to come to some understanding with her before they landed in London and got to Durley House.

She was dressed sexily, too, though less obviously than Gina. Her long navy skirt had a slit up the side, running to mid-thigh, where kinky bone buttons went up to her waist. The matching navy knit top was very clingy, with more of the buttons to attract the eye. The big difference was her figure, which was not as spectacularly female as Gina's.

Perhaps sensing his attention, Paige turned to him with an inquiring look. 'Is there a problem?' she asked, a soft, sympathetic tone in her voice, inviting confidences.

He'd never once spoken to Paige Calder about his wife, and he wasn't about to start now. It was none of her business. Even when he'd been dallying with the idea of making a sexual arrangement with Paige, he would never have given the excuse, 'My wife doesn't understand me.' Nor would he have allowed such an arrangement to impinge on his marriage. His home life was sacrosanct. No one was welcome to touch it.

'No. No problem,' he said, firmly shutting the door on the questions floating around in Paige's shrewd grey eyes.

She was a smart woman, extremely quick on the uptake. The lack of marital harmony was all too evident, but Reid's disclaimer put it out of discussion.

'I was wondering if it might not be more *conve-*

nient for you—' a meaningful look loaded with sexual innuendo '—if I can be moved into a separate apartment at Durley House. Or stay somewhere nearby.'

So whatever went on between them wasn't under his wife's nose, and they couldn't get caught out, either. Reid got the message loud and clear. Paige was still holding the door open for discreet fun and games if he was so inclined.

It brought home to Reid the gross deceit involved in adultery. It made him feel a real hypocrite, he, who had always prided himself on his honesty. As much as he had justified a little adultery on the side in his own mind, deciding it would be a pragmatic course to take, he was intensely glad now that Gina had turned the wheel on it and he didn't have it on his conscience.

'I see no reason to change our current accommodation plan,' he said flatly. *And a lot of reasons not to*, he thought. 'Gina was so adamant about not interfering with anything, she'd probably be upset at the thought of putting you out, Paige.'

Upset and suspicious. Very suspicious. And Reid didn't want Gina suspicious. Especially when there was no longer any cause to be. He hoped Paige was getting *that* message loud and clear.

As far as he was concerned, their sharing the apartment at Durley House was a congenial business arrangement, innocent of anything more personal. That was how he'd presented it to Gina and that was how it was going to be.

'Well, if you change your mind, Reid, I'm happy to go along with whatever you want,' Paige subtly persisted, the invitation still out against all signals.

'We'll see,' he said dismissively.

Her persistence vexed Reid. He wanted to snap, *Give up, lady,* but he'd brought this situation upon himself by allowing a certain warmth and laxness to creep into their relationship. The birthday luncheon… Gina had been right to zero in on it as getting too familiar with another woman. He had justified that, too, but no doubt about Gina's female instincts when it came to her territory. They cut through the camouflage and got straight to the core.

She was his wife.

His wife.

And Gina was certainly letting him know it.

There was no doubt in his mind it was Durley House and Paige that had triggered this mind-screwing revolution in his marriage. He couldn't help being sceptical about it. Yet, what if behind the jealousy and the possessiveness there was a genuine desire to be more of a wife to him?

What if Gina simply wanted to be closer to him, to please him, to forge a happier intimacy between them? Maybe there was a chance—a real chance—for something more than there'd been in their relationship, more than he'd become resigned to. In his heart of hearts he craved more. Couldn't he allow the possibility?

He had to acknowledge Gina was taking everything he said to heart and putting it into practice with a dedication that surely deserved some show of appreciation from him, whatever her motives.

Reid set aside his glass of champagne.

He unbuckled his seat belt and rose to his feet.

Paige looked up at him inquiringly.

He coolly excused himself and turned to move down the cabin. Gina was looking at him, her face bright with expectancy, patently wanting, hoping for him to come to her.

It suddenly thumped him in the gut how beautiful she was. A plethora of vivid memories leapt through his mind—Gina holding their first baby, shining with mother love, Gina on their wedding day, aglow with love for him, Gina when he had first seen her, in the shopping mall at Bondi Junction, happy to have a Christmas job selling personalised children's books, taking pleasure in delighting mothers and their little ones with stories using their names.

Beautiful. Even more so now, coming into mature womanhood, yet still with that look of appealing innocence in her eyes.

He smiled at her, a broad, appreciative male smile for the beautiful woman she was.

Her face lit up, her lovely amber eyes sparkling with golden pleasure, her smile a pure beam of joy.

It warmed Reid's belly and smoothed out knotted nerves.

The guy beside her glanced curiously from her to Reid to her again, but Gina was totally unaware of his interest. As Reid walked around the aisle to her side of the centre row, he couldn't help his gaze dropping to the soft mounds and peaks of her breasts, caressed by lime green cloth where his hands wanted to be.

Her skin started to flush. When he looked up there was anguished uncertainty in her eyes. He sensed the questions tumbling through her mind. *Have I done right? Am I doing right? What is right?*

He saw her recognise the simmer of desire in his eyes, saw relief sweeping her tension away. She relaxed, and her expression focused in on secretive, intimate pleasure, shared with him and him alone.

He bent and kissed her—his wife, who was playing the sexy siren for him. Her mouth was soft and sweet and giving, and the urge to claim fierce and passionate possession was strong. It was a wrench to have to draw back and act the civilised man.

'Everything okay with you here?' he asked, taking her hand and giving it a strong, reassuring squeeze.

'Yes.' Such a look of happy satisfaction in her eyes. 'Edward…Edward Harrow—' her hand fluttered in introduction '—has been very kind in showing and telling me things.'

'Thank you for looking after my wife,' Reid said

with a warmth that completely nonplussed the man who was probably wondering why they were sitting apart.

'Not at all,' he said, recovering quickly. 'A pleasure. Lovely lady.'

'Yes. I'm very lucky.' Reid smiled at Gina again. 'Try the caviar when they start serving dinner. It's superb with all the accompanying extras. Say yes to the glass of vodka, too.' His smile widened to a grin. 'Pretend you're Russian.'

She laughed. 'All right, I will. Thanks, Reid.'

It was a deep-throated, full-bodied, happy laugh, Reid thought. He wished he could have shared this kind of exchange with her all the way to London, and mentally kicked himself for being a stiff-necked, self-defeating fool. So what if it didn't last? Even a passing pleasure was better than none.

'Enjoy yourself,' he said, and meant it.

He returned to his seat on a buoyant wave of benevolence.

A little while later he heard Gina say, 'I'll have the caviar, please.'

It made him feel good.

They might be sitting with other people but they were sharing.

Maybe they *could* increase the sharing, and not just temporarily, if Gina was not screwing with his mind and was genuinely embracing the changes she had instigated. Reid was more than willing to give it a chance. He'd hoped it could be like this when he married her. If a second honeymoon was what she wanted, he'd more than meet her halfway.

Hope, he reflected, was an irrepressible emotion. It never knew when to lie down and die.

CHAPTER TWELVE

IT WAS six o'clock Monday morning when they landed at Heathrow Airport. Gina had not found the long flight arduous. In fact, it had been wonderfully exciting, with good things happening all the way.

The service had been excellent and constant. Superb food and wine and a tempting array of exotic drinks had been on offer. She had especially enjoyed the Citrus Royale, a most refreshing soft drink of fruit juices mixed with 7-Up, and the Mandarin Coffee, rich and creamy and spiced with a heavy dash of Cointreau and the essence of orange.

Reid had helped her select two movies on her personal video, both of them engrossing enough to make several hours slide by quickly and enjoyably. He'd also given her one of his sleeping pills, so she'd had at least five hours' solid sleep.

She'd been so warmly and wonderfully encouraged by Reid's attitude towards her, his caring about her comfort and pleasure, coming by her seat many times to check if she wanted or needed anything and setting her atingle with a look, a kiss or a touch that seemed to say he wished he had her to himself. Perhaps she should have swapped seats with Paige Calder. Yet how could she have known if that might be stepping over the line Reid had drawn?

It was better this way. She didn't feel wrong about coming with him now, or apprehensive about spending the next two weeks in what was foreign territory for her. Reid wasn't hating her presence on this trip, or grudging it or tolerating it for the sake of peace. Perhaps all her positive initiatives were bearing fruit. He certainly seemed to have had a change of heart. It was as though he'd decided to make this time as good for her as he could.

Their arrival at Durley House, however, was somewhat crushing to her high spirits. Paige Calder took over. She had been here before and slid straight into her personal assistant role, checking their requirements with the woman on reception, giving a light breakfast order for eight o'clock, leading the way to their apartment, showing Reid and Gina to the master bedroom, suggesting Reid have first use of the bathroom for his shower and reminding him they would need to be on their way by eight-thirty for their first meeting.

Gina felt decidedly superfluous. Telling herself this was how everything would have run if she hadn't come, she resolved once again to keep her mouth shut and stay out of the way. She unpacked for herself and Reid, at least being helpful to the extent of having his clothes laid out ready for him when he emerged from the bathroom.

The master bedroom was certainly big enough for both of them. Gina couldn't help smiling over the huge bed with its massive pile of white pillows, many of them lace-edged decorator items. Easy enough to get lost in this bed if togetherness wasn't desired. Getting lost was not on Gina's schedule. Not whenever Reid could make himself available to her.

The furnishings were warm and welcoming, luxurious in a nice, comfortable way. The bed and windows were draped in complementary red and white fabrics. There was a Laura Ashley feel about the room, a little fussy and old-fashioned with lots of furniture in polished wood, a big wardrobe and chest of drawers, a large dressing-table in front of the window, lovely antique tables holding lamps on either side of the bed.

The grouped pictures on the wallpapered walls, various little knick-knacks around the room and small vases of flowers added the homey, personalised touch one didn't find in big hotels. Gina could easily imagine herself in one of those grand English country houses, even though she was in the heart of London.

The kitchen was quite spacious and functional with all the utensils and appliances that might be required. Gina made a mental list of what to buy when she found a supermarket—fruit, cheese, biscuits and anything special that appealed. No, not a supermarket, she decided, grinning delightedly at the prospect of discovering all the delicacies of the Harrod's food hall. She would surprise Reid with lots of tempting goodies.

Having made herself a cup of coffee—neither Paige nor Reid wanted one—she carried it through to the drawing room, which was absolutely lovely. Here the extravagant drapes on the windows matched a many-cushioned chintz sofa. A bowl of tulips, freesias and other spring flowers graced a long coffee table that served two splendid wing chairs as well as the sofa. A bookcase provided plenty of reading, and a pretty marquetry desk invited writing letters or post-cards or memories in a diary.

As an elegant, private venue for entertaining, Gina doubted it could be bettered. And there was no question it provided a cosy home atmosphere. Reid's personal assistant had not steered him wrong on either count.

However, when Paige left the bathroom after her shower and swanned into the drawing room on her way to the second bedroom, which was located on the other side of it, Gina's hackles began rising over one extremely obvious area where Reid could have been steered wrong.

The fluffy white bathrobe covered Paige from shoulder to knee but left little doubt she was naked underneath it, and a loose tie belt was not the most secure fastening in the world. One tug and the robe would fall apart. Beads of moisture still clung mistily to the little hollow between her collarbones, and the musky scent of some very expensive perfume wafted from her. Her silky blond hair had been pinned into a sexy tousle on top of her head, with wispy tendrils escaping and trailing damply down her long, graceful neck.

Despite this general state of deshabille, she had stayed in the bathroom long enough to apply perfect make-up. No clothes, but perfect make-up. It added to the fresh vitality she was exuding, suddenly making Gina feel jetlagged and jaded.

'The bathroom's free now if you want it,' Paige said, stating the obvious with a condescending little smile. 'Sorry to have kept you waiting, but it's important I make a good impression today. For Reid's sake. They do match the P.A. against the man, you know.'

'Well, I'm sure you'll do Reid proud,' Gina said coolly.

'They match the wife, too.' Her gaze flicked to the green jacket Gina was still wearing. 'I could give you a few tips on what's appropriate and what isn't, since Reid will be inviting people here later on in the week.'

Gina willed back the tide of heat that threatened to flood her face. How dare this woman imply criticism of her choice of clothes? Imply that she knew better what would be good for Reid! Gina's eyes blazed.

'You look after your business, Paige, and I'll look after mine,' she said in icy dismissal.

A quirky little smile. A bitchy little smile. 'I was only trying to help. Reid's business is surely yours, too.'

Gina seethed. By what right was this woman being so familiar?

'It's my opinion that Reid is more than capable of standing on his own two feet without help from either of us,' Gina said loftily. 'He made it this far by himself.'

'It never hurts to ease the way,' came the silky advice. 'Even self-made men appreciate a lift now and then.'

'And that's what you supply, is it, Paige? A lift?' *To their manhood, their ego, and everything else,* Gina thought with resentment.

'I do hope so. It's what I'm paid for—to lift the burden. Taking care of details, removing obstacles and smoothing the path.'

'Oiling the engine,' Gina put in sweetly.

Paige nodded smugly. 'You could put it like that.'

'Is there a limit to the needs you fulfil?' Gina drawled, hating this conversation, *hating* it, but driven to keep it going, to find out the worst.

A sly gleam. 'It rather depends on my employer. I must say Reid is very considerate. And generous.'

It was a struggle for Gina to hide her mounting fury. The memory of the birthday luncheon was like a flicking whip. She tried a condescending smile of her own. 'That happens to be his nature. Don't take it personally.'

'Well, it is nice to work under him,' Paige answered, an insidious twinkle of amused one-upmanship in her eyes.

A chill suddenly froze Gina's anger. Her mind went ice-cold. Did *work under him* mean what she thought it meant?

'I don't think I've ever met such a kind-hearted man,' Paige went on. 'Reid lavished so much attention on you during the flight here, it must have made you feel great to be his wife.'

She made *wife* sound like a second-class citizen. Was that pity in her eyes? Contempt? The chill sliced into Gina's heart.

Another condescending smile from Paige as she added, 'I've always thought generosity covers a multitude of sins.'

Definitely pity and contempt.

'If you'd like my help on anything, please let me know,' she finished, the perfectly polished personal assistant.

Why not slit my throat to help me bleed? Gina wondered, too stricken to reply.

Reid stepped into the drawing room, looking so heart-catchingly handsome in his best three-piece business suit, Gina had to concede most women would be tempted to set their cap at him. Paige

Calder, however, was doing more than that. She was throwing it into the ring.

And Reid had stepped into the ring with her by agreeing to this apartment. That was what gave Paige the right to this snide familiarity. Gina suddenly had no doubt about that. Not even a smidgen of doubt. And the knowledge of Reid's complicity in this situation drained off the good feelings from the nice things he'd done for her on the plane, leaving a sick emptiness.

For how long had this sort of thing been going on?

There'd been other business trips since Reid had employed Paige Calder, all of them interstate in Australia, a few days in Melbourne, a week in Perth, overnighters in Brisbane. She hadn't even asked if his personal assistant had accompanied him. Until Durley House had come up. How blind had she been? *The wife is always the last to know.*

The phrase kept pounding through her head, followed at last by a further thought.

Was the fight worth fighting?

'I think I will have a cup of coffee, Gina, if there's still one going,' Reid said warmly.

She looked at him, her husband, living a lie with her. Strange how one could actually know something in theory, yet faced with it—faced with it, it was something else.

He frowned and glanced sharply at Paige, who was still hanging around in her bathrobe, which had probably been deliberate, marking time with Gina until Reid came and appreciated the available picture she presented, a more appealing picture than his wife of seven years, who was looking rather worn at the moment.

This was neither the time nor the place for a showdown, Gina decided, inwardly recoiling from saying or doing anything in front of Paige Calder. She pushed herself out of the deeply cushioned chintz sofa and picked up her cup and saucer from the table, pleased not to clatter them together. Her insides were a churning mess.

'It's only instant coffee, Reid,' she said, her voice working but seeming to come from a long distance. 'No trouble to get you one.'

She felt him scanning her face with urgent intensity, but it didn't induce her to meet his gaze. She didn't want to see anything. She knew what had been intended here. He couldn't make that go away and he couldn't make it better for her.

He started to reach out a hand to touch her as she passed him by to go to the kitchen. She instinctively flinched. Her recoil caused him to stiffen. Gina didn't care what tension she left behind. She wanted out of that poisoned room.

'You'd better get moving, Paige,' Reid said curtly. 'The breakfast you ordered will be here in fifteen minutes.'

'I have my clothes laid out. It won't take me long

to throw them on and do my hair,' she answered, her voice a sultry lilt.

'Do it then.' It was an order.

The double clicks of two doors shutting, Paige's, presumably, and the door to the drawing room as Reid left it to move across the hall to the kitchen.

Gina already had the electric kettle switched on and was tipping a sachet of coffee into a cup for him. She felt hopelessly choked up. There were tears burning behind her eyes. She wished Reid would leave her alone to come to terms with a marriage that could be far more fractured than she'd realised. What kind of man housed a wife and a mistress—or would-be mistress—under the same roof?

It showed such a lack of respect for her intelligence. A lack of respect for many things Gina held dear. She wasn't sure she could go on with this attempt at a second honeymoon, wasn't sure she wanted to. Funny how different it was, knowing something instead of just suspecting it. It gave her a keen appreciation of the saying *having the mat swept out from under your feet.*

'Did Paige say anything to upset you?'

His voice came from the doorway. A direct question, loaded with concern.

What could she repeat? The words all sounded innocuous, even praiseworthy. It was how they were said and the context in which they were said that made them heart killers. Besides, if she made an accusation and Reid reasoned it away, it would make everything worse. Better to remain silent until she'd settled it in her mind.

'No,' she replied, reaching for the sachets of sugar and willing Reid to stay precisely where he was because she couldn't trust herself not to react violently if he came near her, and she wasn't ready to make a stand. She might never be ready. Time to think was what she needed.

'But you are upset,' Reid persisted, clearly not liking the vibrations he was picking up.

Upset was such a weak word for what she felt. Desolate, lonely, frightened, stepping into uncharted territory in a foreign land with no close and trusted family to turn to for guidance or comfort.

'I feel…very tired all of a sudden,' she answered. Like the weight of the world had descended on her shoulders. 'My bones are aching,' she added for good measure. 'I think I'll have a long soak in the bath now you've both finished in there.'

The kettle whistled. She poured boiling water over the coffee granules and stirred. She heard Reid start forward to get the cup and quickly picked it up to meet him with it. She needed to hold something between them. Her body was trembling with a terrible sense of vulnerability. She'd given so much in the past few days, all she could, and he'd put Paige Calder in a position to insult and demean her.

'Here you are.' She thrust it at him, managing a glassy-eyed smile.

'Gina.' He scanned her anxiously. 'Is it only jet lag?'

'I'm sure a bath is what I need to freshen me up and iron out the kinks.' She moved past him, desperate to reach refuge. The thought of facing Reid or Paige either singly or together was too hurtful.

'Gina, if something's worrying you…' His unease was palpable. He didn't want to let her go. After all, he wouldn't want all the good work he'd put in on the plane wasted.

'I'll be fine.' The door to the bathroom was right in front of her. 'My turn now,' she tossed brightly in his direction, not waiting for another word from him before opening the door, barging in, closing and locking it behind her. She ran for the taps to the bath, turning them on full bore, not wanting to hear anything more from Reid, not wanting him to hear if she burst into tears.

She sat on the edge of the bath, hugging in her pain, shaking her head over how naive she'd been. Even sitting with Reid in the back seat of the chauffeured car that had brought them here from the airport, she'd been riding on a wave of hopeful happiness, believing their marriage was well on the way to being fixed.

But where was hope when there was deceit?

It was like water rushing down a plug hole.

CHAPTER THIRTEEN

REID stared at the bathroom door, knowing he had been shut out. The door made it physical fact, but the mental and emotional shutting out had already been in process. He'd seen it, felt it, and Gina's denial of anything wrong simply didn't wash. It was another defence to keep him away from her.

The shock of it was how much he cared.

A week ago he might not have even noticed her shutting him out. If it had impinged on his consciousness he would have shrugged it off as a mood that would pass, nothing to concern him. He'd become highly practised at not letting much touch him. He'd told himself it was easier than working himself into a lather over things that weren't about to change anyway.

But they had changed. And it was suddenly terribly important not to have doors shut between them. They'd been opened, and he wanted to keep them open. He cared about that one hell of a lot.

The caring was thumping through his heart so strongly, his whole chest felt like a punching bag. His stomach was screwed into knots, and his mind was pounding. Why this sudden, wholesale rejection of him? What had triggered it? She'd flinched away from him. It was such an extreme reaction, making him feel like a piece of slime she couldn't bear to brush against.

A deep cold seeped into his bones. He had to shake off a premonition that what Gina had started between them was ending before he'd really got a grasp on it. Everything within him recoiled from accepting that. Whatever had gone wrong had to be stopped, turned around.

Paige, he thought, in spite of Gina's denials. It had been Paige and Durley House that had started them along this road of change. Here they were at Durley House *with* Paige, and the two women had been alone together in the drawing room before he'd walked in. Mood and attitude didn't turn around this fast without being driven by powerful feeling, and Paige had stirred powerful feeling in Gina on two other highly memorable occasions.

Gina might be blowing something right out of proportion, but he very much wanted to check out what had transpired between the two women. He glanced at his watch, impatient for the opportunity to talk to his personal assistant. She shouldn't be much longer getting dressed. Breakfast was due in five minutes.

He carried the coffee Gina had thrust at him into the kitchen, not wanting it any more. It was tainted with negative loading. The memory of how different she'd been earlier made the change so much more poignant.

The ride from the airport had been a delight. He'd put Paige in the front of the Mercedes, beside the chauffeur, wanting to have Gina to himself in the back seat of the car. She'd been glowing with happy excitement.

It had felt good, just holding her hand and watching her enthuse about the trip and what she planned to do today. There'd been no problem about touching him then, no sense of distance between them. She'd eagerly interlaced her fingers with his, automatically squeezing them during bubbly bursts of feeling.

He looked at the hand she'd held and flexed his fingers, remembering the sense of holding something precious and not wanting it to slip away from him. The awareness of having a second chance at this marriage was very strong. He wanted it to work more, he realised, than he wanted anything else in his life.

He needed to know what was happening with Gina so he could correct it. He recollected being preoccupied with business issues as he'd stepped into the drawing room. Nothing had hit him straight away. Gina and Paige had appeared to be in conversation.

He tried to reconstruct the scene in his mind. Gina, sitting on the sofa, a glossy magazine open on her lap, Paige, still wrapped in one of the complimentary bathrobes after her shower, standing by an armchair on the other side of the coffee table. He'd vaguely heard Paige offering any assistance Gina might want or need, nothing offensive in her tone, nothing to alert him to the shock of what followed his casual request for the coffee Gina had offered earlier.

The look she'd turned on him…

Even in memory it gave him the weird sense he'd changed from Dr. Jekyll to Mr. Hyde right before her eyes. Instead of seeing him, she seemed to see a stranger she didn't know, didn't trust and didn't want to be near, someone it was safer to evade. Which was precisely what she had done, escaping into the bathroom.

His meditation on this intensely provoking puzzle was interrupted by the doorbell, heralding the arrival of their second breakfast of the day. One had been served on the plane, but that was over three hours ago. The croissants Paige had ordered would have been welcome if his stomach was less cramped with frustration.

As Reid opened the door to the waiter, Paige opened the door into the drawing room, inserting herself into the hostess role again. She'd overdone that earlier, possibly offending Gina then, though there'd been no overt sign of it at the time. Nevertheless, he'd have a word to Paige about toning down her officiousness, especially in front of his wife.

The bathroom door remained ominously shut. Behind it taps were still running.

The waiter lifted a loaded tray and proceeded to

the drawing room, where Paige supervised the laying of the table. Reid knocked on the bathroom door.

'Gina, breakfast is here, and the croissants are warm. You could leave having your bath for a while—'

'No.' An emphatic cry, then in two choppy bursts, 'I'm not hungry. Thank you.'

Leaving no room for argument. He wanted to ask if she was all right but suspected that question would get short shrift, too. Nothing productive was going to be said through this door. He tried the handle. The door was not only shut, it was locked.

As he stood contemplating what that meant—nothing good—Paige saw the waiter out of the apartment. Since she was the only person who might give him answers, he moved into the drawing room, ready to settle himself at the table as soon as she returned.

'Your wife not joining us?' she asked.

'No. Not hungry.'

'Well, she does have the choice of eating at any time.'

Not like us, her eyes said.

Reid bridled against the togetherness Paige was projecting, even though it was perfectly reasonable in the circumstances. There was a complacency in her attitude that implied Gina's presence was not required. Not desired, either. Superfluous baggage they could well do without.

Had she made Gina feel that this morning?

Guilt wormed through Reid as he held out a chair for Paige. He had probably set that tone himself with his insistence this was first and foremost a business trip, and Gina had inadvertently reinforced it with her rejection of Paige's offer to swap seats on the flight. Nevertheless, he didn't like Paige thinking she was more his partner than Gina was. Paige Calder was nothing to him—nothing!—compared to Gina.

As he saw her seated, her perfume hit his olfactory nerves. It was a heavy, exotic scent. Too intrusive, he thought, half inclined to stick his head out of a window and breathe in some fresh air to clear the smell of it out of his nose. He was fast coming to the conclusion Paige was altogether too intrusive.

He sat down, shook out a serviette, selected a pot of English marmalade and broke open a croissant while he considered his next move.

'Shall I pour your tea?'

Reid barely held himself back from snapping that she wasn't his wife. Paige was definitely overdoing the hostess role. 'No, I'll do it later,' he said tersely.

Maybe he was being ultrasensitive. No, damn it! He didn't care if he was. He didn't want Paige adopting some pseudo-wife role with him. It was a mistake, agreeing to this apartment in the first place. Sharing work hours was fine. He must have been mad to consider anything more. No, he'd been letting the brain under his belt do the thinking. Carnal stupidity.

'I've reconsidered the suggestion you made about

separate accommodation, Paige,' he said. 'In fact, I'll call the desk right now and see if another apartment is available for you.'

Surprise…pleasure…triumph?

He had only a brief glimpse of her response before he turned to reach for the telephone on the side table behind him, but Reid didn't care for what he saw. He'd thought of Paige as a subtle player. It dawned on him that sly was closer to the truth.

It took several minutes to make the arrangements. He was in luck. A one-bedroom suite would become available later today. Miss Calder's luggage could be transferred for her then.

Paige was delighted with the news. Whether she'd be equally delighted at being left to herself outside of business hours was another matter. Reid didn't care. Paige Calder held no rights to his private life.

She assured him it would be no trouble to repack before they left this morning. She hadn't taken much out of her suitcase, anyway. Being an experienced traveller, she did not carry an extensive wardrobe with her. Unlike his wife, Reid interpreted, whose ultra-large suitcase was big enough to contain the kitchen sink as well as her clothes closet.

So what? Reid thought. There was no reason for Gina to limit herself if she didn't want to, and every reason for her to feel happy about what she'd brought with her. A second honeymoon did not require efficiency.

'Did you make any plans with my wife this morning?' he asked, hoping to draw out the information he needed.

'No. How could I? I'll be busy with you, Reid.' A touch of smugness there.

'I thought I heard you offering help,' he prompted.

'Oh, only in a general way,' she tossed off carelessly. 'It is her first trip here.' Condescending.

'Was that all you talked about?'

'What else?' She gave him an archly innocent look. 'I did remark that the bathroom was free. She looked as though the long flight was catching up with her.'

No, something else had affected Gina. Jet lag might be part of it, but it hadn't been the prime mover.

He looked at Paige Calder's smooth face and bland expression and knew he didn't trust her.

That was a shock, too.

His brain buzzed with the realisation he'd put this woman in a position of trust and she could do him a lot of damage if he wasn't very, very careful. God only knew what damage she'd already done with Gina.

He talked about the coming business meetings throughout the rest of breakfast. When Paige went to her bedroom to pack, Reid returned to the bathroom door. Paige had undoubtedly made Gina feel shut out, and this was her way of not interfering with anything, shutting both of them out. Nevertheless, Reid was deeply uneasy with the situation. He felt a pressing need to forge a rapprochement with Gina before leaving for the day.

He knocked. 'Are you okay in there?'

A pause, then flatly, 'Yes. It's a nice, deep bath.'

'Mind if I come in for a minute, Gina? I'll be leaving soon.'

A longer pause. 'I'm in the middle of washing my hair, Reid. I don't want to get out. You just go on and have a successful day.'

It sounded reasonable. He wished he could believe her. The door was solid. She wasn't going to unlock it, and the macho impulse to break it open could only end in futility. Thumping it wasn't going to do any good, either. It would draw Paige, and Gina would probably die before revealing her feelings in Paige's hearing.

He hated leaving her in a negative mood her first day in London. He had a strong urge to hang in here, send Paige on ahead to the meeting. On the other hand, time could often sort out the more distorted shapes of a problem.

'Gina, I'm having Paige moved to another apartment,' he said, hoping that information would help. 'A porter will come and collect her luggage once the guest who's leaving has checked out. It should be done by lunchtime. We'll have this apartment to ourselves. Okay?'

There was some muffled sound.

Maybe she *was* washing her hair.

He could call her later, let her know he cared. He wanted her to know he was thinking of her and she was important to him. Of prime importance to him!

'I'll leave numbers where you can reach me on the notepad beside the phone in our bedroom,' he called through the door. 'Don't hesitate to use them if you want me for anything. Any time of the day, Gina. Just ask for me. I'll leave instructions for you to be put through wherever I am.'

No response.

'Gina?'

'Yes?' Reluctant.

Reid hated feeling helpless. He gathered determination. 'We'll talk tonight,' he said, conveying unshakable purpose.

He meant it. With good communication they could resolve most things. Getting Paige out of the apartment would help. They would be assured of absolute privacy, and Gina would surely appreciate his desire to promote intimacy between them.

The silence on the other side of the bathroom door was disappointing. Reid could only hope Gina would be in a more receptive and responsive mood tonight. He pondered what else he could do while he waited for Paige to be ready. Inspiration didn't strike until they were in the lift.

'Would you order some flowers for me?' he asked the woman on the reception desk.

'Of course, Mr. Tyson,' came the obliging reply.

'A basket of red roses. Three dozen. To be delivered here and set on the dressing table in the master bedroom of my apartment.'

'Certainly. I'll see to it.' The woman made notes.

'I'd like to leave a message to be attached to the basket.'

'Would you like to write it yourself, Mr. Tyson?' The woman opened a drawer, took out a classy note card with matching envelope and offered them to him, smiling encouragement.

'Thank you.'

He thought for a moment, then wrote, *Looking forward to being with you tonight. I love you. Reid.*

CHAPTER FOURTEEN

GINA ached to go home.

She dragged herself out of the bath, pushed herself through selecting some fresh clothes and dressing in them, did her best to concentrate on packing everything she'd unpacked from her big suitcase, and all the while she played through her mind what would happen if she did take a taxi to the airport and caught the first flight home, the questions it would raise, the misery of trying to explain, the upset it would cause everyone.

She couldn't face it. Not yet. Not until she'd sorted through where she was now and what might be her next best step.

She couldn't face staying here, either. A shudder ran through her. She wasn't ready to talk to Reid about anything. Not while the hurt was still so raw.

The ache to go home went hand in hand with the hurt, and neither was going to ease in a short time. Her tired and sluggish mind finally latched on to the one hotel she knew in London, the hotel where Reid had stayed before he'd given up on their marriage. At least it was familiar. Le Meridien had over two hundred rooms. Today it had one for her, and Gina gratefully took it.

Relieved to have a bolthole, however temporary, she finished gathering up her luggage and moved it near the door of the apartment, ready to go. In checking around for anything she might have forgotten, her gaze drifted over the bedside table, halting at the notepad on which Reid had written his numbers.

Did he care about her at all?

Or did he only care what would happen with his children?

Tears blurred her eyes. She should never have come on this trip. It was a terrible mistake. Blind hope that her marriage could be turned into something different, something real and true and special. She'd felt Reid had moved away from her. The bitter truth was he'd moved *on* from her.

She hadn't understood, but she understood now. It made sense of everything—why he hadn't believed in what she was trying to do to improve their relationship. It had gone past that for him. He'd even told her it was too late. Then, once they were on the plane and he was stuck with her for the duration of this trip, he'd put a good face on what was inescapable, and she'd been the gullible fool, wanting to swallow it.

But she couldn't swallow any more of it. She was sick to her soul. She wished she'd never found out, wished she'd stayed at home, wished… Hopeless, futile wishing. What was done was done and couldn't be undone.

Reid was the blind one now if he thought moving

Paige Calder to another apartment would gloss over the situation. All it did was remove the deceit from under her nose. And he was the one who had castigated her about living a pretence!

She wiped the wetness from her eyes with a weary hand. Who would have thought she had so many tears in her? They should have all been shed in the bath.

Well, she was ready to go...almost. One last thing weighing on her mind, the problem of letting Reid know where she was staying. A total vanishing act was needlessly cruel. She didn't want him worried about her. She simply wanted to be left alone.

It was so hard to think. It was amazing she'd managed to get herself organized to this extent. The notepad with his numbers kept drawing her gaze, but she didn't want to speak to him. No, she couldn't handle that. Not yet. In the end she picked up the pad and wrote what she hoped was a clear message to Reid. She found an envelope in a correspondence folder on the desk in the drawing room and sealed the note in it, ready to hand in at the desk.

Then she called for a porter.

At reception a different woman was on desk duty. Change of shift, Gina realised, glad to be saved any embarrassing explanations. She handed over the envelope with instructions that it be given only to Reid Tyson, not his personal assistant.

The porter took her luggage to the street and stayed with her to hail a taxi and see her safely on her way.

As the taxi driver stowed her big bag in the boot of his car, a florist's van pulled up behind him. A delivery boy popped out with a beautiful basket of roses.

Red roses for love.

The sight of them put a sharper edge on her hurt, reminding her of the foolish and futile gesture of sending a similar basket of roses to Reid last week. She turned her back on them, stepping into the taxi and nodding for the porter to close the door.

She didn't know when love had slipped away from her, but it was gone.

Her marriage was dead.

She wished her heart would stop bleeding.

CHAPTER FIFTEEN

REID sat in the plushly cushioned alcove he'd booked at Rules, the oldest restaurant in London and one of the most celebrated in the world. He'd hoped its reputation might appeal to Gina. Its location, in Maiden Lane, Covent Garden, lent romantic colour, as well. It was here that the beautiful actress, Lily Langtry, was wined and dined by the Prince of Wales. Reid felt he needed every advantage stacked on his side.

Each minute ticking by stretched his nerves. There could be people of note around him right now, yet only one person's presence counted to Reid, and if Gina didn't walk in here tonight, he had no idea what to do next.

For the past five days she had blocked him out of her life. He knew his messages were delivered to her room at Le Meridien. Not once had she granted him a reply. He'd thought of staking out the hotel lobby and waylaying her as she came or went. The image of her recoiling from him was a strong deterrent. He knew in his heart she had to choose to meet him. No good would come of forcing something she didn't want. The words she had written to him were burnt on his brain. *I need time apart from you. Please let me be. I shouldn't have come. A Mistake. Sorry.*

Sorry...

Reid especially hated that word. The mistakes were his, damn it! Not hers. He'd tried to tell her so. Was she reading any of the messages he'd left for her? Did she even know he was here at Rules, waiting, hoping, desperately wanting her to come?

He checked his watch again. Three minutes past eight. Held up in traffic? It wasn't far from the hotel in Piccadilly to Covent Garden. Gina had a thing about punctuality. She'd never understood social lateness. If a time was given, that was the time one should arrive. It offended her sense of order to be late.

The fear Reid had tried to keep at bay began sinking its teeth into him. The longer a rift went on, the more entrenched feelings and attitudes could become. This was not looking good.

Today was supposed to be their last day in London. Tomorrow they were scheduled to catch the Eurostar train from Waterloo to Paris. If she didn't meet him here tonight, would she be at Waterloo Station tomorrow? If not, what the hell was he going to do?

He passed a hand over his forehead, needing to press something magical out of his brain. As he pinched tired eyelids, he fiercely willed Gina to come through the door and relieve his misery. Please, he prayed.

'If you'll follow me, madam?'

Gina nodded, somewhat intimidated by the black-suited, bow-tied dignitary who was offering to usher her to her husband's table and feeling a rush of relief that Reid was here ahead of her. She was dreadfully nervous. She had lingered outside, in two minds over whether to attempt this meeting. It was bound to be stressful. Still, it had to happen sooner or later, and a public restaurant should keep it civilised.

And what a restaurant! Lovely, rich polished wood everywhere. The bar they passed was magnificent. Mellow lamps giving off a warm yellow light. And the walls covered in framed pictures—drawings, paintings, portraits and cartoons of famous people. The tables dressed in starched white linen and gleaming silver and glasses, chairs upholstered in dark red, black-suited waiters wearing huge white aprons. A feast for the eyes everywhere she looked, a ready fund of distraction if she couldn't bear looking at Reid.

They reached an archway. At the far end of the room, occupying an alcove table and a deeply padded banquette seat, was the man who'd drawn her here, the man she'd married in love and faith in a future together. It hurt, looking at him and knowing it was over.

His head was bent, a hand covering his brow as though nursing a raging headache. Then he glanced up and saw her, and her feet instantly faltered. The blaze in his eyes encompassed shock, relief and a fierce hunger that leapt out at her and squeezed her heart, frightening her with its intensity.

It was as though he was starved for the sight of her, and he rose to his feet so quickly, Gina thought he was going to charge across the room and grab her so she couldn't escape. He visibly restrained himself, pulling back the leg that had started forward, straightening his shoulders, remaining by the table while lifting an arm in a genteel gesture of invitation and welcome.

She saw his throat move in a convulsive swallow. Hers did the same. It was not an easy meeting for either of them. What would happen in the future—especially with their children—was at stake.

Yet as she moved forward, consciously putting one foot in front of the other, Reid's gaze darted over her, keen to take in every detail, as though she, and only she, was the focus of his caring and attention. It was a strange sensation, being noticed so strongly after being mostly ignored.

She was wearing the same clothes as when she'd ached to be noticed by him—black satin trousers and the tiger-print chiffon tunic with the gold chain belt. And a bra. Appearing sexy had not been on her mind tonight. It was confusing and oddly exhilarating to have Reid's eyes eating her up as though she could not have dressed in a more sensually provocative fashion.

Too late, she thought, savagely dismissing confusion. They were at the crossroad.

He, of course, looked class from head to toe, his

grey lounge suit showing up the charismatic combination of blue eyes and black hair. Gina doubted there was anyone as handsome in the restaurant. It was always flattering to be linked with Reid. Even tonight, despite his betrayal of their marriage, she couldn't deny a little flutter of pride in him. And a craven wish that the years could be turned back to when he did love her.

'Thank you for coming,' he said, the words sounding deeply felt. Caring.

Gina choked up. She nodded and slid onto the banquette across the table from Reid, grateful to sit down, aware her legs were beginning to feel wobbly. *Don't be fooled*, she fiercely chided herself. Of course Reid cared. He would care very much what happened next. He did love his family.

He resumed his seat. Champagne was poured into a glass for her before they were left alone. She sipped the wine, needing something to settle her down and ease the tension. It gave her something to look at, as well. She shied from meeting Reid's eyes this close to him.

'How was your week?' she asked, determined to be civil.

'Hellish,' he answered, a dark throb to his voice.

She flicked a nervous glance at him. 'I'm sorry if I messed you up. I didn't mean to. I just wanted out of the situation,' she said quickly.

'I know. I'm sorry you were put into a hurtful position, Gina. It was blindly stupid mismanagement on my part, and I regret it very deeply.'

A prepared speech, she reasoned, struggling not to let it crack her defences. However sincerely it was delivered, it didn't change anything. Nothing was going to change anything. She had to accept that and move forward.

'I guess overlooking me and my feelings had become a habit with you, Reid,' she said in excuse for his blindness. Irony curled her mouth. 'The wife who's a fixture. Taken for granted until it gets up and bites.'

'That's not true,' he retorted sharply.

It drew her into looking squarely at him, her scepticism plain for him to see. 'You're not going to pretend, are you, Reid? This meeting is a waste of time if that's your plan.'

He returned an incredulous stare, then shook his head in slow, helpless despair. 'Have you read any of the messages I've left for you since Monday, Gina?'

A stubborn defiance surged. She could feel it. She wanted to shut him out again, where his criticism couldn't reach her. 'I did ask you to leave me alone,' she tersely reminded him. Her eyes glittered with angry accusation. 'It wasn't much to ask in the circumstances, I would have thought.'

'The circumstances weren't what you believed them to be,' he said quietly, his eyes pained.

She shook her head in patent disbelief. 'Please don't take this line, Reid. It's beneath both of us.'

He grimaced. 'You really haven't read anything I've written you.'

'Today's note,' she corrected him, refusing to let him put her in the wrong. 'That's why I'm here. I know you'll be off to Paris tomorrow and—'

'Do you plan to come with me?'

Her recoil was automatic, her body stiffening in her seat, her eyes flaring. She felt bitter rejection and scorn at the idea she might accompany him and Paige. 'No, I won't,' she said coldly. 'I came here because I thought we should come to an understanding.'

'Understanding,' he mocked. 'What a wonderfully euphemistic word when a marriage is in trouble! Especially when communication has been steadfastly denied.'

That stung. 'Do you want a post-mortem on your failure to tell me where you were at, Reid?' she shot at him.

'I don't want a post-mortem at all,' he declared emphatically, his frustration breaking through. 'This marriage is not dead for me, and why you want to kill it off so damned quickly—'

'*I* kill it off!' It was monstrous of him to turn it around onto her! 'Just because *you* want to have your cake and eat it, too, you think I'm prepared to swallow your—your *infidelity* and turn a blind eye? Go on as though it means nothing to me?'

'I have not been unfaithful,' he stated vehemently.

Oh, the bitterness boiling up from a blanket denial that had to be false. Gina could barely form coherent words. 'You expect me to believe *that* after what Paige Calder said? After how she carried on to me? And with the set-up at Durley House? Not to mention her so-much-more-important-than-me birthday lunch?' She heard her voice growing shrill and grabbed the glass of champagne to loosen her throat.

'I know I'm at fault,' Reid conceded.

'Well, that's big of you!' Outrage burned off her tongue. 'My God! You didn't even have the decency, the fair-mindedness to give our marriage a chance. You decided, by yourself, that I wasn't up to the mark of satisfying you sexually so you went about planning something else. That's the guts of it, isn't it?'

He took a deep breath. He looked sick. His eyes searched hers, looking for some softness in the underbelly of her savage dismissal of his pleas.

'I wasn't unfaithful to you, Gina,' he repeated quietly. 'I thought about it. I didn't do it.'

'Why? Because I found out?' she scoffed, feeling he'd been unfaithful in spirit if not in action, and she didn't believe him, anyway.

'Because I didn't want to.'

In a way, that struck true. If it was true. In his self-centred, self-sufficient world, only what he wanted would count in the end. 'Not out of any sense of caring about me,' she said derisively.

'Very much caring for you, Gina,' he said softly, his eyes boring into hers with urgent intensity. 'And caring about making the best of our marriage.'

'That wasn't how it looked to me,' she retorted. She'd done all the caring and the work on it. He'd resisted her efforts except when it suited him not to. 'Please, just stop it!' she begged, hating this pointless and poisonous dissection of what had gone wrong.

'Gina, if you'll just give me a chance—'

'It's useless, useless!' she cried, anguished by his pursuit of a compromise. It wouldn't wear. It was too repulsive to her. 'Can we please get onto something useful?'

He expelled a long, ragged sigh. 'What would you suggest as useful?'

'How we're going to act in front of the children when we get home.' It was a matter of deep anxiety to her. 'I don't know if you've called them this week. I've only spoken to them about the tourist stuff I've been doing.'

'Yes, I called.' He gave her a wry look. 'It was a relief to find them all still talking to me normally.'

Gina frowned. Didn't he know her better than to think she would badmouth him to his children? They loved their father. It was precisely what made a break-up so difficult, losing him as a constant in their lives, the ready support he provided on issues relating directly to the children.

'Don't do this to us, Gina.'

The low, intense words sliced into her heart, then she saw his flagrant hypocrisy in putting the onus on her. She hadn't done anything, except her level best to make up for her failures of experience and savoir-faire. It wasn't she who'd turned to someone else because she wasn't getting all she wanted from her marital partner.

She curled her fingers around the stem of the flute glass, gripping tightly, tipping the champagne to and fro in the long, narrow goblet. The urge to fling it in Reid's face was strong. Was a man always supposed to have his sins forgiven for the sake of keeping the family together?

'It's not too late to try again,' he pressed, reaching across the table to touch her hand in appeal. 'I promise you...'

'Where did you park Paige Calder tonight?' she fired, her eyes stabbing him with venomous resentment. Promises meant nothing when they got in his way. She released the glass and snatched her hand from any possible contact with his, dropping it into her lap and clenching it in silent fury.

His face tightened. His eyes flared with a blaze of purpose. 'I have no idea where Paige Calder is. She is out of my business and out of my life.'

Sheer surprise tripped the question, 'Since when?'

'I knew she'd upset you on Monday morning, but I wasn't sure of my ground until I confronted her that evening after reading your note. It was a shock to discover what a nasty piece of work she was. I couldn't get rid of her fast enough. I wrote her a cheque that paid out her year's contract with me, and we parted company then and there.'

'On Monday?' It was difficult to take in, Reid's acting so quickly and ruthlessly because…because of the upset to her? Or because his marriage was endangered?

'Gina, whatever Paige Calder insinuated to you was for her own ends. Not mine.'

That did make sense, even to Gina's overwrought mind. Paige would have wanted Reid's wife out of the picture, whereas Reid could not afford and didn't want to let the mother of his children go.

He gestured earnestly. 'Before I left that morning I ordered a basket of roses to be sent to you at our apartment with a message that I was looking forward to being with you that night. And loving you. You can check it with Durley House. I did not have Paige on my mind. Or in my heart.'

A basket of roses? The one she'd seen arriving at Durley House as she'd left?

She shook her head at the awful irony of it—the moment just missed, Reid trying to reach out to her as she'd tried to reach out to him.

Perhaps he had put Paige out of his mind and heart, and the woman had been fighting to hold on to him. 'You must have given her reason to think—'

'No.' He leaned forward in passionate persuasion.

'People twist things to suit themselves. I was pleasant to her. Nothing more than that.'

He was glossing over the telling factors. 'Durley House…'

'She made it sound highly attractive. And it is. Agreeing to share the apartment was the mistake. It placed her too close to me. Made me vulnerable.' He shook his head in self-recrimination. 'She could have created even more havoc for me if you hadn't come on this trip.'

'What do you mean?'

'Setting me up for blackmail. As it was, she went to work on you, wanting you sidelined so you wouldn't get in her way.'

Gina wasn't sure what to believe. 'Why would she want to blackmail you?'

'Power. Some people get off on it, Gina. She's one of them,' he said with bitter certainty. 'I've been in touch with her former employer. I told him how untrustworthy I'd found her, and he eventually admitted she has the screws on him. I've sent instructions that the locks be changed on the executive offices at home. Paige is not to be allowed access to them.'

This new picture of Paige Calder was bewildering. 'You said her references were most impressive.'

Reid snorted derisively. 'Easier to write a top reference than be the victim of malicious mischief. This is a woman who doesn't care what damage she does,

Gina. No conscience about it. She plays to win and enjoys turning the screws.'

Yes, she did, Gina thought, remembering the sly amusement in the shrewd grey eyes as she'd twisted the knife in Gina's heart with her sly comments.

'A very dangerous woman,' Reid concluded.

Evil. Feeding off others. Gina shuddered, seeing how Paige Calder might have manipulated their lives, given more of a chance than she'd had. As it was, she had succeeded in driving a wedge between them, showing up the frailties of their marriage. Those certainly existed. Yet with goodwill between her and Reid, and left to themselves, might they not try to forge something better?

How genuine was Reid in wanting to?

She looked at him, her eyes swimming with doubts, a tenuous hope kicking into her heart.

His response was instant, as though his whole being had been tuned in to picking up that first stirring of hope. He leaned forward, his arms on the table, palms up in appeal, blue eyes on fire with the need to convince.

'Gina, I swear to you there's only one woman in the world I want—' his voice throbbed with passion, drumming for the entry she had denied him up until now '—and that woman is you.'

CHAPTER SIXTEEN

TO GINA'S mind, the waiter's arrival at their table with the menus was impeccably timed. She was suffering a tumult of feeling, stirred by Reid's revelations and declarations, and she was afraid of making a hasty response that might be rued later on.

There'd been too much pain this past week to suddenly dismiss it all as Paige Calder's fault. Or to let a few passionately spoken words have the effect of a miracle drug, making everything better. The situation was not as bad as Gina had believed, but it certainly wasn't resolved.

She was not about to fall into Reid's arms and forget the hurts, the loneliness, the sense of being wanted only for some things and not others—the compartmentalised wife. And *wanting* her wasn't enough. Great sex generated a comforting closeness, but she needed to feel loved on more than a physical plane.

She half-listened to the waiter enthusiastically list the specialties of the house. The wild game dishes sounded amazingly exotic. Some other time Gina would probably be fascinated to read through the entire menu, but not tonight. Food was the last thing on her mind. She selected two of the specials listed by the waiter and handed him the menu.

Reid did the same.

The waiter departed.

Reid leaned forward, electric energy flowing from him, determined to win her over now that the issue of Paige was disposed of.

Gina leaned back, pulling against his powerful charisma. 'It's not that easy, Reid,' she warned him, her eyes flashing with resentment at so many of the assumptions he'd made recently.

He opened his hands, inviting her to elaborate. 'What do *you* want, Gina?'

It was difficult to put into words. Somewhere in their marriage, Reid had withdrawn from her, and she'd felt lost. For months she'd been wandering around in a wilderness she didn't understand. She ached for Reid to take her hand in his and make her feel secure in his love again, but how could she feel secure without understanding why he had left her to fend on her own?

'Were you deeply in love with Suzy Telleman, Reid?'

The unexpected question and the use of his first wife's name were a double jolt. Reid thumped back in his seat, his chin lifted at an aggressive angle, disapproval tightening his face. He winced as though she'd crossed the line of good taste. His eyes tried to freeze her off the subject.

'That's over, Gina. Finished with,' he stated dictatorially. He always dismissed it.

Not tonight, Gina thought grimly, and said with very deliberate emphasis, 'No, it's not finished with.'

He looked needled. 'I assure you—'

'If it was, you wouldn't have used her to make judgments on my actions. Whatever she did, whatever you felt about her, affects how you view me, Reid.'

'No, it doesn't. It shouldn't.' He frowned over his mixed denial. 'Damn it! It *is* different with you, Gina.'

'Then why are you handing me rules that have obviously come out of your experience with her? All that stuff about this is your space and this is my space and here's where the line is drawn. Whatever happened to giving and taking?'

He gave a sardonic laugh. 'Well, Suzy knew all about taking, but giving was a concept she never came to grips with. I guess when I felt you weren't giving to me—' he made an apologetic grimace '—it pulled me back into that old scenario with her.'

'Did you love her, Reid?' It disturbed Gina, the question, Where did love go? If one couldn't be sure of it, life would be very lonely.

He was reluctant to answer. Eventually he grudgingly muttered, 'It was on another level, Gina. I'm not particularly proud of it. Call it a phase of my life when success and the fast lane went to my head.'

'I want to know about it,' she urged. 'Sometimes you react in certain ways, and I don't know why. If you shared that chunk of life you won't let me look at, I'd understand you a lot better.'

He didn't like it. She saw the initial retreat in his eyes, the hard flash.

To Gina, it was a critically important issue—the difference between trusting her or keeping her at a distance by holding his own counsel. To have him unseal this private compartment and let her into it was a huge step.

She kept looking at him expectantly, making him aware she would not be content to let this go. It was not his sole territory any more. He had reached back to it and brought it into their marriage. It needed to be exorcised.

'Gina, my life with her and my life with you…it's chalk and cheese, believe me.'

It was an appeal to let it be. Gina would have none of it. 'Then talk about it, Reid,' she bored in relentlessly. 'Be sure of it yourself, because you put me in the same basket as her last week, and I don't want that to happen again. I don't like getting the fallout of what some other woman did to you.'

He nodded soberly. 'Fair enough.'

It still took him a while to start. He finally plunged into it with an air of distaste. 'Suzy and I were both what you'd call high-fliers when we met, arrogantly confident of seizing the world and making it ours, grabbing the best or what seemed the best of everything. We collided at various social functions, found each other physically attractive and became one of the beautiful couples other people envied. We had a celebrity wedding you wouldn't believe...'

Gina listened to the cynicism in his voice, the description of how they frenetically filled their lives with shallow associations, useful contacts and status possessions that he valued less and less, until they were meaningless and there was nothing left to feel good about.

The tale took them through the dinner they'd ordered, neither of them eating much, Reid intent on satisfying Gina's need to understand, she too busy sifting the information he was giving her to concentrate on food. Both of them declined a sweets course. Coffee was served as Reid wound up his exposition.

'So to answer your initial question, love didn't really enter into it. It was more ego than anything else. As I said, I'm not proud of it.' He reached across the table and took her hand, pressing it possessively, his eyes locking very intently on hers. 'And I know that's not what I have with you, Gina.'

She left her hand in his, comforted by the warmth and strength of purpose emanating from it. 'What did you first see in me, Reid?' she asked, instinctively reaching back to the meeting he'd engineered. 'What brought you to me?' she added quickly, refining the question.

She'd been working on a Christmas job, selling personalised books for children. A sales stall had been set up in the middle of the shopping mall at Bondi Junction. It was designed to catch the interest of passers-by. Reid, however, had not been passing by. He'd met his mother at the coffee shop a few metres from where Gina was dealing with customers.

When his mother had departed, he'd bought a book, ostensibly for a niece but mainly to introduce himself, make Gina's acquaintance and ask her for a date. Since a gorgeous Prince Charming did not step into a girl's life every day, Gina had been dazed into agreeing. Indeed, it never entered her head not to agree. She'd been breathless, dying to meet him again, wondering if she'd somehow dreamed him.

Now he was sitting across from her—her husband of almost seven years—and she watched the tension slip from his face as his mind tunneled back to that time. A reminiscent smile softened his lips. The purposeful blaze of his eyes simmered down to a glowing warmth, embers of a yesterday that had been free of any constraint between them.

'The way you smiled at the children,' he answered, nodding as though affirming the memory. 'You were beautiful, but I've seen many beautiful women who've left me cold. It was how you smiled at the children that got to me. Caring shone out of you. Real caring.'

Children. Were they the top priority in his life?

He suddenly grinned, his eyes dancing a twinkly tease. 'But it was the way you smiled at *me* that blew off the top of my head. No artifice. So open and full of joy and wonder. It was like a rainbow on the edge of my vision for the rest of the day, and I kept thinking, pot of gold, man. You'd better reach out and haul her in as fast as you can.'

She laughed. Couldn't help herself. Then she heaved a long, rueful sigh. He could be Prince Charming, all right. When he made the effort.

'What about you, Gina?' he asked softly. 'What did you feel about me?'

'It's hard to say.' She laughed again, nervously this time, her eyes meeting his shyly. 'You'll think I'm silly.'

'No, I won't,' he said seriously. 'I'd like you to tell me.'

She took a deep breath, wryly thinking it wasn't easy to communicate private feelings. Yet it was the failure to do so that had brought them to this perilous moment in their marriage. It was something they both needed to practise. Often.

'When you first spoke to me, when you looked right into my eyes, I felt tingly all over. Even my toes and my fingertips and my scalp. It was so strange. Nobody else ever did that to me. It was like being touched by a magic wand.'

He looked bemused. 'Can I still do that? Make you feel tingly all over?'

'You did on the flight here, when you first got up from your seat and came to see if I was okay. You looked at me… It was like you were seeing me again after a long time of not really seeing me.' She shrugged, feeling somewhat silly and self-conscious. 'If you know what I mean,' she muttered off-handedly.

'I do,' he said fervently, surprising her with his certainty. His eyes darkened. 'It comes from wanting and feeling wanted, Gina. As for its being a long time, I'm sorry, but the plain truth is I lost all sense of being wanted by you. The children seemed to fill your life and—'

'But I did want you, Reid. I always did,' she expostulated.

He shook his head, pained at the necessity for saying what he felt. 'It wasn't expressed in the way I needed it expressed,' he said quietly.

'I'm aware of that now, Reid, but how was I supposed to know?' she cried. 'You were the first man in my life in any intimate sense. My father never spoke about sex to me. My mother was too much the lady to let him express an attitude about it in front of me. I was his little princess until the day I married you. And since then he's been in Queensland with his brother, helping to run the boat chartering business. So where do I learn such things, Reid, if not from you?'

He frowned, mulling over what she'd told him, not rushing into a reply. 'I thought it would come naturally if the feeling was there naturally,' he said slowly.

'I didn't have what you'd call a free-wheeling up-bringing in raw nature,' she gently mocked. 'Every-thing to do with sex was cover up, cover up, cover up. That's what I learnt, Reid, and it's not easy to break free of it.'

He expelled a heap of pent-up feelings in a long sigh. 'You've been doing great, Gina,' he said, warmly approving. 'I'm sorry I didn't help.'

'Oh, it was my fault mainly. Being pregnant so much made me even more self-conscious about my body. I looked so awful I couldn't see how you'd feel any desire for me. It got to be a habit, hiding it from you.'

He looked astonished. 'But you were beautiful when you were pregnant. Gut-wrenchingly beautiful!'

She laughed self-deprecatingly. 'How can you say that?'

'It's the truth.' He still looked amazed. 'Gina, to any man you are a stunningly beautiful woman. You embody all a man thinks of as *woman*. Even more so when you were pregnant. To me, you've always been the most beautiful woman in the world. The queen of women!'

She was too stunned to reply.

Reid shook his head in rueful bemusement. 'Clearly I am criminally negligent for not letting you know it. For not ramming it into your head so often you couldn't help being convinced of it. It was so obvious to me...' He sighed. 'My fault.'

She sighed. 'Faults on both sides.' But she felt wonderfully uplifted by Reid's insistence she'd never been unattractive to him. 'We should have done a lot more talking to each other, Reid.'

'And a lot more touching. Which reminds me. You know that room you booked for us—' his mouth quirked '—love in the afternoon that I so stupidly passed up?'

She flushed. 'Well, I was trying to reach out and make things better between us.'

'On that score you can absolutely count on getting every assistance from me in the future. And to show my intense desire to try, too, I booked us a special room for tonight.'

His eyes locked onto hers and the tingle started, spreading like wildfire to every extremity of her body but mainly settling around her stomach, making her wish they were intimately connected, drowning in the sensations that made thinking unnecessary and irrelevant.

He squeezed her hand. 'I want very much to make love with you. Right now. Can I take you to your hotel, Mrs. Tyson?'

She knew the melting, mindless ecstasy of physical intimacy wasn't everything. After it came the rest of living together. But right now it felt like the best possible start to reaching out to each other anew.

'Yes,' she said. 'Yes, you can.'

CHAPTER SEVENTEEN

QUEEN of my life.

The lovely phrase swam through Gina's mind again as she lay languorously amongst sumptuous pillows, idly gazing at the fabulous drapings on the magnificent four-poster bed, finding it incredibly erotic to be lying in nude abandonment amongst the richest furnishings she'd ever seen, in the Royal Suite at the Lanesborough Hotel.

A smile softened and lingered on her kiss-sensitised lips as she remembered saying, 'This isn't my hotel, Reid.'

'It is tonight,' he'd replied, his voice husky with desire, his eyes eating her up, telling her she was the most beautiful woman in the world to him, the one he wanted, the only one. 'I want you to feel all that you are to me—' his smile a caress of love '—queen of my life.'

The Royal Suite, booked in the hope he would win her back to him, booked to celebrate and make memorable the beginning of their second honeymoon, booked to show her how much he cared, how much she meant to him, an act of faith in their future together.

A low laugh gurgled from her throat as she wriggled away from the delicious but almost unbearable sensations Reid was arousing, softly stroking the soles of her feet.

'Tingly?' he asked, enjoying his view of her from where he lay sprawled across the bottom of the bed, happy to play at leisure, slowly and sensually, now that their first long and intense coming together had taken the urgent edge off their need to feel at one with each other, united, indivisible, fears and doubts dissolved in a deep fusion of loving.

'Enough, enough,' she gasped.

'No, not nearly enough,' he purred, guiding one twitching foot to his mouth and nibbling her toes. 'I must pay proper homage. I shall start by kissing your feet...'

Queen of my life.

'Then bit by bit work my way upwards.'

Gina's breath hissed out on a long, quivery sigh. He could do such wicked things with his mouth and hands. Wickedly wonderful. Tonight he seemed committed to giving her every possible pleasure, revelling in her responses to him, sipping at them, exulting over them, embracing the totality of making love to every part of her, sweetly, thoroughly, intensely.

He caressed the delicate hollows of her ankles, stroked the curved line of her calves, tantalised the backs of her knees with feather-light fingertips, kissed the soft flesh of her inner thighs and gently, so gently moved her legs apart to kneel between them. And his eyes said, *I'm kneeling to you now, queen of my life.*

Her courtier, lover, consort, husband.

Then he bent to pay the most exquisite homage of all to her womanhood, and she felt herself melting with the mounting intensity of the excitement he wrought inside her, her muscles convulsing in need for the hard, solid shaft of appeasement that was so gloriously part of him.

'Come now,' she cried. 'I want you, want you, want you…'

'Yes…' A hiss of exultation as he surged over her, into her, the wanting a deep beat that bucked and plunged and pounded with the power of two lives pulsing as one, wanting nothing else but this wild affirmation of belonging to each other deeply, beyond all possible barriers, differences, troubles and tribulations. The passion of possession.

King of my life. It was a lilt of joy dancing through her when he fell into her arms, spent from giving his all, and she fiercely embraced him, holding in the flooding warmth of his giving, savouring the strength and the splendour of the man he was, loving him.

The thought came to her that they mustn't ever let this—what they felt tonight, what they had tonight—lapse into something less. It was so good, precious, to be cherished and nurtured.

This kingdom was theirs, this marriage, and they could have lost it. Best never to forget that sobering reality. They could have lost it. They had to be far more conscious of the giving and taking, wanting what was best for both of them, reaching out, being there, listening and above all, loving.

Reid stirred himself to kiss her, long and lingeringly, and he carried her with him as he rolled onto his back, his arms wrapping her to him, holding her close, safe and secure. His chest rose and fell in a deep sigh of contentment, and his breath wavered softly through her hair as he murmured,

'Queen of my life…'

She felt so happy.

Reid not only made her feel beautiful. He made her feel loved.

CHAPTER EIGHTEEN

IT WAS good to be home. Reid viewed the chaos in the family room with happy benevolence. Every souvenir, map, brochure, postcard and tourist book Gina had collected on their trip was strewn across the floor, as well as the toys she'd fallen in love with and declared too marvellous to miss. The children were in seventh heaven, and Reid took immense pleasure in their pleasure.

Patrick was engrossed in a photographic book on Versailles, every so often looking up to ask his mother questions about it. Bobby was pretending to be a Beefeater from the Bloody Tower, marching around the room, watching how the heels of his new sneakers from London flashed with lights. And Jessica, smugly content to sit on Reid's lap wearing her raincoat from Paris, was picking at the plastic fish and flowers and combs and pegs and all the other startling objects that decorated the amazing technicolour coat, crowing a frequent chorus of 'Look, Dad-da... Dad-da, look!'

It was always good to be home, Reid thought, but this time it was extra special. He was acutely aware that all this could have been lost, the wonderfully complete sense of a family unit in harmony, secure in the natural bonding of love. It could so easily have been diminished or destroyed altogether.

He resolved to be far more careful of it. There were both inner enemies and outer enemies to contend with, and he had to be watchful that neither gained the power to unravel the magic fabric of what he had here in the home and family he and Gina had built together. It was too late to start counting the value of something once it was lost. Best to always be conscious of and appreciate it, because it would never come his way again.

'I'm going to wear my new sneakers when we go to the gym tomorrow, Grandma,' Bobby declared, suddenly breaking into what was clearly an aerobics routine.

'The gym?' Reid quirked an eyebrow at his mother, who was sitting on the sofa with Gina, looking through a mountain of photographs. 'You've been going to the gym?' He couldn't help feeling an incredulous bemusement at the thought of his rather plump and very dignified mother in an aerobics class.

'Now don't you laugh, Reid,' she chided him. 'Steve says if I can stay on my new diet, which is really not difficult at all—'

'That's right, Mr. T.,' Shirley called from the kitchen. 'We're all on the new diet. It's protein rich, low in fat, no starchy carbohydrates after four o'clock in the afternoon. It's very good for you.'

'And you sleep better at night,' Tracy chimed in with obvious enthusiasm. 'Even Bobby. He's sleeping like a top.'

'Steve says it's because we're working our metabolism in the morning, when we should, and easing off in the evening so our bodies rest better,' his mother declared. 'I seem to have so much more energy, and it's a lot of fun doing the exercises and the weights.'

'Weights?' Reid couldn't believe it.

'Yes. Grandma's pumping iron, Daddy,' Bobby put in with authority.

'They're to tone up my muscles,' his mother explained.

'You want muscles?'

'I want to lose my flab. I've had it too long and I'm sick of having it. I'm only sixty, Reid. I would like to be a svelte sixty. Why not?'

'Why not, indeed?' He grinned at her, happy she was doing something to make herself feel good. 'Go for it, Mum.' His eyes bestowed both approval and admiration. 'You can be a svelte seventy, too.'

'Oh!' Her face flushed with pleasure. 'I'm so pleased you said that, Reid. Your sisters think I'm silly, going to a gym at my age.'

'They're probably envious that you've got the guts to do it.'

She laughed. 'I must say it's been an education meeting Steve. He's a great motivator.'

'Who, might I ask, is Steve?'

'Steve is *gor…geous,*' Shirley proclaimed from the kitchen with a highly expressive roll of the eyes.

Tracy's cheeks pinked as she excitedly informed Gina, 'He's taking me dancing this Friday night.' She jiggled her slim hips. 'He says I'm a great mover.'

'There you are, Tracy. Nothing ventured, nothing gained,' Gina said warmly, her gaze travelling to Reid, sharing with him a more private pleasure in that truth before answering his question. 'Steve comes to clean our swimming pool once a week. If a model agency ever discovered him, he'd be a goldmine.'

'We all fancy him like mad,' Shirley called out.

Gina smiled at Reid. *Not me,* her eyes said. *There's only one man in the world I want and that man is you.*

Reid took a deep breath. He wished he could sweep her off to bed and make wild, delirious love to her, but it could wait until tonight. The desire for it wasn't about to be taken away or subjected to a change of heart or mood or attitude. The week in Paris had assured him, beyond any possible doubt, that the wanting was very, very mutual. It was great to know. It was like having the rainbow there all the time, the shining promise that was not an illusion. It was real.

'How do I get big muscles like Steve?' Bobby demanded of Tracy.

'Well, maybe you should ask your father that, Bobby,' she said with a deferring smile at Reid. 'He knows everything.'

But he didn't. Even as he chatted to his endlessly inquisitive son, he thought of the things he hadn't known and the trouble it had caused, the wrong assumptions he'd made about Gina and the faulty judgment in trusting—even liking—Paige Calder. Over the past few weeks he'd been stunned to come face-to-face with different realities to those he'd formed in his mind.

He didn't know everything. He hadn't even known his mother was not comfortable being plump, that she was fed up with her flab and wanted to have a more svelte shape. Reid decided that knowing everything shut the door to too many things that were really worth knowing. An open mind brought a lot more rewards.

He looked at his mother and thought he should spend some time getting to know her better—Lorna Tyson the person, not just his always-there mother.

He looked at his children and hoped he could help them open all the doors life had to offer.

He looked at his wife, his beautiful Gina, queen of his life.

She glanced up, her eyes catching his, and she smiled her golden smile.

Love, he thought, and knew one thing very clearly.

It was love that gave his life meaning, and he was never going to let it go.

AUTHOR NOTE

Many of my stories have focused on the emotional journey taken toward the commitment of love and marriage. But what happens afterward? However rosy the future might look for two people starting out with the intention of staying together, it is all too easy to lose the original magic of loving and wanting each other on the long and complex road ahead of them. So many other factors intervene—some of them divisive and destructive—and the ability to reach out and communicate can be eroded and never regained.

The betrayal of love can come in many forms, and it is always devastating. In this story, Gina and Reid managed to bridge the gap that had opened up between them, forging a better understanding and a deeper appreciation of the feelings they shared. In doing so, they were forced to face truths about themselves that they had suppressed or deliberately kept hidden from each other, not wanting to reveal anything that might make them look a lesser person than they wanted to be in the other's eyes.

The Secrets Within…

They are so powerful…those secrets…and in the wrong hands they can be explosive. What might Paige

Calder have done if Reid had put himself in her manipulative web? How does a woman get to be so careless of others' lives? What happened to make her like that? If we looked far enough, closely enough, would we understand why she took that path?

The Secrets Within... It is the title I've used for my novel published by MIRA Books. The story revolves around two families, linked by a long heritage and marriages made to sustain that heritage. It is about what was lost and what was gained in the interwoven relationships, what was done and what was held back. It harnesses every powerful force that families can and do wield over their members—loyalty, love and hatred, ambition and obsession, rejection and rebellion, betrayal and vengeance—and explodes into revelations that force something different to emerge.

You may be shocked as the secrets of these families are dragged out of hiding and the truth unfolds, but you will see and recognize and understand the all-too-human needs and emotions and passions that drive these people to do what they do. You will feel the pain of reaching out...the pleasure of touching...the power of communication.

The Secrets Within is a much broader canvas, a darker, richer, more complex tapestry of lives than I've ever written before—a different journey. I hope you'll find it a compelling one, fascinating in its insights, heart-tugging in its emotional intensity. Nothing about this story is predictable, not even the end. I do promise you this, however…it is unforgettable.

Emma Darcy

Miranda Lee is Australian, living near Sydney. Born and raised in the bush, she was boarding-school educated and briefly pursued a classical music career before moving to Sydney and embracing the world of computers. Happily married, with three daughters, she began writing when family commitments kept her at home. She likes to create stories that are believable, modern, fast-paced and sexy. Her interests include reading meaty sagas, doing word puzzles, gambling and going to the movies.

THE MILLIONAIRE'S
MISTRESS
by
Miranda Lee

CHAPTER ONE

HE WATCHED her from the safety of distance, annoyed with himself for watching her at all.

She was cavorting in the pool with a group of young bucks, revelling in their admiration, flirting outrageously with all of them.

He couldn't take his eyes off her any more than they could, his narrowed gaze captivated by that long tawny blonde hair, those flashing blue eyes and that lushly laughing mouth.

The laughter died on her lips when one of the young men playfully pulled her under the water. She came up spluttering, struggling to push the mass of thick wet hair out of her face. Whirling away from her admirers, she swam with petulant strokes over to the ladder, where she hauled herself upwards, her nose in the air, water cascading from her curves—her perfectly proportioned, glisteningly gorgeous curves.

Once out of the pool, she flipped her hair over and slowly wrung it out like a towel, bending forward as she did so, her breasts almost spilling out of her bikini top, which was slightly askew.

He cursed as he felt his flesh automatically respond. She was everything he desired—and despised. A high-spirited, high-class rich bitch, with beauty to burn, a body to die for, and a soul undoubtedly as spoilt and selfish as sin.

He didn't know her name. He didn't need to. It

would be something like Tiffany, or Felicity. Maybe Jacqueline. Perhaps even another Stephany.

Her name didn't matter. *She* didn't matter. What mattered was that he wasn't yet immune to her type.

God, would he never learn?

His sigh was weary. He should not have come. This sort of empty partying was not for him. He'd grown past it. He wanted more these days. And he wouldn't find more here.

Putting his drink down on a nearby table, he turned from the window and went in search of his host.

'But the night's still young!' Felix exclaimed when his esteemed guest said his goodbyes.

'Sorry,' he returned. 'It's been a long week.'

'You work too hard at that bank of yours.'

'Undoubtedly.'

'You should learn to relax more, Marcus,' came the unwelcome advice. 'Why not stay a little while longer? Have another drink and I'll introduce you to the Montgomery girl.'

'The Montgomery girl?'

'Justine Montgomery. I saw you watching her a moment ago. Not that I blame you. She's a peach. Ripe and ready for the picking.'

Justine…

Yes, that suited. It had a snooty air to it, just like its owner. As for her being ripe and ready for the picking… Marcus only just managed to suppress a cynical laugh. He had no illusions about the Justine Montgomerys of this world. The odds were she'd been picked from the tree many years before. Picked and handled and devoured in every way possible.

He'd met plenty of Justines over the past ten years or so. He'd even married one.

A small shudder ran through him at the memory.

'I don't think so, Felix. Girls like Miss Montgomery are best admired from a distance.'

'Don't let your marriage to Stephany sour you. Not all women are as fickle or as faithless as her.'

'Thank God for that. Though I would hardly categorise Miss Montgomery as a woman. She doesn't look a day over twenty-one.'

'That's because she isn't. But so what if she's young? Stephany was only twenty-one when you married her, wasn't she?'

'Exactly,' came his dry reply.

'You don't have to marry the girl, you know.'

'Oh, yes, I know that. Only too well.'

'That's not what I meant. Don't judge the daughter by the father. Grayson Montgomery might be amoral, but Justine's a very sweet girl.'

Marcus' laughter was cold and hard. 'Too sweet for me, I think. I like my peaches a little less…er… ripe. Still, if I ever run into Miss Montgomery again, I'll remember your recommendation. Now, I really must go. I have a board meeting first thing tomorrow morning.'

Justine parked her silver Nissan 200SX Sports in the double garage, and zapped the roll-down door shut behind her. Her father's car space was empty and she frowned. Where on earth could he be at midnight on a Sunday night?

A Saturday night would have been different. He played poker with his racing buddies most Saturday nights, to all hours of the morning. It was not unknown for him to stay out all night, going straight to his Sunday golf game without returning home.

But Sunday evening he usually reserved for his wife. Still frowning, Justine scooped up her carry-all from the passenger seat and ran up the back stairs to the first floor of the house—and the bed-rooms. Seeing the light on under her mother's door, she stopped and knocked softly.

'Mum? Are you awake?'

'Yes, darling. Come on in.'

Adelaide Montgomery was perched up in bed against a mountain of pillows, a blockbuster novel in one hand and a half-eaten chocolate in the other. At fifty-seven, Justine's mother was still a very at-tractive lady, meticulous with her hair and face. But her once hourglass figure had succumbed to more than middle-age spread over the past few years or so. She was always bemoaning her increased weight, blaming it on everything from early meno-pause to hormone replacement therapy.

'Mum, you naughty lady,' Justine reproached when she saw the large box of chocolates beside the bed. 'You're supposed to be starting a diet this week.'

'And so I am, darling. Tomorrow.'

'Daddy not home yet?' Justine asked, levering herself up onto the end of her parents' huge four-poster bed.

'No, he's not. And I'm going to have a word with him when he does come too. When he rang to let me know he wouldn't be home for dinner, he could have indicated he might be this late. Just as well I'm not a worrier.'

Which she wasn't, Justine conceded. Her mother

never worried about anything because she never took responsibility for anything. Grayson Montgomery was the head of the Montgomery family in every way. He ran the household, hired and fired staff, made all the decisions and paid all the bills. Neither mother nor daughter knew much about his business dealings, other than the fact he ran a high-powered financial consultancy and worked very long hours.

A handsome and charismatic man, Grayson spoilt his wife and daughter shamelessly in material things, but, in truth, didn't spend much time with either of them. Never had.

Justine sometimes wondered what sort of relationship her older brother would have had with his father—had he lived. But Adelaide Montgomery's firstborn hadn't lived. Her beloved little Lorne had died, a cot death when he was only ten months old. From what Justine still gathered from family whispers, her mother had had a breakdown over her son's death, and vowed never to have another baby.

When Justine arrived, nearly ten years later, Adelaide had by then perfected her 'non-worrying' mode, and became a splendidly indulgent, rather scatty-headed mother. Justine had been allowed to run wild; the very opposite to the normal smothering reaction to a previous cot death in a family.

This lack of mothering, on top of her father's many absences, meant Justine had grown up with a serious lack of discipline. She'd brilliantly failed most of her exams at school, despite her reports saying she was exceptionally bright. This she had proved, by putting her head down during the last six months of her final year of school—a male classmate had raised her hackles by calling her a blonde bimbo one day—and achieving a surprisingly acceptable pass. Enough to get her onto a degree course at the university not far from where the Montgomerys lived at Lindfield.

She had already spent a delightful three years on the college campus, joining every club it had, partying and having the most fantastic fun. Unfortunately, her frantic social life had resulted in her failing her exams again. In fact, she'd failed her first year two years in a row. At the beginning of this year, when she'd tried to sign up to repeat the first year of her degree course yet again, the dean had suggested she might like to try some other subject. She couldn't think what, and had wangled her way back for a third try, her dazzling smile achieving the dean's agreement with remarkable ease.

Thankfully, she hadn't let him down, and was confident she had sailed through this time. She'd happily finished her last exam this week and was looking forward to moving on to her second year at long last.

'How did you enjoy the party, darling?' her mother asked vaguely as she munched into another chocolate, then turned the page of her book.

'Oh, it was all right, I guess. The same old crowd. Just as well I went in my own car, though, and didn't let Howard pick me up like he wanted to. Truly, he's getting to be a real pain. Just because I've been out with him a couple of times, he thinks he owns me. I was having a perfectly nice time in the pool when he came up behind me, pulled me under the water and tried to take my top off. I was furious, I can tell you. I can't stand being manhandled like that. The way he was carrying on, any-one would think we were sleeping together.'

Adelaide blinked up from her book. 'What was that, dear? Did you say you were sleeping with someone?'

Justine sighed. She could say she was sleeping with the entire male faculty at the university and her mother would not react normally. Truly, one day something would happen that would shock her out of the fog she lived in.

'No, Mum. I said I *wasn't* sleeping with Howard. Howard Barthgate,' she added, when her mother looked vague for a moment.

'Ah, yes. The Barthgate boy. And you're not sleeping with him? That does surprise me, I admit. Such a good-looking boy. But that's the way to re-ally catch them, darling. Don't sleep with them. You couldn't do better, you know. His father has squillions, and Howard's his only son.'

'Mum, I am *not* going to marry Howard Barthgate!'

'Why ever not?'

'Because he's an arrogant, snotty little creep.'

'Is he? I thought he was quite tall when I met him. Oh, well…whatever you think best, dear. Someone else will come along. A girl like you will always have men trailing after her.'

'What do you mean? A girl like me?'

'Oh, you know,' Adelaide said airily. 'Rich. Single. Sexy.'

Justine was surprised by this last adjective. Most mothers would have said pretty, or lovely, or beau-tiful. Justine was not stupid. She saw herself in the mirror every day and she knew she was a good-looking girl.

But sexy? Now she'd never thought of herself as that, mostly because she wasn't all that interested in sex. Never had been really. While all her girl-friends' hormones had been raging for years, she'd sailed along with myriads of boyfriends and dates, but nothing beyond the kissing and minor groping stages.

Actually, it was her aversion to even *minor* grop-ing which stopped her from allowing more. She hated all that heavy breathing stuff. The thought of hot fumbling fingers pawing at her breasts, or a wet sloppy mouth slobbering all over her gave her the heebie-jeebies.

Justine always made it quite clear on the first date that if the boy thought she was going to come across at the end of the night, he could find himself someone else to take out. She had no intention of giving a man sex just because he bought her dinner, or took her to a movie. Only true love, she reasoned loftily, would make such an intimate and yukky act bearable.

Despite this highly unique stance for a nineties girl, Justine still had a great social life, never lack-ing in invitations or escorts. Her life was full of fun, without complication, without the emotional traumas which seemed to come with a sexual re-lationship. All her girlfriends told her tales of woe about their various boyfriends and lovers.

Frankly, Justine thought sex was more trouble than it was worth.

Of course, there *was* an irritating faction within her female friends who thought differently on the subject. Trudy, who lived two streets away from Justine and who'd been her best friend for yonks, was simply mad about men and sex. Only last week she'd assured Justine that one day some hunky guy would come along and sweep her off her feet and into bed before she could blink an eye.

Justine had scoffed at such an unlikely scenario. He'd have to be a man in a million, that was for sure, with a darn lot of sex appeal and know-how. Nothing at all like Howard Barthgate. Dear heaven, she wouldn't be going out with the likes of *him* again!

Dismissing Howard from her mind with her usual slightly ruthless speed, Justine jumped up from her mother's bed. 'I think I'll go make myself some hot chocolate. Want some?'

'No, thank you, darling. Hot chocolate's very fattening,' her mother said with all seriousness as she popped another milk *crème* into her mouth.

Justine kept a straight face with difficulty as she left the room. Truly, the woman was incorrigible. But she was such a dear, with not a mean bone in her body. Justine would not have had her any other way. It quite wonderful to have a mother who loved you to death but who didn't interfere. Justine liked running her own show. She liked it very much.

Her smile was full of indulgent affection as she skipped down the sweeping central staircase, sliding her hand down the carved mahogany banister on the way and thinking of all the times she'd slid more than her hand down that perfectly polished and thankfully sturdy construction. What a wonderfully carefree and punishment-free childhood

she had had! Some people called her spoilt and wil-
ful, but Justine didn't see it that way. She thought
she was the luckiest girl in Sydney, and maybe even
Australia!

The front doorbell rang just as she jumped off
the bottom step into the marble-tiled foyer. She
stood there for a moment, startled. Who on earth
could be calling at this time of night?

A strange chill invaded Justine as she made her
way with uncharacteristic hesitation towards the
door.

'Who is it?' she asked through the door, a burst
of nerves making her voice sharp.

'The police, ma'am.'

The police! Oh, my God...

She shot back the door chain and wrenched open
the door, paling at the sight of the two uniformed
officers standing on the front porch. Their serious
faces betrayed that their mission was not a pleasant
one.

'Mrs Montgomery?' the older officer queried
with a frown.

'No. Mum's upstairs in bed. I'm Justine
Montgomery, her daughter. What is it? Has something happened to my father?'

When Justine saw their exchanged glances her
head began to swim.

Pull yourself together, she ordered herself. Mum
is going to need you.

'He...he's dead, isn't he?' she blurted out, a silent scream in her head.

The officer nodded sadly. 'I'm truly sorry, miss.'

'I...I suppose it was a car accident,' she choked

out, thinking how often she'd chided her father for driving too fast.

The two police officers exchanged another, more meaningful glance, and Justine stiffened.

'Er…no, miss. Not a car accident. I'm sorry. I really think that—'

'Tell me, for pity's sake!' she interrupted. 'I need to know the truth!'

The older officer sighed. 'Your father had a fatal coronary in a Kings Cross club where gentlemen go to be…er…entertained.'

Justine rocked back, gripping the front door for support, her eyes wide upon the bearer of this almost unbelievable news.

'Let me get this straight, Sergeant,' she said slowly, her mouth parched. 'Are you saying my father died in a brothel?'

He looked painfully embarrassed and reluctant to repeat his news. 'Um…yes, miss,' he finally admitted. 'That's what I'm saying. Look, I realise this has come as a shock. Unfortunately, there—'

'Who's that at the door, darling?'

The policemen broke off. Justine whirled round.

Adelaide Montgomery was coming down the stairs, sashing her dressing-gown, a frown on her plumply pretty face. 'Is there anything wrong?' she asked worriedly in her little-girl voice.

Justine watched her mother blanch at the sight of the two policemen at the front door, watched as Adelaide's eyes filled with panic and fear. She clutched at the neckline of her robe with both hands as she swayed on unsteady feet. 'Oh, dear God, no! Not Grayson…'

Justine hurried to hold her mother before she fainted, knowing that their lives would never be the same again.

CHAPTER TWO

'A BOARDING house!' her mother exclaimed in horror. 'You want to turn my home into a boarding house? Oh, no, no, no. That would never do, Justine. It's out of the question. Goodness, whatever will my friends think?'

'Who cares what they think?' came Justine's frustrated reply. 'Most of them are just fair-weather friends anyway. How many phone calls or visits have you had from your so-called friends lately?' Justine asked her mother. 'How many invitations? They all came to the funeral, mouthing platitudes of sympathy and support, but as soon as they found out all our money was gone, they dropped us like hot-cakes. It's as though we've suddenly got a brand on our foreheads. *Poor*, it says. *To be given a wide berth.*'

'Oh, Justine, you're imagining things. Why, only yesterday I received an invitation in the mail from Ivy, inviting us both to Felix's fiftieth birthday party this coming Saturday evening.'

Justine refrained from pointing out that that was probably Trudy's doing, Ivy being Trudy's mother. The invitation had been suspiciously late. Yesterday was Wednesday, after all. No doubt Trudy had made a fuss when she'd found out Justine and her mother were not on the guest list for her father's party and insisted her mother ask them.

Justine didn't like Ivy Turrell one bit. She was

an awful snob. Her husband wasn't much better. Felix had made a fortune selling insurance, and only invited people to his home who could be of benefit to him. Naturally, there'd been a time when the well-to-do Montgomerys had always been on the Turrells' guest-list. Not so for much longer, Justine thought ruefully.

'People are giving us a little time to get over our grief,' her mother went on, seeing through her usual rose-coloured glasses. 'We're not *really* poor, and it's only been two months since your father...since he...he...' She slumped down on the side of her unmade bed, her hands twisting together in her lap. 'Since the funeral,' she finished in a strangled tone.

Justine sat down beside her, sliding a comforting arm around her sagging shoulders.

'Mum, we have to face facts. We *are* poor, compared to the people we've been mixing with. Okay, so technically you still own this house and its contents. But we have no income any more. And Daddy died owing nearly half a million dollars.'

'But I don't understand,' her mother wailed. 'Where did all the money go? I inherited a considerable amount from my parents when they passed away. It all came to me. I was their only child.'

'Daddy spent it all, Mum. And in a way, so did we. Neither of us ever asked where he got the money for our generous allowances, did we? We never budgeted, never went out to work ourselves, never questioned our lifestyles of sheer luxury. We just accepted all this as our due,' she finished, waving around at the opulent bedroom, with its silk furnishings and antique furniture.

'But Grayson never liked my asking him questions,' came the tremulous excuse.

Justine patted her mother's hands. 'I know, Mum. I know.'

'He…he used to get angry if I asked him questions.'

Bastard, Justine thought bitterly.

She'd once loved and admired her father, but not any more. She knew the real man now, not the smiling sugar-daddy who'd obviously thought being a husband and father was covered by keeping his wife and daughter's bank accounts topped up. The truth was he'd shamefully neglected his family, relying on his empty charm to keep sweet the women in his life.

Justine was forced to accept now that her father had married her mother for money, never love. Grayson Montgomery's greed had been as prodigious as his lust. One of the worst rumours she'd heard since his death was that he'd taken advantage of several elderly and very wealthy widows who'd consulted him about investments, worming his way into their affections and becoming a beneficiary in their wills—money which he'd subsequently frittered away.

Justine didn't doubt any of it. She only had to look at their own dire financial situation to know the truth about the man. Over the last few years, her father had cashed in every viable asset to bankroll his increasingly expensive lifestyle. His rampant gambling plus regular visits to high-class call girls *had* cost quite a bit. He'd died with no life insurance, a considerable overdraft and a massive personal loan on which the family home had been

offered as security. His Jaguar had since been repossessed, as had her mother's Astra. Only her own
Nissan was unencumbered. But even that would
have to go. Justine would have to trade it in next
week, for a cheaper, smaller model.

'We really don't have *any* money?' her mother
asked tearfully.

'None, I'm afraid,' she confessed. 'Daddy's bank
is also threatening to sell the house so they can
recoup their losses. They will, too.'

Her mother's eyes flooded with tears and her
shoulders began to shake. 'But this is my home. My
father bought it when he married my mother sixty
years ago. I was born here. Brought up here. All
my memories are here. I…I couldn't bear to lose
this as well.'

Justine could see that. It had been *her* home as
well, since her grandparents had passed away. She
didn't want to sell the house, but someone had to
be practical; someone had to face reality and do
something to make ends meet!

Like her mother, Justine had spent her entire life
not having to worry about a thing, and it hadn't
been easy for her since her father's death. But oddly
enough, in adversity Justine had found hidden
strengths of character she hadn't realised she possessed. One was a determination not to succumb to
self-pity.

'Which is why I'm trying to save it,' she pointed
out firmly to her mother. 'The boarding house idea
is the only solution. Even so, we're going to have
to auction off some of the contents to reduce the
loan. I thought I'd start with the things Grandma

left me in her will. They're quite valuable, you know.'

Up till today, Justine's mother had simply refused to face what her husband had done, both in life and in death. She'd gone along blithely pretending that everything would come out right in the end if she buried her head in the sand long enough.

Justine watched now as she struggled to accept reality. Unfortunately, her mother's ingrained habit of ignoring unpalatable facts was simply too strong.

Instead of facing their situation, she became stroppy. 'Part with your grandmother's legacy? Absolutely not! I won't hear of it! I...I'll go down to the bank manager myself tomorrow and explain. I'm sure he can wait till we both get jobs and can repay your father's debts.'

Justine could not believe her mother's naïvety! Who on earth was going to employ a fifty-seven-year-old woman who'd never worked in her life? Her own prospects weren't much better!

'Mum, neither of us have skills to offer an employer,' she explained patiently. 'I'd have *some* chance because I'm younger. But nothing fancy. Even if I was lucky enough to get a job in a boutique or a supermarket, my salary would not even touch the sides of the loan repayments. Our only chance is to run a business. We have five spare bedrooms in this house if we share this one. Daddy's study could be made into a bedroom as well, since it has a very comfy convertible sofa. The university is just down the road. We could bring in good money by renting all six rooms to students who want full board.'

'But who would do all the cooking and cleaning? You let Gladys and June go last week.'

'We'll have to do it together, Mum. We can't afford a cook. Or a cleaner. Or a gardener, for that matter.'

'Oh, no, not Tom too,' Adelaide protested.

'Yes, Tom too. We just don't have enough money to pay him. Fact is, Mum, we don't have *any* money left at all. The electricity bill came in this week, and the phone bill is still unpaid since before Christmas. They're threatening to cut us off by the end of the week. We're going to have to sell a few things today to pay those bills and buy some food. Some personal things we don't really need.'

Adelaide's head jerked up, her eyes pained. 'Not my mother's jewellery!'

Justine sighed and stood up. 'It might come to that eventually, but, no, we'll hang on to Grandma's jewellery for a while. We wouldn't get a fraction of what it's worth, anyway. I was thinking of taking a car-load of clothes down to that second-hand clothing store which specialises in designer labels. Just our evening dresses to begin with,' she added when her mother looked appalled. 'I doubt we'll be getting invited to too many dinner parties or fancy dos in future.'

'What about Felix's birthday party?' her mother challenged with a burst of petulance. 'I'll have you know that that invitation said "black tie". What are we going to wear if we sell all our evening clothes?'

'Very well, we'll keep a couple of evening dresses each,' Justine compromised. 'But we'll have to sell some day wear instead. Shoes and bags included. Do you want me to go through your wardrobe and sort something out, or will you?'

Adelaide began shaking her head from side to side. 'This is terrible. Whatever is to become of us?'

'Nothing too terrible, if I can sell my boarding house plan to the man I'm going to see this Friday morning.'

Adelaide glanced up with that blankly childlike expression which made you want to protect her. 'Man? What man?'

'A man in a bank. Not the bank who's threatening to sell us up. One of those merchant banks which specialises in low-interest business loans. Trudy's given me the name of a loans officer there whom she knows personally. It seems he's *simpatico* to damsels in distress.'

Actually, Trudy hadn't put it quite like that.

'Wade has an insatiable appetite for women,' she'd said. 'He'll do anything to get his leg over. I was at a New Year's Eve party the other week and he boasted to me of the loans he'd granted last year in exchange for some slap and tickle. I think he was trying to impress me with his boldness. Didn't do a bad job, either. Given his penchant for female flesh, you'd be sure to qualify for one of his loans.'

'I'm not *that* desperate, Trudy,' Justine had said, shuddering at the thought of giving sex for a loan. That was no better than prostitution!

'No one's suggesting you have to actually come across, Jussie. Of course *I* might, just for the hell of it,' Trudy had added with an impish grin. 'Wade *is* a handsome devil. But I can understand that a girl like you, who's waiting for true love to strike, would not even consider such an outrageous idea!

'So just smile and flirt and flatter the sexy scoundrel. And give him the impression that he'll be amply rewarded if he sanctions your loan. With that face and figure of yours he'll be drooling at the mouth, his brains firmly in his pants as he puts pen to paper.'

'But what will happen when I don't deliver?' Justine had pointed out.

'Oh, he'll be seriously peeved. No doubt about that. But he can hardly go to his boss and complain, can he? Believe me when I say that the head of that particular bank would not take kindly to one of his employees using his position to rubber-stamp loans in exchange for sexual favours. I've met Marcus Osborne. Father's had him over to the house on a couple of occasions. He's a formidable man at the best of times. Ruthlessly ambitious but straight as a die. If he ever finds out what Wade is up to, poor Wade will be out on his ear.'

And well deservedly, Justine had thought at the time. She still did. But she also saw she had no alternative but to keep her appointment with the lecherous Wade or let the house be sold. All Justine's other banking options had finally run out. After a myriad of phone calls, only one other loans officer had consented to see her during the past week, and he'd actually laughed at her idea.

The memory of that laughter hardened Justine's resolve. Come ten o'clock tomorrow morning, she was going to sashay into Wade Hampton's office, ready to do anything to achieve her goal and save her family home. If she had to humiliate herself a little, then she would. If she had to surrender some of her infernal pride, then too bad. If she had to beg, then…

No-no, she would *not* beg. That was going too far.

So was actually sleeping with the man. Good Lord! The very idea!

'What are you going to wear?' her mother asked.

'What?'

'For your appointment with this man in the bank. What are you going to wear?'

'I'm not sure. I haven't thought about it yet.'

'Then perhaps you should, before you sell off all your decent clothes.'

The word 'decent' struck a certain irony with Justine. Decent was not the look she would be striving for tomorrow, not if she wanted Wade Hampton's brains to be addled from the moment she walked into his office. She needed to wear something very bright, very tight and very sexy.

A certain lime-green dress popped into her mind. She'd bought it whilst shopping with Trudy—always a mistake. Trudy was a bad influence at the best of times. Admittedly, the girl did have an infallible taste for the kind of clothes which made men sit up and take notice.

This particular dress was made of a double knit material which clung like Howard Barthgate. It had a modest enough neckline but was appallingly short, the tight, straight skirt curving provocatively around her derrière. Justine had only worn it once, to lectures late last year. When she'd sat down and crossed her long tanned legs to one side of her cramped desk, the poor professor's eyes had nearly popped out of his head.

Would Wade Hampton's eyes pop out as well?

Justine cringed at the thought, but beggars couldn't be choosers, she'd found out. The rules of her life had changed. She was now playing a new game. It was called survival.

Oddly enough, the thought enthused her. She jumped up from the chair, full of new determination.

'Come on, Mum. Time for us to go downstairs and have a hearty breakfast. We have a lot of work to do today!'

CHAPTER THREE

MARCUS sat at his desk, angrily tapping his gold pen on the leather-inlaid surface, his eyes not properly focused on the paper in his right hand.

He still could not believe the gall of that young man! Not a hint of remorse, or conscience. He hadn't even cared about being dismissed on the spot, without a reference.

Of course he came from a moneyed family, with plenty of the right connections and contacts. He didn't *need* his salary. He hadn't had to work his finger to the bone to make something of himself, to drag himself out of the gutter of abject poverty and succeed against all the odds. Wade Hampton's job as loans officer was really just a fill-in, a way of passing the time till he inherited the Hampton family fortune.

The Wade Hamptons of this world had no idea how the other half lived. They were born with silver spoons in their mouths and grew up without having to toe the line in any way, shape or form.

Even Marcus's diatribe this morning over his lack of moral fibre had not made a single dent in the young man's insolence and arrogance.

When Marcus had been told of Hampton's tendency to approve loans not on the merit of the business venture but on the sexual co-operativeness of the client, he'd seen red. The thought that the reputation of the bank was being besmirched behind his back was like salt rubbed into a raw wound. If there was one thing Marcus valued above all else it was his good name, and the good name of his bank. Yet here was an employee, using his position of power to virtually blackmail women into his bed.

Not that Hampton had seen it that way.

'Blackmail?' he'd scorned when this accusation had been thrown at him. 'I don't have to blackmail women to go to bed with me. Not the second time, anyway,' he'd smirked. 'There's nothing wrong with what I did. Everyone was happy. Me. The ladies. And your stupid old bank. Not one of my loans has ever been foreclosed. It's only stuffed shirts like you who think combining business with pleasure is a crime. God, just look at you. You dress like an undertaker. And you act like my grandfather. I'll bet you haven't been to bed with a bird in donkey's years.

'But that's *your* problem. As are my appointments for today,' he'd declared as he whirled and strode for the door. 'I'm outta here!'

A good fifteen minutes had passed since Hampton's departure, during which time Marcus had instructed his secretary to inform Personnel of the situation, then get him a computer printout of the loans officer's appointments for that Friday, all of which had been done with her usual efficiency.

It was Marcus who was not operating with *his* usual efficiency. The appointment list had been in his hands for a full five minutes, yet he hadn't been able to concentrate on the names. Hampton's comment about his sex life—or lack of it—still rankled.

How long *had* it been since he'd been to bed with a woman?

Too damned long, came the testy realisation.

Clenching his teeth, Marcus dragged his attention back to the paper in his hands, his eyes widening, then narrowing when he spied the first name on the list.

Hampton's ten o'clock appointment—his first for the day—was none other than Miss Justine Montgomery!

Marcus's surprise was only exceeded by his curiosity. What on earth was the wealthy Miss Montgomery doing coming to *his* bank for a loan? She must know they specialised in business loans. What use would she have for such a loan?

Did she fancy herself going into some small business to pass her idle hours away till she landed herself a rich husband? An art gallery perhaps? Or a fashion boutique? A trendy coffee shop?

Marcus could only guess. There was one way of finding out for certain, he supposed. Take the appointment himself and ask.

The thought of seeing Miss Montgomery again—and in a position where he had the upper hand—held an insidious attraction. Marcus began to appreciate what Hampton had found so appealing about his job. To have a woman—especially an incredibly beautiful young woman—beholden to you. To have it in your power to give her something *she* wanted in exchange for something *you* wanted...

Marcus's pulse rate quickened as he contemplated such a corrupting scenario. Justine Montgomery had lived on in his memory since that warm November night two months before, when he'd surreptitiously watched her almost naked body emerge from that pool. He still recalled every inch of her physical perfection, from her impossibly long legs to her tight little bottom to her lushly nubile breasts.

How would you like to go to bed with *her*? the devil whispered in his ear.

He stood up abruptly, took a fob watch from a pocket in his waistcoat and checked the time. Five to ten. He had two options. He could have Miss Montgomery's appointment rescheduled to a later date with another loans officer. Or he could go downstairs to Loans and see her himself.

His experience-honed instinct for avoiding trouble warned him to have her rescheduled, but when he glanced up and glimpsed his reflection in the wide semicircular window which wrapped around behind his desk, Hampton's insults once again jumped into his mind.

He glared hard at the man glaring back, the pompously dressed stuffed shirt who believed combining business with pleasure was a crime...

His reflection faded from his conscious mind as another vision took over, that of Justine Montgomery's lovely yet startled face as he laid out the terms for her getting a loan. His mouth dried as he imagined the moment when he first drew her into his arms. He could actually feel her initial reluctance, feel the fluttering of her heart against his chest.

Till he kissed her.

After that there was no more resistance, only the most delicious surrender as she melted against him...

Marcus gritted his teeth as the painful hardening in his trousers brought him back to reality. He knew

he would never do such a disgusting thing as blackmail her into his bed. But he couldn't stop thinking
about it. There was something darkly compelling
about the idea of having Justine Montgomery in his
sexual power.

Common sense and professionalism demanded
he steer well clear of the girl, now that his carnal
desires were engaged.

But both were poor arguments against the excitement which beckoned just one floor down.

Not that he was going to try to coerce or corrupt
the girl, Marcus reassured himself as he stuffed the
fob watch back into its pocket and strode from the
room. Nothing—not even the most desirable female
in the world—would induce him to stoop to such
low behaviour.

The possibility that the incredibly desirable
Justine Montgomery might try to coerce or corrupt
him had yet to occur to Marcus Osborne.

Justine glanced at her watch as she stepped from
the lift. Five to ten.

Scooping in a steadying breath, she straightened
her shoulders and walked with her head held high
to the large reception desk straight ahead. Not normally a nervous girl, she had to admit to wild flut-
terings in her stomach that morning. It would have
been so easy to turn and flee. But fleeing was out
of the question. Anyone with a brain in their heads
could see her mother might have another breakdown if she lost her home on top of everything else.
Justine had listened to the poor love cry herself to
sleep last night, the awful sounds reaffirming her

determination to get this darned loan if it was the last thing she did.

The pretty brunette behind the desk stopped tapping on her PC and glanced up as Justine approached.

'May I help you?' she asked politely.

'I'm Justine Montgomery. I have a ten o'clock appointment with Mr Hampton.'

'Oh, yes, Miss Montgomery. Wade's away from his desk at the moment, but I know he's somewhere in the building. I'm sure he'll be with you in a moment. I'll take you along to his office and you can wait for him there.'

Mr Hampton's office was minute, more of a walled cubicle than a real office. Justine settled herself in the single chair which faced the less than impressive desk to await the loans officer's arrival. She recrossed her legs several times, none of the positions finding favour. Her long stockingless legs still felt awfully overexposed. She tried sitting with her knees pressed primly together but knew that looked ridiculous.

Steeling her nerves, she dropped the handbag she'd been clutching in her lap down by the legs of the chair and crossed her legs one last time, steadfastly ignoring the way the skirt rode up dangerously high. Another glance at her watch told her it was one minute past ten.

Two minutes later, she heard firm footsteps coming down the tiled corridor. She twisted her head round just as a man strode in and closed the door behind him.

Justine blinked, trying not to look as taken aback

as she was. But surely this couldn't be Wade
Hampton!

For starters, Justine had been expecting someone
much younger, not a man in his mid-thirties!
Trudy's taste in men usually ran to the toy-boy
type, with pretty-boy looks, longish hair and wickedly dancing eyes, trendy dressers who smiled at
the drop of a hat and oozed a type of cheeky sex
appeal.

Justine could not help but stare as *this* man
stalked into the room, his face seemingly set in concrete. No smile of greeting softened that hard
mouth, or those deeply set black eyes.

Admittedly he *was* a handsome devil, with a
strikingly sculptured face, a sensually shaped mouth
and deeply set dark eyes which sent shivers down
her spine. But that black pin-striped suit, though
impressively tailored, was anything but trendy, and
his ruthlessly cut black hair was plastered back like
Michael Douglas in that movie *Wall Street*.

He looked about as warm and as approachable
as a Kremlin advisor on nuclear waste, hardly the
type to be susceptible to flirting or flattery, *or* a
short, tight lime-green dress!

'Good morning, Miss Montgomery,' he said
brusquely, his handsome face coldly unreadable.
'Sorry to keep you waiting.'

He moved around behind his desk and sat down,
his dark eyes immediately dropping to scan the application form he'd carried in with him. It was a
full minute before he glanced up at her.

'So how may I help you, Miss Montgomery?' he
asked quite curtly.

The dean had spoken to her in a similarly cool

fashion when she'd gone to him for permission to repeat the year. Yet he'd warmed to her soon enough once she smiled at him.

Justine found that same smile, flashing it for all its worth at the loans officer. 'I have a business proposition to put to your bank, Mr Hampton. I think it's a very good proposition and one which would benefit both of us.'

Marcus just sat there for a long moment, frozen to the chair.

She thought he was Wade Hampton.

Understandable, considering. He hadn't enlightened her otherwise, although he'd meant to, before the sight of those incredible legs had distracted him.

His eyes washed over her more thoroughly, taking in the provocative little green dress, the highly glossed mouth, the beautiful but overbright eyes. She was either nervous, or excited. Or both.

Marcus's suspicions were instantly aroused. Did Miss Montgomery know of Wade Hampton's reputation for being a loans officer of easy virtue? Had she come here today armed with that knowledge, ready and willing to barter her delectable young body in exchange for a business loan of some kind? Was that what she meant when she said her proposition could benefit both of them?

The possibility gave a serious push to his already teetering conscience. But, dear God, she was breathtakingly beautiful, even more when she smiled.

Beautiful but bad, came the silent reminder.

Well, he didn't know that for sure, did he? Not yet. And, if he were honest, he wouldn't mind so much if she was bad. Not now, at this very moment, with his loins aching. Who knew what she might do if she'd come here ready and willing to be *really* bad? The various scenarios such thinking evoked did little for his already painful arousal.

Marcus stared at the object of his darkest desires for a few more moments before deciding not to tell her who he was. He settled back as best he could in Hampton's narrow chair and waited for her to put her foot further into her pretty mouth.

'Is that so?' he said, steepling his fingers across his chest and trying not to eat her up too much with his eyes. But it was difficult not to wonder just how far she would go if he dangled the right carrot in front of those full sensual lips of hers.

He had to clear his throat before going on, not to mention his mind. Damn, but the girl was a temptation all right. If the devil wanted to send someone to corrupt him, he could not have chosen anyone more perfect.

'Perhaps if you could outline your proposition to me,' he said, 'I would be better able to judge its benefit to both of us.'

Justine heard the sardonic edge in his voice, and hesitated. He knew—knew she was going to flirt with him, knew she was going to subtly offer herself as part of the loan package. He was sitting there, waiting like a big black spider for her to walk into his web.

Pride demanded she jump up straight away and stalk out of there.

But pride was not going to get her a loan. It would be cold comfort when she went home and explained to her mother that the house would have to be sold. Pride would not be of much value to Justine when they carted her mother off to some sanitarium or other.

Practicality won over pride. As did pragmatism. Who cared what he thought of her? The man was a creep. A user and abuser of women.

Well, it's *you* who's going to be used this time, buster, Justine thought. She flashed another winning smile at him, then launched into an explanation of her present financial situation.

Hampton frowned when she told him of her father's death and subsequent debts, the frown deepening when she revealed the other bank's intention to sell up the house and recoup their losses.

'Can they do that?' she asked abruptly.

'They're within their legal rights. Will the value of the house cover the entire debt?'

'Oh, easily. It's worth a million at least.'

'Mmm.'

'My mother doesn't want to sell, Mr Hampton. And neither do I. If you could see your way clear to taking over the loan at business rates and giving me a little time, I have a plan whereby I'm sure I can repay the entire loan.'

His dark eyebrows arched. 'Really. Perhaps you'd better tell me about this plan.'

'I'd be glad to. Firstly, I could substantially reduce the loan within a few short weeks by auctioning off some the house's contents.'

'I see. And how much do you think you could raise this way?'

'I'm sure I could cut the loan down to two hundred thousand dollars.'

'How did you plan on repaying the final two hundred thousand?'

'In the normal way, with monthly repayments.'

'You'd still be looking at repayments of two thousand dollars a month. Where will the money come from to make those repayments, Miss Montgomery?'

The logical question led Justine into an outline of her boarding house project. To give Hampton credit, he listened politely, asking her relevant questions about how much she thought she would get for each room, and what her weekly profit might be. Clearly he didn't just rubber-stamp any old loan, regardless of the fringe benefits.

'I'm sorry, Miss Montgomery,' he said at last. 'I'm afraid we can't help you. Your plan just *isn't* financially feasible. It has too many variables. I really think it would be in your best interests for you and your mother to sell the house and buy something smaller with what money is left over.'

'But I don't *want* to live in anything smaller,' Justine suddenly snapped, shock and nerves getting the better of her.

One of those straight black brows arched.

Justine gritted her teeth. She should be simpering at him, not snapping. Flirting, not flaring up. God, but it was hard to grovel.

'My mother hasn't been well,' she tried explaining. 'She's still grieving for my father and it would break her heart to lose her home. Please,' she pleaded, looking straight into his eyes and breaking her vow not to beg. 'I know I can make a success of this.'

For a moment she was sure she had him—and

without having to humiliate herself too much. But then he wrenched his eyes away, snapping forward on his chair.

'I am not unsympathetic to your position, Miss Montgomery,' he said, looking back at her. 'If you had a steady job to back up your boarding house plan, I would have no hesitation in sanctioning this loan. But you've listed your occupation as a university student. What exactly are you studying?'

'I've been doing a degree in Leisure Studies.'

'Leisure Studies,' he repeated drily.

Justine supposed it did sound a bit empty.

'I'm specialising in Tourism Management,' she elaborated. 'It's much more complicated than it sounds. And should lead to a well-paid job. Eventually.'

'And how long have you to go?'

'I've…um…just finished my first year.'

'Only your first year? Yet your application form says you're twenty-one—twenty-two next month. What did you do when you left school? Travel?'

'No. I…er…failed my first year a couple of times.'

'I see,' was his dry remark.

'No, you don't,' she defended sharply. 'I'm not dumb, Mr Hampton. I just didn't apply myself properly. I was too busy having fun. But I can do anything, once I apply myself.'

'Anything, Miss Montgomery?' he mocked.

Justine bristled. 'Well, almost anything,' she snapped. 'I doubt I could be a brain surgeon. But running a boarding house shouldn't be beyond me. My mother would help.'

'I thought you said your mother hadn't been well.'

'She's not physically sick. It's more of an emotional problem, one which would be solved if she could stay in her home.'

Justine waited for him to say something but he didn't. My God, for a supposedly inveterate womaniser, he wasn't making this easy for her. Maybe he enjoyed watching women grovel. Maybe he got a kick out of reducing them to pathetic pawns in his sick little power game.

She swallowed, pushed the remnants of her pride to the back of her mind, then took the plunge. 'I'll try to get a job, Mr Hampton. I will do anything you want. *Anything*,' she repeated, making strong eye contact and promising him all sort of things with her eyes and her softly parted lips.

Once again he said nothing, although he did stare at those lips. Justine's stomach tightened, her mouth drying in the face of his unnerving silence.

'If you give me this loan, Mr Hampton,' she added shakily, 'you will have my undying gratitude.'

'But I don't *want* your gratitude, Miss Montgomery,' he said quite coldly.

Justine felt her face flame into embarrassed heat as those hard black eyes looked her over. Never before had she felt so small, or so irritatingly lacking in confidence. Confusion reigned supreme. Her heart was racing, her stomach turning over and over.

'Then what *is* it you want?' she threw at him in her fluster.

Let *him* be the one to belittle himself now,

Justine thought raggedly. Let him say it out loud, show the world what sort of man he *really* was, not this coolly controlled customer who looked as if he'd never put a foot wrong in his life!

Then she was going to get up and walk out. She might even report him to his boss. What was his name? Osborne. Marcus Osborne. Yes, she'd go and tell Mr Marcus Osborne the kind of man he had in his employ!

'I want you to go home and convince your mother to sell the house,' he shocked her by saying in a harsh tone. 'Then I want you to go and get yourself a proper job. But, most of all, I want you to stop playing provocative and potentially dangerous games. You think I don't know what you were getting at just now, Miss Montgomery? You're not the first beautiful young woman to tempt me. And I dare say you won't be the last!

'There is no quick and easy way in life, Justine,' he lectured on while her mouth dropped open. 'Not if you're a decent human being with values and standards. Don't go down your father's path. You're far too young and far too beautiful to sell yourself so cheaply.'

Justine went bright, bright red. Embarrassed beyond belief, she grabbed her bag and jumped to her feet. 'I don't know what you're talking about. If you don't want to give me the loan, then just say so. There's no need to insult me.'

'Very well. I'm not going to give you the loan.'

'Fine. Then I'll get the money some other way!'

Marcus watched her whirl round and flounce out. He almost called her back, almost told her that he'd changed his mind and the loan was hers.

But of course that was impossible now. He'd done his dash in more ways than one. But by God, there'd been a moment there, a deliciously dark moment, when he'd almost taken her up on her none too subtle offer.

Just think, Marcus, he mocked himself. You could have been taking her out tonight if you'd played your cards right. Taking her out, then taking her back home, to bed, maybe for the whole weekend.

And what did you do?

You wimped out.

He muttered an expletive under his breath.

Now all he had to look forward to this weekend was Felix's fiftieth birthday party.

He hated parties these days, but sometimes he just had to get out of the house—that bloody awful house which he'd bought for Stephany and which she'd graced for less than twelve months. He'd sell the darned thing if it wasn't such a good investment.

Marcus scowled at himself anew. Is that all you think about, Marcus? Good investments? Returns on your money? There's more to life than money, you know.

Or so his beloved wife had thrown at him the day he'd thrown her out.

Which was ironic, because she'd certainly needed plenty of cold hard cash to support the lifestyle she'd grown accustomed to. Women like her always did.

His mind turned to Justine Montgomery once more. He'd felt sorry for her there for a while. Her father might have been a rotter but he'd still been her father. It must have been pretty terrible to have him not only die, but to die in debt and disgrace.

Any sympathy had been dashed, however, when she'd said she had no intention of moving to a smaller house. Not for girls like her a simpler life, or a simpler house. Heaven forbid!

Her boarding house plan was laughable. Did she have any idea how much work would be involved in running such an operation? Did she think she could manage to do it on the side whilst continuing her degree in Leisure Studies?

Her choice of degree was deliciously ironic as well. Girls like Justine Montgomery made an art form of 'leisure'. They didn't have to study the subject. It came naturally to them. As did bartering their bodies for betterment of their circumstances, although mostly it was an advantageous marriage on their minds, not a miserable loan.

Why, you're a cynic, Marcus, came the none too surprising self-realisation. Not to mention a self-righteous holier-than-thou bore. Even with her tarnished soul, Justine Montgomery has more life and fun in her little finger than you have in your whole body.

'Oh, shut up!' he growled, and got to his feet. 'I don't need this.'

Too right, that merciless inner voice shot back. What you need is some decent sex!

CHAPTER FOUR

'MUM, you're not ready!' Justine exclaimed on going into her mother's room and finding her sitting on the side of the bed, still in her bathrobe, her hair in rollers. Yet it was right on eight-thirty, the time they'd agreed to leave for Felix's party.

Adelaide gave her daughter a wan little smile. 'I've decided not to go, darling. But *you* go. Goodness, but don't you look gorgeous? Red is definitely your colour. And I love your hair up like that. You look so sophisticated.'

Justine ignored the barrage of compliments, seeing them for what they were: her mother's way of deflecting her attention from the reality of the situation, which was that she was slumped down on her still unmade bed, trying to be bright and brave when in fact her eyes were once again shimmering with tears. She'd cried on and off since Justine had told her yesterday the house would probably have to be sold. Cried and just sat around, looking defeated and depressed.

Justine had hoped the party tonight might buck her up. She hated seeing her mother like this, so unlike her usual happy if scatty self.

'Oh, no, you don't, Mum,' Justine said, knowing firmness was sometimes the best way with her mother. 'I'm not going by myself.' She walked over to where a beaded black crêpe gown was draped over the gold velvet chair in the corner. 'Is this the

dress you're going to wear? Come on, let's get it
on you and then I'll help you with you hair. It won't
matter if we're late. Parties never get going till well
after nine anyway.'

'I can't wear that dress,' Adelaide said bleakly.

'Why not?'

'It doesn't fit me.'

'Doesn't fit you,' Justine repeated, clenching her
teeth down hard in her jaw. They must have taken
thirty evening gowns of her mother's down to the
second-hand shop yesterday, and one of the two
dresses her mother had chosen to keep didn't fit her.
Truly, 'vague' did not begin to describe her sometimes!

'Then what about the other dress? Where is it?'

'It doesn't fit me either. Neither of the dresses I
kept fit me,' her mother confessed on a strangled
sob. 'I didn't realise how much weight I'd put on
since your father's funeral. I...I always eat when
I'm unhappy. I was so pretty and slim when
Grayson married me. He loved me back then; I'm
sure he did. But after my baby boy died, I started
to eat and I...I... Oh, God, it's no wonder your
father never wanted to come home. It's all my fault
he went with other women. Everything's all my
fault!'

Justine's heart felt as if it was breaking as she
watched her mother dissolve into sobs. She rushed
over to her, gathering her close, hugging her
fiercely. 'Don't cry, Mum,' she choked out. 'Please
don't cry. Nothing's your fault. Nothing! Daddy
didn't deserve you. He wasn't a very nice man. In
fact, he was quite wicked. We're well rid of him.
But you've still got me. We're going to make it

together, Mum, don't you worry,' she went on, fired up with renewed resolve. 'I haven't given up yet on getting that loan.'

Her mother glanced up at her through soggy lashes. 'You haven't?'

'Not by a long shot! There are other banks, aren't there? Other establishments which lend money? Felix's party will be full of influential people to-night, moneyed men with plenty of contacts. I'll keep my eyes and ears open and who knows? I bet I have some good news for you by the time I come home.'

Justine leant over and swept a handful of tissues from the box beside the bed. 'Now, dry your eyes, Mum. And don't give up hope. Your daughter has just begun to fight!'

Justine's newly found optimism wavered during the short drive to the Turrells' place. It was all very well to spout positive aspirations, quite another to put them into action. Giving her mother false hopes might have done the trick for one night, but what would happen in the morning, when she *didn't* have any good news?

Justine sighed, then sighed again when she turned into the leafy street which housed the Turrell mansion. It was lined with cars, not a spare parking spot in sight.

Negotiating a U-turn, Justine finally found a place to park in the adjoining street, the lengthy walk back bringing her attention to the tightness of her skirt. Keeping this little red number had been a bad choice, really. It wasn't at all versatile and could only be worn on really warm evenings.

She'd spotted it in the window of a very exclusive boutique back at the beginning of spring, the red colour attracting her attention. She always kept an eye out for a red dress in the months leading up to Christmas, because she liked to wear red at the big Christmas party her mother threw every year.

Naturally, this year there hadn't been any Christmas party. Justine had found the dress when she'd gone through her wardrobe, and just couldn't bring herself to sell it for a fraction of its value, unworn. It had cost a small fortune, being an original design made from raw silk.

Still, she now regretted keeping it. She should have kept her little black crêpe number along with the black velvet. People didn't remember black, whereas they could see her coming in this red for miles. Dumb choice, Justine. Dumb, dumb, dumb!

By the time she'd manoeuvred her way up the steep front steps in her high heels and rung the front doorbell, Justine was wishing she'd stayed home with her mother.

Trudy opened the door, scowling at the sight of the latecomer. 'So *there* you are! I was beginning to think you weren't coming. And after I'd twisted Mother's arm to get you an invite. Where's your mum?'

'She didn't feel up to it. A headache.'

'Oh, well, perhaps it's for the best.'

Justine bristled. 'How do you see that?'

'Oh, you know my mother, Jussie. She's not the most tactful woman in the world. She'd probably put her big foot in her mouth and say something to offend your mum. She's not sweet-natured like me, darling. She's a natural bitch.'

Justine had to smile. 'You *are* sweet-natured, Trudy. I sometimes wonder if Ivy's your mother.'

Trudy grinned and drew her friend inside, shutting the door behind her. 'Do you think I might be adopted?' she quipped.

'Could be.'

'What a cheery thought! Come on, let's go upstairs and install your purse in my room, then we'll go get a drink and toast the success of plan B for you tonight. At least you're dressed for it,' she added cryptically, her finely plucked eyebrows waggling at Justine's red dress.

Trudy set off up the sweeping staircase at speed, Justine struggling to keep up. 'Plan B? What on earth's plan B?'

'Finding you a rich hubbie. After all, plan A at the bank obviously didn't work.'

'How do you know it didn't?'

'Aside from my lack of faith in your vamping abilities?' came Trudy's dry remark. 'One look at your face on the doorstep, darling, and I knew the truth. You *do* wear your heart on your sleeve sometimes. Not that that dress has sleeves. Actually, it doesn't have much of anything, does it?' she added with a wry sidewards glance. 'So what happened? Did you chicken out yesterday?'

'Not at all. I did everything you told me to do, bar throw myself naked across his desk. I even wore my lime-green dress. He still knocked me back.'

'*Wade* knocked you back?' Trudy was incredulous.

'He not only knocked me back, he gave me a lecture on moral values.'

'I don't believe it!'

'Well, he did.'

They'd reached Trudy's bedroom, which was as large and luxurious as the rest of the house. Frankly, the Turrell mansion made the Montgomery residence look like a miner's cabin by comparison.

Trudy took Justine's purse and put it down on her white-glossed dressing-table, then proceeded to primp and preen in the gilt-framed mirror above it. Trudy was not traditionally beautiful, but she was very attractive, with a voluptuous figure and big brown eyes.

'Maybe someone at the bank was finally on to him,' Trudy mused as she replenished her lipstick and sprayed some perfume down her considerable cleavage. 'Maybe he had to put on a show.'

'Maybe. I can only tell you it was ghastly. I wanted the floor to open and swallow me up, I can tell you.'

'Gosh, how awful for you. Poor Jussie.' Trudy still looked more amused than sympathetic. 'As soon as I've finished here, we'll go and get some champers. Then we'll put plan B into action. I presume Howard Barthgate is out?'

'Yuk!'

'Pity. He fancies you like mad.'

'Not since I lost all my money, he doesn't! I haven't heard from him once. Look, I have no intention of adopting your plan B, Trudy Turrell. Even if I did, I wouldn't let *you* pick me any candidates. From your description of Wade, I at least expected him to ooze sex appeal and charm, but he was as cold as a cucumber sandwich.'

'He must have been putting on an act.'

'I don't know about that. If he was, then he's a damned good actor.'

'You have to admit he's a good-looking devil, though.'

'Yes, I suppose so. Those dark eyes of his certainly sent shivers up and down my spine.'

'Really? Well, that's a first with you, isn't it? From what you've told me, men usually leave *you* pretty cold. Maybe you've met your match at long last.'

'Don't be silly!' Justine refuted. 'I despise men like Wade Hampton.' Which she did. Yet, in truth, she hadn't been able to get the man out of her mind, though her skin still crawled with embarrassment whenever her thoughts turned to him.

'Right, I'm ready,' Trudy said, spinning round and linking arms with Justine. 'Let's go downstairs and knock 'em dead!'

Trudy led Justine down the sweeping staircase and along the wide, tiled hallway to the huge living room, where the bulk of the party-goers had gathered. Justine glanced around, noting that most of the people inside were middle-aged, the younger ones having gravitated out to the pool area on the terrace.

Her gaze landed on Trudy's mother, who looked like mutton dressed up as lamb in a blue satin strapless dress. She had that plastic smile on her overpainted face and was gazing in rapt attention up at a man who had his back turned towards Justine. Not Felix. This man was taller, with black hair and broad shoulders.

Suddenly he turned side-on, and Justine nearly died.

'Oh, my God!' she gasped. 'Why didn't you tell me he was here?'

'Who?'

'Wade Hampton, that's who!'

'Wade? Here? I don't think so. He wasn't invited.'

'Well, he must have come with someone else, because I can see him right over there as clear as a bell.'

'Where?'

'Over there, talking to your mother.'

'Are you crazy? That's not Wade! That's Marcus Osborne!'

'What?'

The two girls stared at each other for a long moment before the penny dropped for both of them. Justine was horrified while Trudy laughed.

'Dear God, Jussie,' she giggled. 'How did you manage to mistake Marcus Osborne for Wade? Oh, heavens, that's funny. No wonder he gave you a lecture when you came on to him. Oh, I wish I'd been a fly on the wall yesterday! What a riot!'

'I don't think it's funny at all!' Justine fumed, glaring over at the man who'd deceived her not accidentally but quite deliberately. He'd known darned well she'd thought he was Wade Hampton when he'd come into Wade's office and sat down at Wade's desk.

But had he informed her of her mistake? Not on your nelly! He'd waited for her to make a none too subtle pass, then cut her down to size. Clearly he'd heard of Wade's little pecadillos and decided to sit in on the action for himself for once.

'I guess we can cross Marcus Osborne off the list

for plan B as well,' Trudy mocked by her side. 'I think you might have blotted your copybook with him a tad, which is a pity. He's filthy rich, and conveniently divorced. You sort of fancied him too, didn't you?'

Trudy nudged a momentarily speechless Justine in the ribs. 'Maybe you're into older men, Jussie. Maybe that's why none of the boys you've gone out with ever got past first base. You probably need a more mature male to turn you on—some cold-blooded brooding banker with loads of unleashed passion. Recognise the description? By golly, our cold-blooded brooding banker *does* look smashing in that tux. I didn't realise how handsome Marcus was till this moment.'

'Handsome is as handsome does,' Justine muttered darkly. 'As for his turning me on, the Arctic will melt before he turns *me* on.'

Trudy was right, though. That dinner jacket and dazzling white dress shirt *did* suit him, much more so than the funereal pin-striped number he'd worn the previous day. Suddenly he looked younger, and sleeker, and, yes, sexier, if you went for the coolly sophisticated type. Which she didn't!

Hatred fizzed and bubbled along her veins as she glared at him.

'You're blushing, Jussie,' Trudy teased.

'No, I'm not. It's my blood pressure boiling. Now, if you'll excuse me, I have something to say to our banking friend. Something which won't wait!'

Justine's blue eyes narrowed as she set off across the room. If Marcus Osborne thought he could get away with treating her in such a shabby fashion, then he could think again!

CHAPTER FIVE

MARCUS felt the hairs on the back of his neck stand on end. Ivy was prattling on about how lovely it was to see him, and how he really should get out more, but his mind was no longer on his hostess. He could see something out of the corner of his eye, someone in red.

He turned his head ever so slightly, then froze. Dear God, it was Justine Montgomery, marching towards him, her furious face telling it all. Clearly someone had told her his true identity, and she was intent on having it out with him.

Anger did become her, he thought ruefully. As did movement. Her obviously braless breasts undulated beneath the provocative little red dress she was wearing, their unfettered curves held precariously in place by the halter-necked style. His flesh stirred uncomfortably, and he was thankful to be wearing a jacket.

'I'd like to talk to you,' she snapped as she ground to a halt beside him.

'Justine, *really*!' Ivy protested haughtily. 'It's very rude to interrupt.'

'And it's very rude to pretend to be someone you're not!' she declared, glowering up at the object of her fury.

Whilst Marcus could admire her courage, he had no intention of letting the girl defame him in public.

'Good evening, Miss Montgomery,' he said with

cool politeness. 'It's very nice to see you again. Yes, I agree with you. Such pretence *is* reprehensible, but the fact is I didn't realise till after you left the bank yesterday that you thought I was Mr Hampton during our meeting. A most regrettable occurrence and one I must apologise for.

'Ivy, my dear,' he said, addressing himself to his hostess, 'I have some banking business to discuss with Miss Montgomery. Do you have somewhere we could talk privately for a few minutes?'

He congratulated himself on successfully disarming his adversary, at least long enough to shepherd her away from prying eyes and flapping ears. But no sooner had a curious Ivy left them in Felix's study than those big and very beautiful blue eyes narrowed again.

'That was a lie!' she accused. 'You knew darned well I thought you were Wade Hampton yesterday, didn't you?'

'Not to begin with,' he hedged.

'Soon enough!'

'Not till it was too awkward to tell you the truth.'

'Oh, codswallop! You knew what I was going to do and you deliberately set out to trap me. What I'd like to know is why, Mr Osborne? Did you enjoy watching me make a fool of myself? Did you get a thrill out of my belittling myself in front of you?'

What could he say?

'Don't be ridiculous. Of course not.'

'I don't believe you,' she raged on. 'But no matter. I just wanted you to know that I had no intention of delivering anything I might have appeared to promise. Not for Wade Hampton or for you.

Especially not for you, Mr Osborne. Wild horses wouldn't get me into bed with you!'

'Is that so?'

'Yes, that's so. I don't go to bed with men for money. And I especially don't go to bed with men who have ice in their veins instead of blood!'

'I'll keep that in mind, Miss Montgomery,' he said coldly. 'But let's not get into a slanging match. Believe me when I say I didn't deliberately set out to trap you yesterday. Mr Hampton's misuse of his position had just reached my ears and I was… upset.'

'Upset?' she sneered at him. 'Men like you don't get upset! They have their egos put out, that's all. You humiliated me! And you *enjoyed* humiliating me!'

Marcus stiffened, indignation obliterating any guilt he was feeling. Who was *she* to judge him? He only had *her* word for it that she hadn't been going to deliver. Frankly, he didn't believe that for a moment. She was like the thief who wasn't sorry for what he'd done but was darned sorry he'd been caught.

What really irked Marcus most was that she wasn't in any dire financial situation which might have warranted such extreme action. He might have been sympathetic if she'd been in real need, if she and her mother were down to their last dollar. But both of them could live quite comfortably on the left-overs if they sold the house and repaid that debt.

But, no, they had to have it all. The high-class home to go with the high-class lifestyle. The final nail in Miss Montgomery's coffin was that she was here tonight, swanning around in a dress worth more than a working-class girl could spend on her wardrobe in a year!

Marcus recognised designer labels when he saw them. That little scrap of red silk she was almost wearing had not been bought off the rack. It had big dollars written all over it, not to mention sex.

Marcus couldn't keep his eyes off the way it hugged her perfect figure, displaying everything she had to offer a man. Justine Montgomery was no misunderstood innocent. She was a clever, calculating, conniving creature, who wanted what she wanted and was frustrated at being thwarted.

'I didn't humiliate you,' he pointed out frostily. 'You humiliated yourself.'

Justine glared at him and thought she had never hated a man so much. Her heart was hammering wildly in her chest. She was actually quivering from head to foot. Yet *he* was standing before her like a marble statue, his face a stony mask, his eyes as hard as ebony. His cold indifference to her distress forced her to regroup and control her temper. In a fashion.

'You're right,' she admitted shakily. 'I did. But at least I had a good reason. What's *your* excuse?'

'*My* excuse?' he said in an almost startled fashion.

'You don't have one, do you? Men like you don't think you need one. You're above explanations, and excuses, and apologies. Yesterday you gave me a lecture on moral values. But I wonder, Mr Osborne, if your own life would bear too close an inspection. Are you as pure as the driven snow? When was the last time you slept with a woman for reasons other than true love? When was the last time you made a successful investment using information you gleaned from an inside source?'

Justine was taken aback when an angry red slashed across his cheekbones. 'I have never done any such thing!'

'What?'

'Been guilty of insider trading. As for sleeping with women for reasons other than true love... true love is a rare commodity these days, Miss Montgomery. However, I do try to choose bed-partners I both like and respect.'

'Which should narrow prospective candidates down considerably, I would imagine,' she shot back, piqued by the fact he neither liked nor respected *her*.

'I don't usually have any trouble.'

'With such impossibly high standards?'

He glared at her and she quaked a little in her high heels. Goodness, but he *was* a formidable man. Trudy had been right there. But oh, so self-righteous!

'Have you quite finished, Miss Montgomery?'

'No, I damned well haven't! You think you're so superior, don't you? Sitting up there behind your undoubtedly big desk in that big bank of yours and deciding who'll be bailed out and who won't. You no doubt sacked Wade Hampton for what he'd been up to, but you weren't any better yesterday. Apart from your vile deception, you didn't give me a fair hearing. You didn't listen to my proposition with an open mind. Your ugly preconceptions blinded you to what was actually a legitimate business proposition.'

'Come now, Miss Montgomery, do you honestly expect me to feel confident that someone like you could run a boarding house of that size?'

'Someone like me? What do you mean, someone like me?' Justine suddenly saw red. 'Oh, I get it! You think I'm useless. Some spoilt, lazy little rich bitch who's never done a proper day's work in her life.'

'*You* said that. I didn't.'

'But you *think* it,' she snapped.

'If the cap fits, Miss Montgomery...'

Justine was genuinely taken aback. She opened her mouth to tear some more strips off him, then closed it again. She supposed he had a point. She *was* a spoilt little rich bitch. And she *hadn't* done a proper day's work in her life. Not for her living, anyway. But she wasn't useless. And she certainly wasn't lazy.

Suddenly it was important for her to prove that to this man who thought he knew it all! Her chin lifted and she set determined eyes on him.

'I challenge you to give me a chance to prove you wrong, Mr Osborne. Give me that loan and give me six months. If I don't meet my repayments during that time then I'll sell up the house and call it quits. Six months, Mr Osborne,' she repeated. 'It's not much to ask for. As I mentioned before, the house is worth over a million. You've got nothing to lose.'

'You really think so?' he said archly.

'Yes, I do. Look, I promised myself once I'd do anything for this loan but beg. And I won't beg now. But if you don't give me that loan, Mr Osborne, I hope you go to hell and burn there for all eternity!'

He laughed. He actually laughed. Justine just stared at him. For while he was laughing his face had been transformed from that of a cold-blooded devil to a wickedly attractive one. His black eyes gleamed and that hard mouth was softened by a display of dazzlingly white teeth.

'Very well, Miss Montgomery,' he said, a disturbingly charming smile still playing on his lips. 'I know when I'm beaten. Come to the bank first thing Monday morning and we'll work something out.'

Her mouth actually dropped open. 'You mean that? You honestly mean that?'

'I'm not in the habit of saying things I don't mean. You can have your loan, and your six months. Though not a minute more. Make no mistake about *that*! Now, perhaps we should get back to the party? Our hostess will be wondering what's become of us.'

'Oh, I can't stay now.' Justine was almost too excited to stand still. 'I have to go home and tell Mum. You've no idea how happy this is going to make her.'

Quite overcome with relief and joy, she rushed forward, reached up on tiptoe and kissed him on the cheek. 'Thank you, thank you, thank you, you darling man,' she gushed, and with one last dazzling smile, whirled and fairly danced out of the room.

Marcus stood there for a long moment, then reached up to touch the spot where her lips had rested. It was moist and soft, the only soft thing about him at that moment.

He had to laugh again, both at his fierce arousal and at the girl who'd caused it.

Darling man, indeed!

He knew exactly what she thought of him. He'd seen it earlier in her eyes. They'd been as contemptuous of him as he had been of her.

But money spoke a universal language with girls of her ilk. Come Monday morning she'd be smiling at him some more, smiling and flirting with him like mad, as she had yesterday in Hampton's office. No doubt he'd get the full force of her blinding charm now that she was going to get what she wanted.

After all, getting what she wanted was the name of the game for females like her.

But this time Marcus had every intention of getting what *he* wanted as well, which was the delectable and delightful Miss Montgomery.

There would be no question of bribing or blackmailing her into an affair. He would simply ask her out, as he would ask out any woman he was attracted to, then let things take their natural course.

Marcus had no doubt that Justine Montgomery would say yes to his dinner invitation, and whatever he wanted for afters. She would be keen to keep in good with her banker, especially once she saw how difficult it was going to be to make those monthly repayments. If there was one thing he could rely upon, it was that she would do *exactly* what he predicted.

Six months, she'd demanded. Well, six months

should just about do it for him, he decided cynically.

He recalled what Felix had said that first night he'd set eyes on her.

'You don't have to marry the girl...'

He finally appreciated the wisdom behind Felix's advice. He was so right. He didn't. If and when he ever contemplated marriage again it would not be to a girl who'd been brought up to think that a huge house was her birthright, along with a designer dress for every occasion.

Marcus wondered what she would wear on Monday. Not that lime-green dress again. Something more sophisticated, and subtle. She would want to impress him with her sincerity, and her seriousness.

Black, he guessed. Women always wore black when they wanted to be alluring without being obvious.

A knock on the study door was followed by Felix popping his head inside. He glanced around before coming into the room. 'Ivy said you were in here with Justine Montgomery.'

'I was.'

Felix's eyebrows rose and Marcus smiled a wry little smile. 'No, nothing like that, Felix. We were just discussing business. Miss Montgomery is in need of a loan.'

'Yes, so I'd heard. Trudy told me. She also said you'd already knocked Justine back but that you'd both been in here so long she thought Justine must have moved on to plan B.'

Marcus stiffened inside while he kept his eyes calm. 'Plan B?'

'A back-up plan if Justine didn't get that loan. Plan B was to find herself a rich man to marry in a hurry.'

For some reason, confirmation of Justine's character irked Marcus more than it should have. He'd already known what she was, hadn't he?

'I haven't forgotten how attractive you found her once before,' Felix was saying. 'I thought perhaps you might have been acting on that attraction…'

'Sorry to disappoint you, Felix. I was only offering Miss Montgomery that loan, not seducing her.'

'That's surprisingly generous of you, Marcus, considering her less than ideal circumstances. But you don't fool me, old chap,' he added, smiling lasciviously. 'You're usually hard-nosed when it comes to banking business, but I suspect it's passion, not compassion which has spurred you to such an uncharacteristic gesture. And she *did* look delicious in that red dress, didn't she?'

'I'm afraid I didn't notice what she was wearing, Felix,' Marcus said with a deadpan expression as he walked towards the study door.

Felix followed Marcus out of the room, laughing.

CHAPTER SIX

JUSTINE was kept waiting an unnervingly long time before she was ushered in to see Marcus Osborne on the following Monday morning. She must have sat in his secretary's office for over half an hour, long enough for her to start worrying that he might have changed his mind about giving her the loan.

Trudy would have laughed at her concern. On the phone yesterday she'd inferred Justine had it made because their esteemed banker secretly fancied her. Where she got that stupid idea from, Justine could only guess. That girl was obsessed with sex. Marcus Osborne didn't even *like* her.

Oddly enough, Justine found it hard to fathom her own feelings towards *him*. Trudy had been way off the mark when she'd accused her of being turned on by the man. Justine was sure she wasn't, even though she conceded he'd looked strikingly handsome in that black dinner suit last Saturday night. And kind of sexy, in that darkly brooding fashion Trudy had mentioned.

Justine had thought about him often over the weekend, with mixed emotions. She still resented his deception of the previous Friday but she had to admit she no longer hated him. How could she, when he'd magnanimously changed his mind and given her the loan? What she seemed to want more than anything, now, was to make him change his mind about *her*. She wanted him to look at her with respect, wanted him to see she wasn't stupid or lazy, that she *did* have some character.

But she feared that was going to be hard to do. He had preconceived ideas about girls like her. She could see that. It worried her a lot that in the time which had elapsed since Saturday night Marcus Osborne might have reconsidered his impulse to give a loan to someone he obviously believed was superficial and possibly irresponsible.

Once Justine got the nod to go in to his office, that worry soared. She plastered a bright smile on her face and bravely ignored the butterflies in her stomach as she walked in.

The room was a far cry from the small walled cubicle he'd filled so intimidatingly on the previous Friday. Huge and rectangular, it was dominated by an equally huge semicircular desk behind which curved a complementary semicircle of glass.

In the middle of this circle, with his back to a view of the city skyline, sat Marcus Osborne.

He looked every inch the president of a prestigious merchant bank, his suit much more stylish than the pompous pin-striped number he'd sported for their last interview. Charcoal-grey and possibly Italian, it was a single-breasted two-piece with a sheen similar to its wearer's sleek black hair. His tie was an elegant grey and blue stripe, his shirt as white as his teeth.

His hard dark eyes surveyed her slowly as she crossed what felt like an acre of grey carpet. Justine might have been wrong but she gained the impression her appearance pleased him, and her confidence received a well-needed push in the right direction. She was glad now that she'd taken her mother's advice and dressed conservatively in a neat little black suit with short sleeves and brass buttons down the front. Her hair was up in a classy French roll and stylish gold earrings graced her ears.

'Sorry to keep you waiting, Miss Montgomery,' he said from his large leather chair. 'Do sit down.' He waved towards the group of three smaller upright chairs facing the desk.

She beamed at him as she selected the middle one. 'Please don't keep calling me Miss Montgomery,' she said sweetly as she crossed her legs. 'I hate that kind of formality. Call me Justine.'

His smile soothed her nerves some more. He wouldn't be smiling if he was going to knock her back a second time.

'Delighted,' he said. 'And you must call me Marcus.'

'Marcus,' she repeated, smiling her relief at the way things were going. She could not have borne to go home today and tell her mother it had all fallen through again. The poor darling had been so excited by the good news on Saturday night. It had totally revitalised her. She'd been a real help to Justine yesterday, mucking in with the housework, and even cooking dinner. Adelaide had also promised to do all the cooking for their boarding house venture, which perhaps was just as well, Justine thought ruefully. Cooking was not her forte. Though she could always learn. She'd told Marcus she could do anything when she put her mind to it, and so she could!

'You haven't changed your mind, I take it?' she asked.

'Not at all,' he returned smoothly. 'When I give my word, it's as good as my signature.'

'That's wonderful!' she exclaimed. 'I was a bit worried you might have. I suppose there are forms I have to sign?'

'Not at this juncture. And it's your mother who'll have to sign, since she's the legal owner of the house. I called you in to get some more details of your plans. First of all,' he went on, leaning back against the leather chair, 'exactly what contents are you going to sell to reduce the debt?'

Justine was glad she'd come fully prepared. 'I've made a list,' she said, diving into her handbag and extracting a folded piece of paper. She stood up to slide it over the wide desk. 'There are several items of antique furniture, some eighteenth-century silver and six paintings by well-known Australian artists. I've put a fair price against each item. As you can see, the total comes to over three hundred thousand, though naturally some of that money would be lost in commission at auction.'

She watched with some satisfaction when his face showed surprise. 'You have some very fine pieces of furniture here. And these paintings are exceptional.'

'You know something of antiques and paintings?'

'I've made an in-depth study of most investment methods. Really good antiques and paintings never lose their value, I've found, provided you don't pay too much for them in the first place. Who bought these? Your mother?'

'No, my grandmother.'

'Who did you get to price them for you?'

'No one. I priced them myself.'

When his eyebrows rose, she added, 'My grandmother was quite an expert and gave me an extensive education in art and antiques before she died.'

'I have to admit I'm impressed, Justine. *Very* impressed.'

Justine shone under his compliment. 'I'll contact an auctioneer this very afternoon,' she told him, anxious to impress him some more.

'No, don't do that. I'd be interested in buying what you have here myself. That way both of us get a bargain by avoiding commission.'

'But that's marvellous!'

'Naturally I would like to see them first. Would you be home this afternoon? Say around two?'

Justine hesitated. She'd been going to sell her car this afternoon. Still, that could wait. No way was she going to knock back an offer like this! Not only would it save her a lot of work, but Marcus was right; it would save her a lot of money.

Her smile was eager. 'Yes, of course.'

Yes, of course, Marcus thought wryly. He had no doubt she would say 'yes, of course' to pretty well any of his suggestions, including the dinner invitation he would smoothly slip in towards the end of the afternoon.

So far she'd been totally predictable, from the little black suit she was wearing to her whole demeanour. She hadn't wasted any time getting them on a first-name basis, and in throwing around some more of those dazzling smiles of hers. All the contemptuous glowers of last Saturday night had been banished, her eyes stopping short of outright seduction but showing a definite eagerness to please.

Admittedly, that list with its prices attached *had* come as a genuine surprise. The girl knew her subject. So did he. Marcus wasn't a fool. He recognised a bargain when he saw it.

Maybe this uncharacteristic episode in his life wouldn't cost him as much as he'd been fearing. For of course he could not actually give her that crazy loan with bank money. They'd think he'd gone mad! He would have to finance it through his own personal pocket.

But what the hell? he thought recklessly. She enchanted him, despite everything. Enchanted and aroused him unbearably. It was as much as he could do to sit here, acting the cool, controlled banker. He felt anything but controlled in her company. His mind would not give him any peace. It kept wandering to tonight, to that moment when he would at last have the opportunity to draw her into his arms and kiss her.

Unless, of course, an opportunity arrived earlier...

'Excuse me for a moment, Justine,' he said abruptly.

He pressed a buzzer on an intercom system, his secretary answering straight away. 'I'd like you to cancel all my appointments after lunch, Grace.'

'*All* of them?'

Marcus could understand Grace's shock. He'd never taken an afternoon off.

Well...not since that day he'd gone home on a hunch and found Stephany in bed with her lover.

The memory popped into his mind with all its

usual explicitness, but oddly enough there was no accompanying pain, and hardly any bitterness. His amazement was only exceeded by his gratitude towards the exciting young creature who was even now looking at him with a flatteringly focused interest.

A lot of people had told him that the way to forget Stephany was to find someone else. It seemed they'd been right. Not that he planned on marrying her. He wasn't *that* much of a fool. If darling Justine had actually moved on to plan B with him—and it *was* possible—then she was doomed to disappointment. Still, the fringe benefits of her trying to hook him were insidiously attractive.

'Yes, Grace,' he said firmly. 'All of them.'

'Very well, Mr Osborne. Oh, before you go...'

'What?'

'Gwen just rang. She's had a little accident. Sprained her ankle. The doctor says she'll be off her feet for a fortnight. She said to tell you she'd miss you. Anyway, I'll organise a temp to fill in, but I thought you'd want to know.'

'Yes. Thank you. Ring the florist, Grace, and send her some flowers. Include a note saying Marcus hopes she makes a swift recovery and that he's already looking forward to her return.'

'Yes, Mr Osborne.'

Marcus turned off the intercom and glanced up, startled to see Justine frowning at him. It came to him that she might be puzzled over his sending flowers to some woman who declared she would miss him. He didn't *have* to explain, but he didn't want her to have any reason whatsoever to reject him as a potential husband or lover. No way did he want her thinking he had some other lady-love in his life. The only lady-love Marcus wanted in his life for now was Justine herself.

'Poor woman,' he said. 'She's one of my cleaners. Does this room every night. Cleans this whole floor, actually. We often have a chat when I work late. Her husband is unemployed at the moment and she has five children. So she's the sole breadwinner.'

Marcus looked at Justine across his desk. To give her credit, she could adopt a sweetly sympathetic face when required. Truly, she could look almost angelic at times.

'Oh, dear,' she murmured. 'That's tough. Will she get sick pay?'

'Yes, of course. She's regular staff.'

'Let *me* do her job while she's away!'

Marcus was stunned by her request. And quite put out. Good God, the last thing he wanted was for her to spend every night cleaning his damned bank. He had other plans for her evenings.

'You don't know what you're asking,' he said curtly. 'Gwen cleans this whole floor. She works from six till midnight five nights a week. It's very hard work.'

'You think I'm afraid of hard work?' she flung at him, clearly affronted.

He didn't think she was *afraid* of it. She just had no idea what it entailed.

'Well, I'm not!' she insisted. 'I can do it. I know I can.' She leant forward in the chair in an appealing fashion, her lovely face both eager and enchantingly earnest. 'The university doesn't go back for another two weeks. I intend to put an ad in next Saturday's *Herald* offering full board. I would imagine I'll get plenty of takers, given the convenience of our house to the campus, but we won't be getting any money in for three weeks at least. I could do with two weeks' pay, I can tell you.

'Please, Marcus,' she pleaded, when he said nothing.

He stiffened as her use of his first name curled around his heart like a clinging vine, squeezing out feelings he'd never wanted to feel again for any woman. His immediate reaction to this unexpected weakness was immediate and fierce. He didn't want her touching his heart, damn it! The only part of him he wanted her touching was much lower.

Suddenly there was a perverse appeal in the image of her down on her hands and knees, cleaning and polishing the surfaces where he walked, and sat, and leant. It kept her firmly where he wanted her kept. In his carnal desires. Nothing deep or dangerous.

Marcus saw now that an intimate little dinner date tonight would have been a mistake. They'd have talked too much. He didn't want to get to know her—except biblically. There was no reason why he couldn't conveniently work late these two weeks, no reason why he couldn't have her in his office instead of his bed.

'Very well,' he said, fighting to keep his equilibrium in the face of his wildly flaring desires. 'You can have the job.' He flicked on the intercom before his conscience could get the better of him. 'Grace? Forget about finding a temporary cleaner. I have someone here willing and able to do the job. She'll be right out with her particulars. You can take her down to Personnel and sign her on as a casual.'

'Yes, Mr Osborne,' Grace said dutifully.

'You *are* willing and able, aren't you, Justine?' he couldn't help saying in slightly mocking tones. Though it was himself he was mocking.

You've lost it, Marcus. You've finally lost it.

She bristled at his tone. 'I told you once that I could do anything if I set my mind to it. You didn't believe me then and I see you don't believe me now.'

'Seeing is believing, Justine.'

Her blue eyes narrowed, and that lovely bottom lip of hers jutted forward. 'Yes,' she pouted. 'It will be, won't it?'

CHAPTER SEVEN

'YOU'RE going to work as a *cleaner*!'

Justine prayed for patience. 'Only for two weeks, Mum,' she said, and walked across the kitchen to open the refrigerator. She hadn't long been home from the bank, and desperately needed a cool drink. It was terribly hot outside.

She found a can of chilled cola in the door. The last one. She'd have to go food-shopping soon or they'd be eating the paint off the walls!

'But…but,' her mother was stammering in the background.

'But what?' Justine said frustratedly, only just managing not to slam the refrigerator door.

'Do you think you'll know what to do?' Adelaide asked uneasily.

'Oh, not you too!' She ripped the ring-top off the can, then tipped it up to her mouth.

'What do you mean? ''Not you too…'''

The cold cola didn't cool her temper, which had been steadily rising along with the day's temperature. It had been the hottest summer on record for a hundred years, according to the silly weather man her mother devotedly listened to every evening.

'Marcus doesn't think I can do it, either. But I'll show him,' she vowed. 'I'll show him if it's the last thing I do!'

Justine threw some more cola down her throat.
'Marcus?'

'Marcus Osborne,' she elaborated irritably. 'The president of the bank. The man at Felix's party the other night. The man I saw today. Mr Sanctimonious! My God, what I wouldn't give to wipe that superior smirk off that disgustingly handsome face of his.'

'*Disgustingly* handsome?'

'Yes!'

'How old is this disgustingly handsome man?'

'Mid-thirties or thereabouts. It's hard to say. Sometimes he looks younger, sometimes older.'

'Married?'

'You're just as bad as Trudy!' She shook her head in exasperation then downed the rest of the cola.

'Really? In what way?' her mother asked vacantly.

'She's trying to marry me off to him as well. She thinks he fancies me, which is as far from the truth as you can get. I embarrassed him into giving me the loan the other night and now he probably regrets it, but he's too much of a gentleman to go back on his word. He thinks I'm an irresponsible nitwit and he's waiting for me to fall flat on my face. I dare say the only reason he's offered to buy the paintings is to prevent his looking a fool for giving me the loan in the first place!'

'He's going to buy the paintings?'

'*If* he likes them. He's shown interest in the antiques as well. He's coming here this afternoon to look at them.'

'What if he doesn't like them?'

'He will. Men like Marcus Osborne measure

everything in profit and loss. All those things are bargains, Mum, and well he knows it.'

'You really don't like him, do you?'

Justine thought of him, sitting in that big leather chair, looking oh, so impressive, but oh, so super-cilious. 'He rubs me up the wrong way.'

'Is that all. Well, he's a man, dear, isn't he? Men often rub women up the wrong way. It's the nature of the beast. But it's often the most annoying men who are the most attractive. From what you've said about him, being Mr Osborne's wife would be a much better job than being his cleaner.'

Justine laughed. 'The day I become Mrs Marcus Osborne I'll walk naked down the aisle!'

Her mother gave her an irritatingly knowing little smile. 'That should make for an interesting cer-emony, darling. You'd better wear a long veil.'

'Very funny, Mum.'

'I'm not trying to be funny. It's just that I've never seen you so rattled by a member of the op-posite sex. Usually you're very *laissez-faire* about them while they're running around in circles trying to impress you. Are you sure your Mr Osborne isn't trying to impress you, but in a more subtle, grown-up kind of way? Since he's in his mid-thirties, then he *is* a man, darling, whereas all your other admir-ers have been mere boys.'

Justine gritted her teeth. 'Mum, I will only say this one more time. Marcus doesn't fancy me. He isn't trying to impress me. He's a banker through and through, with ice where his blood should be. The only woman he's ever really fancied, I'll bet, is Dame Nellie Melba!'

'He's into opera?'

'He might be, but that's not what I meant, Mum. Melba happens to be one of the lucky ladies who grace our bank notes! I'm sure he kisses her image goodnight every evening. Now, no more talk about our esteemed banker. All that does is raise my blood pressure, along with my temperature. I'm going to go have a long, cooling shower and find something negligible to put on before I dissolve into a puddle.'

Marcus pulled up outside the Montgomery residence in his pale grey Mercedes and looked over at the house. It wasn't a mansion, but it was a distinctive two-storeyed stone residence, sitting on a large block and surrounded by a lovely garden. It was also at the bottom of the street backing onto a bushland reserve which overlooked the Lane Cove River. It would bring well over a million at auction in this prestigious North Shore suburb, and in such an attractively private position. Justine was right. He was on a certain bet lending money with such a desirable property as security.

Feeling not at all soothed by this knowledge, he opened the car door and was immediately assailed by the heat. Everyone had been complaining about the long, hot summer, but weather didn't bother Marcus in the main. His life was mostly spent indoors and in air-conditioning. His house and his car were air-conditioned, as was the bank. He did go sailing on a Sunday, but you never seemed to feel the heat on the Harbour.

Despite the blistering afternoon sun, he dismissed the momentary temptation to take off his jacket and tie, determinedly ignoring his discomfort as he

strode across the pavement and let himself in
through the front gate. He sighed with some relief
once he reached the shade of the portico, though
the long wait for someone to answer the doorbell
didn't do much for his composure. Beads of per-
spiration started forming on his forehead, which he
dabbed at ineffectually with his pocket handker-
chief.

His discomfort increased when the door was
wrenched open and there stood the daughter of the
house, wearing nothing but the shortest of denim
shorts and a strawberry-coloured tube-top. Her
lovely face was scrubbed free of make-up and her
long blonde hair lay darkly damp and tangled
across her bare shoulders, suggesting a recent
shower and shampoo. A hairbrush in her hand, plus
her dismayed expression, showed he'd taken her by
surprise.

'You're *early*!' she accused.

'It's right on two by my watch.'

The grandfather clock which stood in a nearby
corner suddenly started to strike the hour.

'Oh, my God, so it is. Sorry. Time seems to have
gotten away with me. I *was* going to change before
you arrived.'

Change? He didn't want her to change. He
wanted her to stay exactly as she was, although it
was a struggle to keep his eyes cool as they brushed
over her bare shoulders, then dipped down to take
in the disturbingly explicit outline of naked breasts
beneath the ribbed red top. Difficult not to stare at
her prominent nipples. Downright dangerous to
think what he'd like to be doing to them.

'There's no need,' he said, a touch thickly. 'What you're wearing is fine.'

'It's certainly a lot cooler than what I was wearing this morning. Aren't *you* hot, dressed like that?'

Marcus's smile was strained, to say the least. 'I have felt cooler,' came his huge understatement.

'Then come inside and take your jacket off, for heaven's sake.'

Swallowing, he came into the relative cool of the cavernous foyer and allowed her to help him out of his jacket.

'*And* that silly tie,' she added, and held out her hand.

He imagined he wasn't the first man she'd encouraged to undress. Neither would he be the last, he kept reminding himself. 'Are you sure you won't tell on me?' he said wryly as he tugged the tie loose and lifted it over his head.

Her beautifully defined eyebrows arched in surprise, possibly at the flirtatious note in his remark. 'Is there anyone to tell? Aren't you the big boss at that bank of yours?'

'Yes and no. I *am* the president of the bank, but I don't own it. I'm answerable to the board.'

'I presume the board demands their president always wears a suit during work hours?'

'They would view my dressing casually with disapproval.'

She gave a dry little laugh. 'I'll just bet they would. But the board's not here, is it? You're playing hookey for the afternoon. From the sound of that secretary of yours this morning, you don't play hookey all that often, do you?'

'I'm a novice at the game, I must admit.'

'Well *I* was an expert when I was at school. The first hookey-playing rule is that you dispense with your uniform. No one can have fun wearing a uniform. Now give that tie to me. I have a feeling you'll put it back on as soon as my back is turned.'

He obediently placed it in her hand then watched as she hung both the jacket and tie in a coat closet under the stairs. Marcus's mouth dried at the sight of her from the rear. Truly, those denim shorts should be registered as a lethal weapon, along with that devastating top!

'And the second rule?' he asked on her return, congratulating himself on his outward composure.

'Oh, there isn't really a second *rule*. What comes next is up to the individual. You just go with the flow. Playing hookey is all about doing what you want to do instead of what you *should* be doing.'

'And what was it that you wanted to do when you played hookey, Justine?'

She smiled a rueful smile. 'Ah, now that would be telling. You already think I'm the silliest most irresponsible girl who ever drew breath. I don't want to give conviction to your suspicions. Let's just say anything was preferable to going to school on the days we had Mrs Bloggs for personal development and sex education classes.'

Marcus watched the way her mouth twitched with amusement, the way her eyes lit up with wicked pleasure at the memory. No doubt she hadn't needed any classes in either subject. She'd preferred to substitute practical experience for the theory.

He wished he'd been a boy going to *her* school around that time. He'd have gladly played hookey with the delectable Justine. There hadn't been any girls in the institution for boys he'd attended. No lady teachers, either. The place had been staffed by hard-nosed brutal teachers who hadn't heard that the laws regarding corporal punishment had been changed.

But he didn't want to think about that now. He wanted to focus his attention on this deliciously irrepressible creature whose path he'd fortuitously crossed.

He could no longer judge her harshly. She was what she'd been brought up to be. But there was no evil in her. No malice or cruelty. She wasn't another Stephany. She was like a breath of fresh air wafting in the window of his boring banking life.

All of a sudden he was sick and tired of the bank, sick and tired of working eighteen-hour days. He wanted to have fun, wanted to play hookey…with *her*.

He might have pulled her into his arms then and there, might have kissed those lovely lips senseless if a woman hadn't suddenly appeared in the hallway—a woman Marcus guessed was Justine's mother.

She looked him up and down as only a mother can. 'Mr Osborne from the bank, I presume?' she said, coming forward with her hand outstretched, and smiling suddenly. 'How do you do? I'm Adelaide Montgomery. Justine's mother.'

'How do you do, Mrs Montgomery?' He shook her plump little fingers while taking in her general appearance.

Overweight and overdressed, she was the perfect example of a pampered lifestyle. Still, for all her obvious over-indulgence, Adelaide Montgomery possessed a childlike charm in her smile which belied her background and made one instinctively like her.

'Oh, do call me Adelaide. Justine and I don't stand on ceremony, do we, darling?' she said, linking affectionate arms with her daughter.

'In that case, call me Marcus.'

'What a wonderfully masculine name! Well, I'll love you and leave you in Justine's capable hands, Marcus. She can take you around and show you everything. I just wanted to say hello and thank you for helping us out like you have. It's men like you who renew one's faith in humanity. *And* bankers,' she added with another of those sweet smiles.

'Don't forget to speak to Tom when he arrives, Mum,' Justine murmured, and her mother's face fell.

Marcus was wondering who Tom was when the older woman looked wistfully up at him.

'Tom's our gardener,' she said. 'At least, he *was* our gardener. Justine says we can't afford him now,' she added in a soft and heart-wrenchingly sad little-girl voice. 'I don't know how I'm going to bear to tell him he's not wanted any more...'

Marcus almost opened his mouth and offered to pay for the damned gardener himself, so great was this woman's ability to stir his long-dormant male protectiveness. Not like her daughter. She stirred *other* male feelings.

'Mum, I don't think we need discuss this in front of Marcus,' the girl herself muttered in a tight-lipped fashion.

Her mother reacted with a guilty fluster. 'No. No,

of course not. Sorry. You're so right, darling. Forgive me. I forgot. We have to solve our own problems.'

'Yes, Mum. We do. Now, I must get on with showing Marcus Grandma's things. I have to go to work tonight, remember?'

'Yes, yes, of course. I'll see you later, perhaps, Marcus? We might have afternoon tea together.'

'I'd like that,' he said.

Justine's mother went off down the hallway, looking chastened. Marcus felt angry with Justine, till he looked at her and saw her own distress. He suddenly appreciated the magnitude of her problems, plus the immense responsibility she'd taken on her slender shoulders.

His urge to pull her into his arms was no less strong, but now his desire was mixed with some sympathy. He wanted to soothe as well as seduce, which was not exactly an easy mix and did not sit well with him.

'Sorry,' she sighed, on seeing his frown.

'You've no reason to be sorry,' he said brusquely. 'I understand what you meant now. She's not strong, is she?'

'No.'

'She wouldn't be able to cope if she had to sell, would she?'

'Not very well. Come on, I'll take you upstairs and show you what's there first.'

She took off at a pace, Marcus hurrying to keep up. He didn't say anything till they reached the landing. 'About the garden, Justine...'

'No!' she said sharply, spinning round to face him. 'I don't want your charity, Marcus. You've already done more than enough. Mum might not be able to cope but I can. I'm young and I'm strong. I can mow a lawn if I have to. And weed a garden bed. Or don't you think I'm capable of that, either?'

'I think perhaps you're taking on far too much,' he prevaricated.

'Maybe I am and maybe I'm not. But that's for me to decide, isn't it? Or do you think I need some man to hold my hand?' she snapped at him.

He thought what she needed was a man's hand across her backside!

'I think what you need, Justine,' he said instead, 'is a friend.'

'A friend!' she snorted. 'I'm afraid friends have been a little thin on the ground around here since Daddy died. I used to have loads of friends. *And* boyfriends. But there's not one I could even ask to mow the lawn now. Not that I would!'

Marcus frowned. This was not what he'd been expecting. He'd thought any pass he made would have been readily accepted, and even encouraged, not misunderstood. Hadn't she flirted shamelessly with him since his arrival?

What game was she playing now? Hard to get?

He was forced to bypass the subtle for the straightforward. 'What about me?' he suggested.

'You!'

Her stunned surprise irritated the death out of him. 'Yes, of course. Who else did you think I was talking about?'

CHAPTER EIGHT

JUSTINE was floored. 'But… But…'

'But what?' he said smoothly. 'Is there any reason why we can't be friends, Justine? You just admitted there wasn't any jealous boyfriend in the wings who would object. As for my part, I am safely divorced, with no other lady-friend in my life at the moment.'

His dark gaze roved over her and Justine's stomach flipped right over. She wasn't a fool. He didn't mean a friend like Trudy was her friend. He meant boyfriend. Though 'boyfriend' seemed a highly inadequate word for a man like him. 'Lover' was more like it.

Marcus Osborne wanted to be her lover.

Good God!

Trudy had been right all along. Marcus *did* fancy her. He'd probably given her the loan and offered to buy the paintings and antiques *not* because he was fair, or compassionate, but because he lusted after her.

Which made him not much better than Wade Hampton, really. He was simply more devious.

Justine should have been outraged. The girl who'd gone to the bank last Friday would have been. The girl who'd swanned into Felix's party on Saturday night would have torn strips off him. The girl who'd visited him this very morning at his office would have reacted with disgust.

But something had happened to that girl since then. Lord knows when, or how. Her mother had been right when she'd said Marcus rattled her more than any member of the opposite sex ever had. He did.

She'd certainly acted out of character from the moment she'd opened the door just now. She'd babbled on, flirting with him in a way, and actually undressing him to a degree. Had she done that because subconsciously she'd wanted to touch him, wanted to see if the breadth of his shoulders was real or just clever tailoring?

They had felt real enough.

She stared at him now and wondered what he'd look like without any clothes on at all. The thought flustered her even more. She could feel the blood in her veins heating, flushing her throat and her face.

Dear heaven, had Trudy been right about this as well? Could it be that underneath her fury and irritation she'd been sexually attracted to Marcus all along?

Disbelief warred with reality, which was that the thought of Marcus lusting after her, wanting her so badly that he would do anything to have her—lower his standards, break his precious rules, risk his self-righteous soul, even—quite blew her away.

Her bewilderment was total.

'Justine?' he prompted. 'Is there a problem?'

'Why would you want to be my friend?' she blurted out. 'You don't even like me.'

Their eyes met and she could not tear her own away. His suddenly smouldering gaze held her effortlessly, mercilessly, sending her pulse-rate wild.

'Justine,' he said thickly, and reached out to run the fingertips of his right hand down her cheek.

She could not move, her eyes widening as his head bent, closing the distance between his mouth and hers. He was going to kiss her, and she was going to let him.

Justine squeezed her eyes tightly shut, as though by closing them she could almost pretend this was not happening to her. She couldn't possibly be going to stand there and let Marcus do this. It was unthinkable!

A small moan escaped her mouth as his lips brushed hers. When he lifted his mouth away, another moan followed, a strangely pained protest. The thought that he might leave it at such an appallingly brief kiss brought a rush of dismay so intense that she reached up on her toes and pressed her lips back against his.

He groaned. Immediately his hand, which had been hovering lightly against her face, slid down around her throat to firmly cup the nape of her neck, holding her mouth captive under his. His other hand snaked around her waist, settling in the small of her back and pulling her hard against his body. She was pinned to him, their bodies touching everywhere, chest to chest, stomach to stomach, thigh to thigh.

It felt incredible. *He* felt incredible. His body, his heat, his mouth moving restlessly over hers. She'd never experienced anything like it, had never known a kiss could evoke such a wave of excitement and longing. She wanted more, more of the kiss, more of him. Her mouth flowered open with a tortured little moan this time. And he needed no further invitation.

His tongue darted forward, then dipped deep.

Where other male tongues had previously brought revulsion, his brought a raging, reckless rapture. She could not get enough of its driving hunger. When he went to withdraw, her hands clutched at his shoulders and she claimed his lips back with hers, sending her own tongue into his mouth with a desperation which would later stun her.

Marcus finally wrenched his mouth away and wrapped her to him, hard. 'Remind me not to kiss you anywhere in public,' he rasped into her hair, his chest heaving against hers. 'Hell, Justine...'

Justine didn't agree. This wasn't hell. It was heaven.

'Kiss me again, Marcus,' she whispered, and lifted her face up to his.

He cupped her face and started kissing it all over. She closed her eyes once more and sucked in breath after breath of much needed air, little 'ohs' escaping her mouth when he pressed his lips to each eyelid.

'God, I want you,' he said thickly, and returned to her parched, panting mouth at long last. 'Tell me you want me too,' he insisted, while his lips hovered over hers and she was simply dying with anticipation and excitement. 'This isn't just gratitude, is it? Tell me this is real, Justine. Tell me!'

'Yes,' was all she could manage, her head spinning, her heart pounding. 'Yes,' she repeated, and melted into his mouth once more.

Elation crashed through Marcus when he heard her admission and felt her surrender. No one, he thought triumphantly, could pretend that well. She wanted him, wanted him as much as he wanted her.

His kiss was hungry and demanding, her response everything he could have wanted it to be.

Dear God, but she was a highly sexed creature. The sounds she made. The way she moulded her body to his. He could only imagine what she would be like when he was inside her. Just thinking about it sent his own arousal into overdrive.

His arms tightened to lift her slightly off her feet and sweep her from the landing into a nearby room, his mouth never leaving hers. It was a bedroom, he noted out of the corner of his eye, a large bedroom with a huge four-poster bed. He pulled her down with him onto the cream-quilted bed, and tried not to think of her mother downstairs.

Soon, kissing her mouth wasn't nearly enough. He had to touch and taste the rest of her. His passion was out of control. *He* was out of control.

So, it seemed, was she.

She didn't stop him when he peeled that provocative little top down to her waist and exposed those perfect breasts to his eyes, and then his lips. She moaned and arched beneath him with an almost liquid abandon as he licked the soft pink nipples into pointed peaks of obvious pleasure. She gasped when he sucked one deep into his mouth and gave it a lover's nip, groaning when he released it.

'You like that?' he rasped, propping himself up on one elbow and staring down at her.

'Yes,' she admitted, her eyes wide upon him.

Yes, indeed, he thought ruefully as he made a concerted effort to get himself under control. As much as he would have adored to strip her totally, right here and now, common decency demanded he stop. Her mother could come upstairs at any moment.

But it was almost impossible to turn his back on the passing pleasure she offered. I'll stop soon, he promised himself, then watched her face while he trailed the back of his right hand across her exquisitely swollen breasts, revelling in her sharply inward gasps, exultant at the flaring of her nostrils whenever he contacted her still wet nipples. He took one between his thumb and forefinger, rolling it to an even more erect and sensitised state.

Her lips fell raggedly apart, her big blue eyes gradually growing heavy with desire. She looked lost on a sea of sensuality, utterly incapable of stopping either him or herself. He had no doubt she would do anything he asked, regardless.

Did she always respond with such total abandon? he wondered, the thought rattling him for a moment before he swept it ruthlessly aside. What did it matter if she did? This was what he wanted from her, wasn't it? Sex on tap till his mad desire for her had burnt itself out. Who cared what she did with other men? The last thing he wanted was to become emotionally involved with the girl.

'Justine!' her mother suddenly called up the stairs. 'Are you up there?'

Marcus swore under his breath, deserting her to swing his feet onto the floor and stand upright. Justine, he noted wryly, took several seconds to snap out of it. When she did, she sat bolt-upright, blushing furiously as she yanked her top back up over her still betrayingly aroused breasts.

Marcus almost smiled at that blush. It seemed

even the most liberated girl found embarrassment in the face of possible discovery by a parent. Did that sweet mother of hers think Justine was still an innocent little virgin?

Marcus imagined Grayson Montgomery hadn't been under any such illusion about his daughter when he'd been alive. Such a man of the world would have recognised her inherent and undoubtedly well-explored sensuality. *Any* man would.

Marcus watched her frantic straightening of the quilt, noting ruefully that she was unwilling to meet his eyes. He actually found her guilty fluster quite enchanting, perhaps because it was so at odds with the wanton creature who a moment before had been lying there, naked to the waist, oblivious to everything but his hands upon her.

'Justine?' her mother called again, her voice decidedly closer.

CHAPTER NINE

JUSTINE groaned, gave the quilt one last agonised glance and dashed for the landing, determinedly avoiding Marcus's darkly amused eyes.

'Right here, Mum. What do you want?'

Her mother was halfway up the stairs, puffing. Justine felt more than a little breathless herself. She thanked God her mother had called out instead of coming up first.

'Tom's here. We'll be out in the back garden if you want us. How are things going with Marcus? Did he like what you had to show him?'

'I certainly did,' Marcus answered, coming up to stand next to her on the landing, his hands reaching out to curve over the railing.

Justine went hot all over as she stared at those hands which a minute before had been doing such incredible things to her. She could still feel her nipples burning beneath her top.

'Excellent,' Adelaide chirped, and waddled back off downstairs.

Justine stood frozen by Marcus's side, confusion rampant within her. Common sense warned her this wasn't true love come at long last. Not in a million years!

Her feelings for Marcus were extremely powerful all the same. And very disconcerting. What she'd felt on that bed had been mind-blowing. She'd never experienced anything as exciting, despite not feeling comfortable with being so out of control.

Marcus didn't seem to be suffering from any such confusion. Or discomfort. Once her mother had disappeared, he turned her straight away and took her into his arms once more, kissing her till her head was reeling.

'Are you always like this with women?' she asked breathlessly when he finally let her mouth go.

'Like what?'

'So…wicked.'

He laughed. 'Now, that's the pot calling the kettle black, isn't it? I didn't notice you stopping me in there. Or now.' He trailed kisses across her cheek to her ear, blowing softly within.

'You do things to me,' she admitted, shuddering wildly. 'Things I've never felt before…'

'In what way?'

'In *every* way.'

'Mmm. Tell me more,' he murmured, and bent to nuzzle her neck.

'Maybe it's you who should be telling *me* more,' she said huskily.

He straightened and stared down at her with narrowed eyes. 'What are you talking about?'

'Did you give me that loan because you wanted to get me into bed?'

'Will I get my face slapped if I say yes?'

'No.'

'Then, yes. I did. In part.'

Again, disgust was very much absent from her reaction, even with his admitting the worst. She thrilled to the evidence of his passion for her, a passion which must have gone against his grain.

She hadn't forgotten that he didn't think too highly of her.

'I fought the temptation from the moment I saw you last Friday,' he confessed wryly as he ran a tantalising fingertip around her mouth. 'I might have succeeded if you hadn't been at that damned party, wearing that damned dress. Do you know how you look in that red dress? Do you have any idea what it did to me?'

'No…' How could she? Today was the first day she'd been introduced to the pleasures of the flesh. But she'd glimpsed its power now, and could well understand the compulsion to put aside thoughts of right and wrong in exchange for such pleasures.

'Come with me now,' he urged darkly, his finger trailing down her throat towards her still aching breasts, 'and I'll show you.'

'Now?' she repeated breathlessly.

'Yes. We can go to my place. It's not all that far. No one will be there. We'll be alone.'

As much as she wanted to, the image of herself surrendering her whole body to Marcus, of his taking her virginity, of his finding out she *was* a virgin, brought a wave of sheer panic.

'I…I can't do that.' She whirled out of his arms and away from his disturbing touch.

'Why not?' he demanded sharply. 'You said you wanted to earlier. What's changed all of a sudden?' His face hardened, his black eyes glittering coldly. 'Don't start playing the tease with me, Justine. I'm not in the mood and it doesn't suit you.'

'I'm not. I just…you're…you're rushing me. I *hate* that!'

One of his eyebrows arched, and a sardonic smile

twisted his mouth. 'You want to make me wait, is that it?'

'I…I think I want to make *myself* wait.'

'Ah…'

She had no idea what that 'ah' meant, except that it sent a startlingly sexual shiver running down her spine.

'And you call *me* wicked,' he murmured. 'All right, have it your way. When will you go out with me, then?'

When…

Justine knew his asking her to go out with him was the same as his asking her to go to bed with him. It was a fair enough presumption, she supposed. She'd led him on, no doubt about that. And, in truth, she wanted Marcus to be her first lover. She could see now that her waiting for true love was a silly romantic dream, fuelled by a belief that she would need an incredibly deep and special love to surrender her body in total intimacy to a man. She'd thought in terms of making a sacrifice, never participating in the act for pure pleasure.

What she'd felt with Marcus this afternoon already was pure pleasure. Well…maybe not so pure…but definitely pleasure—pleasure she could not turn her back on.

But along with a natural fear of the big event lay a fear she might scare him off, once he discovered her lack of experience. Justine could see he thought her a right raver. It was an understandable conclusion, given the way they'd met and the circles she moved in. Virginity was a rarity. Promiscuity more the norm. These days boyfriends *expected* to sleep with their girlfriends—maybe not on their first date, but sooner or later.

Marcus was a mature man. He wanted a mature sexual relationship with her. He would move on to another more willing woman if she said no.

Justine was amazed at how sick that thought made her feel.

'When, Justine?' he growled.

'Saturday night,' she blurted out.

'Saturday night! My God, that's an eternity away. Why not tonight?'

'I have to work tonight, remember? And every night this fortnight.'

'Damn! I knew that was a bad idea when I agreed. Look, what say I arrange for someone else to do it? We can spend each evening together, instead. I'll give you any money you need.'

'No.'

'What do you mean, no?' he demanded irritably.

'I mean, no, you are not going to arrange for someone else to do my job. And, no, you are not going to give me any money at all! I aim to earn what money I need in life. Legitimately. As I told you once before, I don't go to bed with men for money.'

Oh, no? Marcus thought cynically. He doubted he'd be here with her at all if he wasn't who he was, with a bank at his disposal.

'You also said wild horses wouldn't get you into bed with me,' he pointed out dryly, watching for a sign of guilt, looking for any evidence that her passion was not mutual but merely practical. After all, if she wanted him as much as she seemed to, why the delay in consummating their desire for each other?

In truth, he doubted her asking him to wait was an erotic game, designed to increase the intensity of her sexual satisfaction. He'd found the games women played were more about power than pleasure. *He* was the one to be teased unbearably by the wait, to be brought to a pitch where he would do anything she asked just for release. He wondered if she'd already moved on to plan B, wondered how much was real and how much was just an act.

No matter, he thought darkly. Saturday night would come. And, by God, so would he!

'I think I should get on with showing you the things you came to see,' she said abruptly, before throwing him a troubled glance. 'That's if you really *do* want to buy them. You're not going to confess you only came here this afternoon to seduce me, are you?'

Seduce *her*? What a laugh that was! She needed about as much seducing as Mata Hari. He'd never known a woman to go up in flames so quickly. In hindsight, he could not possibly see how she could have faked that scenario on the bed. Her body spoke an automatic and instinctive language under his touch. He had been its master there for a while. My God, the way her nipples had sprung upright at the lightest touch. The way she'd moaned. And writhed.

Hell, he had to stop thinking about that, or he'd end up in the funny farm by nightfall, let alone by Saturday night!

'I'm not going to confess another single thing,'

he growled. 'I take it you won't reconsider my suggestion to give this a miss for now?'

'You take it correctly!' she pronounced firmly.

'Then let's get on with it,' he muttered.

It was a very trying afternoon. Marcus found it hard to keep his mind on proceedings to begin with, though once he recognised the value of what he was being offered his long-trained mercenary nature came to the fore.

The paintings she showed him were by well-known Australian artists, and quite rare. Worth every cent she'd put on them, and possibly more. The antiques were just as rare, mostly small and quite unique tables. There was an eighteenth-century walnut and rosewood inlaid gaming table that would have brought a small fortune at auction. The workmanship was so outstanding Marcus felt guilty taking it for the price. When he said so, however, she waved a dismissive hand.

'I'm happy with the price I put on everything. I'm also happy thinking that they're going to someone who will value them. I know you'll look after Grandma's things as I would have, especially the paintings.'

'They're yours, Justine?' he asked, frowning. 'Not your mother's?'

'Everything I've shown you is mine. Grandma left them to me in her will. I didn't like to sell Mum's things. She's lost enough already.'

He was touched, and at the same time perturbed, especially when it looked as if she was suddenly fighting back tears. 'Justine, if you don't want to sell these things, please say so.'

'There's no question of wanting to, Marcus, but

having to, I'm afraid. It's either this or lose the house, and I know Mum couldn't bear that.'

He frowned further. Was she manipulating him here? Angling for more of his help? Playing on his sympathy? She claimed she wanted to survive on her own, but was that true?

Plan B popped into his mind again. A wealthy husband would solve all her problems. Marcus was almost tempted to offer himself, since she wouldn't take his money otherwise. Wives didn't seem to have any trouble spending their husbands' money.

But the possibility she might say yes, plus the inevitability of another divorce, kept his mouth firmly shut on that subject. As Felix had once told him oh, so wisely. 'You don't have to marry the girl…' He didn't. He just had to wait till Saturday night. Meanwhile, he would offer an option for her to repurchase any of her grandmother's things in the foreseeable future, since he would be keeping them as an investment for some years to come.

'Justine, I…'

'Please don't go making any new offer I'm going to have to refuse, Marcus,' she snapped. 'I only took your loan because I believe I can pay it back. And I accepted your offer to buy these items because I knew you were getting your money's worth. No charity was involved, simply a fair exchange. You once told me there was no quick and easy way in life. I believe you now. Daddy's death has made me face lots of things about myself. Yes, I was a spoiled little miss with a silver spoon in my mouth. I never had to do without, or budget, or work for a living. But I'm learning. And I'll learn more, if you let me.'

She drew herself up tall and set uncompromising eyes upon him. 'You want to be my friend? Fine. I'd like that. You want to be my boyfriend? That's fine too. I'll bet you're great in bed. What I don't want is for you to become my sugar-daddy. That I *don't* need. Okay?'

He was impressed, both by her speech and her sentiments. As long as they were for real...

'Believe me,' he said, 'the last thing *I* want is to become is your sugar-daddy. I wasn't going to offer you money. I simply wanted to say thank you.'

She gave him a wary look. 'For what?'

'For giving me the opportunity to possess and enjoy some very unique treasures. I promise to look after them for you, and if you ever want to buy any of them back again, they're yours at the same price.'

Her eyes flooded with tears and she looked away, blinking rapidly.

Marcus could not help but be moved. She was a more deeply feeling girl than he'd previously given her credit for. He actually began to believe that everything she was doing wasn't so much a matter of selfishly clinging to a comfortable lifestyle, but out of genuine caring for her mother and her home.

He placed a comforting hand on her disturbingly bare shoulder, but didn't say anything. Words were impossible as he battled the urge to haul her into his arms once more.

She threw him a brave smile through soggy lashes. 'Sorry,' she said, and dashed away the last of the tears with the back of her hand. 'It's not like me to be weepy. Thank you so much for that offer.

That's one I won't refuse. You're so right.
Grandma's treasures *are* unique.'

Marcus let his hand drop away from her satiny
smooth flesh, his stomach contracting at the thought
that the most unique treasure of all he wanted
to possess and enjoy was Justine Montgomery herself. He just hoped the price was not going to be
too high.

CHAPTER TEN

'NO!' TRUDY gasped over the telephone after Justine had related a slightly edited version of the day's events. 'I don't believe it!'

'But you were the one who said Marcus fancied me in the first place!' Justine protested.

'That's not the part I don't believe, silly. It's your fancying him *back* I don't believe.'

'I know. I find that hard to believe myself. He's just left and I simply *had* to tell someone. I couldn't tell Mum. She's still got Tom with her.'

'Who's Tom?'

'Our gardener.'

'I thought you said you couldn't afford a gardener.'

'We can't. But he's insisting on doing it for nothing. He says he doesn't need the money and that he would be at a loss without the work. I have a feeling he's sweet on Mum. He's a widower, you know. I think she likes him too. She was all atwitter over afternoon tea. And she didn't gush over Marcus like I thought she would. Tom got all her attention.

'Anyway, enough about Mum and Tom. I rang you up to talk about Marcus and me. I need your advice about something. Trudy, I'm going out with him next Saturday night and he's going to have a fit when he finds out I'm a virgin. I just know he will.'

'My God, you're going to sleep with him on your first date? I mean, this is *you* we're talking about, isn't it, Jussie, not me?'

'Yes.' Justine sighed. 'It's me.' She knew it sounded totally out of character, but she also knew she wouldn't be able to resist Marcus if he started making love to her.

And he would. She just knew he would! He hadn't wanted to take her to his house this afternoon to play chess!

'My God, what did he *do* to you today? Put a spell on you or something?'

Perhaps, Justine conceded. She was totally bewitched and besotted with the man. He'd filled her every thought since he'd left the house only fifteen minutes earlier. Yet already it felt like a lifetime.

'He's not what I thought he was,' she said. 'He's…he's…'

'A banker,' came Trudy's dry remark. 'Never forget that. And he was once married to the biggest trollop since Jezebel. Or so Father said. I didn't know her myself. Father says he's once bitten ninety times shy. He won't marry you, Jussie.'

'But I don't *want* him to marry me.' The very thought had never crossed her mind!

'This is *me* you're talking to, remember? I know you, Jussie. If you fancy the guy that much, I'll bet my bottom dollar you're already falling in love with him. Once you've lost your virginity to him you'll be head over heels and thinking about foreverland. Especially if he proves to be a good lover—which thankfully, I doubt.'

'He *will* be a good lover,' Justine said, quivering

at the memory of what he'd done to her on her mother's bed.

'You sound very sure of that. Good Lord, what *did* he do to you today? I don't believe this. I was only joking the other night when I said you might be turned on by that cold-blooded devil.'

'Marcus is not at all cold-blooded.'

'She's defending him now,' Trudy muttered on the other end of the line. 'The other day she hated him!'

'I was wrong about him.'

'Maybe you weren't.'

'I thought you'd be pleased. You've been at me for ages to give sex a fair go.'

Trudy was disturbingly silent at the other end.

'I'm not in love with him!' Justine insisted.

'Mmm.'

'I see there's no point in asking for your advice, then,' she snapped, and hung up.

The telephone rang back straight away and she reluctantly answered it, knowing her mother was out in the garden with Tom.

'I'm sorry,' Trudy said. 'I'm a bitch. But I don't want you to get hurt. Look, I know I used to tease you about your waiting for true love to come along, but underneath I thought it was rather sweet.'

Justine's chin began to quiver. Before she knew it, she'd burst into tears.

'Don't cry, Jussie,' Trudy begged. 'Please don't cry.'

Justine got a hold of herself pretty quickly. Truly she was having an emotional day. First she'd cried with Marcus over her grandma's things. Now she was crying over her lost romantic dream.

'I'm all right,' she sniffled. 'Really.'

'No, you're not. You've had a rotten time lately, and you deserve to have some fun. Go out with Marcus by all means, and go to bed with him, if you want to. Just keep a lock on that tender heart of yours. You're not made for casual sex, Jussie. If you were, you'd have been doing it all along.'

'He probably won't want me when he finds out I'm a virgin,' she wailed.

'I wouldn't be too sure of that,' came Trudy's dry reply. 'He might want you all the more.'

'Oh? I would have thought he'd run a mile.'

'Why?'

'Because my virginity will shatter all his preconceptions about me. Plus all his expectations. He disapproved of what I did at the bank last Friday, but he was tempted all the same. He believes I know my way around a man's bedroom, not to mention a man's body. He says he wants to be my friend, Trudy, but I think he only wants a fling with a young woman of the world!'

'Mmm. I think you could be right.'

'I can improvise with the foreplay part. I've read enough to have some clues. But that's not going to help much when it comes down to the act itself. I don't want him to know that I haven't done it before. Is there any way I can get around that?'

'Gee, Jussie, I don't know…'

'What happened in your case?'

'It hurt like hell.'

'Oh, golly.'

'But I have a girlfriend who swears her first time was a breeze. No pain. Nothing. There again, she was a mad horsewoman—switched to riding men with no trouble at all!'

Justine closed her eyes. This was a crazy and embarrassing conversation.

'This is silly, Trudy,' she said. 'Maybe I should just tell him the truth.'

'Perhaps that would be for the best.'

'You think he'll dump me then, don't you?'

'I think he'll think twice.'

'Good. That's what I want him to do. Last Friday at the bank I convinced him I was something I wasn't. I'd like the opportunity to redress that opinion.'

'You want his good opinion?'

'Yes.'

'Oh, dear…'

'I'm *not* in love with him!'

'I heard you the first time.'

'Nobody ever believes me,' Justine wailed.

'I believe you. Now, hang up, Jussie, or you'll be late for work. It's gone four-thirty. Didn't you say you had to be at the bank by six?'

'Yes, but it's not far. Only down at Chatswood.'

'Don't forget, it's peak hour traffic. He's not going to be there tonight, is he?'

'Marcus, you mean?'

'Who else?'

'I don't think so. He had the rest of the day off. Why?'

'Men like him always work late. Even later if they fancy the cleaner.'

'You have a wicked mind.'

'Yeah. And I'm only a girl. Imagine what kind

of mind a man of thirty-five has. What are you going to wear?'

'They supply an overall at the bank.'

'An overall's good. Very hard to undress a girl in an overall.'

'I'm not going to listen to any more of this.'

'All right, but don't say I didn't warn you.'

'I won't!'

'I'll ring you tomorrow. Better still, I'll drop round.'

'You do that. You can be useful for once and help me sell my car.'

'Sell your car! But you *need* your car.'

'I need *a* car, not one worth what mine is worth. I'm going to trade down and bank the difference. You've no idea how much it costs to live, Trudy.'

'Tell me about it tomorrow.'

'Don't come before noon. I'll be wrecked after tonight.'

'Mmm,' Trudy said salaciously.

'Oh, stop that!' Justine snapped, and hung up again.

Marcus had no intention of going back to the bank when he left Justine's place. He drove home and went for a long swim, which cooled his blood as well as his ardour. He climbed out after twenty laps, suitably deflated, dragged on a bathrobe and set about making himself a snack and some coffee. He switched on the television and settled back to watch the five o'clock news while he ate.

The newsreader came on. She was pretty and blonde, with a nice smile. But not a patch on Justine, whose face would launch a thousand ships...her figure, a million. He would never forget the sight of her perfect pink-tipped breasts, or the way those breasts had responded to him. He could still see her in his mind's eye, lying semi-naked on that luxurious quilt, her eyes shut, her lips parted and panting.

Marcus swore violently. He'd been doing quite well, trying not to think about her. Now she was back, tormenting his mind and his body. The thought that later this evening would find her alone in his office at the bank brought devilishly wicked temptations. He felt compelled to go there, to see her in the flesh. No one would think anything of his turning up, not even Justine. He had every reasonable excuse to return to the bank today.

'Had to work late,' he imagined himself saying to her when she came in. 'Missed far too many hours this afternoon.'

His smile was self-mocking. He wondered what she'd say if he told her what he was really thinking. 'Missed you already, sweetness. Can't wait till Saturday night. Care for a session on the boardroom table?'

No.

That was what she would say to him. No.

Marcus was not about to put himself into a position where he might look desperate. Or like a fool. Which meant he would just have to wait patiently till Saturday night before making his next move.

Clenching his teeth hard in his jaw, he pointed the remote at the TV screen and consigned the blonde newsreader to oblivion, then rose to get himself another cup of coffee.

*   *   *

Justine wanted to cry. She'd been stuck in a traffic jam for fifteen minutes, yet she was less than fifty metres from the tall blue glass building which housed the bank. A couple of times she'd been tempted to leave her car where it was and just walk. But she couldn't, could she? She was trading the darned thing in tomorrow. She *needed* the car. It was worth more money to her than two weeks' work as a cleaner.

Her insistence on doing this cleaning job that morning had been more a matter of pride and stubbornness than desperate need, despite what she'd said to her mother and Trudy. She'd wanted to show Marcus that she wasn't lazy, that she was prepared to work hard. And now she was going to be late.

Damn, damn and double damn!

At long last the car ahead moved, and although it was at a crawling pace the line of traffic eventually crept through the lights, where the presence of shattered glass all over the road indicated an earlier accident.

What rotten luck, Justine thought. Finally she was able to turn off the highway into the car park driveway. She whipped down the ramp, where she was stopped by a barrier and a security guard, who told her officiously that this was a private car park and not a racetrack. Justine kept her cool, flashed him one of her winning smiles, then showed him the pass the personnel manager had given her that morning.

'I'm a relief cleaner,' she explained. 'This is my first night. There was an accident up the road and it's made me late.'

The guard frowned at her expensive car, shrugged, then directed her to a reserved though now empty parking space in a corner by the lifts. She was only twelve minutes late on arrival on the sixth floor, where she hunted frantically for the cleaner who was supposed to tell her what to do and how to do it.

Justine located her in the very cubicle which had been the scene of her first embarrassing encounter with Marcus. After explanations and apologies, the woman—who was around fifty and called Pat—kitted Justine out in a grey overall and supplied her with a mobile cart full of cleaning equipment, along with a huge set of keys.

The seventh floor was her domain, she was instructed, and each room was to be securely locked after being cleaned. She was to start at the far end of the corridor, where the boardroom and the big boss's suite were, then work backwards. Vacuuming and dusting the rooms was on the agenda every night. *Nothing* was to be touched in any of the offices, except the rubbish bins which required emptying. Lastly, the washrooms were to be cleaned. There were four on the seventh floor. Mr Osborne had a small *en suite* bathroom attached to his office as well.

'I stop for a cuppa and a bikkie around eight-thirty,' Pat told her at the lift doors. 'I'll give you a call. Oh, and don't worry if some of the rooms aren't empty. The fellas in this 'ere establishment are workaholics and slave away into the wee small hours of the night. Just clean around 'em. They'll hardly notice.'

Pat gave Justine a sharp look. 'Er...I take that

back. A fella would have to be dead not to notice you, lovie. You'd better tie that hair of yours back. And don't smile too often. You only have five hours to get around the whole floor, and being chatted up is not on your list of jobs.'

Justine wound her hair up into an untidy and hopefully unattractive knot on the short ride up to the seventh floor, then wiped her lipstick off with the back of her hand. She hadn't come here to be hit upon by some yuppie bank executive. She'd come to clean, and to prove something to herself and Marcus.

The lift doors opened and she stepped out into the hushed corridor, pushing the cleaning cart before her. Pat had been right. There were lights on in a few of the offices. A door on her right suddenly opened and a man in a grey suit hurried past, not so much as giving her a glance. He looked very harried.

Was this what Marcus demanded of his employees? she wondered. Ten-hour days and tunnel vision? Was this what Marcus himself was like most of the time? She recalled how startled his secretary had been when he'd said he was taking the afternoon off. Obviously he didn't play hookey from work too often.

Her mind turned momentarily to his marriage and the reasons for its failure. Trudy had called his ex-wife a trollop. But Trudy called every second female a trollop! Maybe Marcus had never been home, and his wife had strayed out of neglect. Such things happened.

She would ask Trudy tomorrow to find out whatever she could from her father about Marcus's marriage and the woman he'd married. She wanted to know how long the marriage had lasted and how long it was since his divorce was finalised.

Justine recoiled at the sudden appalling thought that there might have been children involved. She didn't want Marcus to have children. Actually, she didn't want him to have had a wife, either. She certainly didn't like the idea of his ever having been in love before.

But he's not in love *now*, you fool, came the savage voice of reason. Certainly not with *you*! He's struggling to like you. He wants to get you into bed, darling. That's the bottom line. He admitted it. You tempted him last Friday and he finally acted on that temptation. Keep that thought in mind and don't start turning this into a romance. It's a matter of chemistry, not true caring, of lust, not true love.

Justine's stomach contracted, and her heart did as well. Oh, God... Was Trudy right? Was she falling in love with Marcus? Had she *already* fallen in love with him?

She didn't know. How could she? She'd never fallen in love before, had no idea what it felt like. Wasn't it more likely she'd fallen into lust? After all, whenever her thoughts turned to Marcus, sex was not far behind. She could not stop thinking about what it would be like, being with him. Saturday night could not come quickly enough.

Her resolve to tell Marcus she was a virgin wavered considerably in the face of the possibility he *might* run a mile once he knew her lack of experience. That was not what she wanted. Not at all. She wanted his mouth back on hers, and his hands, and every other part of his body!

A disturbingly erotic shudder rippled through her.

Dear God, this will never do, she decided shakily. She had to stop thinking about him or nothing would ever get done here tonight.

But not thinking about Marcus was impossible, especially once she pushed the cart down the corridor to the reception area where she'd sat that very morning, waiting to see him. Although the lights were still on, his secretary's desk was now unattended, her computer turned off, her chair pushed back.

Grace was not a young woman, a fact which had pleased Justine at the time. If his secretary had been a glamorous young piece Justine knew she would have been jealous.

Was jealousy a sign of love? Or just lust? Whatever, it was certainly a sign of feeling something. Boys had often accused her of being heartless over the years, of caring for no one but herself. Justine had shrugged off their accusations as sour grapes because she hadn't cared a whit about *them*. She would not have been jealous of any girl ensnaring Howard Barthgate, or any of the boys she'd gone out with. But the thought of Marcus admiring or being with any other female brought jabs of real pain.

Justine shook her head at herself. Lust or love, it was not a very nice thing to suffer from. She decided she didn't like it one bit!

Marcus lasted till twenty past six. His third cup of coffee was left to go cold on a side table while he dashed to his room and pulled on underpants before dressing in what came quickest to hand—a pair of grey trousers which had just been returned from the drycleaners and were hanging on the wardrobe door. He grabbed a navy silk shirt from his shirt drawer and fumbled appallingly with the buttons. Grey socks and black leather shoes proved not so difficult, but were still irritatingly time-consuming.

Another precious minute was wasted trying to put some order into his pool-damp hair, which had a tendency to kink and wave when wet. Usually he blow-dried it straight. Tonight he didn't have time, or the patience. Despite his rush, it was still twenty five to seven by the time he backed out of the garage and pointed in the direction of the Pacific Highway. As he accelerated away, he thanked his lucky stars that he'd bought a house close to the bank. Ten minutes and he'd be there!

Not quite. There must have been an accident earlier, for the traffic was backed up and moving very slowly.

Seven had come and gone by the time a very frustrated Marcus pulled into the underground car park under the concrete and glass skyscraper which housed his bank, only to have the security guard flash him an anxious look.

'Gee, Mr Osborne, you said you'd gone for the day. I…er…I let someone else use your parking spot. A new cleaner. Pretty little thing. She was running late because of the traffic. Sorry, Mr Osborne, but I didn't think you'd mind. The spot next to your usual is empty.'

He didn't mind at all—till he saw what kind of a car Justine was driving.

Marcus slid his Merc into the spot next to the sporty Nissan and glared across at the sleekly silver lines. He knew exactly what such a car was worth, especially one so new. Hardly the sort of transport a girl needed when she was down to her last dollar, when that very morning she'd begged to be allowed to work as a cleaner because she needed the money. Even if she didn't own the car outright, the insurance alone would be quite high, much higher than an ordinary little runabout which would have sufficed for her needs.

Clearly Justine wasn't about to compromise the parts of her life which showed her status to the world at large. Her home. Her car. Her wardrobe.

There was no longer any doubt in Marcus's mind that Justine intended to put plan B into action in the not too distant future. Everything else she was doing were merely stop-gap measures, designed to keep the wolf from the door till she could land herself that sugar-daddy husband she'd seemingly scorned.

But was the object of her manipulations yours truly? he speculated caustically. She was certainly working hard to change his bad opinion of her.

Marcus suspected, however, he was another stop-gap measure—someone to satisfy her highly sexed nature till a suitable marital candidate came along. She'd have to be a fool to think *he'd* marry her, given the manner of their initial meeting.

Justine Montgomery might be a lot of things, but not a fool.

No. She'd decided to kill two birds with one

stone, supplying herself with a lover while conveniently keeping him sweet over the loan at the same time. Then, when plan B succeeded, she would have done with both in one fell swoop.

Or maybe not? Marcus pondered darkly. Maybe, if he pleased her in bed, she might plan to keep him on as her lover. It would not be the first time an ambitious young woman had married one man to better her financial position while entertaining other males on the side.

Marcus rode the elevator up to the seventh floor with fire in his eyes, and in his belly. If Justine thought she could use him, then she had another think coming. It was *her* who was going to be used. Ruthlessly. Smoothly. Mercilessly.

CHAPTER ELEVEN

JUSTINE was finding cleaning more complex than she'd thought it could possibly be. There was so much equipment on her cart. Pat had assumed she knew what was used for what, and she did recognise some of the products, but the others required a good reading of the label before she understood their purpose and the right method of application, which slowed things down somewhat.

Marcus's washroom had proved more difficult than his office, but she was proud of the job she'd done and was standing in the doorway, admiring the sparkling surfaces and smudge-free mirror, when Marcus's face suddenly appeared in that mirror, right behind her left shoulder. She almost dropped the can of spray-on polish she was holding.

'My God, Marcus!' she exclaimed, whirling to smile shakily up at him. 'You almost scared me to death then. What on earth are you doing here?' she demanded to know while her eyes ran over his startlingly casual yet still elegant clothes. He looked sinfully sexy in that navy silk shirt, the open neck revealing a hint of dark hair on his chest. Justine had never thought she would like a hairy-chested man. Now it seemed a most desirable asset.

'I had to get something from my office,' he said, his dark eyes running over her in return, their expression dryly amused by *her* appearance.

In truth, the overall she was wearing was much

too big for her slender frame, and lacking shape altogether. A grey colour, it was like a boiler suit, with studs which snapped shut down the front from the neck to the groin.

'Yes, I know,' she said, a mixture of embarrassment and arousal heating her face. 'I look ridiculous. Pat couldn't find any smaller ones.'

'You still look a damned sight cuter than Gwen did,' he said, his eyes raking over her once more..

But not with amusement this time. A raw, naked passion blazed in their black depths, both shocking and exciting her.

She took a somewhat shaky step backwards, which he seemed to read as a silent invitation, for he followed her into the *en suite* bathroom and shut the door behind them. Justine just stood there like a frightened rabbit while he took the spray can from her frozen right hand and deposited it on top of the toilet.

She wanted him to kiss her, but she was afraid all of a sudden. There was a dark intensity about Marcus—an almost angry quality—which she found both unnerving and disturbing. But, for all that, she was powerless to stop him, her body already filled with a deep longing to feel his mouth and hands on her once more.

He obliged. Oh, how he obliged, kissing her with a hunger which rattled her brain and took her breath away while his busy hands were snapping the overall open and peeling it back till it fell off her shoulders and pooled onto the white-tiled floor, leaving her standing there in nothing but her joggers and undies.

It momentarily crossed Justine's befuddled mind

that her very sexy-looking pink satin half-cup bra
and French knickers did not present a virginal image, neither did the way she suddenly began un-
dressing Marcus with as much indecent haste as
he'd stripped her.

His shirt buttons were proving decidedly difficult, so he simply ripped the shirt apart from under
her fumbling fingers, sending buttons flying everywhere. Four frantic hands disposed of his trousers,
Justine's eyes blinking wide at the size of the bulge
in his underpants.

It was a sobering moment when he took her hand
and held it to him, letting her feel the harsh outline
of his stunningly large erection. There was no way,
she realised, that he wasn't going to hurt her, no
way she could hide her virginity. Not that she really
wanted to. She wanted him to know how special
this was for her, how special she found him.
Whether it was true love or not didn't matter. It
was still the first time any man had made her feel
like this.

'Marcus,' she rasped, her tongue feeling thick in
her mouth. 'I…I…'

'Don't talk,' he ordered brusquely, and bent to
dispose of his underpants before straightening.

Justine could only stare in awe at the power of
his naked male body with all its aggressive sexuality. Her mouth dried as she tried to imagine such
a formidable shaft buried deep inside her, her heart
stopping for a moment.

But then he took her hand again and wrapped it
around his straining flesh, urging her to stroke its
satiny length, to feel its strength as well as its
strangely stirring vulnerability. She did what he

wanted, and watched as his eyes closed on a moan
of raw, ragged pleasure.

The sound found echoes in her own body. Soon
she was burning with desire, any idea of saying
anything that might stop him swept away by her
own unstoppable yearnings.

When he pushed her downwards and pressed
himself against her lips, she took him blindly into
the heat of her mouth, no thought entering her head
but that she wanted to please him, to give him
pleasure. He stopped her all too swiftly, lifting her
back up to cup her face and stare into her passion-
glazed eyes with a hot and almost disbelieving
gaze.

'You're a witch,' he growled, before his head
bent to take a fierce possession of her lips, his
tongue ravaging the depths of her mouth with a
wild and frenzied passion. She gasped for breath
when he finally abandoned her mouth, but there was
to be no peace for the rest of her body. He grabbed
her upper arms in a bruising grip and hoisted her
up to sit on the vanity, pushing her legs apart and
moving between them. He kissed her neck while he
dragged her bra straps off her shoulders, peeling
them downwards till the satin cups gave up their
swollen inhabitants to his questing and quite rav-
enous mouth.

'Oh, God,' Justine moaned when he swept his
tongue over each rock-hard nipple. Her back arched
to offer her breasts up to be licked and sucked more
easily; her hands pressed palms-down on the granite
surface at her sides. Her eyes closed in ecstasy, her
head tipping back, her lips falling softly apart. It
felt better than it had that afternoon, the sensations

electric and compelling. She panted his name, moaned her dismay when he stopped, her head snapping forward to dazedly watch him yank off her joggers then peel her panties down her legs.

Now she was totally naked, and he was parting her legs again, exposing her totally to his gaze. An intoxicating mixture of shame and excitement flooded Justine as he touched her there while watching her face. A wild heat claimed her cheeks, and her lips fell raggedly apart. But it was *him* she was soon wanting inside her, not those tormenting, teasing fingers which quickly drove her insane.

'Marcus…*please*,' she groaned, and actually moved her legs wider, begging him with her body as well as her eyes.

'All right, witch,' he said thickly. 'If that's what you want. But that won't be the end to it. Not by a long shot.'

She gasped her shock when his head began to bend towards the liquid fire between her legs. For that was not what she wanted at all! Naturally she'd read of such an activity, had heard Trudy wax lyrical about it. In truth, she was sure at some other time she might enjoy it with Marcus. But not right now, not when she was desperate to have him inside her, to hold him to her and feel their flesh as one. She was sure now it wouldn't hurt. His fingers had slipped inside her so easily. She knew she was very ready.

'No,' she groaned, and his head jerked upright, dark eyes startled.

'No?'

'No,' she repeated. 'Not that. Not right now. I want *you*, Marcus. Only you.'

'But I don—'

'Marcus, please,' she broke in, and cupped his face with her hands, using the leverage to slide her bottom to the edge of the vanity, wrapping her ankles around his hips and drawing him towards her. 'Do it. Now. I can't wait another moment.'

'God help me,' he groaned, and did what she wanted. Swiftly. Passionately. Roughly.

Justine couldn't help it. She screamed.

CHAPTER TWELVE

MARCUS sat at his desk, his head in his hands.

The sound of water running had his head slowly lifting. He stared at the washroom, with its firmly shut door, and thought of her pale, pain-filled face; of his own shocked self stumbling back from the vanity, of his staring down at the bright red spot on the white tiled floor.

He hadn't known what to do, or to say. Yet he *had* said something, hadn't he? Some thoughtless obscenity. And she'd looked up at him with such scorn in her eyes.

'Just go,' she'd flung at him, pressing her knees together and wrapping goose-bumped arms over her bare breasts. 'Get out!'

So he had. And now he was slumped at his desk, his largely buttonless shirt hanging limply around him, his mind in chaos.

But, good God, how could he have known, or guessed? Virgins didn't waltz into a bank and practically prostitute themselves to loans officers! Virgins didn't let men they hardly knew caress their bare breasts while their mothers were downstairs! Virgins didn't willingly go down on a man in a washroom, damn it!

Marcus groaned at the memory. Her sweetly eager lips had driven him instantly insane, had sent him hurtling towards that point of no return so that he'd had to stop her. Even then he'd been beyond rational thought, had succumbed to a recklessness totally alien to his character. When she'd begged him to just do it, he'd brushed aside his usual passion for protection to embrace a different passion, namely Justine Montgomery, the breathlessly beautiful, wickedly wanton, deliciously decadent daughter of the equally decadent Grayson Montgomery.

But the Justine Montgomery he'd thought she was didn't exist.

A virgin! He still could not believe it. How had it come about? How could a girl looking like her, responding as she did to a man's touch, reach almost twenty-two without having intimately known a male body?

Different if she'd been locked in a convent somewhere. Or been raised in a strictly religious community. The circles she moved in, however, were not exactly renowned for their shrinking violets!

The washroom door opened and Justine walked out with her head held high, her eyes still full of scorn.

'I was right about you,' she said, with more than a touch of bitterness. 'Trudy was wrong.'

Trudy? Now, why would Justine be talking to Trudy Turrell about her relationship with him?

Marcus's brain finally snapped back into gear.

Trudy Turrell.

Plan B...

'I said you'd run a mile once you found out,' Justine went on scathingly.

Marcus thought that would be a damned good idea, if good old plan B was at the bottom of all this. Had Justine been trying to trap him with a pregnancy just now? Had all her so-called eagerness been just part of the plan to ensnare a rich husband for herself? Had her seemingly stunning responses all been an act?

If they had, then by God, she was the greatest faker he'd ever met!

Yeah, right, Marcus, the cynical voice of experience argued back. You're God's gift to women, aren't you, my boy? They can't resist you. They always love you just for yourself, and never for what you can do for them. She couldn't possibly be faking it, could she? She's been saving herself just for you. Waiting for Mr Right to come along before she gives herself in true love.

Huh! And I'm Little Lord Fauntleroy!

The more likely truth is that she's a mercenary ex-rich bitch who's always seen her virginity as a marketable commodity to be bargained with, or sold to the highest bidder in marriage. Don't forget her silver car, that cynical voice reminded him. And her home. And her designer clothes.

She wants it all. *That's* the bottom line. Let's face it, Marcus, her fancying you *was* very sudden, and so very, very convenient, wasn't it?

Marcus's heart hardened with his thoughts.

No female was going to make a fool of him a second time. Yet, dear God, he still wanted her—maybe more than ever. No matter what her motives, the thought of being her first lover, of taking that beautiful body and bending it to his will, was incredibly arousing.

But there would be no pregnancy. And no marriage.

'You should have told me,' he said.

She looked away from his searching eyes, hugging herself defensively. 'So it seems.'

'Why *didn't* you, Justine?' he persisted, wanting to see if she could come up with a smooth lie, instead of the truth about plan B.

She shrugged. 'What does it matter now?'

Marcus had his answer. He was amazed at how much it hurt.

Her eyes were mocking as they turned to meet his. 'I presume Saturday night is off?'

After all she'd put him through? Hell, no! He stood up and walked smoothly over to her, congratulating himself on his own acting ability. His arms curled over her shoulders and he looked down into her immediately wary eyes. 'Now, why would Saturday night be off?' he murmured, the warm smile on his face belying the coldness in his heart.

'You're…you're *not* going to run a mile?' she asked, with what might have been a heart-wrenchingly touching manner…if it had been genuine.

'Of course not. Now that I'm over my initial shock, I find myself enchanted by the thought of your not ever having been with another man. My only regret is that I was so rough with you just now. Though you have to admit my assuming you were a woman of the world was hardly my fault, my love,' he added, with just the right amount of gentle reproach.

She blushed delightfully. Now, that was a skill worth having, he thought cynically. Being able to conjure up a blush at the drop of a hat.

Aware of his still simmering frustration, he bent to press light kisses to her cheek, her nose, her mouth, struggling all the while not to be taken in by the soft gasps of seeming delight she made.

'I...I should have told you,' she confessed breathlessly against his lips.

'Mmm. Never mind. No harm done.' Now he kissed her properly, though still carefully restraining his hunger. Damn, but she was a good kisser, he conceded, marvelling at the way she let her body melt into his, at the way she seemed so desperate for his tongue in her mouth.

And who knew? Maybe, having held her sexuality in check for so long, she was now unable to control it. Perhaps Pandora's Box had been well and truly opened. It was a tantalising thought, and one which Marcus would savour for the rest of the week.

'You're not angry with me?' she managed to say between kisses.

'Not in the slightest,' came his quite truthful reply. For anger was no longer his prime emotion at that moment. Hell, he had to get out of there fast or he'd be right back where he started, and still without any protection at hand.

But it was Justine who stopped the kissing, drawing back to stare up at him with gratifyingly glazed eyes. 'I...I must get back to work, Marcus.'

'Must you?' Already his body was demanding he coerce her back to his place, where he could be alone with her at his leisure.

'Please don't try to stop me,' she said shakily, as though reading his mind.

'*Could* I?' he drawled.

'You know you could. But if you like me at all, Marcus, please don't. Not now. Not tonight.'

Her voice broke, as if she was on the verge of tears. As he looked down into her glistening eyes Marcus felt his own heart squeeze tight.

Hell, he agonised, and looked away quickly. Not that. For pity's sake, not that.

He whirled to stalk back behind his desk, buttoning the one remaining button on his shirt and tucking the tails firmly into the waistband of his trousers. 'Very well,' he said curtly. 'I have to do some work myself, anyway. Though I think I should do mine at home, don't you? Remove myself from this occasion of sin.'

'Occasion of sin?' she repeated blankly.

'That's being within touching distance of you, darling Justine,' he said drily. 'If you'd spent time in St Andrew's Home for Wayward Boys, you'd know all about occasions of sin, and the many ways us wayward boys encountered them. You had "occasion of sin" written all over you from the moment you walked into this bank. My blood pressure still hasn't recovered from that lime-green dress you were almost wearing.'

Damn, she was blushing again. How did she *do* that? The guilt it evoked in him was incredible! What he needed was a change of subject. And a change of scene.

'Before I go,' he said as he swept up his car keys from the desktop. 'What day can your mother come into the bank to sign all the papers for the loan?'

'Oh. Um. Any morning this week, I suppose. I could drive her in.'

In the silver sports, he thought acidly.

'I'll have Grace ring you tomorrow to confirm,'

he said. 'She can also arrange a mutually convenient time for the removalist to come.'

'Removalist?'

His irritation knew no bounds. What was wrong
with the girl? Where had her brains gone to all of
sudden?

'For the paintings and antiques, remember?' he
said. 'I'll get Grace to make the arrangements and
give you the details when she rings.'

'Will *you* ring me tomorrow?' she asked.

One of his eyebrows automatically lifted. 'Do
you want me to?' he said, wondering what she was
up to now. Maybe she'd changed her mind and
wanted to see him sooner than Saturday night. If
she did, then that might mean she really wanted
him. Him, Marcus. Not him the high-profile president of a bank and potential partner for a gravy-
train life.

'Yes, of course.'

There was no 'of course' about it. She was beginning to confuse him again.

'Right,' he said testily.

'Why do you say it like that?'

'Like what?'

'Like you're angry.'

He sighed. The last thing he wanted was to make
her suspicious of *his* motives. 'Justine, love,' he
said. 'I'm not feeling too good right now. Men
don't like to be taken that far and then have to stop.
Sorry if I was short with you, but I'm in considerable discomfort. It's called frustration, not anger.'

'Oh.'

That damned blush again! And it worked every

time, making him question everything he believed about her.

'I think I'd better go,' he said.

'Oh, Marcus, I'm so sorry,' she apologised, and took a tentative step towards him.

His fists clenched into balls at his sides lest he surrendered to the temptation to take her in his arms once more.

'I'll ring you tomorrow,' he promised, then marched determinedly from the room.

'I told you he'd show up at the bank last night,' Trudy said scathingly on the way to the used-car lot. 'I'll bet he didn't go there to work at all. I'll bet it was just to seduce you. Which he seems to have done with surprisingly little resistance from you, I might add. I'm surprised you're making him wait till Saturday night to finish what he started, if you were enjoying yourself that much!'

'I am too,' Justine had to admit. 'But you've no idea how much it hurt, Trudy. One minute I was in ecstasy, and then in agony. I thought it would take me at least the rest of the week to recover.'

In more ways than one. She'd been in shock afterwards, both physically and emotionally. It had taken her some considerable time to get her thoughts and feelings together. How she'd finished her cleaning job after Marcus left, she'd no idea. When she'd finally arrived home she'd run herself a bath and lain in its soothing warmth for ages before going to bed.

Unfortunately, although exhausted, she hadn't been able to sleep, the memory of Marcus's love-making fuelling her mind and re-inflaming her

body. She'd tossed and turned for hours in a fer-
ment of frustration and longing. Lust, like fire, she
finally accepted, could be a good servant but a very
bad master. She could well understand why Marcus
had been so irritable afterwards.

'Well, if you'd told him you'd never done it before, like you said you were going to,' Trudy
hissed, 'then it wouldn't have hurt so darned much.
He'd have known to be more gentle. From the
sound of things you'd been acting like you'd been
doing it since puberty, so what did you expect? On
a vanity! Good Lord! You've truly shocked me,
Jussie.'

'I shocked myself, believe me.'

'You've certainly got it bad. Either that, or
Marcus is a far better lover than I had him pegged.'

'I told you he'd be a good lover.'

'Yes, well, maybe I was wrong there. But I
wasn't wrong to warn you off him. Dad says he's
very bitter about his first wife. He says you've got
very little chance of marrying Marcus Osborne!'

'Trudy! How many times do I have to tell you?
I have no wish to marry Marcus. I don't love the
man; I just want him to…to…'

Justine tried not to colour guiltily when her friend
flashed her a truly scandalised look.

But she wasn't about to be a hypocrite. Or a naïve fool. By morning, she'd accepted that her feelings for Marcus were strictly sexual. What she was
suffering from couldn't possibly be love. Love was
warm and tender and sweet. Love was safe and secure. It didn't hurtle one along darkly compelling
tunnels into a world where shame and excitement
mingled to ignite one's flesh into uncontrollable

flames, where you begged mindlessly for the burning to be stoked even further, where only the most excruciating pain could douse that seemingly unquenchable fire.

Justine had no doubt that Marcus could take her back to that point of no return whenever he wanted, and the next time there would be no excruciating pain to stop proceedings. The barrier of her virginity was gone, banished to the wilderness where once she'd walked in total ignorance of the pleasures of the flesh. She'd tasted the full potential of those pleasures now, and there would be no going back.

Still, having discovered the intensity and power of her sexuality, Justine found the future a little frightening, and somewhat confusing. Her feelings about Marcus were often mixed up. Saturday night seemed both too close and too far away.

'Do you think we might abandon the subject of men and sex for the next hour?' she said impatiently as she eased her Nissan over to the kerb outside the first of the used-car lots she planned to visit. 'I have a car to trade in.'

Trudy was about to argue when she spied a salesman walking in their direction. A very tall, very handsome salesman. Her switch to seduction mode was focused and immediate.

Justine shook her head as her friend bolted out of the car. Trudy had a hide accusing *her* of acting in a promiscuous fashion! Marcus was her first lover whereas this poor, unsuspecting salesman would probably become another victim in Trudy's hapless male harem!

*   *   *

Three o'clock that afternoon found Justine the proud owner of a neat white seven-year-old Pulsar, plus a sizeable change-over cheque, which she banked before coming home and finding the rates notice in the mail. She rolled her eyes at the amount, and slid it in the drawer where she kept all the other unpaid bills. At least now she had enough in her account to cover all their living expenses for a few months, with some rainy-day money left over.

'Mum!' she called out. 'Where are you?'

'Out here, darling,' came the lilting answer from the direction of the back yard.

The sight of her mother on her hands and knees in the garden, happily weeding, surprised Justine. Not so much the sight of Tom, standing nearby watering, and watching her mother with the tenderest look on his face, his eyes soft, his smile sweet.

Justine's heart turned over, then twisted slightly. Now, *that* was the look of love, not the darkly glittering gaze Marcus had bestowed upon her last night. Or that smoulderingly sexual smile which sent her into a tailspin.

'Hello, Justine,' Tom said on seeing her.

'Hi, there, Tom. It's hot again today, isn't it?'

'Not as bad as yesterday. But we could do with some rain. The gardens are beginning to suffer, what with the water restrictions and all. You can only use a hand-held hose during the day, you know. No sprinklers.'

'It's been a long, hot summer all right.'

'Yet we're only at the end of January.'

'Still, you've got the garden looking lovely, Tom. I'm only sorry we can't pay you.'

'You couldn't pay me for what I get while I'm

here, my dear,' he said softly, so that her mother could not hear.

Justine didn't say a word, just smiled at him. He smiled back, and Justine thought what a really nice man he was. He had lovely eyes. A soft brown, they showed intelligence and kindness. He was not as handsome as her father, but still a fine figure of a man.

Her mother glanced up from her weeding, her face rosy-cheeked, her pretty blue eyes sparkling. 'Did you and Trudy find a nice new little car, dear?'

'Not new, Mum. But little, and much more economical. And Trudy found herself a nice new boyfriend.'

'That girl! Speaking of boyfriends, Marcus rang earlier, by the way,' she added with a knowing little smile. 'He said he'd ring back.'

'That's nice.' No use denying Marcus was about to join the boyfriend category. She just hoped her mother didn't start thinking an engagement ring and wedding bells were to follow.

Despite her attempt at cool sophistication, the sudden sound of the telephone ringing sent Justine's heart leaping and her stomach contracting.

'That'll be him now, I don't wonder,' her mother said. 'Aren't you going to go in and answer it?'

'Yes, but it's too hot to hurry.' Justine took her time, not picking up the receiver in the hallway till the phone had rung a dozen times.

'Hello?' she said nonchalantly.

'Miss Montgomery?' a woman's voice answered.

Justine's instant and very intense disappointment showed what a fool she was to think she could play at being a woman of the world. The truth was she'd been dying to hear from Marcus all day, to feel reassured that he still wanted her after sleeping on his discovery that she was a virgin.

'Yes,' she said rather wearily. 'Who is this?'

'Grace Peters here. Mr Osborne's secretary. I've organised a removalist to call at your house Friday morning at ten, Miss Montgomery. Does that suit?'

'Yes. Yes, that's fine.'

'And Mr Osborne can see Mrs Montgomery tomorrow morning at eleven, if that suits as well?'

'Yes, that should be fine too.'

'Splendid. Now Mr Osborne would like to speak to you himself. I'll just put you through.'

'Justine?'

She clutched at the phone. Just his voice was doing worrisome things to her body, especially her knees.

'I'm ringing, as asked,' he said on a drily teasing note.

'Yes. So you are.' She was astonished at her coolly composed reply. Amazing when she was in danger of dissolving onto the carpet. Still, if she was going to have a strictly sexual affair, then it was imperative she keep a semblance of control over the situation.

'I did ring earlier but you weren't home,' he volunteered. 'Your mother said you were out shopping with Trudy. Since I can't imagine that particular young lady being acquainted with supermarkets I assume you were conducting an end-of-summer raid on the Double Bay boutiques?'

Justine pulled a face at the sardonic note in that last remark. Obviously Marcus still thought she was an irresponsible idiot, using what little money she had left on clothes. 'I don't have the money for such frivolities as fashion,' she pointed out. 'If you must know, I was busy trading in my car for a cheaper model.'

Silence at the other end.

'Marcus? Are you there?'

'Yes. Yes, I'm here. Sorry. Grace came in for a second. What was that you were saying? Something about trading in your car?'

'Yes. I've been going to do it for ages. Dad bought me a silver Nissan for my twenty-first last year, you see. Paid cash for it, which was darned lucky, otherwise it would have been repossessed like poor Mum's car. But it was an unnecessary expense to run and maintain. The insurance alone was horrendous.'

'So what did you buy instead?'

'A used Pulsar.'

'Did you have it inspected?'

'No. Why should I?'

'Did you get a warranty with it?'

'Twelve months. Oh, for pity's sake, don't go all macho male on me and start asking me a million mechanical questions about the darned thing. It's a car with four wheels and will get me from point A to point B and that's all that matters. You're the one who said I should live within my means and that's what I'm doing.'

'Mmm.'

'What does ''mmm'' mean?'

'It means I wish I could see you tonight.'

Justine's breath caught in her throat. 'I…I wish you could too.'

'God, Justine, I—'

'No, Marcus,' she broke in. 'I have to go to work. Stop trying to tempt me.'

'What about tomorrow? Meet me for lunch.'

A quickie at lunchtime? Oh, no. That was not what she wanted at all! 'No, Marcus,' she said firmly. 'Saturday, and not before. Pick me up at seven.'

'Seven…'

'Is that too early?'

'No,' he said drily. 'Not nearly early enough— unless you're talking about seven a.m.'

'I'm not.'

'I didn't think so. In that case I won't be ringing you again before then. It's far too…disturbing.'

The thought of him sitting behind his desk in a state of acute arousal gave Justine a perverse jab of pleasure. She didn't stop to analyse too deeply why she wanted him to suffer, but she did. Maybe she wanted some revenge for his propelling her out of her innocent and largely happy world, where sexual passion and frustration had been alien concepts and emotions.

'In that case, don't *you* work late any night this week,' she said tartly. 'Because I find *that* disturbing!'

'Mmm. Now, that's a very provocative confession, Justine. Brings all sorts of possibilities to mind about desks and deliciously polished boardroom tables.'

She flushed at the images he evoked. Thankfully, he couldn't see her flaming cheeks.

'I think your board of directors would expect their esteemed president to restrict his activities in that room to mergers of a more financial kind, don't you?' she countered.

Marcus laughed. 'We'll see, Justine. We'll see. I'll give you a reprieve for this week. But I won't promise the same for next week. That might be a different story.'

Justine couldn't even begin to think about next week. Saturday night was as far as her thoughts would extend at that moment.

'Will you be coming in with your mother in the morning?' he asked.

'Do you need me?'

'Would you care to rephrase that?'

'Is my presence strictly necessary?'

'No.'

'What a pity! I was about to iron my lime-green dress.'

'I'm not sure if I'm relieved or disappointed. That dress exposes more leg than your shorts did yesterday.'

'Not to worry. I'll wear it on Saturday night, if you like. I might have to, anyway.'

'What do you mean…have to?'

'Well, if this heat keeps up, I have the stunning choice of the lime-green or the red silk I wore to Felix's party. They're the only summery dresses I kept.'

'Kept?'

Justine bit her bottom lip. Darn! She didn't want Marcus to think she was crying poor-mouth, or looking for pity.

'Justine? Explain, please.'

When Marcus got that tone about him, there was nothing to do but obey. 'Look, I had to sell most of our going-out clothes to get some cash for food, and to pay the phone bill, otherwise I wouldn't be talking to you now. It's not a big deal. Mum and I didn't need dozens of glam dresses, anyway. I didn't expect to be going out much for a while, to be honest, so if we're to date on a regular basis then you'll have to put up with seeing me in the same things over and over, I'm afraid. Sorry.'

'There's no need to apologise, Justine,' he said tautly. 'No need at all.'

'Good, because I didn't mean to. It's a habit with females, that's all, saying sorry all the time when there's absolutely no need. Though I *was* sorry I hadn't told you I was a virgin last night.'

His sigh could have meant anything, but Justine automatically concluded it meant something bad.

'If you want to call it quits,' she said sharply, 'then just say so.'

'I don't want to call it quits.'

'Then what's the problem?'

'Who says there's a problem?'

'You sighed.'

His laugh was dry. 'So I did.'

'Well?'

'A sigh is just a sigh, Justine. Don't read so much into it. I'm tired. I didn't get much sleep last night. I doubt I'll get much sleep for the rest of the week.'

'Oh.' She quivered at the thought of his lying wide awake in bed, thinking of her, wanting her, needing her.

'Marcus,' she said, and her voice was low and husky.

'Yes.'

'Don't be late on Saturday night.'

'Don't worry,' he said ruefully, 'I won't be.'

CHAPTER THIRTEEN

HE *WAS* late. Seven minutes. But it was enough for Justine to have a taste of how she would feel if he never came, or if he ever decided to wipe her from his life altogether.

Devastation did not begin to describe her feelings. She spent those interminable seven minutes pacing to and fro across the lounge room and peering anxiously through the curtains, grateful that her mother was relaxing in a bath upstairs after her afternoon's gardening, unable to witness her daughter's uncharacteristic agitation.

Justine tried telling herself that sexual frustration was the reason for her fear-filled state, but somehow that didn't wash. Realisation dawned once Marcus pulled up in his Mercedes and she almost burst into tears with relief.

'Oh, my God, I *am* in love with him!' she wailed aloud.

Dropping the curtains, she clutched her bag to her chest and tried not to cry. Though whether it was from delight or dismay now, she wasn't sure.

Get a grip on yourself, girl, common sense demanded very quickly. So you're in love with him. That's nice. But he's not in love with you, so don't go winding romantic dreams around him. Trudy warned you good and proper. He's not going to marry you. All he wants is an affair. Right? Got that? Good!

137

An artificially composed Justine went to answer the doorbell at seven minutes past seven, having schooled her face into a perfectly understandable pout. She swung open the front door, ready to lambaste him for being late, but her words of reproach died at the sight of him.

He was wearing black. All over. Not the bleak, funereal black of that pin-striped suit he'd been sporting at their first meeting. A devilishly dark and sleek black, which screamed sin and sex from every angle.

She tried to keep the hunger out of her gaze as it swept over him, absorbing each wickedly elegant detail.

Lightweight woollen trousers proclaimed Italian tailoring. A black silk shirt, with long sleeves and an open neck. Shoes and belt fashioned in black leather. Combined with his flashing ebony eyes and sleek black hair. He looked like every woman's fantasy of a bad-boy lover come true.

It took several seconds for Justine to appreciate that the sight of *her* in her red silk dress had rendered him just as speechless. She tried to guess what *he* was thinking as he took in every inch of her from her upswept hairdo down to her outrageously high red heels. By the look of the smouldering expression in those deeply set dark eyes of his, he was as aroused by her appearance as she was by his.

The thought sent her blood fizzing through her veins.

'I think the lime-green would have been preferable,' he muttered at last.

'As would your pin-stripes,' she countered drily.

His eyes clashed with hers and a wry smile lifted the corners of his mouth. 'Shall we skip dinner in favour of a late supper?' he drawled. 'A late…*late* supper?'

Justine hesitated. It was one thing to plunge into an affair with him when it had just been a matter of sex. Would she survive giving him her body in true love? This was a new experience for her in more ways than one. Frankly, it terrified the life out of her.

Marcus saw her hesitation and frowned. What was she playing at *now*? Was he to be teased some more, made to sit and wait over a long drawn-out dinner he had no appetite for? Was she hoping that by the time the big moment came he'd be so blind with lust and longing he'd promise her anything? Marriage, even?

This last thought brought him back to cold, hard reality with a jolt. There he'd been, worrying about her all week, about his own selfishly wicked intentions, about how she constantly seemed to be smashing all his preconceived ideas after her. He'd even begun to believe her feelings for him might be genuine, that she had no mercenary plans in mind.

But if that were true then she would not be hesitating now; she'd be wanting him as badly as he was wanting her. There would be no hesitation, no game-playing.

'If you're desperate for dinner,' he grated out testily, 'then we'll have dinner.'

'I…I'm not desperate for dinner…'

'Then what's the problem?'

'The problem? I…I guess I'm a little nervous,' she confessed.

Marcus sighed. He hadn't thought of that. No matter what her motives, she hadn't been to bed with a man before. He was so sure himself it would be fantastic that he hadn't stopped to think she might be worried about the outcome.

He picked up her hand and drew it to his mouth, pressing his lips to each fingertip. 'Trust me,' he murmured thickly, and felt his desire for her kick back to where it had been all week, tormenting him every minute of every day.

She didn't say a word as he drew her down the front path to the street, where he settled her into his car; nor on the twenty-minute drive to his house; nor in the time it took to guide her from the triple garage in through his front door.

She made no comment over his house, as luxurious as it was. There again, girls like her were used to luxury, he reasoned. They took such things for granted.

The first words she spoke came when he led her into the master bedroom and turned her to him.

'I won't sleep with you in the same bed as you slept with your wife.'

He was taken aback, both by her shakily delivered pronouncement and the obvious emotion behind it. Was it jealousy which inspired such a sentiment? He hoped it was. Jealousy was real, not contrived. Jealousy he empathised with. The thought of Justine going from his bed to any other man's brought such a black jealousy that he hadn't yet confronted its full meaning.

He pulled her into his arms, his mouth barely

inches away from her. Her eyes glittered and he saw her hunger matched his.

'It's not the same bed,' he growled. 'I bought a new one after I threw her out.'

'Oh,' she said. 'That's all right, then.' And, sliding her arms around his waist, pressed herself against him.

Marcus's mouth crashed down on hers, passion rampaging through him like a river in flood. It was a battle to control the primitive urge to rip the clothes from her body and surge into her where they stood. She didn't help when she moaned deep in her throat, or when her nails began to dig into his back.

He wrenched his mouth away at last to drag in a much needed breath, but his name on her lips brought him swiftly back. His hands shook uncontrollably as they moved to undo the single button at the back of the halter-necked dress. When he felt it give way he groaned, the knowledge that shortly she would be naked bringing a white-hot haze down over his brain. His already teetering control shattered totally. With a harshly primal cry, he scooped her up into his arms and carried her over to the bed.

Justine exulted in his animal-like force. This was what she wanted, what she needed. To be given no time to think or to worry. To be swept away on the passion of the moment.

She lay there, wide-eyed and head whirling, while he stripped her then joined her on the bed.

His hands stroked possessively over her nakedness, heating her flesh and her blood. She gasped under his caresses, then moaned, wriggled and writhed. Her legs fell wantonly apart, inviting more intimacies.

He knew exactly where to touch to drive her wild. And how to touch. His fingers eventually gave way to his lips, and finally his tongue. Her first climax brought cries and shudders. Her second, a tortured sob. Her third, pleas to stop.

He did. But not for long, stripping himself and drawing on protection in no time. Before her breathing even slowed a fraction he was looming over her, magnificent in his nakedness, awesome in his need. The memory of the pain he'd caused last time brought a moment of panic. So when he bent his mouth to her breasts instead, she sighed her relief.

But his tongue on her nipples soon brought moans, not sighs. He laved them mercilessly, then tugged at them with his teeth till they burned with a white-hot heat which blazed a furnace through the rest of her body. When he moved between her legs she was no longer thinking about pain, so great was her craving to be as one with the man she loved.

And there was no pain as his flesh fused with hers, despite his filling and stretching her to the full. Her legs automatically wound around his waist, their bodies becoming blended and moulded in a single unit.

Justine moaned softly when he began to move, then when he cupped her face and kissed her at the same time, his tongue surging in a parallel rhythm with his penis. It was so much more intimate than anything she could ever have imagined, so much more emotionally moving. She clung to him with her hands and her heart, then finally came with him.

'Oh, Marcus,' she cried, her mouth bursting from his as her body clenched and unclenched his in a series of deeply satisfying spasms. 'Darling Marcus…'

'Darling Marcus' didn't allow himself the pleasure of staying inside her after he was done, rolling from her before he ended up losing more than his control. But, dear God, she tugged at his heart, made him want to say stupid things, promise stupid things.

He got up immediately to stride into the bathroom and do what he had to do. Afterwards he glared in the vanity mirror and warned himself not to let her lack of experience corrupt his common sense. Virginity did not necessarily equate with innocence. Or ignorance. She still might be faking it.

But what kind of girl would fake what had happened out on that bed? Such a devious action didn't equate with the Justine he now knew: the daughter who loved her mother and her home with such a selfless passion; the girl who'd sold her car and her clothes to make ends meet; the proud and high-spirited creature who took a cleaning job rather than ask her wealthy lover for money.

Marcus scowled at his reflection, with its wary eyes and sour mouth. The trouble was he'd hugged his lack of faith in females to himself for so long it was difficult to give it up—difficult to be open to real feelings, difficult to accept the possibility that Justine might not be trying to manipulate him for her own ends.

Damn it all, he could not stand his suspicion and distrust any longer. It was getting in the way of what he wanted, which was Justine in his bed—not just for a night, but every night. He wanted her as he'd never wanted Stephany. And he wanted her to want him back the same way. Obsessively. Possessively.

Maybe it was love. Maybe it wasn't. Whatever, he couldn't turn his back on it any longer. He had to embrace it. Had to!

Justine could not feel sad as she lay there. Or even regretful. Making love with Marcus had been too wonderful to spoil it with negative thinking. He might not love her, or want to marry her, but she felt sure he liked her now. Maybe he even respected her a little these days. He certainly wanted her. There was no doubt about that in her mind.

The bathroom door opened and she turned to look at him. God, but he was lovely naked. A real man. Broad shoulders. Narrow hips. Long, muscular legs. And the most incredible chest, with a matting of soft dark curls in its centre.

Her eyes lifted to his and her stomach lurched. He'd looked at her with desire before, but this was something else. His narrowed eyes held hers as he came forward and lay down beside her and began to kiss and stroke her anew. Yet with a strangely restrained passion this time. There was nothing remotely rough in his lovemaking this time. His touch was gentle, his mouth teasing, his tongue softly tantalising.

Slowly, skilfully, he rekindled the fires within her, taking her to that point of no return where her own passion took over and *she* became the aggressor, pushing him onto his back and bending her mouth to him as he had to her.

* * *

Marcus gasped when her lips brushed over his straining flesh, clutching at the quilt lest he go all noble and stop her. He hoped and prayed that the part of him which ached to surrender mindlessly to her own seemingly mindless passion would prove much stronger than the stupidly spoiling feelings which kept besieging him. This was what he wanted, wasn't it? For her to be so turned on, so carried away that she would do anything he asked of her, anywhere, any time? Such a scenario had plagued him ever since he'd met her. He wanted it. Hell, he needed it. Only then would this madness have a chance to burn itself out and leave him in peace.

He didn't want to love her. He wanted it to be nothing but lust. A passing passion. A quenchable fire.

Her lips were moving intimately over him and everything inside him lurched.

Dear God, girl, don't do it, he found himself thinking in an agony of ambivalence.

For at the back of his mind, in that place reserved for the harshest of truths, he knew if she did, if she took him into the heat of her mouth, if she reduced him to a screaming, mindless mess this way, then he would be lost in her for ever.

He moaned when her lips parted, groaned when she started to take him in. The physical sensation was delicious, the emotional impact devastating. She was doing it. Dear God…

His muscles tensed as he fought the tempestuous feelings which threatened to overwhelm him. But he was powerless against her passion, and his own. *She* was supposed to become *his* victim. Instead, he was on the verge of being the vanquished one. A slave to her superior will. Hers, in love and in lust.

Her mouth and hands were masterful, and merciless. They brooked nothing but his total surrender.

Marcus fought the good fight for what felt like an interminable time. Perhaps it was only a minute or two. She stopped for a second, giving him a moment's respite, making him think he might survive this after all. But then she glanced up at him, blowing him away with the look of blind adoration in her passion-filled eyes.

Now, instead of stopping her, he urged her back to his burning flesh and just let go of everything he'd been battling to contain. His body. His heart. His very soul.

CHAPTER FOURTEEN

MARCUS stood beside the bed, staring down at her nude body. She was curled up in a foetal position, her left arm covering her perfect breasts, her lovely hair spread out on the pillow, the curve of her bare bottom looking childlike.

Yet there'd been nothing childlike in the way she'd responded to him. She'd been all woman.

How many times had he had her already? He'd lost count. He'd imagined making love to her countless times might rid his body both of his passion for her and those other more disturbing feelings.

It hadn't worked. He was still flooded with the same emotional weakness every time he touched her. There really wasn't any point in denying it any longer. He loved her.

So what are you going to do about it, Marcus?

He didn't know yet. There was no rush to do anything, he supposed. No reason to reveal this unexpected development in their relationship. He really needed time to think about his feelings further, time away from the corrupting and confusing influence of her flesh.

His gut crunched hard as he thought of how that flesh felt. He really could not get enough of it. He walked around the foot of the bed, his gaze still hungry upon her.

But enough is enough, Marcus, he lectured himself. Besides, it won't work. Even when it's over, you'll still want her again. And again. And again.

It was going on three o'clock. They'd been making love on and off for several hours, their torrid matings punctuated only by coffee and a couple of revitalising swims in the pool. They hadn't eaten anything except each other. Their conversation had been the talk of lovers. Basically empty but complimentary. Flattering. His especially.

Of course he hadn't told her he loved her. Neither had she even come close to saying the same in return. But he was in no doubt that her sexual feelings for him were real. The mechanics of orgasm could be faked, he knew. But not the gush of liquid heat which flooded her. Neither could she engineer the way her nipples lengthened and hardened at his touch, or the way her eyes would darken and grow heavy.

He didn't think a faker would be quite so accommodating, either. There was nothing he'd demanded that she hadn't done with an abandon which had stunned and enthralled him.

He groaned at the memory, grimacing as he felt his body begin to ache one more amazing time. He really had to wake her and take her home. But he couldn't. Just thinking of her responses had him lying down beside her and stroking her silky flanks till she uncurled on a low moan and snuggled against him.

'It's late,' he murmured, and kissed her on the shoulder.

'Mmm,' was all she said, and she kissed him on the chest.

'I really should take you home, Justine.'

'I don't want to go home.' She licked at a nipple, then nibbled at it till he gasped.

'I want to stay here with you for ever,' she sighed against his skin.

Marcus frowned. Was this the first sign of plan B? He decided to test her.

'What do you mean?' he asked carefully. 'Are you saying you want to move in with me?'

Her head shot up, her hand pushing her hair out of her face. 'Good heavens, no. I can't do that. I have a boarding house to run. I didn't get round to telling you, but we had so many enquiries today from the ad in the *Herald*. I could fill each of those rooms ten times over. It was just a…a wish, that's all. I know I have to go home.'

Perversely, he felt disappointed. If she was in love with him, she would jump at the chance. If she had marital designs on him, she'd be doing cart-wheels!

He almost wished she *did* have designs on him.

'What if I asked you to?' he said, and waited in an agony of anticipation for her answer.

She sat up and blinked at him. 'But why would you do that? I wouldn't have thought you'd like that idea at all.'

Hardly the answer of one besotted. No, *he* was the only fool around here who was besotted!

'I don't see why not,' he drawled, and reached out to tweak her nearest nipple, his male pride soothed by the sight of its instant response. If nothing else, she was in lust with him at least.

Or was it lust itself she was enamoured of? That newly discovered dark side of herself which could drive one to go to the bed with the strangest partners? Since Stephany's departure Marcus had found carnal solace in the arms of women he hadn't particularly liked. Maybe Justine was doing the same.

The thought that she might not particularly like him at all was quite crushing.

'What is it that you want of me, Justine?' he was driven to ask. 'What are you expecting from our relationship?'

Justine heard the edge in his voice, and the emphasis on the word 'expecting'. Oh, dear heaven, he thought she was angling for marriage. As much as she loved the man, marriage had not even entered her head!

How could it when she already knew marriage was the last thing Marcus wanted? Trudy had warned her of this, warned her not to fall in love with him. If he had even a hint of her true feelings, she wouldn't see hide nor hair of him again.

The concept of never making love with Marcus again, of never experiencing what she knew only he could make her feel, brought forward a brutally pragmatic response to his question. Better she lie than lose him. Better she fulfil the role he wanted her to play than have no part in his life at all.

'Expecting, Marcus? I'm not sure what you mean. I'm not expecting anything from you but what you offered.'

'And what was that?'

'Your friendship. And your body, of course,' she added with a saucy little smile.

'My body...'

She stroked down his chest and over his half-erect penis, her heart leaping along with his flesh.

It was still hard to believe how love had changed her perception of sex. She found it all so delicious. Nothing embarrassed her with Marcus. Everything seemed perfectly natural yet at the same time unbearably exciting. She loved the feel and taste of his body, loved arousing him, loved hearing him groan and tremble deep within her.

He rolled away from her and sat up on the side of the bed. 'Tell me about plan B,' he grated out.

Shock tripped her tongue for a moment. 'Plan…B?'

His glance over his shoulder was harsh.

'Please don't act obtuse. Felix mentioned your plan B on the night of his party. He implied I was the first cab off the rank.'

She stared at him, her heart hammering in her chest. Dear God, had he been thinking all the while that she was trying to ensnare him into marriage? Did he believe the things she'd been doing in this bed tonight had been inspired by greed and not genuine feelings? Had he demanded and enjoyed such intimacies with her suspecting she was nothing but a cold-blooded ambitious little bitch?

If he did, then he could go to hell!

'Firstly, it wasn't *my* plan,' she ground out in an agony of dismay and disappointment. 'It was Trudy's. Some ridiculous idea she had about my catching myself a rich husband. At one stage she thought you might be a suitable candidate, but I soon set her straight about that, believe me.'

He had the hide to actually look offended! 'You don't think I'm suitable husband material?'

'You have to be joking. You're far too bitter and

cynical about women. A woman would have to be crazy to want you as her life's partner.'

'Is that so?'

'Yes. When I marry it will be to a man who loves me to pieces and thinks I'm the best thing since sliced bread. A man who would never question my motives because he knows I love him back the same way. I've seen first-hand what happens when someone marries for money, not love. I want no part of such a sick bargain.

'So, do stop worrying, Marcus darling,' she flung at him, barely controlling her temper. 'I have no designs on you personally, or on your bank balance. I just want your body. But if you're not careful, I might not want that any more, either. I'm sure I will very shortly develop an aversion to being intimate with a man who thinks I'm nothing but a gold-digging tramp!' She scrambled off the bed and began scooping up her clothes from the floor.

'Justine,' he said frantically as he followed her around the room. 'Please don't be angry. I'm sorry. I…'

'Oh, I'm not angry!' she spat at him before he could voice a single more insincere word. 'I'm bloody furious! To think I waited this long, just to give my virginity to a cynical bastard like you!'

When she went to brush past him on her way to the bathroom, he grabbed her upper arms and forced her to face him, her bundle of clothes a convenient barrier between their naked bodies. Temper, it seemed, was no barrier to desire. Or love. Justine could not believe she still wanted the man!

'You're right,' he growled. 'I *am* bitter and cynical about women. I admit it. And I hate it as much

as you do. Hate the stupid, narrow-minded, prejudiced view I formed of you the very first night I
saw you.'

Justine was taken aback. But it hadn't been *night*,
the first time they'd met. What on earth was he
talking about?

'Yes. I see you're confused. I'm not talking about
that day you came into the bank. I'd seen you once
before that—at one of Felix's parties. Last
November, it was. You wouldn't have seen me. I
was inside, with Felix. You were frolicking in the
pool, surrounded by young male admirers.'

'And?'

'I watched you for a while…'

Justine remembered that night very well, since it
had been the night her father died. She vividly recalled being in that pool, recalled Howard's silly
antics, pulling down her top underwater. She especially recalled flouncing out of the pool like the
spoilt little miss she'd been back then.

She thought of Marcus watching her and her
cheeks pinkened with embarrassment. 'I suppose I
looked pretty silly,' she said.

'I thought you looked incredibly beautiful,' he
said, dark eyes gleaming hotly. 'I wanted you so
much it was almost unbearable. Felix noticed my
fascination and said he'd introduce me to you, but
I chose to leave instead. I'd already tagged you as
another Stephany, you see…'

Justine's heart twisted at the pain in his eyes.
'She must have hurt you a lot, Marcus.'

'She destroyed my dreams.'

'Your dreams?'

'Yes. But that's another story, and not one you'd

be interested in. I'm simply trying to explain that when you came into my bank that day I was programmed to believe the worst of you. Not that that made any difference to my wanting you,' he added ruefully. 'If anything it seemed to make things worse. Instead of despising you, I desired you even more. I was severely tempted to abandon every standard I valued for just one night with you.'

'Goodness!' she exclaimed.

'Well, I've had my one night now and I want you more than ever. I adore everything about you, Justine. Your enthusiasm for life. Your spontaneity. Your passion.'

'Don't you mean sex?'

'That, too. Marry me, Justine. Marry me.'

She gaped up at him. 'Marry you! But I...I can't!'

'Why not?'

'Because...because if I do, you'll destroy *my* dream.'

'What's that? Your boarding house plan? Good God, Justine, as my wife you won't have to bother with that. I'll clear your debts. Hire your mother a housekeeper. Neither of you will have to worry about a thing for the rest of your lives.'

Justine wanted to slap his arrogantly insensitive face. Couldn't he hear himself? He was no better than her father, or Stephany. No talk of love, just money. She resisted the urge to cry, or scream, settling for straight talk instead.

'No, Marcus,' she said firmly. 'You've got it all wrong. My dream has nothing to with houses. It's about love.'

'Love?'

'Yes. You sound as though you've never heard of it, despite it being a four-letter word! The fact is, Marcus, I promised myself I would never marry except for love. *True* love. Not simply to fulfil a sexual attraction. I'm sorry, but you…you just don't fill the bill.

'Thank you for asking,' she raced on blithely, before she could do anything stupid like cry. 'But it really wasn't necessary. Men who deflower virgins don't have to marry them in this day and age. I'm sure once you think about it later you'll be relieved I didn't take you up on your impulsive offer. After all, you don't love me, Marcus. You simply want to make love to me, which you can still enjoy, quite frequently and free of charge, without the encumbrance of a wife. Because I like making love to you too, darling. You're as great in bed as I thought you'd be. Now I'm going to have a shower and get dressed. Then I think you'd better drive me home before Mum comes after you with a shotgun.'

Marcus stared, wide-eyed, after her retreating nakedness, his head whirling with a perverse joy.

She'd knocked him back. Told him where to stick his offer of marriage, *and* his bank balance. She was nothing like Stephany. Nothing at all!

Except in that she doesn't love you, you fool, the ugly voice of brutal honesty piped up, dampening his exuberance a little. You heard her. She'll only marry for true love.

Then he'd have to make her fall in love with him, wouldn't he?

But how?

Sex? Oh, yes, he'd use sex…at every opportunity. He thought she was great in bed, did she? Well, he aimed to be great *out* of bed as well. She ain't seen nuttin' yet!

Attention? He'd ring her up twice a day.

Presents? He'd send her flowers. Bring chocolates and perfume every time he called. Whoops, no! He didn't want to give the impression he still thought her a gold-digger. Just flowers, then. And nothing over the top.

Flattery? He didn't need to use flattery. He would just tell her the truth—that he thought she was the most beautiful, clever, witty, entertaining, wonderful, fantastic sexy female who'd ever drawn breath!

But what about that old standby…telling her he loved her every other sentence?

Now why was it that Marcus feared that particular truth wouldn't work? No, he would keep those three little words in reserve till the moment was right, till something happened and Justine would see that he really meant them. Then and only then would that tack have a chance of striking home!

Marcus's jaw jutted out stubbornly. He'd overseen plenty of mergers and takeovers in his life. But none as crucial as this. Nothing inspired him more than a difficult challenge. And he had a feeling that making Justine fall in love with him was going to be just that. But making her believe he loved her back might prove to be the emotional equivalent of *Mission Impossible*!

But when Marcus Osborne set his sights on an objective, it had better watch out. He wasn't the youngest bank president around for nothing!

He was bending to scoop up his own clothes when he heard the shower running.

The thought infiltrated that showers were filled with all sorts of erotica. Naked bodies, warm water, shower gel, sponges, back scrubs...

Marcus dropped his trousers and strode towards the bathroom door.

CHAPTER FIFTEEN

'I'LL BE sad to lose you,' Pat said over their eight-thirty cup of tea the following Friday night. 'You're a good little worker, Justine. Make someone a good little wife one day.'

Justine rather agreed with her. But she doubted Marcus ever would. He hadn't repeated his first impulsive proposal of marriage. He'd been too busy taking advantage of her offer to provide him with sex. Gratis. Naturally he had no idea she was in love with him. He thought she was just in lust with him—which, of course, she was as well.

On Sunday evening he'd returned to take her out to dinner again, and they'd actually made it to the restaurant this time. They'd eaten a couple of courses, though for the life of her Justine could not remember what. The sexual tension between them had been distracting in the extreme, both of them falling awkwardly silent during the drive back to Marcus's place.

They hadn't made it to the bed. Marcus had pounced on her in the hallway. She'd had great difficulty finding her clothes afterwards. They'd been scattered through the house. Her panties by the front door. Her lime-green dress beside the leather sofa in the lounge room. Her soggy bra out on the terrace.

Monday, he'd talked her into meeting him for lunch—only of course it had been *she* who was on his menu. She'd chided him when he'd headed home instead of to any eating establishment, but any mild reproach on her part had soon changed to a passion as driven and conscienceless as his.

Tuesday, she'd been breathlessly waiting for him outside his house when he drove up shortly after one, as arranged. The day had been steamingly hot and they'd spent two hours in the pool, making love. It was after three by the time Marcus went back to the bank, with an exhausted Justine left to wonder at his amazing stamina and imagination.

Wednesday, she'd refused to meet him for lunch, a perverse jab of pride demanding she not be so easy. But it had been darned difficult. She'd been on edge all day, the continuing hot weather not helping. She'd kept thinking how she would prefer being in Marcus's pool, with a deliciously naked Marcus, rather than washing sheets and making up beds for the coming boarders. By the time she'd arrived at work that night she'd been deeply regretting her decision. Why deny herself the pleasure Marcus could give her? If she couldn't have his love, then at least she could have his lovemaking.

When she'd wheeled her cleaning trolley into his office to find him sitting at his desk, looking supersexy, despite his wearing that stuffy pin-striped suit of his, she'd surrendered to the devil's whispers and seduced him on the spot. She still blushed at the thought of what she'd done under his desk, with people walking down the corridor a few feet away.

As much as Justine had enjoyed these erotic encounters, *nothing* compared to what had happened on Thursday.

Thursday, Marcus had taken her to an extrava-

gant lunch in a swanky hotel on the Harbour, then
up to a room afterwards—'For some leisurely afternoon lovemaking,' he'd said. His call to Grace
to excuse his presence from the bank for the rest of
the day had been a classic of *double entendre*. He'd
told his secretary that he'd run into a valued client
over lunch who had an exciting new proposition for
him, and that he'd be all tied up for the afternoon.

Justine had had no idea at the time that he'd
meant it literally. He'd seen it in a movie once, and
found the idea a serious turn-on.

'Provided, of course, one's partner can be totally
trusted,' he'd murmured as he'd kissed her into
compliance against the hotel room door.

Justine shook her head as she thought of that
afternoon. Having him at her total mercy had been
corruptingly exciting. And surprisingly informative.
She'd revelled in being able to tease him, in taking
him to tantalising and probably torturous edges, at
which point she'd coaxed answers to questions he
would probably have sidestepped if he hadn't been
desperate with desire. Acute frustration had allowed
her to strip away the controlled façade he usually
hid behind, and all sorts of interesting facts had
come tumbling out of his groaning mouth.

During the course of the afternoon Justine had
elicited quite a chunk of his life story. She'd been
both fascinated and moved. Born to a drug-taking
teenage runaway—father unknown—he'd been
taken from his mother at a tender age by welfare
and well-meaning relatives, and put into a wonderfully warm and welcoming state institution.

There had been no hope of adoption with his
mother refusing to sign any papers, although he'd

been fostered out several times to people who'd seemed more interested in their government cheques than the emotionally deprived boy. Finally he'd been consigned to the home for wayward boys after a bout of bad behaviour which came after news of his mother's death through an overdose— news which had shattered his secret dream of one day having a family of his own.

Naturally, as soon as he'd finished school he left the boys' home, to make his own way in the world. He'd worked his way through university, after which he'd joined the bank as a trainee loans officer. Twelve years later, he'd become the president of said bank.

Justine smiled ruefully at the memory of Marcus's modestly succinct description of his success. To rise to his present position in such a short time had been quite spectacular.

Actually, she knew more about his working history than he knew she did. Trudy had played detective for her this past week, finding out from various sources all she could about Marcus Osborne, banker extraordinaire.

Apparently, during the eighties, he'd been one of the only investment executives to advise his bank not to lend money to the scores of flashy entrepreneurs who'd besieged most of the major banks and glibly conned them into handing over massive loans for speculative deals, but without proper security. When the property crash had come, Marcus had become his bank's golden boy, having saved them a fortune in bad loans. He'd been rapidly promoted, first to vice-president at the age of twenty-eight, then to president at thirty.

His only failure during those years, it seemed, had been his marriage, which had occurred soon after his promotion to president. According to Trudy's sources, Stephany had been the only daughter of another bank president, who hadn't been so fortunate in his decisions and had subsequently been sacked.

Suddenly impoverished, the spoilt only daughter of the family had turned her greedy eyes on the banking man of the moment. Marcus had married her before he knew the selfish soul behind those big and reportedly beautiful brown eyes. Their marriage had lasted only twelve months, with no children.

Justine was no psychologist, but she believed anyone with a brain in their heads could see Marcus's deprived upbringing had been the perfect breeding ground to produce a driven personality with an intense need to succeed in life. But resting alongside his tunnel-vision ambition would lie a deep well of emotional vulnerability.

Love would always present itself as a two-edged sword. He would distrust it, yet crave it as one always craved what one had never had. The only problem would be that he might not know what true love was. The poor darling had had little experience of it, after all.

How easy to confuse lust with love. Or to be fooled by a gorgeous young woman who lavished him with false affection and flattery while hiding her mercenary motives behind a beautiful and distracting façade. Stephany had obviously been just such a woman.

Justine frowned. Marcus had thought *she* was tarred with the same brush for a good while. She hoped he didn't still think that. Hopefully, he didn't. Surely her rejecting his proposal of marriage had shown him she wasn't after his money?

The one subject Justine hadn't been able to coax Marcus into talking about in any detail on Thursday was his marriage, other than admitting he'd divorced Stephany for adultery. Most of what she knew of Marcus's ex was what she'd learned from Trudy—which wasn't all that much. A sudden thought occurred to her, and she glanced at the woman opposite.

'Tell me, Pat, did you ever meet Marcus's... er...Mr Osborne's first wife?'

'Did I ever! Now there was a one. We all cheered the day the boss got rid of her, I can tell you.'

'How long ago was that, exactly?'

'Gosh, it must be nearly two years ago now. Yep. Two years. Heavens, how time flies!'

'What was she like?'

'Lovely to look at. Tall and blonde, with a spectacular figure. Butter wouldn't melt in her mouth around Mr Osborne and any of his business colleagues, but she was a right cow to anyone she considered didn't rate. A snob through and through. I used to clean the seventh floor back then, and I ran into Madam quite a few times times in the evenings. She always looked right through me, as though I didn't exist. Poor Grace used to complain about the way she was treated as well.'

'Do you know what broke up the marriage?'

Trudy had told her rumour claimed there had been more than one affair on Stephany's part, but Trudy hadn't known the particulars.

'No secret there, love. The boss caught her in

bed with the pool-cleaning man. He tossed her out on the spot. Threw all her clothes—and her—out into the street, then had the locks changed.'

'Goodness! But how do you know that for sure? I mean, I can't imagine Mar… Mr Osborne telling anyone anything so personal.'

'Heard it all with my own little ears. Mr Osborne had come back to the bank that evening to work, as was his habit most evenings back then, when Lady Muck came storming into his office and let fly. I was cleaning the boardroom at the time, and the adjoining door was slightly ajar. My ears went bright red, I can tell you. I've never heard such filthy language from a woman in all my life!

'I was right proud of Mr Osborne, though. He never raised his voice once. Just told her quietly to leave. It wasn't till she started screaming out really shocking details of all the other lovers she'd had since their marriage that he called Security and had her forcibly removed. We all felt so sorry for him, being publicly humiliated like that. Everyone on the floor must have heard. We're not surprised that there hasn't been anyone else since then. Mr Osborne is the sort of man who would feel something like that very deeply. I doubt he'll ever marry again. Before his disillusionment, the poor man was totally besotted with that creature.'

Justine's heart sank into a black pit. It was as she'd feared. Marcus would never get over his first wife enough to trust another woman, or to risk his happiness again. But it was crazy to be so upset about something she'd always known. Hadn't Trudy told her *ad nauseam*?

Justine sighed her dismay. Her silly romantic

soul must have been secretly hoping that some day Marcus would fall in love with her and repeat his offer of marriage.

'Why did you want to know, love?' Pat asked. 'Are you interested in our Mr Osborne?'

Justine was taken aback, although it was a fair enough question. 'Oh. Er…well, he *is* a very good-looking man, isn't he?'

'Oooh.' Pat eyed her knowingly. 'Now here's a turn-up for the books. Of course *you're* a very good-looking girl, too. Don't tell me the boss's been giving you the eye while you've been up there cleaning his office?'

'He *has* given me the odd second glance occasionally,' she said, and tried not to look guilty. If only Pat knew. The things that had gone on in the boss's office on Wednesday night would have turned more than her ears bright red!

Justine had expressly forbidden Marcus to work late tonight. She wanted to do a really good cleaning job on her last night, or Gwen would be complaining when she came back the following Monday and found poorly cleaned rooms.

But it had been lonely cleaning his empty office. She missed Marcus. Not just his lovemaking, but the man himself.

Her heart lurched at the sudden unbearable thought that since he would never fall in love with her, then one day he'd be gone from her life. He would tire of her sexually and that would be that!

How on earth would she survive without him? He'd become as essential to her as breathing.

Suddenly she wanted to cry. But that would never do. Not in front of Pat. Plastering a false smile on her face, she jumped up from the tea table. 'Must get back to work,' she announced brightly.

'But what about Mr Osborne?'

'What about him?'

'I mean…what are you going to do about you and him? I mean…this is your last night working here, you know.'

'Yes, I do realise that. I'm afraid I have to accept that Mr Osborne and I aren't meant to be, Pat,' Justine said, her heart catching.

Pat sighed. 'I think you could be right, love. That Stephany piece did a right good hatchet job on him. I wonder what happened to the rotten cow? Probably sailed on to some other rich sucker without a backward glance. Them types don't have a heart. Not like our Mr Osborne. Now, he's soft as mush under that stiff upper lip he likes to put on. Do you know, he sent Gwen flowers, and even visited her personally at home with the biggest box of chocolates? She was quite overcome. Not many bosses would do that for a cleaner.'

'No,' Justine said thoughtfully. 'They certainly wouldn't. Well, I'd better get back to work, Pat. See you later.'

'Yes, see ya, love. And don't be too upset about Mr Osborne. There'll be plenty of fellas for you in the years to come.'

But none that I'll want as I want Marcus, she thought wretchedly as she rode the lift up to the seventh floor. None that I'll love half as much. Justine knew in her heart that there would only ever be one true love for her.

Her mood lifted when she recalled what Pat had said about Marcus being soft as mush under his stiff upper lip. Maybe Pat and Trudy were wrong about his being so damaged that he would never fully trust or love a woman again. He'd asked her once what she wanted of him, but she'd never asked him what he wanted of her. Maybe because she'd been too afraid of the answer. Was it just sex he was looking for? Or could she hope he wanted more?

Trudy had told her to just enjoy the moment and not to hope for anything permanent. But Trudy was a bit of a cynic. She'd also insisted Justine not tell Marcus she was in love with him.

'He'll treat you like a doormat if he knows that,' she'd pronounced on the telephone earlier in the week. 'Truly, Jussie. I did warn you that you'd fall in love with the man once you went to bed with him, didn't I? You're like a babe in the woods when it comes to men and sex, especially men like Marcus Osborne. They eat little girls like you for breakfast. Now, you listen to your old friend, and hopefully you might get out of this affair relatively unscathed, plus a whole lot wiser. *Don't* go saying anything you shouldn't. That way, when he dumps you, you'll at least have your pride intact.'

Pride.

What was pride in the scheme of things if Marcus was no longer in her life?

Be damned with her pride! she decided.

The lift doors opened and she hurried down the corridor. Wasn't honesty worth a try? What if Marcus felt more for her than he'd let on and was just waiting for her to admit the same?

It was a possible scenario, given his background. He'd be wary of committing himself to another woman, especially one with a spoilt upbringing similar to Stephany's. His offer of marriage the other night might not have been a mad impulse of the moment. It might have been a blurted out expression of his deepest desire.

Maybe Marcus loved her…

Truly loved her.

Her heart swelled, then raced with the possibility. She had to know. And she had to know *now*! It would not wait another moment.

Bursting back into his office, she strode over to his desk and swept up his telephone. Punching in the number for an outside line, she then added his home number. She clutched the handpiece to her ear, counting the number of rings at the other end. Five. Six. Seven. Oh, please don't let him be out!

'Marcus Osborne.'

Now that he'd answered, Justine froze. This was a stupid idea. Stupid, stupid, stupid!

'Hello? Anyone there?'

'Marcus?' she squeaked.

'Justine? Is that you?'

'Yes…'

'What is it? What's wrong? Where are you? Aren't you supposed to be at work at the bank?'

'I am. I'm in your office.'

'Oh?'

'I…I *had* to ring you.'

'Well, I'm flattered. Not to mention frustrated,' he added dryly. 'Dare I hope you want me to dash over for a rendezvous in the storeroom? No? Damn. Guess I'll have to wait till tomorrow.'

'Marcus…'

'Yes, my love?'

Her heart twisted at the endearment. 'Am I?' she

choked out, her chest tightening. 'I mean *do* you? Love me, that is?'

Justine had heard of silences being described as deafening. Now she knew what they meant. Marcus's silence screamed through her head for several nerve-jangling seconds.

'Why do you ask?' he said at last, and her chest tightened another notch.

'It…it was important to me all of a sudden.'

'Why?'

'Because…because I want everything between us to be open and above board,' she blurted out. 'I hate thinking of the way we first met. I was worried you might still think I was after something from you.

'Which I am, of course,' she raved on, nerves making her babble uncontrollably. 'But it's not your money, Marcus. Or marriage. Although I wouldn't mind being married to you. Some day. But only if you loved me, of course, and wanted to marry me, because I…I love you, Marcus,' she finally confessed in a rush. 'That's what I'm trying to say. I love you. Oh, God…I hope you're not angry with me for saying so. Trudy said I shouldn't tell you, but…but I'm not Trudy, am I?'

Marcus struggled to control the emotion welling up in his heart, but it was a struggle he was destined to lose.

'No,' he managed at last in a strangled fashion. 'No, my darling, you're not anything like Trudy. And, no, I'm not angry with you, because I…I love you too. How could I not? Oh, God, Justine, I'm getting all choked up here.' He swallowed convulsively and dashed the wetness from the corners of his eyes. 'Do you have any idea how many years it's been since I cried?'

'You're crying?' She sounded dazed. 'Over me?'

'Over you.'

'You didn't cry over Stephany?'

'That bitch? God, no. Once I saw what she was made of I couldn't wait to have done with her.'

'What became of her, do you know?'

'Funny you should ask. I had no idea…till last Tuesday. Grace pointed out this article in the *Herald* to me about a New Zealand banker who was on trial for embezzlement. There was a photograph of his wife going into the court and it was Stephany. I was amused to read he claimed he'd been driven to the crime by his wife's excesses. I almost felt sorry for the poor devil. Leopards don't change their spots, do they? Stephany'll go to her grave conning men out of their money. You don't have to worry your pretty little head about her, Justine. I can't stand the woman. If she stood naked in front of me I wouldn't turn a hair.'

'But…but you must have loved her to begin with, Marcus.'

Marcus heard her insecurity and was tempted to lie. But she'd said she wanted everything to be open and above board between them. Best to start with the truth.

'I thought I did. As a young lad growing up I had this dream of one day having this perfect life, which included the perfect wife on my arm. Stephany played the role of perfect wife-to-be to perfection—till the ring was on her finger. I fell in love with the illusion she created, not the real woman underneath. She fooled me completely with her flattering words and ways. She was also an accomplished actress in the bedroom. I won't deny I was seriously infatuated in the beginning.

'I began to suspect something was wrong right from the honeymoon, when all she wanted to do was shop. By the time the crunch came, and I found out what she really was, the wool had already started slipping from my eyes. Still, for a long time after I discovered the truth about her, I mistook the hurt and bitterness I was feeling for a broken heart. More a bruised ego, I think. Once I fell in love with you, sweet thing, I saw that what I'd felt for her hadn't been true love at all, but a very poor copy.'

'I'm your true love?'

'The truest and the loveliest.'

'Oh, Marcus, now *I'm* crying!'

'With happiness, I hope?'

'Oh, yes.'

'I'm coming over.'

'Marcus, you shouldn't. I still have so much work to do. Please let me do it. I…I promise I'll come over to your place as soon as I've finished.'

'In that case you'd better ring your mum and tell her you won't be home tonight. It's going to take me hours to show you how much I love you.'

'Oh, Marcus… All right, darling. I'll ring and tell her straightaway.'

'She won't come after me with a shotgun, will she?'

'No, of course not.'

'Pity,' he muttered.

'What?'

'Nothing.' Marcus had thought Justine's love

was all he wanted. But it wasn't. He wanted more. He wanted her to be his wife and the mother of his children. And soon, not *some* day.

But she was still so young. He had no right to rush her, no right to insist she change all her plans to fall in with his. He would have to be patient, have to wait for her 'some day'.

Meanwhile…

'You won't change your mind about coming over?' he asked tautly, his body already in an agony of longing to hold her in his arms. 'Promise me.'

'I promise.'

Justine lay in Marcus's arms, listening to the rhythm of his sleep and thinking she had never been happier. Marcus had just made love to her with a passion and tenderness which had brought a different dimension to his lovemaking. There had been a sweetness to each kiss and caress which had touched her soul as well as her body. When he'd finally moved into her, telling her all the while how much he loved her, tears had welled up in her eyes. She'd clung to him afterwards, sobbing. He'd kissed the dampness from her cheeks and she'd seen the love for her shining in his eyes. She was, indeed, his true love, as he was hers.

Okay, so he hadn't asked her to marry him yet, but he would. Some day. When the time was right.

Justine knew that time might be a while coming. Marcus had been too hurt in the past to rush into anything. And, in truth, she wanted some more time to prove to him she was nothing like Stephany. She was actually looking forward to the challenge of running a boarding house, of finishing her degree part-time and completing what the last few months had set in motion—the transformation of Justine Montgomery from spoilt little rich bitch to a grown up and independent woman who could be proud of herself.

She never wanted to revert to being that other silly, empty-headed girl, who hadn't known the value of a dollar or how to do a full day's work. She almost felt guilty now of the way she'd treated Howard Barthgate, and those other boys she'd dated. She'd used them shamelessly.

Not that they had been guiltless. They'd all dropped her soon enough after her father's death, which just showed the depth of their feelings. Actually, boys like Howard Barthgate were a bit like her father, Justine believed. High on charm, but low on conscience. Marriage, to them, was often simply a merger for money. True love was a concept for peasants, and sex, a commodity to be found wherever it was available. She doubted there was a husband in her old social set who was faithful to his wife.

Marcus, on the other hand, was lower on charm but higher on conscience. Justine liked that balance a lot better. She sighed a deeply contented sigh and drifted into a deeply contented sleep.

Her happiness, however, was to be short-lived— disaster waiting with the dawn.

CHAPTER SIXTEEN

JUSTINE woke to the sound of wind, and a branch slapping its leaves on the bedroom window. The clock on the bedside chest said two minutes to eleven, which meant she was already two hours behind the hour she'd faithfully promised her mother she'd be home.

'Marcus,' she said, and nudged him in the ribs.

He groaned.

'Stay there if you like but I have to get up and go home. I have a lot to do today. Our first boarders are arriving tomorrow.'

Marcus yawned and stretched. 'God, what's that infernal noise?'

'It's the wind. But no rain, unfortunately. Clear blue sky again.'

'Crazy damned weather we're having. Almost as crazy as I am about you. Come here and kiss me good morning, you beautiful thing, you!'

'Oh, no, you don't!' Justine squealed, and warded him off. 'I have to get out of here in fifteen minutes or my mother is going to kill me. I promised her I'd be home long before this.'

Marcus grinned and snuck a quick kiss in. 'Was she shocked and horrified when you rang last night?'

'Mum? No. Mum's always let me run my own race. Nothing I do would ever shock her.'

'Wise Mum.'

'I don't know about wise. She's a bit on the scatty side, actually.'

'A darling, though.'

'Yes.' Justine sighed. 'Poor Mum. These last couple of months have been traumatic for her.'

'You underestimate her, Justine. She's a survivor.'

'Perhaps. I think Tom's in love with her.'

'The gardening chap?'

'Uh-huh.'

'Seemed a nice enough bloke.'

'He is.'

'What's the problem, then?'

'Mum was very much in love with Daddy. I don't think she'll ever fall in love again.'

'Funny. People said the same thing about me and Stephany…'

Justine looked sharply at him, and he grinned.

'They were dead wrong, weren't they? Now, off you go to the shower, my love, while I lie here and languish in the memory of last night.'

'Turn on the radio while you're languishing, lazy bones. See if you can get the weekend weather report.'

Twenty minutes later, a shocked Marcus was speeding up the Pacific Highway towards Lindfield, a pale-faced Justine sitting beside him. He hadn't just caught the weather, but the whole eleven o'clock news report. The newsreader's words were still ringing in his ears.

Some nut-case arsonist, not satisfied by the bush-fires which had ringed the rural outskirts of Sydney all summer, had actually set fire to the National Park running along the Lane Cove River. Eighty-mile-an-hour winds had whipped up what should have been a containable blaze into an uncontrollable force, which was burning all in its path.

It seemed incredible that a bushfire should be threatening homes in the inner city area, but that was what was happening, according to the news. Several houses had already been burnt to the ground. Lindfield had been one of the suburbs named where houses had succumbed, and more were in danger. Since Justine's home backed on to the park, Marcus feared it would be one of the first at risk!

Justine's panic increased as Marcus drew nearer her street. The pall of green-black smoke in the sky was appalling. She hoped it was just the result of trees burning, but feared this was an optimistic view. The thought of her home burning to the ground was bad enough. The fear of her mother in danger brought a clutch of nausea to her stomach.

Marcus tried to keep a handle on his fear but it was difficult. Things didn't look good.

Dear God, he prayed, as he hadn't prayed since he was ten years old. Don't let anything happen to Justine's mother. Or that stupid damned house. I promise if you keep them both safe, I won't press or coerce Justine into a precipitous marriage. I'll even keep using protection and not have any convenient lapses of memory.

He couldn't drive down her street. It was blocked with police cars.

Marcus knew without having to be told that the situation was critical. He could actually see the

flames of one house burning at the far end of the
street. It *was* on the other side from Justine's home,
but with the wind it wouldn't take much to jump
that small distance. The sudden realisation that the
wind was going in the opposite direction and had
already done its business on the other side made
him quake inside.

'Oh, Marcus,' was all Justine said, despair in her
voice.

He parked his car down a side street and they
both ran back to the corner of Justine's street, where
groups of people were huddled behind a police barrier, everyone looking shell-shocked.

Justine suddenly grabbed his arm. 'Marcus!
Look, there's Mum! She's all right. Oh, thank God.'

Marcus did. But there was still the question of
the house. Lord knows what would happen if the
darned thing *had* burned to the ground. Adelaide
would probably fall apart and so might Justine. She
was a far more sensitive and sentimental girl than
he'd ever imagined, as evidenced by the sudden
flood of tears in her eyes.

'Don't cry, Justine,' he advised sternly. 'Your
mum doesn't need to see you crying. You have to
stay strong for her, darling, especially if something's happened to the house.'

'Yes—yes, you're quite right, Marcus,' she said.
'Mustn't cry. Must stay strong. It's only a house,
after all. Mum's fine. That's all that matters.'

He was so proud of the way she pulled herself
together, of the determination in her eyes to be
strong and brave for her mother. But he kept a comforting arm around her waist as they moved over to
where her mother was arguing with a policeman.

She didn't sound at all scatty, Marcus thought suddenly. She sounded like a mother frantic about her daughter, but determined to get answers. The policeman was looking very harried.

'But you *must* let me go down there, you stupid man. My daughter said she'd be home first thing this morning and Justine is as good as her word. I won't do anything silly, I promise. But I need to know if my daugh—'

Adelaide whirled when Justine tapped her on the shoulder, saying, 'Mum,' at the same time.

The look in the woman's eyes told it all, and Marcus knew that there was nothing on this earth like a mother's love. He felt momentarily sad for what he'd missed out on, then glad that the woman who would bear his children one day had been reared by a mother as caring as this.

'Oh, Justine!' Adelaide cried, her two chins wobbling. 'I've been so worried.' She clutched at Justine's upper arms, then hugged her tight. 'But you're all right. Tom, look, she's all right. My precious darling is all right.'

'Yes, dearest,' Tom said, coming forward from where he'd been silently standing by.

Justine stared at him when he slipped his arm around her mother's shoulders, her eyes widening when Adelaide slumped submissively against him. The mother tigress of a moment ago was gone, Marcus saw, replaced by the persona Adelaide had long since adopted, that of the fragile female who had to be cosseted and protected from reality.

'The house is gone, Justine,' Tom informed them both.

'Oh, God,' Justine choked out, and Marcus

steadied her with a squeeze. 'Were…were you able to get anything out?'

'I'm afraid not. By the time we got here they wouldn't let us down there. The street had been evacuated and blocked off.'

'What do you mean, when you got here?' Justine looked from Tom to her mother, then back at Tom.

Adelaide blushed while Tom straightened, his eyes clear and unwavering. 'Your mother stayed the night at my house, Justine.'

Marcus might have been amused by Justine's shock at any other time but this. 'She…she what?' she gasped.

'Your mother and I are in love, Justine,' Tom said, with a simplicity which was quite touching, Marcus thought. He liked the man. He was going to be a lot better partner for Adelaide than the likes of Grayson Montgomery.

'In love,' Justine repeated rather blankly.

'Yes, dear.' Her mother joined in at last, looking half-sheepish, half-defiant. 'Like you and Marcus. We're going to be married. Tom asked me last night and I said yes. The wedding will be quite soon. At our age we see no reason to wait.'

'But…but what about the house?'

Adelaide looked wistful, but not too distraught. 'It's very upsetting, I know, and I feel for you dreadfully. I know how attached you were to it, and how hard you fought to keep it.'

Marcus could feel Justine's dismay and frustration through every pore of her body. He knew full well she'd fought to keep the house more for her mother than for herself!

'It's only a house after all, dear,' Adelaide added.

'And it *was* heavily insured. Marcus made sure of that before he sanctioned the loan. Tom said I can move in with him straightaway. I doubt anyone will be scandalised in this day and age.'

'But…but what about your things? What about Grandma's jewellery?'

'All my mother's jewellery is in the bank's vaults—didn't I tell you? Marcus said if I wasn't going to wear any of it then I'd better put it somewhere safe since we were going to invite a lot of strangers into the house. Oh, my goodness, I'd forgotten about that! What are those poor students going to do when they find out their rooms no longer exist?'

'I dare say they'll survive,' Marcus said dryly. And so will you, Adelaide dear, he thought, though I'm not so sure about your daughter. She was looking stunned, the poor darling. She'd lost her home and her illusions in one and the same day.

'I think, Tom, that we should take Adelaide and Justine back to your place,' he advised. 'There's nothing any of us can do here for now. I'll speak to the policemen and find out when we can return.'

Tom's house proved a surprise. Only a few streets away, it was spacious and elegant with a magnificent garden. Tom confided over tea and cake that he hadn't always been a gardener. He had once been a middle-management executive for a large food company, but had been retrenched at fifty-one after his company was taken over. Despite a lucrative golden handshake he hadn't wanted to retire, and had gone into gardening—more as an interest than a career. It was apparent Adelaide would not want for anything by marrying him, either in affection or security.

Marcus was pleased to see Justine looking a little more her old self after an hour or so, though it was clear she was still far more distressed than her mother over the house. Her face was pale and there was a haunted look in her eyes.

He didn't think it was doing her much good being with her mother. Adelaide had obviously shut the door on her old life and home—both mentally and emotionally—and kept talking about Tom and the future with a slightly insensitive optimism.

Marcus suspected that was her way of coping, but it wasn't Justine's. She needed to openly grieve the loss of her home, and everything that home represented. When Marcus whispered that they could go back and look at what was left of the house now, she nodded her agreement.

It was worse than he'd envisaged. A blackened, sodden shell. A fire truck was still there, and they were warned not to touch anything, although it was obvious the thick stone walls weren't in any danger of collapse. Nothing was salvageable inside, everything either reduced to ash, or melted and twisted into unrecognisable shapes.

'Oh, Marcus,' was all Justine said over and over as they picked their way carefully through the rubble, her voice breaking.

It wasn't till she stared up at where the staircase had been that she seriously began to cry. Marcus folded her to him and let her. She needed to cry, needed to let it all out, needed to grieve.

She was deathly silent during the drive home.

His, not Tom's. Marcus wasn't about to let her go back there. Not tonight.

He poured her a stiff drink on arrival and pressed it into her hands.

'Don't be angry with your mother, Justine,' he said as she drank it down.

'I'm not,' she said, sighing. 'Not really. She's only doing what she's always done. Putting her head in the sand and pretending everything will be all right. And it probably will be. Tom's a good man. She's obviously going to be very happy with him. It's just that I feel so desolate. I can't explain it. I have nothing left from my life there. No photographs or mementoes. Nothing. It's as though I don't exist any more.'

'Not exist? Oh, Justine, my love, you exist more than anyone I've ever met. You walk in a room and the air is instantly warmer, the light brighter. You have a living aura around you which is both captivating and enchanting. You *are* life. But I understand what you're saying. I would have dearly loved some photographs of my mother. But, be assured, there are more photographs of you and your past life around than you realise. All your friends will have some. Relatives. Old classmates. Photographers keep negatives for decades, and so do people. We'll get some photographs for you, my love. Meanwhile, I have a little surprise for you—something which I think might make you feel better.'

'What?'

'Seeing is worth a thousand words,' he said, smiling, and led her along the hallway to the large back room which had been empty till a week or so ago.

He opened the door and guided her in, watching as her eyes widened on a gasp of spontaneous joy.

Marcus would always remember that moment, the way her face went from a bleak sadness to blazing happiness in one split second.

'Grandma's things!' she exclaimed. 'Oh, I'd forgotten about them. Oh, Marcus, what a wonderful surprise!' And she ran around the room, touching everything with loving little strokes of her hands, laughing and crying at the same time.

'I won't even make you marry me to get them back,' he teased.

Her head shot up and a mischievous glint came into her eyes. His heart turned over. The girl he'd fallen in love with was back, as bright and bold as ever.

'Was that a proposal I just heard?' she asked saucily. 'Or a bribe? Marcus Osborne, you wouldn't be trying to corrupt me, would you?'

'Could I?'

She started to undulate towards him and his throat thickened. 'Not with things, my darling,' she murmured, reaching up on tiptoe to wind her arms around his neck and press herself against him. 'But make love to me like you did last night and I'll be yours for ever.'

'Is that an acceptance, or another bribe?'

'It's a promise.'

Justine was moved by the expression which came into his eyes. She realised then that her mother had been right. Love was all that mattered. Not a house. Or things. Love.

'Will tomorrow be too soon for the ceremony?' he asked impatiently.

She laughed. 'I don't think a marriage can be arranged that quickly. Not legally.'

'Where there's a will there's a way.'

'Then go to it—pronto. Meanwhile…'

She became his wife by special licence seven days later—Marcus pulling all sorts of strings and claiming a pregnancy as the reason for the undue haste.

As it turned out, technically, he hadn't lied. Their first child—a daughter—arrived eight months and three weeks later, just in time to move into the new house Marcus had had built on the burned-out site—a duplication of the original house from the plans they'd found still lodged at the local council.

It was always a happy house, with a carved mahogany balustrade which the children slid down, but only when their grandmother was minding them. She never seemed to notice their misdemeanours—not like their mother, who was very strict. None of them believed for a moment the stories their father told of their mother being a wild child who had played hookey from school, been an outrageous flirt and who'd worn tight, sexy dresses. That wasn't *their* mother. No way. That had to be some other person.

But when their parents found the privacy of their bedroom at night, and the children were fast asleep, something happened to their mother. In Marcus's arms she became a different woman, a woman who knew she was very lucky to have found her true love in life. They would have been very surprised to see the woman she became then. Very surprised indeed!

Born in London, **Sophie Weston** is a traveller by nature who started writing when she was five. She wrote her first romance recovering from illness, thinking her travelling was over. She was wrong, but she enjoyed it so much that she has carried on. These days she lives in the heart of the city with two demanding cats and a cherry tree – and travels the world looking for settings for her stories.

Sophie is a rising star in Tender Romance™, loved by readers around the world for her emotionally exhilarating stories and fabulous international settings! Her next book is set in the exciting world of European royalty: look out in Tender Romance™ for –

THE PRINCE'S PROPOSAL
by
Sophie Weston
on-sale June 2002

THE INNOCENT AND
THE PLAYBOY
by
Sophie Weston

CHAPTER ONE

'I WON'T,' yelled Alexandra from the staircase.

Rachel cast a harried look at the kitchen clock. The taxi was due any minute and she had not even checked her briefcase. At the table her stepson, Hugh, was munching his way through an enormous plate of toast and blackcurrant jam, ignoring his sister. No help there, then. Rachel sighed and went out into the hall. She looked up the stairs at her grim-faced stepdaughter.

'Look, I've said no and…'

Alexandra's expression darkened even further. 'You've got no right to say no. You're not even my mother.'

This was a complaint that was appearing in their arguments more and more. Rachel would have found it easier to deal with, she was sure, if she had not had a stepmother herself. As it was, half of her sympathised totally with Alexandra. The other, responsible half knew that an adventurous fifteen-year-old needed rules of conduct more than she needed sympathy. As a result their arguments tended to be protracted.

Heaven help me, today of all days, thought Rachel. She resisted the temptation to look at her watch but it was tough.

'I know I'm not your mother, Alexandra. It makes no difference. Any adult would tell you the same.'

'Theo's an adult and he thinks I should go.'

'Any responsible female adult,' Rachel corrected herself grimly. She hesitated, then, choosing her words with care, said, 'Of course Theo wants you to go. You're a very pretty girl.'

She did not add, as she might well have done, And you're going to inherit half your father's business in less than three

5

years. She did not need to. It was there between them already. Her stepdaughter had not forgotten a word of the disastrous altercation after her last evening out with Theo Judd. Rachel could see it in Alexandra's hot eyes.

Her next words confirmed it. 'You think Theo's after my money.'

Rachel pushed her hair back wearily. It was too long. It needed cutting. She had kept it short for nine years but during these last hectic weeks she had not had time to get it cut.

'I don't know what he's after, Alexandra, and that's the truth.'

'He's too old for me. Go on, say it.'

'Do I have to?'

Alexandra almost stamped her foot. 'You just don't know what it's like.'

And that was a problem too. Rachel knew exactly what it was like to be in love when you were too young and the man you loved was too worldly and sophisticated to recognise how vulnerable you were. In fact, she had worked hard at forgetting for nine years. What was more, she would have said she had succeeded, until Alexandra had decided to make a present of her generous heart to a twenty-four-year-old bartender with a line in flash cars and flashier repartee. Trying to induce a little wariness in her stepdaughter had brought back some memories which could still make Rachel wince.

Sidestepping Alexandra's comment, she said, 'I do know that I would not be much of a guardian if I let you stay out till all hours, God knows where, with a man who is nine years older than you are.'

Alexandra could sidestep difficult issues too.

'Dad was twenty years older than you,' she snarled.

It was true. In spite of her anger and worry, just for a moment Rachel was startled into amusement. 'You've got me there,' she admitted. She leaned her arm on the carved wooden banisters and looked up at her stepdaughter straightly. 'Look, Lexy, I know you won't believe me now, but that really was different. Your father and I had both been around a bit. Fifteen and twenty-four is another kettle of fish entirely.'

'You mean I'm a child.'

'No, maybe not a child exactly. But there is a whole world of experiences you have not had yet.'

'And Theo has?'

By the truck-load, if Rachel was any judge. Wisely she did not say that either.

Instead she said, 'Well, he must be well aware of the difference between you and girlfriends of his own age. Even if you aren't.'

Alexandra tossed her head. 'Theo thinks I'm very mature.'

Hell, thought Rachel.

There was a swish of tyres on the wet gravel outside the house. Her taxi had arrived.

Knowing that she was giving in and she should not do it, she said, 'Look, we'll talk about it this evening…'

'Because you've got to rush off to work, right?'

'Because I'm *late* for work,' Rachel said between her teeth. 'Because I'm making a strategy presentation. Because the full board will be there and some of the shareholders aren't happy. Because I have other responsibilities as well as you.'

'You're not responsible for me,' flashed Alexandra. 'I can make my own decisions.'

Rachel sighed. 'Not legally. Look, I've got to go.'

'If my father were alive you wouldn't treat me like this.'

Rachel winced. Even though these were exactly the circumstances which Brian had envisaged when he'd first begged her to marry him, and they'd both thought she had prepared for them, Rachel had been missing him badly in recent days.

The taxi hooted. Rachel stopped glaring at Alexandra and shot into the kitchen. Late as she was, she still checked the briefcase methodically. It was something her own father had taught her to do and she sometimes thought ruefully that she could do it in her sleep. Everything was there.

She pinned up her hair on top of her head without looking in the mirror. Then she stuffed her handbag under her arm and prepared to go.

Hugh looked up from his breakfast. The pile of toast had diminished noticeably, as it always did. So why did he always look as if he were starving? Rachel thought. He saw her worried look and grinned.

'Sock it to them, Super Shark.'

Rachel knew this was meant to be both encouraging and complimentary. She responded accordingly.

'Thank you very much for your support. Hugh...'

He jerked his head at the door. 'Don't worry about her. She'll sort herself out sooner or later.'

'Just as long as it isn't too late,' muttered Rachel, not much comforted.

'Don't worry about it. Lexy can look after herself,' said her sympathetic brother.

'I hope you're right.'

The taxi hooted again, longer.

'Damn. I must go. I'm sorry. I'll see you both tonight,' said Rachel, running.

Too fast, of course. It was blowing a gale outside. The leaves flew up, making her blink against the flying dust. The wind caught at her hastily arranged hair and whipped great hanks of red-gold fronding out of its confining hairpins. She cursed but she did not go back to repair the damage. She had told the children she was late for a board meeting. What she had not told them was that it could just turn out to be the most important meeting of her life.

Now, racing into the waiting taxi, she slipped and fell to one knee on the gravel. She felt the run in her tights at once. But it was too late to go back and change. The unfamiliar taxi driver was already impatient and Rachel was hardly less so. She got into the back seat and slammed the door.

'Bentley's Investment Bank,' she said. 'Old Ship Street.'

All the way to the huge new office block, she could feel the run snaking down her leg. On the sheer dark tights she favoured, it was going to be horribly conspicuous. She would have to keep her legs out of sight under the board table until she could dash out and get another pair. Maybe just before lunch, thought Rachel, running over the timetable in her mind. Then, jumping out of the taxi, she did not duck low enough. Rachel felt her already descending *coiffure* lurch sideways at the impact. It was the final straw.

As the taxi drove off, she swore before turning to steam in through the silent automatic doors.

'Morning, Mrs Gray,' said the security officer, from behind his smart, brass-trimmed desk. He had seen her mishap and could not suppress his grin. 'Bit windy out there.'

Rachel hefted her briefcase under her arm and thrust her free hand distractedly through her hair. Several pins fell out.

'Morning, Geoff. Are they here yet?'

The security guards had the best information network in the bank. Geoff did not pretend to misunderstand.

'The party from the States arrived about ten minutes ago.'

'Oh, hell.'

'Mr Jensen is giving them the tour.'

Rachel stopped fluffing up her hair and scattering pins. 'You mean he knew I hadn't got here?'

Geoff looked wise. 'He was looking for you earlier. Mandy told him you were on your way.'

Mandy was her secretary. Philip Jensen was Rachel's boss—at least on the organisation chart—and he was a panicker.

Rachel sighed. She should have been here an hour ago at least. She had intended to be when she'd put her papers for the meeting into her briefcase last night. But with Alexandra's bombshell at the breakfast table she had temporarily lost sight of her timetable. The fact that it was her own fault did not help. If anything it made it slightly worse.

'Hell,' said Rachel again with feeling.

Geoff grinned and opened the small door at the side of the security guards' cubby-hole. They had their own lift to all floors which no one else was supposed to use. The theory was that it should be available at all times in case of a security alert. As a result, it was known to be the fastest route between floors. In addition, it had the advantage that she was unlikely to meet the board and their honoured guests in the unadorned steel box which served the security force. It was against bank policy but, on today of all days, the offer was irresistible.

'Thank you,' said Rachel with real gratitude, and dived into the prohibited lift.

She made it into her secretary's office without encountering anyone else. Mandy looked up and took in her situation in a glance. She swung round on her rotating chair and extracted a new packet of tights from the pile in the stationery cupboard behind her.

'Traffic?' she said.

Rachel dropped the briefcase thankfully. 'Only domestic.'

Mandy pushed the tights across the desk and surveyed her thoughtfully. 'You've got mud on your jacket.'

Rachel looked down. It was true. There was a great splash of it like a wizard's hand across the front.

'I didn't realise. It must have happened when I tripped. Damn.'

Mandy held out a hand. 'Give it to me. I'll have a go with the clothes-brush. You deal with the extremities.'

Rachel shrugged herself out of the jacket. 'My one designer suit,' she said gloomily. 'Only just back from the cleaners.'

Mandy was surveying the dried mud. 'The check jacket is in your office. If all else fails you could wear that.'

The check jacket was an old friend. So old that its black velvet collar showed its age. They both knew it. Rachel sighed again.

'Philip will be furious.'

'Philip is too terrified to be furious,' Mandy said frankly.

'He'll be so relieved to see you, he won't care if you turn up in dungarees. Go on.'

Rachel went swiftly into the ladies' cloakroom, pulling the remaining pins out of her hair as she went. Mandy soon joined her, bearing the check jacket apologetically.

'Designer clothes need designer cleaning. I brushed the mud off but you could still see the shadow.'

Rachel lobbed the ruined tights into the waste-paper basket and smoothed her skirt.

'Thank you for trying.' She straightened up to face her image in the big mirror behind the hand basins and grimaced. 'It's not going to make much difference anyway. My hair needs surgery. I've lost too many pins to put it up properly.'

'Then leave it loose.'

Rachel fluffed out the red-gold fronds doubtfully. 'Not very professional.'

'Better than everyone in the meeting sitting there wondering when it's going to fall down,' Mandy said, ever practical.

Rachel laughed suddenly. 'You're probably right. I don't want to distract them from my beautiful corporate plan.'

She brushed her hair rapidly. Mandy gathered up the scatter of hairpins and silently laid out Rachel's underused cosmetics. Most of the time Rachel wore no make-up at all unless she was going to some big business reception.

It was Mandy's private opinion that this was a horrible waste. However, Rachel, although in general as friendly and informal a boss as you could wish for, did not encourage this sort of comment. Mandy could never quite work out whether this was because Rachel genuinely did not know how spectacular she could look when she tried. It seemed unlikely. Sometimes Mandy even suspected that Rachel knew quite well and was, for some obscure reason of her own, terrified by it.

Now Rachel made a face in the mirror, reaching out for

the little make-up case. 'Why is painting your face supposed to improve your confidence?'

Mandy perched on the edge of the vanity counter. 'Because it makes you look more like a performer?'

'You mean like a clown?'

'Like a star,' Mandy said reprovingly.

Rachel snorted and wrinkled her nose at her reflection. 'Some hopes.'

So maybe her unawareness of her looks was real. But she had to know how high her professional reputation stood. So why did she not have more self-confidence? Someone somewhere must have done a real number on Rachel, Mandy thought.

She was too tactful to say so, however. Instead, she said, 'Your confidence doesn't need any boosting. Everyone in the bank knows how good you are at your job.'

Rachel laughed. 'That isn't the point. I'm the one who has to believe I'm good. That's what confidence means. And after this morning—' She broke off.

'What went wrong this morning? Homework?'

Rachel ran a small make-up sponge under the tap before replying. A faint frown appeared as she brushed the sponge across the compressed block of pale tan colour.

'No.' She hesitated, then started to sponge on the light make-up with quick, angry strokes. 'It's Alexandra.'

Mandy nodded, unsurprised. She had worked with Rachel all through the last three traumatic years and she did not have to have the family tensions explained to her.

'Being difficult, is she?'

Rachel put the sponge down. 'She thinks she'd like to live with her mother,' she said neutrally. 'Her real mother, that is.'

Mandy was shocked. 'And can she?'

'I don't know. Not unless her mother wants her, that's for sure.'

'She doesn't?'

Rachel picked up a palette of eye-shadows and a small brush. She surveyed herself, hesitating.

'Not up to now. That's why Brian—' She broke off abruptly and leant forward to paint discreet colour onto her eyelids. Mandy bit her lip. When Rachel mentioned her late husband it was usually a sign that she was deeply disturbed.

'How old is Alexandra now?' she asked, tactfully changing the subject.

Rachel gave her a pale grin in the mirror. 'Fifteen going on forty. To judge by this morning's performance, anyway.'

Mandy was surprised. 'How quickly they grow up. I hadn't realised.'

'Nor, according to Alexandra, had I,' Rachel said drily.

'Ah,' said Mandy, enlightened. She had younger sisters. 'She wants to go to a rock concert and you won't let her.'

Rachel's face tightened. 'Something like that.'

'They all do,' Mandy said comfortingly. 'It's just a phase. I had some terrible fights with my father. You grow out of it.'

Rachel flicked the little brush over her other eyelid. 'Do you? I never had any fights like that. Too much of a goody-goody. Never did anything my father wouldn't like,' she confessed.

Except once, said a small voice inside her. Except that last, fatal time when you brought the whole world down on everyone, just because you were determined to show Riccardo di Stefano and his kind that they could not hurt people with impunity.

It was a voice that had been whispering away for three or four days now. It reminded her that even the best-conducted adolescents could make some horrible mistakes. It was a voice she had silenced for nine years and it was disconcerting to find it coming out of the ether now. Especially as it had a disturbing tendency to take her difficult stepdaughter's side in the present argument.

Mandy said comfortably, 'I bet you did. You've just forgotten.' She relieved Rachel of the eye-shadow and handed her a lipstick and lip-brush. 'Alexandra just needs a good fight with authority at the moment. You happen to be the only major authority figure around. Hard on you, but it's not the end of the world. What she needs is a man in her life.'

Rachel shuddered. 'Don't say that. She's jolly nearly got one.'

Mandy was unperturbed. 'We all had boyfriends.'

Rachel paused, the lip-brush arrested halfway to her mouth. Not me, she thought involuntarily. Is that why I'm so bad at dealing with Alexandra? Is it because I never went through the normal stages? Was I just too busy being a good little girl, working hard and winning prizes? Until... The voice again! Why on earth should it start up *now* when she needed all the confidence she could summon up?

She suppressed the voice, applied the lipstick, stepped back and looked at herself critically.

'Well, that will have to do.'

Mandy nodded approval. In spite of the fact that Rachel paid very little attention to her appearance, when you had shining, naturally auburn hair and wide brown eyes, it did not make too much difference, Mandy thought without jealousy. A dash of modest eye-shadow and Rachel's eyes turned the colour of Madeira wine.

'You look gorgeous.'

Rachel sent her a harassed look. 'I wish I looked tidy.' She flicked irritatedly at the loose hair about her shoulders. 'Tidy is efficient. Untidy—well...'

'Philip knows you're efficient,' Mandy soothed.

'It isn't Philip I have to convince.' She looked at her watch. 'Being half an hour late isn't going to help either.'

Mandy laughed and uncurled herself from her perch.

'Don't worry about it. The new boss man has changed all the meetings round, so no one knows who is due to speak when or on what. With a bit of luck no one except Philip will even know.'

Rachel was looking in the mirror, giving a last downward

brush to her neat skirt, but this made her look round. 'New boss man?'

'Genghis Khan in person,' Mandy said cheerfully.

Rachel was aware of a quick lurch in her stomach, as if she were still in Geoff's lift and it had hurtled down to the lowest level of the underground car park. You're paranoid, she told herself. And obsessed. This is ancient history. You'd never have remembered it at all if it weren't for the fight with Alexandra.

She took a firm grip on herself and said casually, 'Which Genghis Khan is that?'

'The main man. Leader of the barbarians in person.'

Her stomach sank below car-park level to somewhere around the seabed.

'You don't mean di Stefano?'

Please tell me you don't mean Riccardo Enrico di Stefano, heir to one fortune and personal creator of another five times the size, patron of the arts, darling of the gossip columns and the man who took confidence into a whole new dimension.

But Mandy was grinning. 'Himself.'

Rachel's stomach penetrated the earth's crust without difficulty and began to swirl around in the molten core. She could feel the heat in her face. She even put up a hand. Her cheekbone was warm under the make-up.

She swallowed. 'What—?' Her voice squeaked. Mandy was looking at her curiously. She swallowed and got a grip on her vocal cords. 'What is Riccardo di Stefano doing here? The bank is only a minority investment from his point of view.'

Mandy chuckled. 'Well, from what I saw when I helped Angela with the photocopying, that's all going to change. I'd say he's going to buy us.'

Rachel stared at her, appalled. Mandy misinterpreted the horror.

'Don't worry about it. He'll probably buy your corporate

plan as well. More likely to than the old board, if you ask me.'

This could not be happening. Something inside her was turning over like a hibernating beast roused out of ice. Old, deep ice. Rachel could feel the faint internal tremors starting again. They were not exactly unfamiliar, but she had not been aware of them for years. Meanwhile, Mandy, unaware, was giving her an encouraging smile.

'You could be right,' Rachel said faintly.

Mandy patted her on the shoulder. 'Of course I'm right. Now go and broke the agreement.'

There was nothing to be done. If he was here already, all her escape routes were blocked.

'Yes,' said Rachel automatically.

She shrugged herself into the check jacket like a sleep-walker and went to the door. She looked as if someone had hit her with a sandbag, Mandy thought. More encourage-ment was clearly called for.

'Cheer up, Rachel. Your tights are whole and your jacket is clean. From here on in, today can only get better.'

Rachel stared at her. For an odd moment it seemed as if she were looking over the precipice of a particularly cold and deadly mountain. Then she gave a harsh laugh. 'I wouldn't put money on it.'

It was bitter. It even startled Mandy out of her cheerful-ness. Then she said bracingly, 'You'll do fine. Bigwigs have never worried you. The bigger the wig, the cooler you get.'

But Rachel was still looking sick. Mandy had never seen her look like that before. She began to be alarmed.

'You can handle yourself,' Mandy reminded her urgently, putting a hand on her arm. 'You know you can.'

Rachel gave a little jump as if she had been brought back to the present by main force. 'I hope,' she muttered.

The sick look went out of her face. But although she was regaining command of herself there was still that shaken look at the back of her eyes. It was almost as if she had received a bad shock, Mandy thought. Which, of course, was ridiculous. It took more than a visiting troupe of American money-men to shock Rachel. Or, at least, it ought to.

Rachel was thinking the same thing. She pulled her jacket straight and squared her shoulders in the mirror.

'Boardroom?'

Mandy said, 'Well, Mr Jensen said he'd like to see you in his office first.'

I'll just bet he did, thought Rachel. If the biggest shark of them all has turned up in person, Philip will be turning to jelly.

'But they arrived and he went straight to the boardroom. Would you join him—er—soonest?'

Panic stations, interpreted Rachel. She did not say so. She was too close to panic herself.

'Right,' she said.

She went, buried in thought. Confidence, she said to herself. That's the thing to remember. You're good at your job. You know that. Everyone else does. Believe it, why can't you? Play to your strengths.

He must never know you even remember. Almost certainly he won't. It is nine years ago. He must have had dozens of girls before and since. It's ten to one that he forgot the whole thing in days.

She almost convinced herself.

She was still frowning in preoccupation as she went along the executive corridor. It was ankle-deep in an expensive carpet and hung with valuable seascapes. Usually Philip's idea of executive interior decoration made Rachel laugh. Today, however, she barely noticed it.

In fact she was so deep in thought that she did not notice the man coming towards her. That was hardly her fault. Although he was tall and loose-limbed, he moved like a cat. On the sumptuous carpeting his tread was noiseless.

So when a voice said, 'Hi there,' she jumped about a foot in the air and came down with her head spinning.

It was the voice from her very worst dreams. Rachel felt

as if someone had thrown ice-water over her. She found herself staring straight into those laughing, green-flecked eyes for the first time in nine years. It felt like yesterday. She stared at him, transfixed.

The man looked amused. 'Rick di Stefano.'

There was not the slightest hint in his voice that he knew they had met before. Rachel registered his open smile: not a glimmer of recognition there. She moistened suddenly dry lips and tried to believe it.

In all those worst dreams of hers Riccardo di Stefano knew her at once. What he did about it varied with the awfulness of the dream but he had never looked at her with the smile of a pleasant stranger.

Rachel gulped. For the first time in years she was unable to think of a single thing to say. Instead, she just went on staring at him, horrified. Not yet, something in her brain was wailing. I'm not ready. Not *yet*.

Her reaction surprised him, she saw. One dark eyebrow rose.

'I startled you. You must have been a long way away.'

Oh, she was, she was. Nine years and a whole ocean away. Impossible to say that, of course. Engage brain, Rachel, she told herself furiously. Engage brain. Or this will go out of control before you've even said hello.

Years of professional negotiations came to her aid at last. The unforgotten past receded, at least for the moment.

She swallowed and said, 'Hello, Mr di Stefano.' It came out a lot huskier than she'd expected but at least it did not sound as if all she wanted to do was run away from him and hide.

He laughed aloud then. 'That sounds very formal.'

She gave him a quick, meaningless smile. 'That's the English for you.'

He smiled back. It was slow and sexy and made his eyes crinkle at the corners as if he was used to staring into the sun. He was not as tanned as she remembered, but the muscles were still as lithe under the city suit—and the laughter as wicked.

'Now, I've always found English formality to be a bit of a myth,' he said easily.

Oh, have you? she thought. Now that she had brought herself back under control she had time to observe him more dispassionately. She disliked what she saw amazingly. Confident, good-looking, intelligent. The things that her stepmother had gloated over all those years ago were still true. Even more so, if you could judge from one quick, resentful look. The charm was still there too—and he knew it. He was even waiting for her to respond to it. Rachel realised it in gathering wrath.

She said smartly, 'I'm afraid I'm rather a formal person.'

Riccardo di Stefano's eyes narrowed. It looked as if he had just registered that there was a real person confronting him in the corridor, Rachel thought, pleased. Her satisfaction was short-lived.

'Have we met before?'

She could have kicked herself. Never start a fight unless you're prepared to finish it, she reminded herself grimly.

She said in her most colourless voice, 'I was away when you were here in September.'

He detected the evasion. Of course he would. He had built up a worldwide empire on management skills, which meant that he would have no problem at all in reading a minor employee's disaffection.

He did not look worried by her attitude. Why should he? His reputation said he had a flair for rooting out opposition at the heart. He would have detected that this minor employee would not present him with any problems he could not deal with. Just let him not detect as well how carefully she had orchestrated her leave in order to avoid his thrice-postponed visit, Rachel thought.

Before he could challenge her further she said, 'Were you looking for the boardroom? You should have turned right out of the lift, not left.'

He was looking at her intently. Before he could question her she said, 'Let me show you.'

For a moment he did not say anything. She could feel him weighing up her reaction, assessing its implications, even its possible effect. Oh, yes, you could see why he was head of a multinational, multi-business empire.

She could have kicked herself. She held her breath, not quite looking at him. But he decided it was not worth probing, in the end.

'Thank you,' he said easily. 'I'd appreciate that.'

She breathed again.

He fell into step beside her. He did not say anything further, but Rachel could feel his thoughtful gaze on her profile. She hoped she kept her expression neutral. By the time they reached the boardroom she felt as if the whole of that side of her face had been irradiated. Doing her best to ignore the feeling, she opened the door.

'Mr di Stefano,' she announced to the room.

It was not necessary. All the men there already knew who he was as well as she did, Rachel could see. And most of them were scared of him. She saw that too.

Well, at least she wasn't scared of him, she thought. Not now. Maybe once. Not any more. It was ironic. He had done his worst to a vulnerable adolescent and she had survived. There was nothing left to be afraid of.

Reminding herself that she was totally unafraid of Riccardo di Stefano was one thing. Meeting his eyes and retaining conviction was something else entirely. Prudently, Rachel kept her head turned away from that piercing gaze. Luckily it was not difficult.

It became obvious that Riccardo di Stefano had come to Bentley's that morning with one object and one only. He was pleasant enough about it but underneath the good manners he was not making much attempt to hide that steely purpose. Philip Jensen was chairing the meeting and managed to deflect four pointed questions. Eventually Riccardo di Stefano changed tack. He stopped asking questions and interrupted Philip in mid-waffle.

'Frankly, it seems to us at Di Stefano that you've lost your way,' he said.

Philip Jensen was unused to direct confrontation.

'If we can just keep with the agenda...' he began fussily.

Riccardo di Stefano pushed the papers away from him.

'Forget the agenda. What's the point of talking about whether to go into Eastern Europe next year when the bank could collapse at any time?'

Rachel gasped. She was not alone. Riccardo di Stefano's eyes swept round the table.

'That sounds like surprise,' he mocked.

Philip recovered. 'Collapse? What are you talking about?'

'Your little adventures into the futures market. You've got enough risk on board to wipe out the bank.'

Philip forgot he was in awe of Riccardo di Stefano. He sat bolt upright and glared. 'That's a preposterous suggestion.'

'Is it?'

Riccardo nodded to a quiet man whom Rachel knew to be his company's London director and who was on the bank's board. The man produced a pile of printed sheets and began to pass them round. The result of Angela's photocopying, presumably. Could Mandy possibly be right about his intending to put in a bid for the whole bank, then?

Rachel looked at the sheets blankly. They were figures of some sort. She was too shaken to focus on precisely what they represented.

The quiet man said, 'I've been saying I wasn't happy with bank strategy for six months. After the last board meeting I was so worried that I talked to Riccardo. He had our research department do a full analysis. These are the results.'

Philip picked up the stapled sheets and flicked through them. Sitting next to him, Rachel saw that his hands were shaking. He was clearly having as much difficulty in focusing on the figures as she had.

He managed, though, and looked up sharply. His eyes went very small and sharp and the tremor in his hands intensified.

'Where did you get these figures?'

Riccardo shrugged. 'Market information and some in-depth deduction. Then the research department in New York did some modelling. This is the result.'

Philip was shaking with anger now. With more than anger—fury.

'You've been spying. This is market sensitive.'

Riccardo looked amused. 'No need to spy. It's all out there in the market if you go looking for it. With Sam on the board, I knew what to look for, of course.'

Philip stood up. 'This is intolerable.'

Riccardo stood up as well. He looked utterly relaxed. How well Rachel remembered that cool, relaxed manner. How well she remembered how effectively he could use it—and with what devastating results. She braced herself.

Riccardo drawled, 'I rather agree.'

Philip blinked. All Rachel's protective instincts urged her to take his shaking hand. She curbed them. It would do no good and Philip would not thank her for humiliating him in public. She looked down at her own copy of Riccardo's figures again.

Riccardo said, 'Face it, Philip. You've driven this bank into the ground. Mismanagement followed by panic. Speaking as a major shareholder, I've had enough.'

Rachel was probably the only person at the table who was not surprised. Even Riccardo's quiet colleague looked taken aback. A general spluttering of indignation and recriminations broke out. Riccardo sat down again, leaning back in his chair. He watched them all lazily.

Rachel lifted her eyes from the papers in front of her. Across the table Riccardo was the only one not trying to make himself heard in the hubbub. The only one apart from her, that was.

Suddenly something seemed to draw his attention to her.

Seeing her silent, he raised his brows. Then he looked directly at her, straight in the eyes. Rachel felt as if she had touched a naked wire. She jolted back in her seat, breaking the eye contact feverishly. But she knew he was still looking at her.

Beside her Philip was roaring, 'Breach of confidence… Complain to the authorities… The bank will sue…'

Riccardo was unimpressed. His lip curled faintly. He said nothing. Suddenly Rachel could not bear it any more. She stood up. The move was so unexpected that it attracted everyone's attention.

If she had ever imagined a scenario like this she would have been alarmed at the thought of taking public initiative away from Philip. But she had never imagined it. And anyway there were older and far more serious things she had feared in her life than Philip Jensen's potentially wounded ego.

So she said levelly, 'Gentlemen, the main item on the agenda was future business strategy. My report is in your folder as item four. I suggest we break to consider Mr di Stefano's analysis. Then we can come back and discuss it. We can look at the strategy options once we've agreed where the bank is falling down now.'

She sat down. There was a murmur of assent.

Riccardo had gone very still. The long-fingered hand on the table was clenched tight. His eyes looked black with an odd blind look in them as if a ravine had suddenly opened in front of him.

His director sent him a quick, enquiring look. Riccardo ignored him.

'How long?' he said at last. He spoke directly to Rachel. His tone was sharper than any he had used so far.

Rachel looked unseeingly down at the papers. She had not the slightest idea. She took a blind stab at a time.

'Three hours.'

He looked incredulous. 'You'll have proposals in three hours?'

Rachel thought, I have proposals now. You're not the only one who knows something has got to be done about this place. But I need time to convince Philip.

She said calmly, 'I believe so.'

It seemed as if everyone in the room was holding his breath. At last Riccardo di Stefano nodded.

'OK. Same place.' He looked at his watch. 'Two-thirty.'

He stood up. Everyone else did the same. As if he were an emperor, thought Rachel. She was not even trying to curb her hostility now. But still she somehow found herself on her feet too. That infuriated her.

Across the room, Riccardo di Stefano looked at her. His dark eyes measured her as if he had only just become aware of her. She thought she saw faint contempt and put a hand to her loose hair self-consciously. His eyes narrowed. Something in that basilisk regard brought Rachel to attention as if she were facing a court martial.

'I look forward to your ideas,' he said softly.

Something light as a feather, deadly as a cobra, slid up the back of Rachel's neck. She managed not to shudder, but only just. Instead she gave him a bland smile.

'I hope to surprise you.'

He laughed aloud at that. 'I'm sure you do. But I have to warn you a lot of guys have tried.'

And failed, was the implication.

Rachel said, 'I like a challenge.'

Riccardo di Stefano stopped laughing. The look he gave her was pure speculation.

'So do I,' he said softly. 'So do I. Maybe we're both going to learn something from this.'

CHAPTER TWO

As THE door closed behind Riccardo di Stefano, Philip sank back in his seat. He looked ill, Rachel thought with compassion. Beads of sweat were etching out a mask on his face. She was not the only one to notice.

'Better let Rachel run with this one, Phil,' said Henry Ockenden, the head of lending.

Philip waved a hand vaguely. Rachel took this as agreement. It looked as if he was not going to need much convincing after all. She got up.

'I'll be in my office. I'll get briefing to you by two at the latest,' she said.

She gathered up her papers and went.

Mandy was at her desk in the outer office. She raised her eyebrows as Rachel steamed past.

'Fireworks?'

'As you predicted,' said Rachel.

'Di Stefano on the attack?'

'And then some,' said Rachel with feeling. 'Call the group; I want a meeting in twenty minutes. Everyone to have a copy of these.' She dumped di Stefano's papers on Mandy's desk.

Mandy picked them up and took them to the photocopier.

'Is di Stefano as gorgeous as they say?' she said, pressing buttons briskly.

The copier warmed into life.

'Worse,' said Rachel crisply.

She turned away. Mandy was too observant. Rachel did not want the other woman to detect that this was not the first time she had had the opportunity to observe at close

25

quarters how gorgeous he was. Or that she would give anything not to remember how gorgeous.

Rachel gave an angry little sigh. Riccardo di Stefano had obviously had no trouble forgetting. So why couldn't she?

Mandy, at the photocopier, was not detecting anything, fortunately. She laughed. 'He looks a heartbreaker all right.'

Rachel stiffened imperceptibly. Not turning round, she said casually over her shoulder, 'I thought you hadn't met him.'

'No.' It was not hard to discern Mandy's regret at this fact. 'He had his mug shot in the papers yesterday. Taking Sandy Marquis out on the town.'

'Sandy Marquis?' The name was vaguely familiar. Then she remembered. 'The model, you mean? The redhead discovered teaching gym to schoolgirls?'

'That's the one.' Mandy looked at Rachel speculatively. 'He seems to go for redheads.'

'He goes for anything female that doesn't run too fast,' muttered Rachel unwarily.

Mandy's eyebrows flew up. This time she was detecting. And accurately.

'You know him,' she said on a note of discovery.

That's what comes of losing your cool, Rachel told herself, annoyed. Aloud she said repressively, 'We've met.'

'Wow.' Mandy was impressed. 'You've been clubbing on the quiet?'

'Of course not. Even if that was how I got my kicks, which it isn't, what time do I have to go clubbing? When I'm not working I'm trying to persuade two adolescents that school isn't all bad.'

Mandy chuckled. 'I don't see di Stefano at a PTA meeting,' she allowed. 'Where on earth did you meet him, for heaven's sake?'

Rachel grimaced. Take it lightly, she adjured herself. It was never important. Don't build it up into something it was not.

She shrugged. 'It was a long time ago. I shouldn't think he even remembers.'

And I'm going to do everything I can think of to stop him remembering, she resolved fiercely.

'Have you said anything to him?'

'*No.*' Rachel was unable to disguise her horror.

Mandy looked even more intrigued. Rachel realised she could be getting herself into exactly the kind of trouble she had hoped to avoid—the kind of trouble that slapped an ice-pack on the back of her neck and sent her normally logical mind into meltdown. She could trust Mandy, of course, but if she told her it was a secret Mandy would inevitably start to wonder what it was all about. It was only human nature. It was also horrifying.

I can't stand that sort of speculation, Rachel thought. How can I avoid thinking about him if every time I put my head out of my office my secretary's asking herself what Riccardo di Stefano was to me in my dark past?

She felt panic rise. It took all her self-control to quell it, to think of a plausible story. It was half the truth anyway.

'Look,' said Rachel, 'I'd be grateful if you didn't mention it. It was no big deal but I was very young.' She managed to sound rueful, even faintly embarrassed. She was impressed with herself. 'It wouldn't do my credibility much good to remind him. I don't want him thinking he's negotiating with a spotty teenager with no control over her temper.'

No hint of the inner panic. Well done, Rachel, she congratulated herself. Mandy was taking it at face value anyway.

'No control...' Mandy stared. 'You?'

'Youth,' said Rachel. She gave a very good shrug, quite as if she did not care. She even managed a light laugh.

That was not quite so convincing, evidently. At least, it did not convince Mandy. 'Did you have a crush on him?' she demanded.

'No,' said Rachel with unmistakable truth. In spite of

her determination to stay cool, she could not repress a shudder.

Mandy was not just a colleague, she was a friend. She saw the shudder and drew her own conclusions.

'Well, if he hasn't remembered yet, he probably won't,' she said comfortingly. 'Not with Sandy Marquis to keep him happy.'

'I'm relying on it,' said Rachel. She went into her office. In the doorway she paused and looked back. 'Oh, we've got a deadline. Two o'clock with Mr Jensen. You'd better find out what the group want in their sandwiches.'

Mandy grimaced. 'Right you are. Action stations.' She was already on the telephone when Rachel closed the door.

The room was uncannily quiet without the hum of the photocopier. Rachel sank down behind her desk and stretched out her legs in front of her. They were trembling.

There was an unfamiliar tension between her shoulder-blades. She bent her head forward and sideways and the tension eased. It did not go away entirely, though. If she was any judge, it was not going to go away until Riccardo di Stefano was safely back on his own side of the Atlantic.

'Blast,' she said.

She rubbed her hand across the back of her neck in an uncharacteristic gesture. The muscles felt like iron. Even as the thought crossed her mind, she remembered another time when she had done the same thing. Her hand fell.

Another time and a whole world away. She got up and went to the window. Outside the rain ran greyly down the window. But the world of her too vivid memory was drenched in sunshine.

Rachel tipped her head forward and rested her brow against the window-pane. How could she ever have thought she had forgotten?

She closed her eyes and let the memories flood back.

She had never wanted to go. She had tried so hard not to. But she had been eighteen and the opposition had all been over twenty-one and had had the big guns.

'It will be the holiday of a lifetime,' her father had said heartily. Too heartily. Rachel had not noticed that at the time, of course. 'You've been tying yourself to your books too much. Now the exams are over you deserve a really good time. Judy and I both want you to go.'

And that had been the first objection. Rachel had never warmed to her father's second wife. Judy felt the same, she'd been sure. Most of the time they'd been polite to each other but that was as far as it had gone. Rachel had frankly been appalled at the idea of going off on a Caribbean holiday with her stepmother for company.

She had not said that to her father, of course. And what she had said had only caused him to persuade harder.

'Judy needs a holiday as much as you do. It's been a tough year, with the takeover and everything. She needs to get away from it all. Sun, sea and a bit of exotic night-life.' He laughed. 'Do you both good.'

Rachel said, 'Exotic night-life doesn't sound like me, Dad.'

But he was not to be deflected. 'Nonsense. All girls of your age want to spread their wings a bit.'

Presumably Judy had told him that. Presumably she had also convinced him that she and Rachel were virtual contemporaries and could not be better friends. None of Rachel's protests had any effect.

'It's very good of Judy to suggest it,' her father said in the end.

His tone had stopped being hearty. Rachel recognised an order when she heard it. He might just as well have said she did not have a choice.

'She's been invited to stay with some very old friends. They have taken a house in the Caribbean. Film-star luxury, I'm told. Judy needn't take you along, you know. Since she's offered, you owe it to all of us to accept gracefully.'

So she went. Later it occurred to her to wonder whether her father was already suspecting his young wife's restlessness. Maybe he'd sent Rachel along to act as some sort of chaperon. Or even as a substitute for conscience. If he had, he had been singularly out of luck, she thought now.

She had not suspected any such thing at the time, of course. To be honest, Rachel had not seen much of her father or Judy, particularly over the last year when her father's company had got into difficulties. Rachel herself had been working furiously hard to get into university. She and her father had met occasionally over the coffee-pot in the small hours. They'd exchanged tired quips. But they had not really talked since he'd married Judy.

So, if there were strains in the marriage, at that time Rachel had not known it. She'd just known she did not like Judy, and she had not been able to imagine why her stepmother would want to take her on holiday.

It had been some time before she'd found out why, but she had. By that time she'd no longer cared. She'd had her own hurt and her own guilt by then. By that time she'd no longer cared about anything except getting away and never seeing any of the inhabitants of the Villa Azul ever again.

Rachel opened her eyes and stared blindly at the London rain. In all the three weeks she had spent at the Villa Azul, it had never rained once, she remembered. She would wake up in the huge colonial bed to a sound like rain, but when she'd rushed to the window it had been to find that the sound was only the wind through the palm trees. She had been so homesick. So hungry for familiar sights and sounds. So alone.

Open-eyed, she stared out at the rain. Alone! She gave a harsh laugh that contained no amusement at all. Oh, she had been alone all right. Until that last night, when she had learned, briefly and unforgettably, that there were worse things than being alone—and that the worst loneliness of all was when you could not reach the person you were with. She felt sick, remembering.

But there was nothing else for it. Now she had started, the whole thing was coming back in cruel Technicolor.

The first time she'd met Riccardo di Stefano she had almost run away. He had been like an alien from another galaxy. Well, they all had been, at the Villa Azul. By that time Rachel had learned to expect every new acquaintance to possess a degree of sophistication she knew she could not deal with. By the time he arrived, Riccardo di Stefano was exactly what she was expecting.

Tall and slim, he arrived in the Caribbean with an all-year-round tan and the inscrutable dark glasses to go with it. His hair was so dark that it looked blue in the glare of the midday sun. He was wearing piratical cut-offs that could have belonged to the ragged urchins in the town, had it not been for the indiscreet designer label at the back of the belt.

He was not bothering with a shirt that day and even to Rachel's jaundiced eye its absence revealed muscles that could only be called impressive. He moved lazily, gracefully, as if he knew every eye was on him and did not give a damn. Rachel loathed him on sight.

The Villa Azul loved him. It was only to be expected.

But by that time she was loathing the Villa Azul and all its inhabitants with a ferocity that she would never have thought possible. It could not have been further away from the relaxing holiday her father had fondly described. There was no possibility of relaxing. Rachel had never felt more on edge in all her eighteen years.

One thing her father had been right about was the luxury, though. Rachel had never seen anything like it. The house party seemed to drink champagne at all hours, change their designer outfits three times a day and have personal trainers and hairdressers in constant attendance.

In fact, at first she thought Riccardo di Stefano was a new fitness expert. Only, then he took off the arrogant shades to reveal even more arrogant eyes. Rachel revised her opinion rapidly.

Slowly he surveyed the company scattered round the pool and the exotic gardens. His expression announced that he was supremely bored. None of the tennis professionals and expert scuba-divers would have allowed themselves to look like that. It would have cost them their job. It did not make Rachel like him any better.

And then their eyes met.

It was oddly shocking. Even on edge as she was, Rachel felt her inner tension go up a couple of notches. She stepped back as if she had walked too close to a fire.

The stranger in the designer rags looked her up and down. Rachel had just come up from the beach to collect some fruit for her lunch. She had not bothered with a wrap because she did not intend to stay. She was going to go back to the beach and carry on reading in the shade of a coconut palm. Indeed, she was still marking the place in her book with one finger.

So all she was wearing was a dark one-piece bathing suit. By the standards of the Villa Azul it was modest to the point of puritanism. But, under that cool inspection, Rachel felt that she might as well have been naked. Her face flamed.

Even across the width of the flamboyant garden, the pirate recognised her reaction. His eyebrows rose. He was clearly amused. Rachel blushed harder, and hated him for it.

Nobody else paid any attention at all. At least, not to her. That was nothing unusual. The sophisticated house party had been bewildered by her arrival. Since then, they had done their best to ignore her. Because, of course, Judy had dumped her the moment they'd got to the estate.

'This is Bill's daughter,' she had said, waving a hand in Rachel's general direction.

After that she'd stripped off and dived into the pool. She had not exchanged more than a dozen words with Rachel since. She had not even bothered to introduce their host.

He was, Rachel discovered, Anders Lemarck and said to be something in oil. The other guests were vague on his profession but very precise on his wealth, which was described as serious. On their arrival, he'd considered Rachel appraisingly, decided she was not worth getting up for and raised a casual hand in her direction.

'Hi, Bill's daughter.'

After that he'd ignored her too. If it had not been for the friendly islanders who ran the Villa Azul, Rachel would not even have had anywhere to sleep.

'Part of my education,' the eighteen-year-old Rachel had told herself. 'Nobody said education had to be pleasant.'

She'd established a routine of swimming and reading, keeping out of the way of the main party as much as she could. Until now it had worked fine. But the piratical stranger was something else.

In spite of herself she could not look away. She stared into the face she did not recognise and knew that she would recognise it anywhere in the world for evermore. It was not just the barbecue-deep tan and insolent eyes. It was something that seemed to look right into the heart of her and imprint his image on her very core. Rachel felt helpless all of a sudden.

If the other guests continued to ignore her, they were more than enthusiastic to greet him. Women in tiny, jewel-coloured bikinis converged on him; men turned from discussing stock-market prices to greet him. Even Anders got out of his hammock to shake his hand.

And I'm no better, standing here like a mesmerised rabbit, staring at him, thought Rachel. She was disgusted with herself. It was a real physical effort to break that eye contact. Even across the garden she could feel his resistance. But she did it.

She turned away and made for the terrace where the luxurious cold lunch was set out. These days, Rachel had learned to mingle with the sophisticated diners with reasonable confidence.

She was bending all her attention on a dish of exotic fruits, when she felt a butterfly touch against her bare arm.

She brushed it away absently. Warm fingers caught and held her own.

Rachel gave a thoroughly unsophisticated squeak and let go of her plate. The pirate caught it neatly, one-handed.

'Don't tell me—you're the discus professional.' His voice was as casual as his appearance. Casual and low and horribly sexy.

He returned the plate to her with an enigmatic smile. Rachel swallowed hard. This was where that education proved its usefulness. She tried to remember all that the holiday had taught her about dealing with these people.

'Thank you,' she said, clutching at the plate. It tilted dangerously and half a mango fell off it. He caught that too.

'Not the discus,' he said thoughtfully. 'Maybe ping-pong?'

Rachel was embarrassed. That education did not seem to have stuck after all.

Annoyed with herself, she said curtly, 'Sorry, no,' and held out her hand for the fruit.

He turned it over with a grimace. 'Is this all you're eating?'

'I like fruit in the middle of the day.' Why did she sound so defensive?

His eyes crinkled at the corners. With half the garden between them she had thought his eyes were dark. Now she saw that they were a swirl of curious, complicated mineral colours, flecked with green. They were also oddly weary.

She thought suddenly, He looks as if he's seen everything in the world. And nothing matters to him any more.

She gave herself a quick shake. This was silly, melodramatic. He was a stranger. And not a very kind stranger, from the expression in those eyes. She did not think he would be kind if he knew what she was thinking about him, anyway.

He looked round at the little groups of people sitting under the trees.

'Who are you with?'

Rachel almost jumped. 'What?' Then she realised what he meant. 'Oh. I'm not. I mean—'

He looked surprised, his brows rising interrogatively. 'You don't eat with the guests?'

'No,' she admitted. It felt like owning up to her lack of sophistication all over again. She looked away.

He buffed his knuckles against the top of her arm.

'No need to look like that. So where do you take your plunder?'

She looked up at that, laughing in quick surprise. At once his eyes narrowed, became intent. Rachel saw that the hand holding the mango clenched. Then slowly, as if in an act of will, he relaxed his fingers and gave her a slow, lazy smile.

'Well? Do you climb a tree, or what?' The laughing voice said he shared her amusement.

'I've got a beach,' Rachel admitted. Laughter always warmed her. The trouble was—and she had not learned enough yet to know how dangerous this was—it also took her off her guard.

'Really? A whole beach?'

'Well, no one else seems to use it.'

The pirate looked over his shoulder at the party again. He shrugged.

'Surprise me,' he said cynically. 'Real sand, real seaweed?' He shook his head. 'Messy.'

Rachel chuckled.

For a moment those strange eyes widened. Then he seemed to shake himself. He looked down at the mango he was still holding. It was looking distinctly the worse for wear.

'You can't eat that.' He summoned one of the house staff by some magic semaphore which Rachel was not quick enough to catch. As the man appeared at his elbow, he said, 'Take this away, will you? And bring some food down to—' He broke off and turned compelling eyes on Rachel. 'Where is this magic beach of yours?'

It was at the far end of the estate, outside the cabin she had been allotted by the staff. There was no point in trying to hide the location. This was the servant who had shown her to her room three days ago. The man nodded.

'Coconut Beach. I know. Gladly, sir.'

The pirate took the plate out of her suddenly nerveless fingers. 'You won't need that. Ben's a professional. He'll bring everything we need for a beach picnic, won't you, Ben?'

'I will, sir.'

Rachel did not at all like the look they exchanged. It was not far short of a grin. She suspected masculine conspiracy. It annoyed her. Worse, it made her uneasy.

But she could hardly prohibit one of Anders' guests from visiting to one of Anders' private beaches.

She said, 'Maybe I won't have anything to eat, after all. It's hot.'

'Plenty of shade on Coconut Beach,' Ben said, thereby confirming Rachel's suspicions about masculine solidarity.

The pirate chuckled. 'Lots of ice in that picnic, Ben. Plenty of nice ice-cold drinks. Oh, and the lady likes fruit.'

The man nodded. 'Leave it to me.'

He went. Rachel found she had an arm round her shoulders. It was warm and sinewy and it felt like iron. Her heart began to slam uncomfortably. She made a move to draw away and the arm tightened as she had somehow known it would. It set her very slightly off balance, so that she had to lean against him.

She looked up, uncertain. He was smiling down straight into her eyes. His expression made her head swim.

'And now take me to the seaweed.'

He took her down the shallow steps of the terrace into the midday glare. Even in her confusion, Rachel was aware of the eyes watching them. For days her fellow guests had seemed barely aware of her existence. Now she felt as if she were in a spotlight.

The pirate seemed unaware. Or, if he was aware of it, he did not care. Still with that long arm round her, he skirted the pool area, with its spectacular apricot-veined marble, and swept her off into the shade of the casuarina trees.

He let her go then. It was not practical to walk along the uneven, sandy path side by side. But he did not stop touching her. The path through the casuarinas was dotted with fallen vegetation—things like cones and scaly brown twigs. He put out a hand to help her skirt them. He brushed away the feathery branches that drooped over the path, holding them back for her to pass. Once or twice, perhaps by accident, his hand brushed her loose hair.

It was flattering. It was also slightly alarming. Rachel ducked her head and made for the beach without daring to meet his eyes again.

They came out through a grove of trees whose name she did not know. They were slim-trunked and fanned out to make a loose canopy overhead. The sun made a sharply etched lace pattern of shadows beneath.

'We could sit here. In the shade,' said Rachel, holding back a little.

In the garden her swimsuit had felt modest until he'd looked at her. Out here, with no companion but the ocean and the pirate, she suddenly needed the covering of shadows.

He shook his head.

'No, we can't.'

'But I'd rather.' Her embarrassment felt like panic. Her voice came out too high, too defensive. 'I can't take too much sun. My skin—'

He looked at her. It was like a caress. It silenced her. The sexy smile grew.

'Believe me, your skin would not like sitting under manchineel trees.'

'What?'

He put a hand against one of the slim branches. It was a large hand, long-fingered and brown as a nut. For no reason she could think of, Rachel's mouth dried.

'Manchineel,' he said. 'Poison apple. Didn't anyone warn you?'

Rachel shook her head. 'What's to warn?'

He frowned. 'Well, the fruit's poisonous, but you probably would not eat that. The leaves give off a sticky sap like lime trees. It's not exactly poisonous but it can irritate the skin. Some people react badly. There have been nasty cases of blistering. The bad thing is to be under the trees when it rains. The rain washes the sap off the leaves onto the people taking shelter beneath.'

'Oh.' Rachel looked at the beach, powder-white in a sunlight so intense that it seemed to hum. The sky was so pale that it was hardly blue. There was not a cloud in sight. She put her head on one side. 'An immediate danger, do you think?'

He stopped frowning and gave a bark of laughter. 'Maybe not today.'

'I'll bear it in mind for the next time it rains.'

'Bear it in mind for the next time you look at your contract,' he said cynically. 'Suing Anders can be lucrative.'

Rachel stared. 'My contract?'

'Working conditions are not supposed to include poisonous trees. Unreasonable hazard, if you were not warned.'

'Working conditions?'

But he was not listening to her. He was running across the baking sand to the shade of the coconut palms. He looked fit and free and utterly at one with the wild landscape. Rachel followed more slowly.

So he had not realised she was a guest. In fact he had made exactly the same mistake about her as she had about him, when she'd first seen him. She thought about the other guests, their casual acceptance of every luxury, their brittle laughter and their dark, dark tans. He had recognised at once that she was a misfit. It was not really surprising, she thought wryly.

By the time she reached the tree he had found her sun-block and towel. He shook the towel free of sand and spread it for her ceremoniously. Rachel laughed and sat down. But the misunderstanding still worried her.

She said, 'Look, I know I don't fit in here—'

He interrupted. 'Why should you? You're twenty years younger than most of them.'

It was closer to thirty years, if she were honest. Most of the house guests were Anders' contemporaries.

'That's not the point.'

He dropped down beside her and Rachel fell abruptly silent. She found quite suddenly that she could not remember what she had been going to say. The pirate sent her an amused, comprehending glance.

'Oh, but it is. You're not here to fit in. You're here to help them convince themselves they're having a good time.' The cynicism was harsh.

Rachel shifted uncomfortably.

'I'm not—'

'Yes, you are.'

He stretched out, propping himself on one elbow, and looked at her. His eyes were not unkind but they had a remote expression. Once again Rachel had the overwhelming impression of weariness.

'What do you think you're here for? To run aerobics sessions? Guide them round the reef?'

She opened her lips to correct him but he waved the suggestion away before she could speak.

'It doesn't matter what it says in the contract. Your real job here is to be their audience.'

'What?'

'Such an innocent.' He sounded almost sad.

Unexpectedly he cupped her face. It was a tender ges-ture, quite without sexual intent. But it set something fluttering under Rachel's breastbone that she had never been aware of before. She drew back instinctively. His hand fell.

She rushed into speech, the words tumbling out, only half-aware of what she was saying. More aware of the small reverberations she could still feel in every nerve and muscle. Aware of the need to hide that schoolgirl vulnerability to his fleeting gesture.

'You don't understand. It's not like that at all. They don't want me as an audience. They don't want me at all. I should never have come. The way they look at me.'

He said quietly, 'You're talking about envy.'

Rachel shook her head violently.

'No, I'm not. You haven't seen it.' She remembered last night's barbecue, the way people's eyes had glazed over as she'd approached. 'It's as if I'm spoiling things somehow. Like I'm an alien or something—some creature that's put a tentacle out of the sea and pulled itself up the beach to spoil the party.'

There was a little silence. Rachel realised she was shaking.

At last he said slowly, 'Spoil the party?'

She made a helpless gesture. 'I know it must sound stupid.'

'No.' He sat up, propping himself against the bark of the coconut palm. 'No, it sounds very lifelike.' She felt his reflective gaze on her face. 'They really didn't know what they were getting in you, did they?'

Before she could answer there were footsteps behind them. The manservant appeared at the top of the slope, bearing a rush basket.

The pirate looked up.

'Our picnic,' he said, amused.

He got lazily to his feet and went to receive it. He exchanged words with the man which Rachel could not catch. Then he brought the basket back to the shade of the tree.

'He'll pick it up later. All we have to do is eat, drink and enjoy ourselves.' He looked at the pale crescent of sand and gave the first unshadowed smile she had seen from him. 'Shouldn't be too tough.'

It was not. They swam, then talked while Rachel unpacked the basket, finding delicacies wrapped in foil and cool-boxes. There was flaked crab in a spice that burnt the tongue, barbecued prawns soaked in lime, wonderful crisp bread, a cornucopia of exotic fruits, and wine—wine such as she had never imagined, sharp and sweet at the same time, the bottle icy cool in its astronaut suit.

The pirate did not eat much, she saw, though he watched her appreciation with lazy amusement.

'It's wonderful,' she sighed at last, licking mango juice from her fingers.

He was propped against the tree.

'You like your pleasures simple.'

'Simple…' She stared. Then, seeing he meant it, she burst out laughing. 'And what would you call luxury?'

He was watching her with an odd, quizzical expression. He shrugged at her question.

'Oh, something with linen tablecloths and at least three Michelin stars. You'd have to wear diamonds.'

Rachel choked. 'I almost never wear my diamonds to swim,' she said gravely.

His eyes crinkled at the corners. 'Why is that?'

'It attracts the sharks. Or so they tell me.'

For a moment the strong face tightened. 'I've heard that too.'

Rachel looked at him. He had been a friendly, easy companion over lunch. So why was she reluctant to ask him about himself? He was self-evidently not the usual type of visitor to the Villa Azul, in spite of his familiarity with the names of the staff and the quality of the company. What was more, he had elected to spend half the day in her company. Her curiosity was perfectly understandable. Yet she sensed a reserve in him which would not permit invasion. And she did not think he would be kind if she intruded too far.

So she did not ask him who he was and what he was doing as Anders' guest. Instead she said carefully, 'Meet a lot of sharks, do you?'

His expression was inscrutable. 'My share.'

Rachel looked away from him. They were facing a view of breathtaking beauty over the pale beach to the Caribbean Sea. In the sun it looked like a cloth of silver. The distant islands could have been painted on silk, as insubstantial as dreams.

She said softly, 'Well, there are none here.'

There was a pause. He neither moved nor spoke. All she could hear was the steady lull of the waves against the shore and the cicadas in the trees behind them. Then he gave a long sigh.

He said slowly, as if something new had occurred to him and he was examining it, 'You could just be right.'

He stretched. Out of the corner of her eye Rachel saw him move. Instinctively she tensed. Something in her had been waiting for him to make a move in her direction ever since she'd first set eyes on him. She had been aware of it, increasingly, all during the afternoon. It was exciting, but it troubled her all the same. She did not know what she was going to do about it.

But her wariness was unnecessary. He was only lowering himself to lie full-length under the palm. He crossed his arms behind his head and tipped his head back. He closed his eyes and made a noise indicative of total satisfaction.

His lips barely moving, he said, 'Wake me up when it gets dark.'

CHAPTER THREE

RACHEL spent the next three hours swimming and sunbathing and reading her novel. The pirate slept deeply beside her. At first she was disconcerted, even slightly piqued. But then she remembered the terrible weariness she had sensed and kept herself as quiet as a mouse in order not to disturb his rest.

Eventually he stirred. Rachel put down her book and looked at him. His eyes opened, drifted shut, stayed closed for a moment. Then they flew wide open, a startled expression in their depths.

'What—?'

Rachel laughed down at him gently. 'You were tired. You ate. You slept.'

His eyes flickered and went dark. His expression became unreadable. He continued to look up at her. Rachel shifted a little, suddenly uncomfortable under that unblinking stare. She tore her eyes away and made a great business of tidying up the last of their picnic. She even tried a little mockery to ease that sudden tension.

'You don't snore.'

He still watched her. For a moment she thought he was not going to reply.

Then he said idly, 'You reassure me.'

Still not looking at him, she wrapped glasses in the napkins Ben had provided and stowed them carefully. A thought occurred to her. She gestured to the picnic basket. 'Would you like something?'

'Well…' His voice became a drawl. 'Maybe I would, at that.'

Rachel was surprised but she peered inside the basket, inspecting the remains.

'Cheese, breadfruit, pineapple— *Oh!*'

He had reached out a lazy hand and pulled at her shoulder. Not expecting it, Rachel fell back onto the sand in a tumble of flying hair. She was twisting her head, brushing hair from her eyes and mouth when the sky above her went dark.

'Pass on the pineapple,' said the pirate, leaning over her. He was amused. He bent forward.

She had been half braced for it all day but now that it was happening it came at her out of the blue. Really, she had the sophistication of a six-year-old, Rachel castigated herself. What was more, now the moment had arrived, she had not the faintest idea what to do about it.

'Oh, Lord,' said Rachel, shutting her eyes.

It was not a demanding kiss. He feathered his mouth over her lips, her brow, her eyelids. He took his time and seemed to enjoy it. Rachel thought she could feel him smiling. She swallowed and tried to relax.

He made a small sound of satisfaction and turned her head so that he could kiss the soft, vulnerable place below her ear. Rachel quivered. Suddenly she did not have to try any more. She was relaxing spontaneously. Her limbs felt as if they were melting, moulding themselves round him. She felt lazy, luxuriously alive to her fingertips.

She thought of the boys she had kissed or wanted to kiss at the occasional party she'd got to in London. It had never felt like this. She was not quite sure where the difference lay but she knew it had felt a world away from this. In London she had felt hot and anxious, terrified—of doing the wrong thing, of being laughed at, of being hurt.

If she was terrified now, thought Rachel dimly, it was not of anything the pirate might do. It was of the way he was making her feel.

He kissed her jaw, so lightly that it felt as if he did no more than breathe on her. Unbidden, Rachel's body jackknifed into an arch. He gave a soft laugh, his hands gentling her down again onto the sand. He slipped the straps of her swimsuit away so that he could kiss her warm bared shoulders.

Her eyes drifted half-shut. She was breathing rapidly. Her head tipped back in an agony of expectation. At last—at *last*—he found her mouth. This time his kiss was shockingly far from gentle.

So far that, in spite of her own body's hunger, Rachel was frightened. Her muscles locked, quite beyond her control. She felt suffocated. She tried to turn her head away.

For a moment he would not let her. His body was fierce on hers. Then, abruptly, he let her go and swung away from her.

Rachel lay there for a moment, fighting for breath. Beside her, the pirate sat up and stared out to sea.

'Crossed wires, I think,' he said at last drily.

Rachel was embarrassed. That annoyed her.

'You mean because you jumped on me?' she snapped unfairly. 'Why on earth did you do that?'

He shrugged, looking bored. 'Jumped on you? It's called a kiss. You should know that by now, even if you don't use them. As for why... Because I wanted to. Don't you ever do things just because you want to?'

Rachel stared up at him, arrested. Her bad temper evaporated, taking embarrassment with it.

'No,' she said slowly, recognising the truth even as she said it.

He looked down at her then. The heavy eyebrows rose. 'You serious?'

She pushed herself away so that there was no chance of touching him and sat up. 'Yes.'

She pulled up the straps of her swimsuit, brushing the sand off her arms and shoulders. He watched her through narrowed eyes.

'You going to tell me why?'

'What?'

'Why you don't follow your instincts,' he said patiently.

Rachel shook her head. She felt odd. That must be why she'd told him the straight, unembroidered truth. Up till then she had not even recognised it herself.

She gave a short laugh. 'Oh, instincts. Something else I've heard about and don't use. As you must realise.'

She kept her head proudly high but she did not quite manage to meet his eyes. The pirate sat bolt upright. He looked at her broodingly.

Finally, he said ruefully, 'It looks like I've got more than I bargained for as well, doesn't it?' He put out a hand as if to touch her face and then changed his mind. 'Want to tell me about it?'

Rachel let out a breath she had not known she was holding.

'Not a lot to tell,' she said carefully. 'That's rather the point.'

She did meet his eyes then. He was taken aback but he did not pretend he did not understand.

'So why haven't those instincts of yours had an outing before? What have you been doing?' he said lightly. 'Living on a desert island? Hiding in a convent?'

Rachel gave a choke of laughter. 'Just about. Going to a girls' college and working for exams.'

'Ah. Working.' He nodded, as if he really did understand then. 'You can do too much of that.'

'All work and no play makes Jack a dull boy,' agreed Rachel. 'So my stepmother keeps telling me.'

At that he did touch her—not her face but her upper arm—running the back of his hand down her warm skin, almost as if he could not help himself.

'So you're at the Villa Azul to learn to play.'

'*No.*' Rachel sounded appalled.

He flung back his head and laughed.

She was confused, blushing. 'Oh, I didn't mean it like that. Not the way it sounded.'

'Yes, you did,' he contradicted her, still chuckling.

'Nothing wrong with that. They're not exactly role models, Anders and his cronies. I should have remembered that. Now, what you need is—'

But Rachel was not to hear what the pirate thought she needed. Ben had appeared, slithering down the slope to them.

'You finished, Mr Rick?' he asked.

The pirate hesitated. Then he shrugged and got to his feet.

'I guess so.' He looked down at Rachel. 'For the moment.'

The manservant gave him a quick look. He said without expression, 'Mr Lemarck been asking where you are.'

'I'll bet he has.'

'You want to talk to him, better be quick. Got a big party tonight. Guest's birthday.'

Rachel stood up too. She held out her hand to the pirate. 'Better be going, then. It takes everyone long enough to get ready for the small parties,' she said wryly.

He took her hand but he did not shake it. He held onto it. 'I guess you're right. I'll see you this evening.'

Ben's expression became wooden.

Rachel said hastily, 'I'm not sure. I've had a lot of sun today. Maybe I'll just—'

The hand holding hers tightened. 'I obviously didn't make myself clear,' said the pirate softly. 'Let me lay it on the line for you. I'll see you at the party. If I don't, I come get you. Your choice.'

Under the manservant's expressionless gaze, he pulled her towards him and gave her a brisk kiss. It was neither passionate nor seductive but it shocked Rachel to the core. It spoke of total possession.

Then he hoisted the picnic basket and set off up the sandy slope. Startled out of his perfect training, Ben exchanged one stunned look with Rachel and then dashed after him. Rachel could hear them arguing about who carried the basket until the engine of the shooting-brake started up.

She gathered up her towel and book. As soon as she was sure that the engine noise had died away and they were not coming back for any reason, she toiled up the slope. The faint evening breeze was just beginning to whip up from the sea but it was not because of that warm current of air that she was trembling when she reached her cabin. She closed the door and leaned against it, trying to collect her wits.

The cabin was at the very far end of the Villa Azul's grounds, half-hidden behind a hedge of bougainvillea and a huge hibiscus bush. A pretty maid, about her own age, came every day to change the linen. Apart from that daily visit, Rachel had been left severely alone, with her palm trees and her sea views. It had suited her very well up to now. This evening, for the first time since she'd arrived, Rachel would have given anything for the company of one of her friends.

But there was no one to discuss the pirate's strange behaviour, still less her own uncertain reaction to it. So Rachel, being a practical girl, climbed out of her swimsuit and into the shower. She was washing her salt-encrusted hair for the second time when she heard the door rattle.

For a moment she froze. Then she heard her name called. It was a woman's voice.

'I'm in the shower,' she called back.

'I'll wait.' It had to be Judy, thought Rachel in surprise.

'Just let me rinse my hair and I'll be out.'

She did so and padded into the main room, wrapping her hair turbanwise in one of the Villa Azul's daily clean towels. She was swathed in another. Her stepmother was sitting at the elegant dressing table, peering at herself in the mirror. When Rachel came out of the bathroom, she swung round.

'I've been swimming,' said Rachel, instantly defensive.

Judy looked resigned. But all she said was, 'I hope you brought enough conditioner. Sea-water is terribly drying.'

Rachel was even more surprised. Judy did not bother herself with her stepdaughter's appearance even in London. Here at the Villa Azul she had done her best to ignore her existence.

Judy read her expression. Briefly, she looked uncomfortable. She started fiddling with the trinkets on the dressing table.

'You'll want to look your best tonight. It's going to be a big party.'

'Even bigger?' Rachel asked drily. She sat on the bed and curled her legs under her, watching her stepmother's reflection interestedly.

Judy ignored the barb, if she noticed it.

'Yes. Anders has got Corporal Lili to play. And the local steel band, of course. Some guitarist for later. Dinner is formal and then there'll be dancing on the lawn.' She drew a long breath and came to what was clearly the ultimate in these delights. 'Lots of Press, of course.'

She sent Rachel a quick look in the mirror and gave a little laugh. It sounded false.

'Of course, I know it's not your sort of thing. No disco or teenage yobs. But it will be a once-in-a-lifetime experience for you. You can't pass it up. Not a party like this.'

Rachel's eyes narrowed. She knew quite well that she could not pass it up. Not unless she wanted a pirate to come looking for her in her private quarters—with consequences she was certain that she was not equipped to deal with. But she did not tell Judy that. She was wondering exactly why Judy wanted her there. She was prepared to be devious to find out.

So she stretched and said, 'Oh, I don't know.' She did not try telling Judy she had had too much swimming and sun. She gave Judy an excuse she would believe. 'I haven't got the clothes for a jet-set party.'

Judy stopped playing with the dressing-table trinkets and swung round.

'I know,' she said eagerly. 'I thought you'd want to borrow. I brought a couple of things over.'

She nodded at the wardrobe and Rachel realised the door was supporting hangers draped in silk and glitter that had not been there before. She considered them for a moment. Then she shrugged.

'I'm not a sequin sort of girl.'

Judy's face darkened. 'Don't be difficult, Rachel. They're both designer names.'

Rachel plumped up the pillows and settled down into them. She was enjoying herself.

'Maybe I'm not a designer girl either.'

Judy's fists clenched. But she knew that Rachel was winding her up. 'If you want to turn up in your jeans, that's up to you.'

Rachel smiled. 'I don't want to turn up at all,' she pointed out.

Judy looked alarmed. 'You've got to.' Her voice rose unattractively. She brought it under control. 'You're as much a guest here as I am. It would be unforgivable if you cut Anders' big party.' Her eyes hard, she said with deliberation, 'People would talk.'

Rachel raised her brows.

Judy drew a deep breath. 'Look, it's my birthday.'

For some reason it sounded like a confession. Rachel stared uncomprehending. Then, suddenly, she saw.

'It's not Anders' big party at all, is it?' she said slowly. 'It's yours.'

Judy looked away, shrugging.

Abruptly Rachel stopped enjoying herself. She sat up. 'What's going on, Judy?'

Judy looked back at her. Her eyes were bitter, though her painted lips stretched into a smile. 'Oh, come *on*, Rachel.'

All Rachel's suspicions suddenly became a certainty. She felt slightly sick.

'You're having an affair with Anders, aren't you? You're not even trying to be discreet about it.'

'You noticed!' Judy mocked.

'So why on earth did you want me along?' Rachel cried.

'Why on earth do you think? To keep your father quiet, of course.'

Rachel's lip curled. 'You mean you still have a use for him?'

To her surprise, Judy did not lash out at that. Instead her eyes fell. For a moment, for all the exquisite make-up and the elegant clothes, she looked haunted and almost old.

'You don't know what it's like,' she said, half to herself. 'Wanting him so much. Never *knowing*…'

'Don't!' Rachel's voice was harsh. In spite of herself, she was curious. 'Why didn't you marry him?'

Judy's incredulous look was answer enough.

'So you still need my father to pay your bills.'

'No. Well, not only that. I need—a place in the world. I'm not like you. You'll have your degree, a career. I haven't got any of that. If I'm not a wife, I'm nothing.'

Rachel's laugh hurt. 'And I thought you were a rich man's mistress.'

Judy shook her head. Her chandelier earrings jingled. 'Holiday fantasy, darling. Real life is back in London, waiting. At least—'

'As long as you don't burn your boats out here,' interpreted Rachel.

Judy was smiling again. 'Of course. Which is why you must turn up this evening. Too many gossip columnists not to. What do you think the papers will say if my stepdaughter isn't there? Do you want your father to read *that*?'

There was a long silence.

'You mean you want me there for the press call,' Rachel said at last.

Judy laughed. 'If that's the way you want to put it…'

She went over to the wardrobe and took down the hangers. 'Try them on. You've never worn anything like this. Come on, Rachel; you're a woman, aren't you? Live a little.'

Rachel just looked at her. Judy lost her temper. She flung the clothes across the end of the bed.

'Please yourself. And if your father doesn't like the gossip—' her tone was suddenly malicious '—you can tell him exactly why you fell down as a security guard.'

She stamped out. Rachel felt sick and rather dirty. She went and stood under the shower again until she felt better. When she came out, her hair conditioned and smelling of orange-flowers, the abrupt Caribbean night had fallen.

There was a knock on the door. Warily Rachel went to answer it. But it was only Stephanie, one of the maids.

'Oh, it's you. Come in.'

Stephanie smiled. 'I came to see if you wanted any help.'

Rachel was suspicious. 'Did my stepmother send you?'

Stephanie looked surprised. 'Nobody sent me. All the ladies want their dresses pressed, taken up, taken down. I thought you might too. What are you wearing?'

Rachel looked with dislike at the multicoloured heap on the end of the bed.

'Oh,' said Stephanie, intrigued.

'Borrowed. From God knows who. Not Judy—she's the wrong size. I'm assured they're *very* expensive.' Even to herself she sounded savage.

'Oh,' said Stephanie again in tones of complete understanding. 'Perhaps you would prefer something else?'

'I'd prefer not to go at all.'

But if I don't, she thought, and the papers pick it up as Judy thinks they will, Daddy will read it and be hurt. I can't do that to him. Not after the year he's had. Oh, why did he send me along? It's crazy, expecting me to chaperon a woman twice my age.

'Then why not stay here?'

'Family obligations,' Rachel said with a ghost of a smile.

'Ah.' Diplomatically Stephanie did not comment further. Instead she was rummaging at the bottom of the chest of drawers. A strong smell of lavender filled the room. Stephanie gave a cry of triumph and stood up with her prize. Rachel stared.

'What's that? It looks like a counterpane.'

Stephanie threw the material away from her. It billowed up and floated down onto the bed, in shades of smoke and copper and gold.

'A sarong,' she explained.

Rachel picked up a corner. 'It still looks like a counterpane. What do you do with it?'

Stephanie showed her, whipping the fine stuff round her over her green-checked uniform and knotting it between her breasts. Rachel regarded it dubiously. Without the green-checked dress, she thought, it was going to be terribly revealing. She said so.

Stephanie laughed and picked up the nearest hanger. She held the sequinned top against Rachel. It was evident that the neckline plunged dangerously low.

'I see what you mean,' Rachel admitted.

'You are not so pale any more. And if you put that wonderful hair on top like this…' Stephanie showed her in the mirror, warming to her theme. 'You need long earrings. Bangles. A gold chain or two.'

Rachel turned away from the sarong material, sighing. 'No jewellery. Sorry.'

Stephanie was not put out. 'I will borrow. You do not need anything valuable. Just the things that the ladies would wear to sit by the swimming pool. I will ask.'

And she was gone.

So an hour later Rachel pushed her way through the casuarina trees at the far end of the garden, feeling extraordinarily exposed and shy. The warm breeze touched her skin, reminding her constantly that her shoulders were bare. She wore long jet earrings, emphasising her pale throat and the soft tendrils of red-gold hair that escaped artlessly from Stephanie's inspired swirl.

But Stephanie had relented as far as further jewellery was concerned. Instead, Rachel had a golden trumpet of hibiscus in her hair and another at her waist. In the mirror she had looked like a stranger—a beautiful, exotic stranger with apprehensive eyes.

She stood for a moment in the shadow of the trees, watching the party. It was obviously as sophisticated as Judy had said it would be. She could not see her host or the chart-topping group he had hired but there was a fair crowd of expensively dressed people on the terrace and round the pool. Rachel noted white dinner jackets and jewel-coloured silks and shrank back into the grateful shade of the trees. She wished herself anywhere else in the world.

There was no sign of the pirate.

She drew a deep breath and made her way to the terrace. Above the background music, the cocktail party buzz and the clink of glasses, her ear caught snippets of conversation.

A long-legged blonde called Helen was saying, 'Sylvie's here.'

Her companion expressed surprise.

'She rang earlier,' Helen said. 'She's with the Lamberts. The yacht docked in St Lucia yesterday. So when she called Anders asked them to the party.' She added in a voice pregnant with meaning, 'She's bringing them over. And Riccardo.'

The companion was satisfactorily impressed. 'Riccardo di Stefano? I thought that was over.'

Helen giggled. 'So does he. So does everyone except poor Sylvie.'

Rachel turned away, wincing for the unknown Sylvie. But the next overheard gossip was even more unpalatable.

'Do you think she'll get him?' a grey-haired woman was

saying. She wore a skintight coral dress with a neckline that plunged to her navel. Everything you could see, and you could see a lot, was as brown as a coconut.

'Judy? Get Anders? Shouldn't think so.'

Rachel stiffened and stopped strolling.

Someone else said, 'He didn't stop her marrying her dull Englishman. Don't see why he should bother now.'

Rachel stood as if turned to stone. Oh, Daddy, she thought. Poor, poor Daddy.

'So why is he giving a party like this for her?'

'Don't be silly darling,' said the grey-haired woman. 'Anders always gives a big party when he's at the Villa Azul. It's supposed to be fun but really he asks all the people he wants to do business with. Kent and I were asked months ago when he started negotiating for the Gregor field. Judy has just hijacked it, that's all. She's trying to manipulate him.'

'Then she's lost her touch,' said a short, dark-haired man indifferently. 'God, you women! Millionaires are dangerous to your health.'

How right you are, thought Rachel. Her skin crawled. A passing waiter held out a tray to her. She took one of the offered glasses, uncaring as to its contents, and took a great gulp.

It was champagne. Of course. Trying not to cough, Rachel turned away. She felt bitterly scornful of the whole party and everyone there.

Then, across the terrace, she saw her stepmother. After what she had just heard, she was almost sick. Hard-eyed, Rachel watched Judy's progress.

Her stepmother was certainly doing her best to act the hostess. She drifted from group to group, putting proprietorial hands on people's backs as she exchanged a few words, summoning waiters to top up emptying glasses, making sure she was seen doing just that. Judy might say she wanted to stay married, but she clearly wanted everyone to see her position at Anders' side more. Rachel's sympathy for her father turned into slow-burning rage.

Judy caught sight of her. She came over, her eyes sharp. The rage seemed to be mutual.

'What on earth are you wearing?'

Rachel did not answer. She was too angry. She folded her lips together tight in order not to say exactly what she was feeling.

Judy glared for a moment, then shrugged. 'Oh, well, at least it looks original, I suppose. Now, dinner—there's a table plan by the bar. I suggest you have a look.'

Rachel nodded.

Judy's voice hardened. 'And try to behave in a civilised fashion. All this glowering is very embarrassing. You're only making yourself look utterly naïve.'

Anders had appeared at the far end of the kidney-shaped pool, talking to knot of people. He looked serious and so did they. Rachel could well believe their conversation was pure business.

Judy caught sight of him. She took no more notice of Rachel. She picked up two glasses of champagne and went purposefully to his side. Rachel watched.

Judy was wearing tiger-striped chiffon and quantities of gold chains which chinked as she moved. Her eyelids, Rachel saw now in the light of the brilliant poolside torches, were as gold as her jewellery. She looked like a Hollywood pattern of a pagan princess. She gave Anders his champagne but she slipped her hand into the arm of another man in the group. Her eyes were challenging.

Her words floated up to Rachel. 'Oh, good. Another lovely eligible bachelor. I haven't seen you for ages, Ricky.'

The man she was standing next to looked down at her. He was tall and elegant in his dinner jacket but something in the gesture made him seem preoccupied. Another of Anders' business cronies pretending to be on holiday, Rachel thought, her lip curling.

Then he turned slightly and the harsh lights threw his profile into relief. Rachel received yet another shock—her worst yet. It was the pirate.

She stood mesmerised. Her hands slowly clenched on the terrace balustrade. It seemed impossible that he should not look up and see her, so intense was her gaze.

Someone else noticed.

'Who's that? Oh, di Stefano,' said the grey-haired woman on whom Rachel had eavesdropped earlier. 'Back from South America, then.' She leaned over the balustrade, peering. 'I heard he'd been ill. Doesn't look it, does he? Heck, he's a good-looking man.'

'Isn't he heaven?' said a girl who answered, to Rachel's surprise, to the name of Monkey. She added wistfully, 'Do you know him?'

Another woman laughed. 'I had a bijou flingette with him in Aspen last year. Heaven just about covers it. Trouble is, it never lasts with him.'

'All that turbulent Italian blood, darling,' said the grey-haired one. 'Can't expect it to last.'

'Italian? But surely…? He sounds American.'

'Fourth-generation New York but the family came from Genoa originally. Great-grandfather was a black sheep, though he made money fast enough. Riccardo always says he was thrown out for seducing the mayor's daughter.'

'It's in the genes, then,' sighed Monkey.

'That and the rest,' said the woman from Aspen. 'Everything he touches turns to gold.'

Rachel wanted to turn away, not to hear the cynical gossip. She had *liked* the pirate. Yet she had to listen.

'Slippery?' asked the grey-haired woman, unsurprised.

'As an eel, darling. Don't know why Sylvie doesn't face it. Like he says himself, he travels light.'

'And does he travel,' agreed the other. She turned to Rachel. 'Known him long?'

'What?' Rachel jumped at being directly addressed. She

pulled herself together quickly. 'Oh, no. We've only just met. I didn't even know his name.'

The other women exchanged glances.

One of them said kindly enough, 'Di Stefano's a heartbreaker. He should leave a baby like you alone.'

Rachel flushed. 'He has. I mean, we only met. We just talked. I—'

I was going to meet him this evening. He was going to come and get me if I didn't come to the party. He slept beside me on my beach this afternoon. He kissed me; he teased me about my instincts. I thought he was *different*.

Well, of course, said a newly awakened, cynical voice in her head. He would not be much of a heartbreaker if he could not manage to convince a girl that he was different. Suddenly her anger took on a new focus, directed no longer at the Villa Azul sophisticates, no longer at Anders, not even at Judy in her predatory gold. Riccardo di Stefano, pirate heartbreaker and liar.

Oh, she would show him, Rachel vowed. She was trembling with outrage. She would make him sorry, as none of the other girls had ever managed to make him sorry. She would puncture that ego, tear off that charming, lying mask, make him *hurt* as he had hurt so many others. And then she would laugh.

CHAPTER FOUR

RICCARDO had said that, in Rachel, he had got more than he'd bargained for with her. He was going to find out how true that was, Rachel promised herself. But first she was going to have to make herself look like the rest of Anders' party people.

She retreated to one of the downstairs cloakrooms and considered the problem in the mirror. She was not alone. The sumptuous blonde called Helen was painting her sultry eyelids with a tiny brush. She ignored Rachel but when the door opened and Monkey came in she gave a little shriek of pleasure.

'Darling. Wondered if you'd be here.'

They air-kissed. Monkey sat down on a little dressing stool and began to make liberal use of the cosmetics set out there for the use of guests. They sat side by side, concentrating on composition.

'Have you seen who's here?' said the blonde, her mouth not moving as she drew a careful outline. 'Ricky.'

Monkey sent her a warning look in the mirror.

'Trust you, Helen. Yes, I've seen him in the distance. He's been spending time with—' She gave up on Rachel's name and nodded her head in her direction.

'Really?' The blonde removed the little brush carefully and turned incredulous eyes on Rachel. 'Have we met?'

'My stepmother is a friend of Anders,' Rachel said curtly.

'Oh.' Helen nodded, understanding perfectly. 'The college girl. You're staying here.'

Rachel nodded. She contemplated the cosmetics critically. Should she go for the natural look or go for the high glamour of Judy and Helen? With the paint-box before her the possibilities were infinite.

Helen was evidently still intrigued by her audience with the pirate. 'You've actually talked to Ricky di Stefano?'

You would think he was a rock star, Rachel thought contemptuously. She shrugged. 'A bit.'

There was a respectful silence.

'It must be because you're clever,' the blonde and sultry Helen said at last, plainly bewildered. 'He's supposed to be the most brilliant trader on Wall Street.'

'No, that's wrong, darling,' Monkey corrected her. 'Money is in the family.'

'Yes, but he quarrelled with his family. Never sees them. He made this million all by himself.'

Monkey looked suitably reverent.

'Could that be why everyone says he's so attractive?' Rachel wondered aloud.

She leaned forward, trying a purple-grey shadow on the corner of her eyelids. A glittery-eyed reflection looked back at her, cool and dangerous.

Helen gave her a dry look. 'Honey, if you don't know why Rick di Stefano's attractive, you're even younger than you look.'

Rachel looked down at the paint-box, willing herself not to blush. She swirled the brush around savagely in some gold-shot bronze shadow. 'He's hardly the most good-looking man around.'

'Oh, looks,' Monkey waved them aside. 'It's the way he makes you feel when he looks at you.' She gave a little shiver which strained the bikini-top to her vibrant dress almost to breaking-point. 'Mmm. All weak and wonderful.'

'He doesn't make me feel like that,' said Rachel defiantly.

The two women looked at each other and laughed. They went out.

Left alone, Rachel darkened her thick lashes, painted dramatic shadows about her madeira-wine eyes, and turned her mouth a luminous browny-gold. When she was satisfied, she stepped away from the mirror, fluffed up her hair and lowered the top of the sarong to a level that was just about decent.

'That will give Judy a run for her money,' she told her reflection with satisfaction.

She might not look like a Hollywood princess but she was young and she had been to enough parties to have learned a certain style. Judy, she resolved grimly, was not going to know what hit her. And nor were any of the rest of those cynical beauties.

And nor was Riccardo di Stefano. Her heart hurt when she thought about him. He had seemed so different. On the beach he had talked as if he and she were on the same side. It was an agony to find that they weren't. He was in the same team as Helen and Monkey and the whole crew of the Villa Azul. How he must have been laughing at her this afternoon.

Well, he was not going to laugh any more, Rachel vowed as she made her way to the pool area. The borrowed sarong clung to her legs as she walked. The night air was cool on her exposed shoulders. She felt like a war maiden, utterly ready to go into battle.

She did not look at Riccardo as she went up to the group.

'Good evening,' she said quietly.

Anders looked up. His surprise was almost comical as he took in her appearance. He pursed his lips in a soundless whistle.

'Hel*lo*, Rachel. Giving the party a chance?' He looked quickly at Judy, who was still clinging to Riccardo di Stefano's arm. 'You look good enough to eat. So when does the ice thaw, sweetheart?'

Judy let go of di Stefano's arm and gave a tinkling laugh. 'Or a refugee from *South Pacific*. Darling, did you think it was a fancy-dress party?'

Two hours ago, Rachel would have blushed and fled. Now, however, she was armoured by her anger—anger and a queer coldness, as if a limb had been amputated and she had not quite begun to feel the pain yet.

So she put a hand to the hibiscus flower in her hair and caressed it. It was an affected, even a flirtatious gesture. It was meant to be. Although she was not looking at him she could feel Riccardo staring at her.

'This, do you mean? I thought it would help me melt into the background,' Rachel said sweetly.

One of the men—not Riccardo di Stefano—laughed. Judy's face darkened.

Anders said quickly, 'I hope you won't, though. Not now you've made up your mind to join us at last.' He said to the others in explanation, 'Rachel has been very tired. We left her to recover in her own time. You will sympathise with that, Rick.'

Rachel did not understand that last remark, but she knew she had run out of excuses to ignore Riccardo di Stefano. Reluctantly, she turned. He was looking stunned. It pleased her. It was some balm to her sore heart.

Di Stefano said slowly, 'Rachel?'

'A relation of Judy's,' Anders said smoothly. He made the introductions swiftly. 'Letitia and Ronnie Lambert. Sylvie Ford. Piers Hilton-Dennis. Riccardo di Stefano.'

'We've met,' di Stefano said curtly, cutting over the polite murmurs of the others.

He did not look very pleased about it. The man who had threatened to come and get her if she did not turn up to the party seemed strangely unenthusiastic now that she was here as instructed, she thought. It turned the knife a little deeper in the wound.

Rachel pretended to study him from under mascaraed lashes. In fact she was startled by the alteration in him. It was not just that he had changed out of his cut-off jeans into the black-tie uniform of the businessman at play. With the dark jacket and trousers had come an indefinable air of authority. He looked older and far more tense, as if his patience was on a very short rein.

Rachel shrugged. It was nothing to do with her if he chose to behave like a chameleon. As long as he did not hurt her, it did not matter what he did. And it was up to her to see that he did not hurt her, at least any more than he had done already. She got back into her new character and held out her hand, prettily.

'Yes, but we didn't introduce ourselves. Hello, Mr di Stefano.' Her whole manner said that he was a generation ahead of her and she was a nicely behaved adolescent. That should get him on the raw, she thought.

His expression was unreadable. 'Hello, Rachel.'

He took her hand. But instead of shaking it he carried it to his lips. It was not a conventional, polite brushing of the air above her knuckles either, but a real kiss. It was quite deliberate and it was not intended as a compliment.

Her careful indifference turned to ashes. Rachel jumped and snatched her hand away. She tried hard not to blush. She was not sure she was successful.

Sylvie Ford looked at her narrowly. She was not unsympathetic, Rachel thought. It was an added humiliation.

Sylvie was a dark gamine beauty with lines round her eyes which revealed that she was not as young as her dress sense invited you to think. Or as carefree. Now she took hold of Riccardo's arm.

'Have you been hiding behind dark glasses again, darling? You know, it's really not fair, going around like a prince in disguise.'

'On the contrary,' he said coolly, not taking his eyes from Rachel's flustered face. 'If anyone was in disguise, it was Rachel.'

Sylvie gave a little crow of laughter. She sounded genuinely delighted.

'Then now you know what it's like. I hope it teaches you a lesson.'

His eyes dropped to Rachel's painted and glowing mouth.

'Do you know, I think it just might,' he drawled.

He lifted his eyes and met Rachel's. Startled, she recognised a rage as great as her own. Only, it was far better controlled. She took a step backwards from pure instinct.

Riccardo di Stefano smiled. It was not a nice smile. And it was very clear whom it was aimed at. Somehow she had managed to turn Riccardo di Stefano into a personal enemy. It shook Rachel to the core. And, although she did not want to think about it now, beyond the shock there was a grief as great as for the loss of a friend.

She was not the only one disconcerted. There was a sharp little silence. Then three of the group started to talk at once.

'Time you looked at the seating plan,' Judy said sharply to Rachel.

At the same time, Sylvie said to Riccardo, 'Darling, we really ought to say hello to Marthe.'

With an apologetic smile at Anders, she began to draw him away. She looked like a small, determined tug towing a liner. Riccardo did not acknowledge anyone, even his host, by so much as a look. But at least he went. When he had gone there was a collective sigh of relief.

'That man gets more impossible every time,' muttered Hilton-Dennis.

Anders looked sharp and spiteful suddenly. 'If he weren't so damned successful, I wouldn't give him the time of day. But face it, Piers—we need men like that. The new generation.'

He glowered at di Stefano's departing figure. Nor was he alone, Rachel saw. From the way he and Sylvie were received, it seemed that the men were at least as resentful as they were admiring. By contrast, the women did not attempt to disguise the fascination he had for them. Which presumably made their escorts even more equivocal.

Not that Riccardo di Stefano noticed. In fact, he did not seem to be noticing anyone very much that night—not his host, not the gamine beauty on his arm, not anyone from the eager groups who greeted him. No one except Rachel.

He seemed as if he could not take his eyes off her. Every time she looked up, there he was, his narrowed gaze fixed on her, his face expressionless.

Rachel stopped pretending to circulate and watched him.

He was neither the tallest nor the most handsome man there by any measure. But there was an indefinable presence about him, like an invisible cloak, which made people turn towards him as if they felt its touch. Was it something to do with the cool, commanding air he had? He was not handsome. He had heavy brows and high, haughty cheekbones that made him look hard and cold as an iceberg.

In fact this evening he was looking so cold that Rachel found it difficult to believe he was the same man who had kissed her on the beach. Yet this was the man that those women she had overheard knew, not the casual pirate.

Could they really find him attractive? she wondered, shivering. You could burn yourself on the ice in his eyes. Yet as he mingled with the party-goers women turned to him as if they needed something from him. Heaven preserve me from ever needing anything from Riccardo di Stefano, Rachel prayed. That would be a cruel trap indeed.

She meant it. In her deepest soul, she was afraid that it was a trap in which she was already snared.

They sat down to dinner even later than usual. Rachel had not managed to find where she was supposed to be sitting but Riccardo took her by the elbow and propelled her into a chair beside his own at Anders' table. From Judy's glare, Rachel inferred that this was not at all what her stepmother had intended.

'Now,' he said.

Waiters brought tureens of some gourmet soup. The smell was delicious but Rachel found she could not eat a mouthful with Riccardo di Stefano watching her. His deep-set eyes had laughter lines at the corners. At the moment he was not laughing.

'What did you say your name was?'

Rachel sat ramrod-stiff. 'Rachel McLaine.'

'McLaine.' He thought about it, then shook his head. 'And not a sports professional to amuse the guests. So what exactly is it that you do for Anders?'

'Nothing at all,' snapped Rachel. She was not so young that she could not spot innuendo. Her loathing of Riccardo di Stefano increased to a new record. 'My stepmother is a house guest.' Thus she neatly disclaimed any association with Anders herself.

He pursed his lips in a soundless whistle, looking across the table at Judy. 'Stepmother, is it?'

Rachel flushed. Even with her intentions towards Anders becoming painfully clear, Judy could not quite keep the hunger out of her eyes when she looked at Riccardo di Stefano.

Rachel said sharply, 'My father thought she needed a break.'

His eyes mocked. 'And you came along for a free ride?'

She hated him so much then. She could think of nothing more satisfying than to confirm all his prejudices.

'And the free beach, the free parties and the free champagne,' she agreed, baring her teeth in a smile that should have turned his blood cold.

It had no noticeable effect. In fact he did not even look surprised. If she had not sensed that deep, controlled anger earlier, Rachel would have said she was boring him. She was so furious that she went on the offensive.

'And what's your reason for being here?'

That did startle him. He did not look pleased but at least this time he looked at her as if he realised there was someone there. It was exhilarating.

'I was on holiday,' he said with bite.

'Was?'

'"A peaceful break" was what they said. No one was supposed to know how to get hold of me.'

Rachel looked round at the party and lowered her lashes as she had seen Judy and Monkey do. She mocked him with an innuendo of her own.

'Oh, boy, did you come to the wrong place if you didn't want to be got hold of.'

Riccardo's eyes narrowed. 'I take it we've met before? I mean before that charming pastoral interlude this afternoon.' His voice was cynical.

That hurt. She was not going to let him see how much. So Rachel widened her eyes at him as innocently as she could manage. 'Well, I've heard a lot of your advance publicity today. Does that count?'

For a moment he looked as if he was about to burst into flames. 'If it meant that you came looking for me, it counts,' he said. He sounded grim.

Rachel quailed. She was not going to let him see that either. 'Why should I come looking for you?'

'The pastoral idyll,' he drawled. 'Rather a good ploy with a man who is known to be looking for—peace.'

Rachel sat very straight in her spindly chair. Suddenly she did not want to play games any more. She spat, 'Just what are you implying?'

'Implying? Nothing. I'm congratulating you on your tactics, Rachel McLaine.'

The drawl was more pronounced and his lids dropped steeply, hiding his expression. But his whole attitude, from the lounging body to the lazy voice, was insolent. Calculatedly insolent, Rachel thought. Only just on this side of downright insult and quite deliberately so.

Rachel would not have believed mere words could hurt her so much. She actually caught her breath at the pain. Then she rallied. She had promised herself she would teach him a lesson. By heaven, he deserved that someone should do just that.

So she said with contrived sweetness, 'I'm flattered, of course. But I don't quite see what there is to congratulate me on.'

'Don't you? Everyone else here does.'

She raised her eyebrows.

'I wouldn't have spent the afternoon with any other

woman here,' he explained in a reasonable voice. 'They know it, too.'

Rachel gasped. For a moment her eyes blazed. Riccardo laughed.

'Your marketing strategy is impressive,' he told her softly. 'It's a great skill—not to let the punter know he is being marketed to. You're a natural.'

Rachel went cold with a fury she would not have believed herself capable of. Her feelings towards Anders and Judy paled in comparison with it. She even forgot her betrayed and hoodwinked father in her outrage.

She said chokingly, 'At least I'm not a playboy. A vain, silly playboy.'

He leaned back in his chair, toying with his wineglass. He did not even look annoyed.

'Rude,' he said, sounding pleased. 'A shift of marketing strategy? Or do you get upset when your target sees through you?'

Rachel had got hold of herself. She managed a smile, though her cheeks felt as if they would crack with the effort. 'Only when everyone else is falling over themselves to lay out the red carpet. I like to think of it as redressing the balance.'

'You're quick to make judgements.'

She put her head on one side. 'Oh, I don't think so. I've been watching a pretty nauseating display ever since you arrived this evening.'

Across the table Letitia Lambert drew in a shocked breath and even her easygoing husband said, 'I *say*, hang on there.'

But Riccardo silenced him with an upraised finger.

'Watching me all evening, were you?' he said softly. 'Now why was that?'

To her fury Rachel found a fiery blush rising to her cheeks. She set her teeth and flung back, 'Doesn't one always watch the main attraction at the circus?'

Letitia Lambert exchanged a shocked look with her husband. 'Ask the waiter how they barbecue the lobster,' she said quickly.

'But we've barbecued our own dozens of times.'

'I want to know how they do it here.'

Ronnie raised a hand to summon a hovering waiter. Riccardo ignored it. He had not taken his eyes off Rachel. He seemed unaware of anyone else.

He drawled, 'Main attraction? Are you trying to flatter me?'

Rachel raised her eyebrows. 'Your standards of flattery can't be very high,' she commented.

He stretched suddenly, his hands clasped at the back of his neck, and gave her a long, slow smile. And what he said was utterly unexpected.

'So why don't you show me some of the high-grade stuff?'

Rachel could not have been more shocked if he had thrown his champagne over her. She blinked, silenced.

There was a short pause. She became aware that other people were watching them openly. Riccardo di Stefano gave her a bland smile. She flushed deeply and turned away. She felt as if she had lost a battle somehow. A public battle.

Waiters came and went, bringing food that Rachel barely touched. She kept her back resolutely turned to Riccardo, talking hard to her other neighbour. She took about as much notice of what he had to say as she did of the food.

The meal finished. Anders made a brief speech, welcoming everyone. He did not, Rachel noticed, mention Judy's birthday.

Afterwards the famous band began to play and the guests started strolling from table to table. The blonde Helen made a beeline for them as soon as Anders sat down. She flung her arms round Riccardo's neck from behind.

'Wonderful Ricky,' she said, nuzzling his ear. 'I waved but you weren't looking. Are you losing your touch?'

He turned and flicked her chin. 'It seems like it,' he said drily.

Helen laughed. 'Oh, not with me, lover. Never with me. But, from what I could see, you haven't cracked the thought police.' And she sent a malicious look across at Rachel.

Rachel stiffened. Riccardo looked from her to Helen and back again.

'You've lost me.' He was drawling, the last word in sophisticated unconcern.

Helen gave a tinkling laugh. 'Didn't you know, darling? Rachel—it is Rachel, isn't it?—is here to make sure that Judy doesn't stray *too* far off the straight and narrow. At least, not while anyone important is looking.'

Riccardo raised his brows. His expression was unreadable. Rachel felt as if her feelings would boil over and scald them all. Abruptly she turned her shoulder and began to talk to her other neighbour. She was aware of Riccardo taking Helen off to dance but she did not look round as they went.

The music became louder and more insistent. Voices rose. More and more people began to dance. Rachel's neighbour went too, with an apologetic look as he was swept off into the crowd.

'Looks like you'll have to dance with me, then, my siren.' The husky voice was low, as if only she was meant to hear. As presumably she was.

There was something faintly threatening about it. Rachel froze. She looked round. Those who were not dancing were talking noisily or sipping champagne so cold that it frosted the glasses. For once, nobody seemed to be taking any notice of Riccardo di Stefano. Except her.

She lifted her chin and looked at him. Throughout the evening his manner could have added several inches of ice to those glasses. Now he was looking warm and lazy and— worst of all—as if it was all her doing.

Rachel sat very stiff in her chair. She was certain that

she was being mocked—and by a master. She did not like it. But this was a new ploy and she did not know how to handle it at all.

Feeling horribly gauche, she said, 'This is not really my sort of party. I don't think I'll—'

Riccardo twirled one of the spindly chairs round and sat down astride it. He smiled at her from under his lashes. Rachel's stomach turned over. She found she was grasping the arm of her patio chair rather tightly. She let it go—but not before Riccardo had seen that convulsive grip. His smile widened. 'I was thinking the very same thing.'

Young and inexperienced she might be, but she was not an idiot. It was quite clear what he was thinking and it was as far away from her own ideas about how to spend the rest of the evening as you could get.

She said levelly, 'I didn't quite finish my book this afternoon. I really want to know what happens. I'd like to read for a bit before I go to sleep.'

She thought he would mock. Once again he confounded her with the unexpected. 'You'll miss the birthday cake.'

'I'm not hungry,' Rachel announced defiantly.

'Aren't you?' He seemed surprised. 'I am.'

He let his eyes smile straight into her own. She could not pretend not to know what he meant. What was more, the sexual challenge might be contrived but it nevertheless had a shocking effect on Rachel. Her stomach turned several back-flips and started to tremble like an earthquake warning.

Humiliatingly, Riccardo knew it. He had to know it. His experience would have told him even if he had not seen the tell-tale tremors of her fingers against the arm of the chair.

His experience was not sufficient, however, to hide the small gleam of triumph in his eyes. Rachel saw it. It fired up all her pride in one glorious surge of anger.

'Stop it,' she choked. 'Just stop it.'

She rose to her feet and bent her eyes on him with a

sulphurous expression. Now they were beginning to attract attention. Rachel was in too much of a temper to notice, however.

'Don't think you can play your silly games with me,' she said, bravely ignoring her scarlet cheeks and trembling limbs. Her tone was utterly contemptuous. 'I'm not one of your fan club. And I don't want to do business with you, either. I don't have to take this. And I won't.'

She stalked off through the tables, horribly conscious of the amused glances that followed her. Riccardo di Stefano was not unconscious of them either. He did not follow her but as she went he watched her. And his expression was no longer amused.

Still shivering with temper—she told herself firmly that it was temper—Rachel skirted the dancers. There was a small group by the pool, not dancing. As Rachel approached she saw the shoulder-borne camcorders and the businesslike cameras. This, then, must be the Press. They looked alarmingly well equipped.

Rachel hesitated. This was the reason why Judy had wanted her at the party. Should she join them? There was no sign of Judy. Anders was sitting on one of the pool loungers, waving a cigar as he held forth. But he was alone apart from his audience.

Rachel was beginning to turn away when one of the photographers saw her. Anders looked up at once. He waved imperatively.

'Damn,' muttered Rachel.

But she went over to him. There was reluctance in every muscle but she went.

'Mrs McLaine's stepdaughter, gentlemen,' he said, urging her into the lounger beside him and putting a heavy arm round her shoulders.

It was all Rachel could do not to shudder. For Daddy, she reminded herself, and pinned on a dazzled smile. For a moment the click of camera shutters almost drowned out the cicadas.

And then the questions started.

'Been to the Caribbean before?'

'How does it feel to be among the beautiful people for the first time?'

'What do you want to be, sweetheart? Model? Actress?'

And then, sneering and somehow gleeful, a voice asked, 'How long have you known Rick di Stefano?'

Rachel unfocused her eyes and looked round at them all as if she were too dim to understand what they were implying. I hate this place and I hate these people, she thought. I'm never coming near people like this ever again as long as I live. I don't care what Judy or Daddy or *anyone* says. Never again.

And then help came from an unexpected quarter. Judy appeared on the terrace. The whole tribe turned their cameras on her. She tossed her hair, laughing. Then she was strolling down the steps to the kidney-shaped pool, unbuttoning her gold dress as she came.

When she arrived in front of Anders and Rachel she stopped. She ignored Rachel, her whole concentration bent on Anders. Her head tilted provocatively. Anders lounged there, looking up at her, not moving.

Judy gave a soft laugh. Rachel was shocked. She had never heard any sound so intimate, so wholly adult in her life, she thought. Then, quickly, Judy shrugged off her gold dress. It fell over his legs. He made no attempt to move it.

Rachel and the whole crew of press men held their breath.

Underneath the evening gown, Judy wore a lacy bikini that left very little to the imagination. Nor did the look she sent Anders.

Rachel shrank back in an agony that was part embarrassment, part something far deeper. She felt desperately shaken. Judy had said Rachel did not understand how she felt about Anders. How right she had been. Looking, flinching, Rachel saw that it was as if there were only the two of them in the whole world. As if Judy did not even remember she had a husband, much less care about him.

With a toss of her head that was frankly challenging, Judy kicked off her shoes and dived into the pool. The cameras swirled round, following her. The oil magnate got to his feet, stripped off his jacket, and followed her.

Rachel could not bear it. The cameras trained away from her at last, she leaped to her feet and ran into the arbour. Straight into the arms of the man waiting in the shadows. The impact knocked the breath out of her.

He kissed her. She knew who it was.

At last he lifted his head. 'It may not be your sort of party,' said Riccardo di Stefano unevenly, 'but you seem to be stuck with it.'

Rachel hauled herself away from him as far as he would let her go. His dark hair was stirring in the faint breeze from the sea. For a moment he represented everything she hated at the Villa Azul.

'Don't bet on it,' she snarled.

'Coward,' he said softly.

That brought Rachel's chin up so sharply that the hibiscus flower in her hair jerked dangerously.

'I'm not a coward.'

His mouth twitched. She was positive that he was laughing at her. Anger came another critical centimetre closer to the surface.

He absently tucked the hibiscus back into place. Rachel felt his fingers, warm and deft, just brush her ear, then touch that devastatingly vulnerable spot behind it.

In spite of her anger at him and all he represented, she shivered with longing. Just for a moment, Riccardo looked startled. His arms tightened.

Behind them there was a sudden surge of laughter. Rachel stood like a steel column in Riccardo's arms. She could not even imagine what Judy had said or done to have caused that ribald shout. She felt ashamed—and desperate that he should not see it.

She said in a hard voice, 'Let me go.'

He shook his head. 'Not a chance. You can either come back to the party and dance with me of your own accord, or I carry you.'

Rachel glared. 'Bully-boy tactics.'

'If you like.' He was implacable.

'I thought playboys stuck to charm.'

He smiled then, as if he was really amused. 'Ah, we do. But only as long as it works. Which, in your case, it clearly doesn't.'

'And nor will throwing me over your shoulder like a barbarian raider,' she flashed.

He burst out laughing. Rachel could have hit him. Or burst into tears. Both possibilities were equally awful to contemplate.

'Oh, why couldn't you—?' She broke off, pain tearing at her.

There was no way she could say what she really felt. She felt betrayed—partly by Judy, whose performance to-night had rocked Rachel to her foundations, but worse— far worse—by Riccardo himself.

He had hurt her, Rachel realised, dazed. He had hurt her more than anyone had ever hurt her in her life. And all because he was not what he'd seemed. No, not even that. It was because he was not what she had thought he was. Instead he was, as everyone else knew, one of the Villa Azul's beautiful people: sophisticated and amoral and cold to the bottom of his soul.

You couldn't say to a man like that, Oh, why couldn't you be what I thought you were? Rachel thought. He would only laugh. And serve her right.

She was shaking as she levered herself away from him.

She said as if she hated him, 'I'm not dancing with you. Or anyone else in this beastly place.'

Riccardo's arms slackened. He held her away from him, a look on his face that said he was going to demand an explanation. Rachel knew she could not afford that.

Before he knew what she was about, she had wrenched herself out of his grasp and fled.

She meant to go straight back to her cabin but she was too restless. Instead she walked along the beach, trying to remember her life in England, the school she had left, the college she hoped to go to if her exam results were good enough. But it all seemed unreal somehow. Her mind kept breaking back to the Villa Azul. The problems it posed were insoluble.

Rachel was kicking up the sand, thinking ferocious thoughts about Judy and Anders, when she realised that the person she was feeling most savage about was Riccardo di Stefano.

What is wrong with me? she thought. Anyone would think I had fallen in love.

She stared out to sea. The stars were brilliant but their reflection was broken up by the restless waves. The breakers looked like stranded monsters reaching for the shore, only to die before they reached it. Seeing it, Rachel shivered. Was she, too, reaching out for something she would never quite touch?

This is nonsense, she told herself. You can't fall in love in a day.

But the poets she had read at school said you could fall in love in an hour, in a moment. She had thought it was silly. She had thought it was just an excuse to write their poems. She thought she had even said so in one of her examination essays. Now—

I'm going home, she decided.

She had an open ticket, which she now realised Anders had probably paid for. Judy must have wanted to keep her options open to stay on. Well, the advantage of that was that she could take off whenever she wanted.

Tomorrow morning. When everyone else is still recovering from the party. I'll get Ben to drive me to the airfield. I'll get the first plane to Antigua or Barbados and then any plane I can back to London.

And then you'll never see Riccardo di Stefano again, said an unwelcome voice in her head.

That's just fine.

But you want to.

No, I don't.

This afternoon you thought he was the most exciting man you'd ever met.

Rachel cast another look at the restless sea and its eternal hungry surge for the shore.

'This afternoon he wasn't Riccardo di Stefano,' she said aloud.

This afternoon he had been a challenging stranger. There had been a hint of danger about him, perhaps—a sense that she did not really know him or what he would say or do in any given situation. But she had not known about his millions, his reputation—or his groupies. It was like recognising a truth one had been hiding from.

It was surprising how much it hurt. Rachel's head went back as if the surging sea had struck her.

Oh, she had to leave the Villa Azul all right. If she did not, Riccardo di Stefano was going to find out that she was in love with him.

CHAPTER FIVE

RACHEL rushed back to her cabin, determined to pack. But when she got there she found a dark figure sitting on the low wall in front of it. She stopped dead. It had to be Riccardo. Her heart leaped into her throat. But she knew this was a confrontation she could not avoid.

She went forward bravely.

'What are you doing here?'

Only it was not Riccardo. It was a short, slim man with one of those cameras that looked like a long-range weapon. Which, she supposed, it was, in a way. He stood up.

'Hi, Rachel,' he said cheerily, as if they'd known each other all their lives. 'That was a great shot I got of you.'

Rachel stopped dead. She thought of all she had heard about the paparazzi. And then Judy's performance tonight. Her heart leaped in an entirely different way. She wished passionately that she was older, more experienced. Or at least less alone. Don't antagonise him, she told herself.

So she said pleasantly, 'I'm glad. When do I get to see it?'

He was surprised. Then he laughed, sounding almost admiring. 'Won't make tomorrow's papers in Europe. Too late. Any day after that. Depending...'

He left it up in the air. She thought, He is waiting for me to protest. So she would not protest. Instead she went up to the little house and put on the terrace light.

'I'll look out for it,' she said over her shoulder, quite as if she did not care.

He followed her, peering into her face. 'Has McLaine's gone bust? Judy left your Dad? Did you know that when

78

you came with her? How you finding life at the Villa Azul?'

She answered the only one that was not a minefield. 'Out of this world,' said Rachel with irony.

He missed the irony. 'Gonna stay?'

She said carefully, 'My stepmother has put a lot of effort into giving me a good time, but we both know it's only a holiday.'

He looked at her, his sharp little face disappointed. 'You saying she came to the Villa Azul so you could party? Pull the other one.'

Rachel smiled. 'Well, if you've done your background research, you must know I've never been anywhere like this before. And without Judy I never would have come now.'

He chewed his lip. 'Yeah. But…'

She looked at her watch as if she were waiting for someone. He picked it up at once, as she meant him to.

'Meeting someone?'

'I think I've already met him.'

She remembered how Helen had looked in the mirror. She attempted the cat-like smile, implying all sorts of things she could not have put a name to.

It seemed to work. He was impressed in spite of himself. 'Rick di Stefano?'

He also sounded as if he did not really believe it.

Rachel's shrug was innuendo all on its own. 'I look forward to the photographs. Enjoy yourself. Goodnight.'

She closed the door firmly behind her.

She thought the photographer might try to follow but all she heard was a disconsolate, 'Night,' as he trailed away. She hadn't closed it properly. The door swung back open again, letting in the sounds of the sea and the cicadas. But the photographer did not return.

Rachel switched on the indoor light. She was trembling. She put a hand to the back of her neck to ease the tension and kicked off her shoes. Her feet felt gritty on the floor. She looked down.

At some point she must have brought in sand from the beach. There were sandal-shaped prints across the floor and a little swirl in the bathroom doorway, where she must have shaken out her beach towel. It crunched underfoot unpleasantly. It could not stay like that.

She went to a cupboard and got out the small besom with which the cabin was provided. In spite of her trials of spirit, Rachel grinned suddenly.

'Hearts may break but the housework still has to be done,' she remarked aloud.

'How very true,' said a voice from the doorway.

Rachel dropped the broom and swung round. Her heart was in her mouth. When she half expected him he was not there and when she had all but banished him from her mind he turned up, rendering her speechless.

Riccardo di Stefano raised his eyebrows at her expression. 'Why so shocked?' he said smoothly. 'You knew I was not going to leave it at that.'

He was right. Her reaction when she'd first seen the photographer proved that. All her borrowed sophistication deserted her. 'Yes. No. I mean I wasn't sure—'

He laughed, not unkindly, and strolled into the room. 'Be sure.' He took the broom away from Rachel's suddenly nerveless fingers. 'Housework can wait.' His voice was no longer entirely smooth.

Without her shoes, Rachel felt even more overwhelmed by his height. She stepped back. Riccardo propped the besom against the wall and followed.

She said hurriedly, 'What are you doing here?'

He laughed.

'I told you—'

'You want to go to bed with a good book. I know.' He sounded amused but there was still that undertone that was not amused at all.

He prowled closer. Rachel's heart beat under her breastbone like a desperate bird. She thought, I am his prey. Before, he didn't really care very much, but now that he is concentrating on me he will be merciless. She also thought, alarmed, I am still in love with him.

Her eyes flickered. Riccardo gave a low laugh.

'I shall have to change your mind.'

Rachel curbed her alarm. He was a civilised man, she told herself. He might like winding her up but he had a reputation to maintain. Apart from anything else, he did not need to force himself on a woman who did not want him. Not with that fan club lusting after him back at the party.

So she waited until her heart had stopped its panicky beating. Then she said steadily, 'It would hardly be worth your while.'

'You must let me be the judge of that.' The undertone was less under control now. Was it anger?

Rachel stared. What reason did Riccardo di Stefano have to be angry with her? If it had been the other way round, she would have had plenty of cause. But he had treated her like a fool, patronised and deceived her from the moment he'd seen her.

She tried to keep it level but her voice sounded horribly young when she said, 'Haven't you had enough fun at my expense already?'

There were green glints in his eyes. 'Believe me, I haven't even started. Come here.'

Rachel was shaken. 'What?'

But he did not order her again. Instead he took one long step forward and took her in his arms. He forced her to look up to meet his eyes. It hurt Rachel's neck. He was too tall, too wide-shouldered; he blocked out everything. In spite of all her good sense, Rachel felt her head begin to swim.

'Don't pretend,' Riccardo said roughly. 'You've been playing me on a line ever since you saw me this afternoon, haven't you? Well, now you've got me. Don't you want me, after all, sweetheart?'

Rachel swallowed. 'I don't know what you mean.'

But her voice was shaky. She had promised herself she would make him sorry. How had he found her out? It was stupid. She regretted it bitterly. She did not think Riccardo was going to believe her regrets, though.

'I don't know,' she said again, helplessly.

He held her away from him. 'You know.' His voice was cynical, even weary. 'Would it help if I told you I heard every word you said to that creature with the camera out there?'

The half-truths she had used to fob off the reporter? What relevance did those have to anything? Rachel's eyes widened.

He nodded, as if she had spoken. 'Yes, it did give you away rather.'

She shook her head, bewildered. 'Give me away?'

Riccardo shook her a little—not hard, just as if he was trying to make her concentrate.

'Up to then, I might have been willing to give you the benefit of the doubt.' He sounded mildly regretful. 'But that was a class performance you turned in out there.'

She was so angry that she forgot that Riccardo di Stefano intimidated her. She fought her way out of his arms and backed to the wall, glaring.

'How kind,' she spat. 'Class performance. I'm really flattered.'

He gave a low laugh. But he did not look amused. His eyes were cold and watchful.

'I can see you are. I take it you've finished your experiment for tonight?'

'What?'

'Experiment,' repeated Riccardo di Stefano casually. 'Isn't that what it was? A little flattery, a little stroking. How much can I get away with without having to pay my dues?'

Rachel realised with an unpleasant shock that he was seriously angry. In fact 'angry' was hardly the word for the cold rage beating at her across the little cabin.

She was tired and not entirely proud of herself but she was still not answerable for her actions to Riccardo di Stefano.

So she tossed her head and said, 'What's wrong with experimenting a little?'

'And this is the girl who took me to task for being a playboy,' he mocked. 'There's a name for what you were doing this evening, you know.'

She shrugged. His eyes flickered. She was suddenly aware of her bare shoulders cooling in the evening air. She lifted her chin and stared straight back in defiance.

'So?'

'So I think that makes us equal,' he said softly.

Quite suddenly, Rachel began to feel thoroughly out of her depth. She looked over her shoulder, harried. She had nowhere to retreat to. He saw her dilemma. His smile grew.

'What do you mean, equal?' Rachel wished her voice had not quavered on the last word.

The green glints in his eyes made him look positively satanic. 'I mean you lost the moral high ground tonight. If you ever had it. Which, with hindsight, I doubt.'

Rachel was pressing back against the wall so hard that she could feel her hair catching on the rough plaster. 'I don't know what you're talking about,' she said contemptuously. But there was a distinct tremor in her voice.

Riccardo laughed. He came so close that Rachel could feel the heat of his body. He leaned forward, one hand pressed against the wall behind her head. If she'd turned her head, Rachel could have touched his flexed knuckles with her mouth. She could smell wine and the crisp cotton of his shirt, and some other odour that was entirely masculine, entirely Riccardo. She caught her breath.

'You are *not* intimidating me,' she announced.

'So I should hope. If you can handle the paparazzi you can handle me. A high-grade diplomat like you.'

He put his other hand on the wall by her head, effectively pinning her in place. Rachel's heart beat fast but she refused to let him see how nervous he was making her. She looked scornful.

'Now who's being childish?'

Riccardo showed no sign of remorse. He said thoughtfully, 'There is a child in all of us. Sometimes a good child, sometimes a naughty one. This afternoon, I thought I was letting a good child down lightly.' He paused and surveyed her deliberately. 'But I am re-appraising the situation.'

Rachel said furiously, 'I am not a child.'

Quite suddenly he was not laughing any more. 'Quite.'

'I—'

In the corner, the broom clattered to the floor with a sound like a gun going off. Rachel gave a small scream, out of sheer tension. Riccardo gave her a disparaging look. But he straightened and lounged away from the wall to pick up the broom.

'What an extensive repertoire you have,' he marvelled. He sounded savage all of a sudden. He threw the broom away from him with quite unnecessary force. 'Home-maker. Diplomat. The siren on combat duty. Now, she was very beguiling. But I think my favourite so far has been the trembling innocent. You're good at that.'

He looked her up and down, where she stood pressed against the wall. There was something in his eyes which froze Rachel to the spot. He smiled. It was not a pleasant smile.

'Which one will it be in bed, I wonder?'

Her mouth went dry. Civilisation was out and anger was in but this was unbelievable. He might be angry with her but he still could not make love to her against her will. She said so.

'Who said it would be against your will?'

'I did,' said Rachel with the firmness of desperation.

She stared at him, quivering. Riccardo was unimpressed, dismissing her protest with a shrug. He hooked a finger into his bow-tie and undid it with a single pull. For some reason the little movement was more threatening than anything else that he had said or done yet.

'You don't mean it,' she said breathlessly. 'I'm not a fool. This is a game to you.'

He lobbed the tie away from him.

Rachel said, 'You're not serious.'

The jacket followed the tie. Neither Rachel nor Riccardo broke eye contact to see where the garments fell.

'I'm always serious when I play games.'

Rachel shook her head. She felt dazed. He did not mean it. He could not. She looked at his expression and realised she was wrong. He meant it.

Riccardo di Stefano cancelled the distance between them and reached for her in one smooth movement.

'Oh, Lord,' she said as her feet left the ground. She clung onto him purely for balance.

He held her against his chest, looking down at her for a moment. His eyes were assessing. 'Ah, the innocent,' he remarked. 'Interesting.'

He strode over to the bed and dropped her unceremoniously in the middle. The front of the sarong came undone at the rough treatment. Neither broke eye contact to take any notice of that either.

He sat on the side of the bed. Rachel struggled up onto one elbow. 'I don't know what you think you're doing—' she began indignantly.

His expression silenced her. To her intense astonishment Rachel felt her bones begin to melt.

'Yes, you do,' he said softly. 'You know exactly. We're going to do something about those instincts of yours.'

His fingers drifted up the side of her bare arm. Something inside Rachel contracted with longing. Her eyes screwed tight shut with the intensity of it.

'Some of them are in working order, then,' said that amused voice in her ear.

She felt his lips on the side of her neck, her collar-bone, brushing aside the tangled sarong. His touch was insistent. He was gentle but utterly determined. And when he reached her quickening breasts she did not even want him to be gentle any more.

She twisted restlessly, her hand tangling wildly in his hair. He lifted his head. Reluctantly, Rachel opened her eyes. He was looking down at her, his chest rising and falling as if he were running a race. She could not bear it. Her head tossed on the pillow, tumbling her hair into crazy disarray. The hibiscus fell away unnoticed.

Slowly, slowly, he raised his head, searching her face. Her gaze was wild. Riccardo met it. He looked implacable. Her lips parted in silent yearning. His eyes flamed.

She felt his breath on her flesh, the beat of his blood. She felt his naked skin, warm as she had never imagined. She trembled, shaken. She knew his need was as harsh and urgent as her own.

Yet, in spite of that, Riccardo was holding back. Rachel felt it, in disbelief. Her fingers clenched like a vice on his upper arms. A groan burst out of her. There was a precipice that she needed to reach, she *had* to reach.

Riccardo seemed to know. He said her name, almost as if he were in pain. And then, and then...

In the end it was not the knowledgeable, dominating man of the world who drove them both over that compulsive edge. It was Rachel herself.

Afterwards he rolled over on his back and stared at the ceiling. Rachel's heartbeat steadied slowly. She felt bewildered. And lonelier than she had ever done in her life.

She thought she would give anything if Riccardo would only take her hand. But his open eyes were fixed on the ceiling fan. He seemed very far away. She realised, with a flash of perception beyond her years, that to be unable to reach the person you were lying beside was one of the cruellest exiles. She did not think she was going to forget that one again.

And there was something else she realised. Judy had said she did not understand. Well, now she did. If Riccardo wanted her there was nothing—*nothing*—she would not do for him. *If* he wanted her. The silence was like a prison sentence.

Rachel folded her lips together and got off the bed. Riccardo turned his head to watch her. She bent her head, rubbing the back of her neck to ease the tension. He shut his eyes briefly.

'Rachel, I didn't mean—'

But she was not to find out what Riccardo had not meant. Because that was when the door of the cabin banged back on its hinges and Judy stormed in.

Nine years later in London Rachel shut her eyes, remembering. Even over the distance of years, her whole body convulsed in an agony of shame.

Later she'd discovered that Judy had just tried to persuade Anders to marry her if she got a divorce. Anders had laughed. Rejected, Judy had been hurt and spitting mad. She'd gone to Rachel's cabin looking for a fight. She'd found it.

For a moment Judy stood in the doorway, frozen. Then pure venom took over. Rachel blinked and shrank.

At once Riccardo stood up. 'Enough,' he said.

Such was his authority that Judy stopped, in mid-vituperation. He strolled forward, magnificently unconscious of his nakedness. Rachel groped round for the rags of her sarong. She was appalled.

'This,' he said to Judy, 'is none of your business. Out.'

And, to Rachel's amazement, her stepmother turned and went. Riccardo turned back to her.

'I seem to owe you an apology,' he said formally.

He was as remote as the moon. The man who had called out her name in something like agony might never have existed. Rachel shrank even more. She did not know what to say. She could not bear to look at him. She was afraid of what she would see in his face: indifference, embarrassment or, worse, regret. She wished he could not see her either.

But he could, and seemed to have no trouble in reading her reactions. He sighed.

'Don't look like that. It's not the end of the world.'

Rachel found herself wishing passionately that it was. She did not say so. She did not say anything.

He hesitated. 'I take full responsibility but—'

Rachel flinched. She could not help it. He was going to say that they had both been carried away and she was not to make too much of it. She almost hated him for that.

But she was still in love with him and it was total desolation. She put out an instinctive hand to ward off whatever he was going to say.

He said quietly, 'I never meant to hurt you. I didn't think.'

Rachel nodded jerkily, not meeting his eyes. 'I know. Nor did I.'

'Well, then—'

'These things happen all the time,' Rachel said, before he could.

But she had read him wrongly.

'No, they don't.' Riccardo was not remote any more, or unreadable. He was furious. 'Not to me.'

She shrugged. 'Then chalk it up to new experience.' She thought she would die of the pain. But she sounded flippant. In fact she could almost convince herself that she was utterly cool and in control. It was some consolation.

He took an impatient step forward, then curbed himself.

'You're beat,' he said curtly. 'We'll talk in the morning.'

But in the morning she was on her way to the airport in Anders' limousine, with her stepmother as escort.

In contrast with her venom of last night, Judy was oddly triumphant.

'You always were a slyboots. A cold, self-righteous, *stupid* slyboots.'

Rachel had not slept. After Riccardo had left she had packed. Then she'd gathered the sarong around her like a shawl and sat in the window, waiting for dawn. She was now too tired to reply to Judy's taunts.

'Sneering at Anders and the rest of us like that. Going off with your books and pretending to be so holy. The crazy thing is, you convinced me. You convinced everyone. We thought you didn't even know what you were passing up.'

Rachel leaned her head back against the cushioned headrest and tried to ignore the shrill voice.

'You won't be so smug now, will you? You're down here with the rest of us now.'

Rachel said wearily, 'I can't argue with that.'

Judy laughed. 'And of all the men in the world! The moment Riccardo di Stefano walked in.'

'No,' said Rachel loudly.

Judy laughed again. 'Oh, yes. We all saw it. You're an open book, you stupid child.'

Rachel kept her eyes very wide and refused to cry. Her ordeal was nearly over. The limousine was pulling up outside the shack that was the small island's airport.

Judy gave vent to one final flurry of malice. 'We'll see what your father says about his idolised little girl *now*.'

Nine years later Rachel remembered exactly what her father had had to say and shuddered. He'd met her at the airport and delivered it in one comprehensive speech. After that, he'd driven her to a friend's house and never seen her again.

For weeks Rachel was numb. Even Judy, when she returned to London, was taken aback. She arranged to meet

Rachel and gave her some money to tide her over.

In fact, Rachel thought afterwards, it was, perhaps, just as well that the practical problems were so enormous. In facing them, she began also to face her own feelings. There was no question of going to university without her father's financial support. So she had to find a job. Although she did not admit it to herself, she was half waiting for Riccardo di Stefano to arrive in London and save her from her predicament. He never did.

In the end she found Brian Gray and his family. She began to go to night school. She passed crucial examinations. Eventually she stopped waiting for Riccardo. Eventually the only thing she wanted was never to see him again. She began to think she would manage that.

Until today. Rachel rubbed her hands over her tired eyes. It was all back, as clearly as if she had only just got off that plane. She bit back a cry of shame. For, whatever she'd thought, then or later, about Riccardo di Stefano's seduction, there was one thing she could not disguise from herself. He was older, more experienced and infinitely more cynical than she, but in one thing they had been equals: she had wanted him quite as much as he'd wanted her.

The fact had been so difficult to live with that she had wiped it out of her memory. Or she had thought she had, until today. That must be why she had been so hard on Alexandra, she realised suddenly. Riccardo di Stefano was not forgotten and poor Alexandra had been picking up the punishment for a younger Rachel's mistakes.

She bit her lip, remorseful. What had happened at the Villa Azul was *history*. It had nothing to do with Alexandra, or with the person Rachel herself was these days. She straightened her shoulders. Anything she might have to say in the future to Riccardo di Stefano was going to be professional and nothing but professional, she vowed.

But that small room, the tangled sheet, the wide shoulders, slick and warm under her hands...

'Forget it,' she said to herself, clenching her fists in concentration. 'Forget it, forget it, *forget* it.'

She banished it. There was a job to be done. She was the one to do it and she knew it. She could not allow herself to be deflected. Rachel had to meet her team for discussion and then it was back into the boardroom.

At first she thought no one was there. That did not surprise her, or worry her. Normally she liked to be early, to set up her presentation. On this occasion she'd thought she would probably have to do it all under the impatient eyes of her intended audience. So it was with a sigh of relief that she registered the empty chairs. Clearly the board lunch was running on.

She began to set up the slide projector and checked that her notes and the slides were in corresponding order. Her notes were on small cards which she could hold in one hand. It was an orderly task and she relished it. She was even humming to herself before an unexpected voice spoke.

'I see you like to be prepared.'

Rachel jumped. She stopped humming. After those vivid memories, the sound of that voice made her feel a little sick. She turned round very carefully.

Riccardo di Stefano raised his eyebrows. He strolled forward.

'I seem to have shocked you. Sorry.'

He did not sound the least bit sorry, Rachel thought. Nor did he look sorry. But he did look curious. Her shock must be showing.

That was dangerous. She pulled herself together.

She said with as much calm as she could command, 'I didn't realise anyone was here.'

His eyebrows rose higher. They were strongly marked. Why hadn't she remembered that? He was not a friendly pirate any more. Today he was looking satanic. Those eyebrows gave him the air of a devil, and what was more, a devil with a special line in mockery.

Had he always been like that? She remembered cynicism and anger and, in the end, a passion that had seared her to the soul. She did not remember mockery.

Stop that, she told herself, shaken. Long forgotten, right?

Of course, he was older, and even more successful these days. He would not be the same person she remembered, any more than she was after all these years. She became conscious that he was watching her narrowly.

The mockery intensified. 'Do I disturb you?'

'Of course not,' Rachel said sharply.

She bent her head and riffled blindly through the memo cards she had just put into order. She could feel him watching that too.

He said in a thoughtful tone, 'You know, I have the oddest feeling about you, Mrs Gray.'

Rachel's mouth went dry. 'Oh?' she said, trying to sound indifferent.

'Yes. Increasing by the minute.'

Rachel concentrated on her task. She knew he wanted her to ask what sort of feeling. She was not going to give him that satisfaction, she promised herself. So she shrugged, not looking up.

'Really?'

'Don't you look at people who are talking to you?' he demanded. There was a distinct edge to his voice.

It was a challenge she could hardly avoid. It made her furious but there was nothing she could do about it. Rachel gave an elaborate sigh and straightened.

She still did not quite dare to meet his eyes. But by dint of looking just to the left of his ear she gave a very fair impression of looking at him directly. Riccardo di Stefano's expression was frankly speculative.

'You're quite sure we haven't met before?'

She did not know what to say. There was a pause. His mouth tilted.

'Because, you know, I have the strangest feeling that we know each other. Very well indeed.'

CHAPTER SIX

RACHEL'S fingers tightened involuntarily. Her hands were sweating. She could feel the stiff little cards getting slippery.

'I told you, I was away—'

'The last time I came by,' he finished. 'Yeah, yeah. But the world is not bounded by Bentley's boardroom. Maybe we bumped into each other some other place? Another time?'

The cards shot out of her hands, fanning out across the carpet in total confusion. Rachel gave an exclamation of dismay and fell to her knees, gathering up the cards clumsily. She had difficulty in getting hold of them. Her hands were shaking.

'Allow me.'

Riccardo di Stefano bent and gathered the cards in one hand, like a gambler. He straightened. Rachel had to get up as well, perforce. He was a lot closer now. He put the cards on the lectern and considered her thoughtfully.

'Thank you,' she said. Her throat hurt.

He ignored that. He was smiling and his eyes were bright green. 'You know, I've heard a lot about you, Mrs Gray. A lot of good things from a lot of people. None of them said you were as jumpy as a cat on a hot spot.'

Rachel was tempted to ask the identity of his informants. For a moment she almost did. Then it occurred to her that it would only prolong the conversation.

She said carefully, 'I think your bombshell this morning was enough to make anybody jumpy.'

He looked amused. 'Yes, that they did mention.'

'Mention?' Rachel was confused. 'What?'

'You think on your feet.'

She could feel the guilty colour in her cheeks.

'Now are you going to tell me why I scare the hell out of you? Or are you going to let me have fun working it out?'

There was no answer to that. Rachel looked down, picking up the cards pointedly. She could feel him looking at the top of her head, feel his annoyance. He was balked and he knew it.

Let him stay balked, she prayed.

He gave a quick, annoyed laugh. 'OK, I get the message. You want to get your presentation in order.'

'That was why I came to the boardroom early.'

'And there was me thinking you were stalking me,' he said silkily.

For a moment she did not realise it was a joke. Her eyes flew up to his in pure horror. She had no time to disguise her reaction. His brows twitched together in surprise. His lips parted as if he was going to demand an immediate explanation.

Rachel leaped in to forestall him.

'Please—I haven't got much time.' She gestured at the lectern, the slide projector.

There was a frozen second when she thought he was going to insist on his explanation there and then, no matter what her excuse. Rachel's head went back and, behind her back, she crossed her fingers in a gesture that was pure childhood superstition.

Then at last di Stefano drew back. Reluctantly, it seemed.

'And I've interrupted you.' His voice was heavy with irony. 'Sure. You've made your point, Mrs Gray. But we still have to get together and sort out where we've met before.'

Rachel suppressed her shiver at that. Instead, she gave him one of her best unfocused smiles and said, 'I look forward to it.'

For a moment his frustration was undisguised. Then he shrugged. 'See you later, then.'

He sauntered out. Rachel collapsed in the nearest chair.

She could not stay there, of course. She had work to do. And work, as she had good cause to remember, was a great therapy. Thank God for work, she thought.

By the time the meeting reconvened, she was in reasonably good shape. Her work was in order again, her speech ready. Philip ushered the men into their seats. Rachel took a deep breath, avoided looking at Riccardo di Stefano, and began.

She had learned that the secret of selling her ideas to the board was to keep her presentations short and let them ask questions. That way they got to think they had thought of some of the ideas themselves. That made them better disposed to accept them. No one had ever noticed this technique before.

But from the amused way Rick di Stefano watched her throughout her brief introduction Rachel was almost certain that he had detected her strategy. He had found her out and, from the way he toasted her silently with his water glass, was amused by it. Maybe even impressed.

For a moment Rachel almost faltered. Rick di Stefano's amusement increased. Hurriedly she pulled herself together and went on.

The questions came on as she'd expected, in roughly the order she'd expected. She took them all, dealing with them as she had planned. Then came the key one.

'But I can't see how we can pay for it. How will we fund this?'

Tread carefully, Rachel; here come the eggshells, she thought. She avoided Riccardo di Stefano's eye even harder.

'A good question, Mr Barron,' she said to the questioner. 'My proposal is that we take funds away from the Eastern European section and put that on a care and maintenance basis. You will see—' she flipped up a chart on the projector '—we have been losing money in that area for some years. I know we all think it is an investment in the future but, with the position as it is, we have to look at nearer horizons. At least for the moment.' She looked around. 'But I'm open to any alternative suggestions.'

Rick di Stefano said lazily, 'What about if you just got more money?'

Rachel folded her lips together. 'Since the purpose of this meeting is to find how to avoid a takeover, I don't see that as a serious question, Mr di Stefano.'

It was the first time her diplomacy had deserted her in a gruelling couple of hours. Philip looked at her, horrified.

He stood up, saying, 'I'm sure it was a serious question if Mr di Stefano asked it, Rachel. Perhaps—'

Rachel was so angry that she looked directly at Rick di Stefano for the first time. 'We've borrowed as much as we can support. If we go for any more we'll have to pay higher interest or pledge assets—either way, our existing lenders will get worried. As I explained. If you've got any options to suggest—apart from selling out, that is—I'd be happy to hear them.'

Rick di Stefano took no notice of Philip either. He gave a low laugh. He seemed to be enjoying himself hugely. 'Some well-wisher might lend you the money.'

'Without additional security? Or taking shares?' Rachel was scornful. 'You're crazy.'

'Rachel!' Philip sounded almost frantic. 'Rick, look, maybe we should take a break and think about this.'

'Oh, Mrs Gray has plenty of thoughts, Phil.' He sounded unoffended, even intrigued. 'Do you want a breather, Mrs Gray?'

'No,' snarled Rachel.

'I thought not,' he murmured. 'Now let us suppose that I, for example, might be willing to lend you the money to fund the change of direction you're talking about here. What would you say?'

'What?' Philip sank limply back in his chair. He looked

stunned. He was not the only one, including di Stefano's own team.

Only Rachel and di Stefano stayed cool. Rachel was wary, while di Stefano was relaxed and maddeningly uninvolved.

'Well?' he prompted.

Since it was clear that Philip and the others were in no state to answer him, Rachel said, 'Why?'

He laughed aloud at that. 'Mrs Gray, you are a delight.'

That brought Rachel's chin up. 'If you are asking me to hypothesise something inherently ridiculous,' she said in her most prissy voice, 'you have to give me a reason why I should waste my time.'

'So I see.' The irony was back. Along with something else. Rachel did not know what it was but she was sure it did not bode well for her. 'Well, let us say that I like Bentley's management style more than I expected. Will that do?'

Seeing the no which was forming on Rachel's lips, Philip rushed into speech.

'Of course, of course,' he said heartily. 'You can do a simulation on the basis of borrowed funds, can't you, Rachel? Do you want to go and put it in the computer?'

'I don't need a computer,' Rachel said evenly.

She looked down at her painfully composed slides and picked up a marker. 'You assume increased inflow of another—what shall I say, Mr di Stefano? One million?'

'One million seems reasonable,' he agreed gravely.

The board gave a collective gasp. You could feel the level of hope rising, Rachel thought. Why could they not see what he was doing? She put a slash through both totals so heavily that she broke the point of her marker.

She went on, 'On the balance sheet you increase borrowing. On the outflow side you use it by retaining the East European desk, maybe add a little lending.' She picked up a fresh marker and adjusted those totals too. 'So the assets go up a little. The liabilities go up a lot. And none of the new business will bring in any profit in this year.' She looked round. 'And may I remind you, gentlemen, it is this year which is critical?'

She must look like a small animal at bay in front of her projector, Rachel thought. A small animal, helpless to turn the herd from its self-destructive course. The board had scented reprieve when, only this morning, it had been expecting extinction. They were not going to question Riccardo di Stefano's motives in offering them this last-minute rescue. And nothing Rachel could say would make them ask themselves what was in it for him.

Oh, he was clever. Presumably this was how he'd made his millions in the first place. Walk in, terrify the board and management, then offer them a little hope; then, later, however many months later it took, gobble them up. Why on earth was she the only one to see it?

Across the room, her furious eyes met his. It was a mistake. It was a mistake of incalculable proportions. His eyes were as green as glass. He smiled.

Her heart lurched up into her throat and then down to the centre of the earth. She thought, He *knows*. She stopped arguing.

Rachel escaped to her office while the rest of the board was still gathering round Riccardo di Stefano, telling him what a wise investment he had just made. If only they knew exactly how wise, Rachel thought cynically. But the bank was the last thing on her mind after that shocking moment of eye contact. Her mouth was dry and her head was pounding like a smith's hammer.

'Hi,' said Mandy, looking up. 'Did they buy your reconstruction?'

'At a price,' said Rachel grimly.

She picked up a bottle of mineral water from Mandy's desk, hauled off the top and drank a long draught straight from the bottle.

Mandy stared. She had never seen Rachel do anything

like that before. Also, there were droplets of water on the second-best jacket lapel. That could only mean one thing: Rachel's hands were shaking.

'High price?'

Rachel lowered the bottle and wiped a hand across her mouth. 'The highest.'

'For you or the bank?' said Mandy prosaically. She did not believe in identifying with her employers.

Rachel gave a little laugh which broke in the middle. 'I wish I knew.'

She shot into her room and closed her door, only to open it a moment later.

'If anyone calls, I've gone. If anyone turns up here, I've gone.'

Quite bemused, Mandy nodded.

She was not bemused for long. A tall and gorgeous predator strolled into her office and paused at her desk. 'Mrs Gray's office? Don't tell me. She's just gone into conference.'

'Er—no,' said Mandy, thinking that corporate raiders should not be allowed to have warm, green-flecked eyes that made your spine turn to treacle. Manfully, she recalled her instructions. 'I think she's gone for the day.'

Riccardo di Stefano gave a crack of laughter. 'She'll regret that,' he said with confidence, and made his leisurely way through Rachel's door before Mandy could stop him.

Rachel was divesting herself of the checked jacket when the door opened. She did not immediately look round. Not, that was, until a voice said in accents of unholy glee, 'Gone for the day? Not worthy of you, Rachel. Really not worthy. You must have known I'd check.'

Rachel spun round from the cupboard, her expression unguarded. Riccardo was leaning back against the door as if he were some waterfront bum propping up the nearest wall for lack of anything better to do. A waterfront bum with a nasty streak, she corrected herself mentally. One who was not going to move out of the way except in his own good time.

'Check?' she said mechanically. 'Why should you?'

'Secret of my success. Never take anything on trust. Particularly where women are concerned.'

Rachel stood stock-still. She was fighting to stay in control. No matter what she thought she had seen in his eyes back there, there was no proof yet that he remembered anything. Work on the assumption that he is still fishing, she told herself. 'I'm sure it's an excellent strategy.'

'It works for me,' he said lightly. But his eyes were not light.

In her shock at his entrance she had half pulled the front of her blouse out of her skirt. Now her hands began to twist unconsciously in the loose stuff. He took in the signs of agitation. The silence lengthened.

'Well, Rachel,' he said at last, 'it's been a long time.'

Rachel felt as if the floor had dropped out of her well-built office. She adopted her most wooden expression. 'I'm afraid I'm not with you.'

'Same old Rachel,' he said tolerantly. 'Beautiful manners and a stone wall behind them. Still we both know the stone wall comes down in the end, don't we?'

She did not answer. She could not.

He added in a thoughtful voice, 'I should have known you'd go far. I don't know why I never thought of looking for you in the financial world. It was obvious that was where you'd end up, with your father to back you.'

Rachel just stopped herself wincing.

'You know, that was a really good pitch you ran just now.'

'Thank you,' she said in a stifled voice.

His smile grew. 'Never let the punter know he's being marketed to,' he reminded her softly.

So he did remember. Suddenly there was no longer any way she could pretend that she did not understand him. Rachel felt herself whiten.

He was impatient suddenly. 'You look as if you're about to face a firing-squad. Sit down, for God's sake.'

She did.

'That's better.' He strolled forward and propped himself on the corner of her desk, looking down at her with un-disguised speculation. 'Little Rachel McLaine. Well, well, who would have thought it?'

Rachel was not playing the social reminiscence game with him. 'Thought what?'

For a moment he looked disconcerted. Then he gave a soft laugh. 'Stop glaring at me. This isn't the Villa Azul. Or do you want to call me a playboy again?'

She was cold with shock inside. But that had been nine years ago and these days Rachel's armour was better. She leaned back in her big swivel chair and crossed one slim leg over the other. 'Does that still rankle?'

Riccardo's eyes still had green flecks in them. Rachel could see them because he was much too close. They still crinkled at the corners when he was amused, too.

'Every day,' he told her solemnly.

Rachel did not want to amuse him. She looked away, biting her lip. 'I'm sorry. That was a fatuous thing to say.'

He smiled. 'Not at all. Nobody likes to be called a play-boy. Especially as it was what my father was saying reg-ularly at the time. It rankled all right.'

'Then I apologise.'

'Why should you? As far as you know, it was true.'

'Not from what I read in the papers,' Rachel admitted ruefully.

He leaned even closer. 'You've been reading my press?' His tone sounded dangerously personal.

Rachel drew back a little. 'We keep a cuttings file on important people. Directors, shareholders, main custom-ers—that sort of thing. The big cheeses in general.'

Riccardo was not best pleased. He pulled a face. 'I don't think I've been called a big cheese before.'

'Not to your face, maybe.'

Faint annoyance crossed his face. 'You don't change, do you, Rachel? Still saying it to their faces.'

'Tell the truth and shame the devil,' she said flippantly.

'Meaning me?'

After what she had been thinking about him earlier, she almost jumped. There was a shocked pause. Then she shrugged. 'If the cap fits…'

His eyes narrowed. 'So I'm still cast as the devil, am I, even after all these years?'

This time Rachel was not quite quick enough to censor her own reaction.

There was no point in trying to disguise her hostility. She said coldly, 'Well, you were hardly my guardian angel, were you? What do you expect?'

For a moment he did not speak. When he did, it was on a note of discovery. 'You blame me.'

She had given herself away. She made a desperate attempt to retrieve her mistake. 'It was so long ago—'

'You blame me.'

She moved restlessly in her chair. 'That's a very dramatic way of putting it. I prefer to say I don't feel much affinity with you.'

That amused him. 'Then things have changed indeed. As I recall it, affinity was the one thing we really had. By the truck-load.'

I will not blush, Rachel thought. She was furious. I *will not.*

She said curtly, 'Then our memories differ.'

'Do you think so?'

He considered her. From another man, in another place, with a different history between them, that look would have been almost caressing. From Riccardo, it was sheer, unmitigated provocation. Rachel felt the hair on the back of her neck rise.

'It seems so.'

He shifted. At once she tensed. She could not help it.

Riccardo saw it, of course. She saw him take note, thought-fully, and then store it away for future use.

'Then we should discuss it, don't you think? Have dinner with me.'

'*No.*' It was pure instinct. It did not even pretend to ordinary social courtesy.

His reaction was unexpected. Oh, she remembered that too. He had never been predictable, had he? He should have been offended by her instantaneous rejection. Instead he looked even more thoughtful. If anything it seemed to please him.

He stood up and turned. He was not touching her—the desk between them would have been too wide, even if he had tried—and he showed no sign of attempting it. But Rachel scooted her chair back as far as it would go. Inside she was trembling as she had not trembled for nine years.

'You misunderstand. It was not an invitation.' His voice was pleasant. He even smiled.

Rachel was incredulous. 'You're ordering me to have dinner with you?'

'Oh, I don't think we need go that far, do you? You're a clever lady. You can read the subtext.'

She was so outraged that for a moment she forgot her inner tremors. She stood up and looked him straight in the eye. 'And the subtext is that my job depends on seeing you socially?'

He threw back his head and laughed. His throat was long and tanned. She remembered that too. Out of sight, Rachel's hands clenched into white-knuckled fists.

'I don't think it will be very social, do you?'

She said stonily, 'You haven't answered my question. Do I lose my job if I turn you down?'

'Of course not. That's illegal, isn't it? Even in this backward country.' His eyes started to dance. 'Have you got your office bugged, by any chance?'

She said nastily, 'Up to now I've never thought of it.'

He pursed his lips in a silent whistle. 'Biting. Very bit-

ing. You really don't think much of me at all, do you,
Rachel McLaine?'

'Gray. My name is Rachel Gray these days.'

'Of course it is.' That did not seem to amuse him quite
so much. 'I can't wait to meet Mr Gray.'

'My husband is dead,' Rachel told him quietly.

Riccardo's eyes were hard. 'Then it will just be you and
me at dinner.'

'I said no.'

'And I said it's part of your professional responsibilities.'

Their eyes clashed. Rachel drew a long shaky breath.

'Get out of my room.' Her voice was so quiet that it
was almost a whisper. 'Unless you want to find yourself
on the wrong end of a sexual harassment charge, don't
come back.'

They stared at each other in silence for a long moment.
Rachel's challenge seemed to hang in the air, like an echo.
She was shaking visibly now. She was beyond caring.
Riccardo's expression was unreadable.

She said, 'I'm not eighteen years old and friendless any
more. This time I'm fighting back.'

Riccardo stiffened. For a moment he seemed to have
turned to stone. If she had not known that he was invul-
nerable on all fronts, she would have said she had landed
a body-blow.

He did not say anything but his eyes narrowed to slits
of ice. Rachel stood her ground proudly. Then he made an
odd abrupt sound, half-laugh, half-protest. And, while she
still stood there braced for a blasting from a man who was
famous for it, he turned on his heel and walked out.

The light was on in the kitchen when Rachel got home.
She went in. Hugh was sitting in the same place she had
left him this morning. This time he was munching his way
through a sandwich the size of a doorstop. Rachel put
down her briefcase and cast her eyes to heaven.

'Heavy day,' he said with a grin. 'Couldn't wait for supper. Even if there is any.'

Rachel jumped guiltily. 'What's in the fridge?'

'One old lettuce and three eggs,' Hugh reported without having to look. He waved the sandwich. 'This is the last of the cheese.'

Rachel laughed but she was remorseful. 'I'm a rotten provider.'

'You could always provide take-away pizza,' he suggested. Hugh adored pizza.

'What about Lexy's diet?'

'She says she's not eating with you any more,' Hugh reported. 'She went to her room. She can have the lettuce,' he added generously.

Rachel sighed. 'Battle still on?'

'Not over till the fat lady sings,' Hugh said peacefully. 'Or until you let her go to whatever it is with Theo Judd.' His interest in his sister's love affairs was remote at best.

Rachel bit her lip. 'It's an all-night party. Tell me honestly, Hugh—do you think I'm wrong?'

Hugh took another mouthful of sandwich. His head shake was not an endorsement of her view. It was a refusal to get involved, and they both knew it.

'You're a great help,' Rachel informed him.

He was unrepentant. 'I'm not my sister's keeper, thank God. Send her back to the wild. That's what she wants.'

Rachel gave a little choke of laughter at this reference to his mother's free-wheeling ménage in southern California. 'But is it what your mother wants? I got the impression she was very busy. And what about Lexy's schooling?'

But Hugh was not to be drawn. He had expressed an opinion, which contradicted all his principles of non-alignment, and he was not to be drawn further.

'I wish I knew what to do,' said Rachel, more to herself than to him.

He finished his doorstop. 'Bin her,' he advised, getting

up and going. In the doorway a thought struck him. He looked back. 'Better still, get yourself a man. We need someone to lay down the law round here.'

He watched her stiffen. Before she could say anything he gave her a wide, wicked grin. Then he raised a hand and clattered off upstairs.

'Male chauvinist pig,' Rachel shouted after him.

'Super Shark,' he yelled back cheerfully.

His door slammed. Rachel hoped he was getting on with his homework. She went back to review her store cupboard ruefully. She had spent the weekend working on her reconstruction plan. The need to eat had simply slipped her mind.

The phone rang. It was the mother of Alexandra's best friend, calling to form a parental alliance in the face of a new offensive on the all-night-party front. She had also been Rachel's mentor in the last two difficult years since Brian had died.

'Oh, hello, Gilly. Gosh, do I need some solidarity,' responded Rachel with feeling. 'Lexy's not speaking to me and there's no food in the house.'

'I'll be over in ten minutes,' said her friend.

She was as good as her word, bringing the remains of a substantial stew and a supermarket bag of staples.

'Burning the candle at both ends,' she diagnosed, stocking the refrigerator and making coffee as Rachel stuffed half a week's dirty laundry into the washing machine. 'What you need is staff. Alternatively get the monsters to do their own washing.'

Rachel poured washing powder into a dispenser. 'Hugh would. Though I'm not sure about the quality control. Lexy wouldn't on principle.' She slammed the door shut and programmed the machine. 'Come on. Let's go and take our coffee where we can't hear the machinery of conscience.'

They went into her study. Rachel took a pile of computer reports off the single comfortable seat and plumped up the cushions.

'I like this room,' said Gilly, settling down. 'Books and a desk and a view of the garden. What more could a woman want?'

Rachel perched on the ancient leather chair by her desk.

'A reasonably stocked fridge,' she said drily.

'Yes, what happened there? You're usually so efficient, I hate you.'

Rachel sighed. 'Too busy. Lexy would have reminded me normally, but she's not speaking to me. Essential war despatches only, at the moment.'

Gilly nodded. 'All-night party? Susanna's the same.'

'Susanna doesn't want to go with Theo Judd.'

Gilly shuddered. 'No, thank God. He's a really nasty piece of work. Susanna thinks he carries a knife.'

Rachel bit her lip. 'So do I. I've seen it. But Lexy doesn't believe me. Or she thinks it's glamorous.'

'What on earth does she think she's doing?'

Rachel pushed back her hair with a weary hand. She had not managed to put it up again all through the day. 'You tell me. Looking for a father-figure, maybe.'

'Theo? A *father*-figure?'

'Well, he's so much older—'

'Alexandra's father didn't have designer stubble and a leather jacket with too many pockets,' Gilly interrupted briskly. 'Or no visible means of support—apart from running these terrible raves, of course. Peter thinks he's a drug dealer.'

Rachel gave her a disturbed look but did not say anything.

'Why else would a man his age want to hang around with a bunch of fifteen-year-olds?' said Gilly unanswerably.

Rachel put her hand over her eyes. 'That's what I've been asking myself. But when I say it to Lexy—'

'She thinks she's old enough to choose her own friends.' Gilly nodded.

'And points out the age difference between Brian and me.'

Gilly whistled. 'Shrewd move.'

'No one said she wasn't bright,' said Rachel bitterly. 'She doesn't work. Her exam results are appalling. But she's bright enough, if she'd only choose to do something about it.'

'And you're elected chief torturer to make her do just that?'

'That's about the size of it,' Rachel agreed.

Gilly shook her head. 'Don't even try. You're on a hiding to nothing.'

Rachel leaned back and closed her eyes briefly. 'Hugh says the house needs a man to introduce some discipline.'

Gilly stared. 'Are you pulling my leg?'

Rachel opened her eyes and shook her head.

'My stars.' Gilly looked at her friend cautiously. 'Is there—er—anyone that Hugh has in mind?'

For no reason at all, Rachel thought of Riccardo di Stefano. She looked quickly down at her coffee. 'No.'

'Oh.' Gilly sipped coffee and debated. 'It's a long time since Brian died. You're very young to lock yourself into contract stepmotherhood.'

Rachel shook her head again. This was a conversation they had had before.

'No time,' she said briefly.

Gilly was sad. 'Oh, Rachel. Still?'

Rachel looked away, feeling a fraud. All their friends thought her marriage to Brian Gray had been a highly romantic union between a middle-aged man and his friendless young au pair. When he'd died, they'd tiptoed around her grief as if the last great love affair had come to an end.

She had never been able to tell any of them that it had not been like that. It had been a marriage of convenience from first to last. Brian had been her greatest friend. She had liked him and trusted him and gone to him for advice when she had felt she could trust no one else in the world. But neither of them had ever been remotely in love.

And when she'd married him he'd already known he was dying.

Rachel had found him alone in the kitchen one night after the children had gone to bed. He'd looked at his wits' end. That was when he'd told her.

'I've been talking to Angela. She doesn't seem to be able to take it in. She's very busy with her new life, of course. Which doesn't include the kids. She keeps saying something will turn up.' He banged his fist on the counter-top. 'But it won't. All I've got is maybe a year to find a solution.'

He had had two years in the end. And the solution had been Rachel.

She had never regretted it. She knew that it had not been a one-sided relationship. Brian had given her support in her education and, eventually, her career. He had helped restore her shattered confidence. And he had provided the best reason in the world for her lack of relationships with men.

Now that reason was gone. So either she had to find another one or face up to experiences she had been running away from for nine years.

She said with an effort, 'I'm a contract career lady too.'

Gilly took the hint. 'Alexandra was saying. Long hours?'

Rachel sighed. 'I thought it was going to be just for this single project. You know—a few weeks doing eighteen-hour days and then back to normal. Only, it isn't working out quite like that.'

'It never does,' said Gilly wryly. 'Whenever Peter does any of these one-off assignments, he always ends up with more work at the end of it.' Her husband was an executive in a multinational company.

'Well, unless I'm very careful, it looks as if that's exactly what's going to happen to me,' Rachel said gloomily.

Gilly was scornful. 'Careful? Huh! What can you do

about it? If they've realised you can work round the clock, they'll jolly well make sure you carry on doing it.'

Rachel knew that, on the basis of her experience as the wife of a seriously successful senior manager, Gilly knew what she was talking about. On the other hand, Rachel had been gaining some experience of her own since she'd started at Bentley's. She allowed herself a small private smile.

'Well, maybe not.' Rachel swirled her coffee round in its mug. 'There are a couple of male egos that might be brought round to seeing things my way. If I approach them in the right way.'

Gilly looked at her with awe. 'You know the right way?'

Rachel looked up. Her eyes danced suddenly. 'I have a working hypothesis. I'll let you know if it works.'

'If it works, patent it,' Gilly advised, getting up. She kissed Rachel briefly on the cheek. 'Don't bother about the casserole. Alexandra can bring it back any time.' She went.

Rachel went to her room and climbed out of her city suit. She hung it up in her understocked wardrobe and put on jeans and a roomy sweatshirt.

There was no sound from Hugh's room, which meant he was wearing his earphones. Rachel gave silent thanks. She knocked quietly at Alexandra's door but was not really surprised when there was no answer. Alexandra was making a point of her right to privacy at the moment.

Rachel went back to the kitchen and geared herself up for phase two of the working day. She checked the washing machine, put Gilly's stew in the oven and started peeling potatoes. Normally she hated peeling potatoes but today she attacked them with a will, as if they were personal enemies. As the peel fell away, she felt an almost blood-thirsty satisfaction.

'Take that,' she said, gouging a particularly stubborn eye out of one of the larger potatoes.

'Talking to yourself now?' said a voice from the doorway.

Rachel looked up. Her stepdaughter had finally emerged from her room and was draped gracefully against the door-jamb. She was wearing a skintight tube-dress that showed an enticing acreage of pale-skinned bosom and ended halfway down her upper thighs. She was presumably going out.

Rachel bit back her immediate reaction and gave Alexandra a pleasant smile. Dealing with corporate raiders all day gave you some grasp of tactics at least.

'Hi. Hungry?'

'I *was*,' returned Alexandra, no mean tactician herself. 'But when you were so late I thought you weren't coming back this evening. So I've made other arrangements.'

Silently Rachel cursed Riccardo di Stefano. If he had not kept her at bay in her office after that meeting, she would have finished her day's work at a reasonable time and been home when she'd said she would be. Not that that would have prevented Alexandra from making a bid to go out with Theo. But at least it would have meant she did not have an excuse handed to her on a plate.

Rachel skewered another eye out of the potato with quite unnecessary viciousness.

Not looking at Alexandra, she said, 'Where's he taking you? And when is he picking you up?'

A faint frown crossed her stepdaughter's face. In matters of detail Theo was proving difficult to pin down. Rachel had discovered this by accident and was using her awareness of it sparingly.

Now Alexandra shrugged elaborately. 'No special time. I said, Let's just hang out.'

'Ah,' said Rachel.

She quartered the potato, dropped the pieces in the salted water with the rest and put the pan on to boil. She rinsed her hands and dried them. 'Pity,' she remarked to the wall. 'Gilly's stew smells good.'

'Gilly *likes* cooking,' Alexandra pointed out. She managed to make this indisputable truth into a rebuke.

'She's also got a cordon bleu qualification,' said Rachel, stung.

'You could have done a cordon bleu course if you'd wanted. It was you who wanted to do that MBA and have a career in banking. Daddy would much rather have had a proper wife who made food look nice.'

'So much for the feminist influence in the younger generation,' muttered Rachel. 'Stop nagging, you little reactionary. Your father wanted me to have the chance to do work that interested me. Just as he wanted you to,' she added with point.

Before his last session in hospital, Brian had mounted a fierce campaign so that Alexandra could study the physics course she'd wanted rather than the biology course that had suited the school curriculum. He had won. It had been good to see his triumph, especially as Alexandra had been delighted with the defeat of authority in the shape of her formidable headmistress.

Reminded now, Alexandra looked uncomfortable. Rachel pursued her advantage ruthlessly. 'By the way, how is school going?'

Alexandra regarded her beadily. 'If you're asking whether I've done my homework, the answer's yes.'

'I wasn't, actually. If I wanted to know the state of your homework, I would ask,' Rachel said levelly.

She reached for the gardenia-scented hand cream which Alexandra had bought her for Christmas when they'd still been in relative harmony—before Theo had appeared. She began to smooth it over her fingers. The potato water had given them the texture of old prunes.

'It just occurs to me that I've got to go to your PTA meeting next week. I could do with some advance briefing.'

Alexandra watched. Eventually she burst out, 'You mean you actually think you'll get there this time?'

This was an unexpected attack. Rachel gaped.

'I've only missed one,' she protested. 'I couldn't help that. The Malaysian deal. I told you.'

'Two others,' corrected Alexandra. 'The one before Christmas—you said it was only a social. And then Hugh's last one.'

'I didn't. I—' Rachel stopped, remembering. She grew indignant. 'The plane was late. I got there in the end.'

'Not in time. Hugh particularly wanted you to talk to Mr Templeton about him doing Russian and Mr Templeton had gone.'

'I talked to his tutor,' said Rachel defensively.

'His tutor's a silly old prat who thinks clever boys do Greek, not Russian,' said Alexandra, with her usual grasp of essentials. 'Hugh needed you to tell him to bog off. You didn't and now he's lumbered.'

One of Alexandra's great strengths as a tactician was to point out the genuine shortcomings of the adults in her life. While they were feeling properly guilty, they forgot the substance of their original argument. Rachel reminded herself of this.

'I'll talk to Hugh about it,' she said.

Alexandra looked annoyed. But she was shrewd enough to recognise that her move had been countered. She shrugged.

'So how *is* school going?' said Rachel, returning with an effort to the subject in hand.

For a moment Alexandra seemed almost uncomfortable. Then she said airily, 'Oh, boring. But I survive.'

'Well, congratulations.' Rachel's tone was dry. 'Now tell me the truth.'

Alexandra sent her a look of dislike. 'What has Gilly been saying?'

Trained by experience, Rachel concealed her surprise. She raised her eyebrows. 'What do you think?'

'She promised she wouldn't split,' said Alexandra with disgust. She glowered but decided to expand. 'It's nothing. I just told the Hornbeam I wasn't wasting my time doing stupid maps for history prep.' She snorted. 'You'd think we were five instead of fifteen. Tracing paper and coloured pens at our age. I ask you.'

'I see.' Rachel folded her lips together in an attempt to curb instinctive laughter. On the whole she was successful. 'And what did Mrs Hornbeam say?'

Alexandra shrugged. 'Stamped and screamed and threatened thumbscrews,' she said indifferently.

Rachel nodded. 'I see. Standard stuff.' She took some more hand cream and applied it absorbedly. 'And how did it happen to come to Gilly's notice?'

'Oh, Susanna didn't do her map-making either. The Hornbeam told Gilly I was a bad influence.'

This seemed to afford Alexandra considerable satisfaction. Rachel comforted herself with the fact that Susanna's parents could not share the form mistress's opinion or they would not be allowing their daughter to spend all her free time with Alexandra. She put down the bottle of gardenia hand cream with resolution, however.

She said carefully, 'You and Susanna are growing up. You need your personal space, I know. And you can do without people like me telling you how to run your personal relationships. I accept that. But when you're young—'

The doorbell rang. Alexandra had been beginning to look mulish but the sharp ring wiped the frown off her face. She stopped even pretending to listen to Rachel.

'Theo,' she said, her face lighting up.

'You can make mistakes that take so much getting over, it's out of all proportion to the fun you had in the first place.'

But Alexandra had already flown to the door. After a moment, Rachel gave a twisted smile. She was not entirely sorry. If Alexandra had been listening she would have demanded an explanation. Rachel was not sure that she had one. Not without explaining Riccardo di Stefano. She did not think she could bear that. Surely there was a limit on the self-immolation required of a stepmother?

CHAPTER SEVEN

RACHEL sighed and followed in her stepdaughter's wake, bracing herself to give stern warning on being home before eleven. It was not needed. It was not Theo Judd on the doorstep. It was the only visitor who was more unwelcome.

'Rachel,' purred Riccardo di Stefano, stepping past an open-mouthed Alexandra and taking both Rachel's hands in his. 'So good to see you relaxed at last.'

It was like a nightmare, Rachel thought. She was utterly unprepared. She had no arguments to get rid of him and no possible excuse for leaving the house herself. In her jeans, with the rumble of the washing machine behind her and the kitchen full of the smell of Gilly's good stew, it was obvious that she had settled down for a family evening at home.

Riccardo assessed the situation in a moment. He discarded his well-cut overcoat and dropped it over an oak chair in the hall. Alexandra followed, her eyes wide.

'How pleasant,' he said, sniffing the aroma of hot food with appreciation.

He strolled into the kitchen with the ease of an accustomed guest. You would think that he was not only invited but absolutely certain of his welcome, thought Rachel indignantly. Such was his confidence that she gave ground before him. She retreated behind the kitchen table. He gave a small nod, as if that was what he'd expected.

'I was going to take you out to dinner,' he announced. 'But that would clearly be redundant.'

Rachel braced herself against a kitchen chair. The warm wood was reassuring somehow.

She said arctically, 'If you remember, I refused.'

Alexandra swung between them, looking intrigued.

'And now I see why,' he said politely.

Alexandra did not like being ignored. She said, 'Rachel didn't cook that.'

Rachel ignored her stepdaughter. She was concentrating all her force on Riccardo. She was shaking imperceptibly—with temper. She assured herself it was temper.

'You know perfectly well why I refused to have dinner with you.'

'Do I?'

'Just as you did at the time. Which is why you turned up here, isn't it?'

Riccardo's eyelids dropped. 'Maybe.'

'Rachel can't cook at all,' Alexandra told him chattily. 'Well, only scrambled eggs and baked beans.'

Riccardo directed a slow smile at Rachel. She could feel the heat of it, like a furnace, like sunshine. Nine years ago, a look like that would have set her blushing furiously. What was it Judy had said? She was an open book? Rachel thanked God for experience and kept her complexion. Riccardo's smile widened.

'Then it's just as well it's not her cooking I'm interested in, isn't it?' he said, not taking his eyes off Rachel.

Alexandra was impressed. Rachel was outraged.

She said crisply to her stepdaughter, 'Mr di Stefano is a business acquaintance.'

Alexandra did not look convinced. Riccardo's attitude did not help. He shook his head reproachfully.

'Business acquaintance? Do you feel that covers it?'

'Yes,' said Rachel hardily.

He put his head on one side, consideringly. 'I would say our relationship is a little more—complicated than that.'

Rachel forgot their audience. She forgot boardroom diplomacy and her beloved career as well. All she was aware of was a great need to tell him exactly where she stood. She met his eyes, her own cold as glass.

'We have no relationship.'

Alexandra, enthralled, held her breath.

Riccardo was not put out in the slightest. 'If that were true I would not be here.'

Rachel gave him a look of undisguised dislike. 'Well, I certainly didn't invite you and I can't think of any reason why you should be here.'

'Can't you?'

She set her teeth. 'Mr di Stefano—'

'Riccardo.'

She ignored that. 'I don't want to be rude—'

'Don't you?' He looked amused.

Rachel ignored that too. She swept on. 'This is my home. I try not to bring work home. I don't always succeed. But I don't encourage colleagues to turn up on the doorstep unannounced. You, if you will forgive me, are—however grand—just another colleague.'

He did not like that. She could see it from the way his face went very still. All vestige of amusement was banished. Suddenly, he looked the ruthlessly successful man she knew him to be.

'More than that, I think,' he corrected her quietly.

It was not—quite—a threat. Rachel went white. She folded her arms quickly across her breast, hugging her waist. Her face felt pinched. Alexandra, she saw, was looking uncharacteristically shocked, and uncertain. Rachel tried to pull herself together.

'We'd do better to discuss this in private,' she said through stiff lips.

Riccardo was not given to remorse. His eyes flicked over Alexandra at last. He looked back at Rachel.

'Quite,' he said blandly.

Rachel decided that she hated him.

The doorbell rang again. This time Alexandra did not dive for it at once. She was chewing her lip, regarding Riccardo with dawning suspicion. She had also shrunk rather closer to her stepmother. Rachel felt sorry for her.

'That will be Theo, won't it?' she said gently.

'Yes.' Alexandra hesitated, still undecided.

'Then you'd better let him in. You invited him.'

'I know. But—'

The bell rang again, insistently. Reluctantly, Alexandra went off to the front door. Left alone, Riccardo and Rachel measured each other like duellists.

He said softly, 'She's very protective.'

'She's very young,' said Rachel sharply.

'But not young enough to be your daughter.'

Her head came up. 'What?'

He said in a musing voice, 'Marriage to a man old enough to be your father. Two adolescent stepchildren. Full responsibility for them when he dies. Plus a demanding climb up the corporate ladder. Don't you ever feel out of your depth?'

Her eyes glittered. 'Do you?'

For a moment he looked taken aback. 'I direct my own course.'

'So do I.'

His brows rose. She thought he was going to challenge her. But then Alexandra came back into the kitchen with Theo and the moment passed.

Theo, as usual, was wearing a black leather jacket and dark jeans that Alexandra, no doubt, thought the height of sophistication. As always he was so much at ease that Rachel wanted to hit him. It deflected her momentarily from Riccardo di Stefano.

'Hi, Mrs Gray. How you doing?'

'Fine, thank you,' said Rachel with restraint. 'You?'

'Can't complain.' He eyed Riccardo di Stefano. 'You want us out, right?'

'No,' said Rachel.

'Perceptive of you,' said Riccardo at the same time.

Theo grinned. 'No sweat. We're on our way.' He flicked a forefinger in Alexandra's direction. 'Get waddling, doll.'

Rachel closed her eyes, anguished. Alexandra, however, found nothing to complain of in this mode of address. She grabbed a crocheted shawl, swung it about her shoulders and flung her arm round Theo's waist. She was positively luminous with glee.

'Ready.'

'Back by eleven,' Rachel reminded her.

Alexandra frowned but the curfew clearly suited Theo very well.

'You're on,' he said. 'Eleven it is.'

They began to go.

'Have a good time,' said Rachel, though it cost her.

Theo gave her an altogether too knowing look over his shoulder. 'We will.'

The front door slammed. Rachel let out a long breath of relief. No longer obliged to contain her frustration, she picked up an oven glove and threw it hard at the opposite wall.

Di Stefano considered the fallen thing with some amusement. 'Don't like the boyfriend?'

Rachel was reminded that she hated Riccardo more than she loathed Theo Judd. 'That's got nothing to do with you.'

'That depends on your point of view.'

She sent him a look of dislike and went round the table to pick up the oven glove. Di Stefano forestalled her. He picked it up and tossed it absently onto the table behind her. Then he took her gently by the arm.

Rachel froze.

'From where I'm sitting, anything that comes between you and your work has rather a lot to do with me,' he said quite gently.

His hand was incredibly warm on her bare arm. It set up a perceptible flutter in her throat. Rachel ignored it, trying to disengage herself.

She said icily, 'Nothing comes between me and my work.'

He did not let her go. 'That's not the way I hear it.'

'What?' She was so startled that she stopped pulling against those imprisoning fingers.

'Philip tells me that you have been very preoccupied recently. He thought—trouble at home. Of course, you're very young to have such a big responsibility. He assumed it was getting you down.'

Riccardo's tone was neutral. He expressed no opinion; he was merely reporting an allegation, awaiting her response. It was all admirably unemotional.

Rachel was unable to match that professional impassivity. She shook herself free from his grasp.

'If that were true, why didn't Philip say anything to me about it?'

Riccardo shrugged. 'Didn't want to add to your burdens?' he suggested indifferently.

'Balderdash. Philip doesn't know a single thing about my burdens. And cares less,' said Rachel roundly.

There was quick gleam of triumph in the dark eyes. It was as quickly masked but Rachel had seen it. It set light to all sorts of vague suspicions.

She said slowly, 'When did Philip tell you he thought I had trouble at home?'

Riccardo had the grace to look uncomfortable. 'He didn't exactly tell me—'

'When?' Rachel was implacable.

'I called him this evening,' he admitted.

'You called him? About me?'

If she thought he would show any sign of decent confusion she was disappointed.

'Naturally.'

She was so outraged that for a moment she could barely speak. 'How dare you?' she managed at last.

'If we are to trust the recovery program to you, I have to know that you are reliable. You are, after all, relatively inexperienced.'

Their eyes clashed. His mouth tilted wickedly.

'In banking, anyway.'

Rachel felt as if she had been hit. Her head reared up. For a moment the kitchen seemed to swing wildly about her. She almost staggered. Something flickered in those strange eyes and he reached out as if to steady her.

This time she had no trouble at all in detaching herself. She shook his hand off as if it were no more than a troublesome insect. She held his eyes with hers.

'I see,' she said softly.

His eyes narrowed. 'What do you see?'

'You think you have some sort of special influence over me.'

'Not influence.'

She paid no heed to his protest. 'Because I knew you when I was young and silly, you think you can walk into my life and hijack whatever part of it happens to amuse you at the moment.'

His face tightened. 'Don't be melodramatic.'

She brushed that aside too. She took an angry step towards him. 'I've got news for you. I grew up.'

'I noticed.'

'I'm not so easily intimidated. Not any more.'

His look was frankly incredulous. 'Are you trying to say you were intimidated the last time we met?'

Rachel set her teeth. 'The last time we met,' she said with precision, 'I was eighteen years old.'

To her astonishment, Riccardo di Stefano looked away. A faint colour ran along the high cheekbones. Could the man possibly be embarrassed?

He said stiffly, 'So I have been told.'

'So don't think you can treat me like a child any more. I've learned a few things along the way, including how to fight my corner.'

The flush—if a flush it had been—was gone. It left him surprising pale under the accustomed tan. 'I am sure you have. But you don't have to fight me.'

'Don't I?' said Rachel. It was a challenge and neither of them pretended anything else.

Riccardo muttered something under his breath. It

sounded explosive and uncharacteristically agitated. He pushed a hand through his hair.

'Rachel, I didn't come here to fight with you.'

She could see herself reflected in the mirror that hung on the wall behind his head. Her eyes were too bright, like those of a child who had been too long at a party. She thought, I've got to get him out of here.

She said, 'No, you came here to remind me about an episode which was over and done with nine years ago. I don't know if you think that puts me in your power in some way. I can only tell you that it does not. Nor does it give you any right to invade my private life—'

He held up a hand, quite suddenly. He was smiling but Rachel had the sudden impression that he was very angry.

'Any invading,' he said, too quietly, 'was done a long time ago and was entirely mutual.'

Rachel snorted. 'Don't be ridiculous.'

'It is not ridiculous. It is the truth. As you would recognise if you would only stop spitting for a moment and talk this over like a reasonable person.'

'I am not,' said Rachel with the calm of despair, 'going to stand here discussing my adolescent disasters with you.'

He homed in at once on the one word that gave her away. She would have recalled it if she'd been able to. But it was too late.

'Disasters?' He took a step forward.

Rachel backed. 'I hate post-mortems.'

Another step forward. She had nowhere else to go unless she swung herself backwards into the sink.

'Why disasters?'

She lifted her chin and met his eyes with as much dignity as she could muster.

'Don't be disingenuous, please. Of course it was a disaster. One night with the last of the all-time playboys? It had to be a disaster.'

He drew in a little breath as if she had punched him unexpectedly. But it did not stop that slow advance on her position. He was now so close that she had to strain back not to touch him. A muscle worked in his cheek.

'I see your point,' he admitted levelly. 'What I don't see is why.'

He put a hand on her waist. It felt hot, burning. Suddenly Rachel was having trouble getting her thoughts together.

'Why?' she echoed.

Another step. No amount of craning backwards could avoid physical contact now. He touched her everywhere—thigh, hip, shoulder. He towered over her, making her look up into his face. It was quite without expression.

'Why it had to be just one night,' he explained.

Rachel stared at him. Desperately she reminded herself that, however practised he was, she had the measure of him. These days she could meet him on his own ground and rout him. Had she not been training herself to do exactly that for the last nine years?

But the last nine years seemed to be dancing away from her. Looking up at him, she could almost smell the ocean again, hear the distant rock band and, closer, the whirr of the old-fashioned ceiling fan above their heads. She swallowed.

Riccardo said, quite kindly, 'You made a mistake leaving like that.'

'L-leaving?'

'I said we'd talk in the morning. I don't like waking up and finding the lady I should be having breakfast with has gone.'

Some vestige of common sense reasserted itself. Rachel gave a crack of cynical laughter. 'Tough.'

He smiled but his eyes were veiled. 'It was. Oh, it was. Especially as we had not done with each other. Had we?'

Rachel reared back, shocked. Riccardo laughed aloud. He touched a finger to her mouth. It was hardly a touch, just a butterfly brush of the very tip of his finger, but it made Rachel shake visibly as if he had branded her.

He saw her reaction and smiled. 'We are not done yet, are we?'

She might be shaking but she had built some defences in the last nine years. Now, at last, she activated them. She pushed at him, head down, outraged. 'Get out of my house.'

He gave ground, his eyes alight with laughter suddenly. 'Are we?'

'Out.'

She drove him back through the kitchen, the hall. He went, throwing up his hands like a defeated duellist. But he did not look defeated. He looked alert and interested and altogether too cool.

'There's unfinished business between you and me, Rachel. You know it and so do I. Nothing either of us can say will change that.'

'Get out. *Now.*'

He shrugged. 'If not now, later.'

Rachel picked up his coat and flung it at him. He caught it one-handed, hesitated for a second, then reached out and took her chin in one long-fingered hand. Rachel let out a screech of sheer animal rage.

And Riccardo di Stefano leaned forward and kissed her hard on the lips. He did not wait to see her reaction.

The next day Rachel was waiting for Philip when he came into his office at nine. He was surprised but he showed no sign of an uneasy conscience.

'Good morning, Rachel,' he said, regarding his personal computer with disfavour. He sighed and turned it on. 'Jolly well done yesterday, by the way. I didn't get the opportunity to say so at the time. Rick was most impressed.'

'I just bet he was,' said Rachel grimly.

'What?' Philip looked up from the keyboard he was squaring up to gingerly. 'Sorry, missed that.'

She sat down on the end of the sofa which Philip kept for his most illustrious clients. Her mind went blank.

It was odd. Rachel had thought out this interview so carefully. When she had told Gilly that she was going to appeal to her colleagues' egos, it had been of Philip that she'd been thinking. She had thought she could get him on her side by showing him a way to score a victory over di Stefano. After yesterday he would be badly needing to do something to restore his self-esteem. Last night she had concocted a strategy step by step.

This morning it was gone. Rachel looked down at her hands and desperately tried to recall what had seemed so obvious last night. She tried to think of a way to approach the subject subtly. Nothing came. In the end she blurted it out baldly.

'I need to know what di Stefano said. About me, I mean.'

As soon as she'd said it, she could have kicked herself. It was about the worst thing she could have thought of. Instead of getting Philip on her side, it immediately set him on the defensive.

He bridled. 'Well, we had other things to talk about. Business strategy in the wider arena—'

There was no point in playing games. Rachel cut him short. 'Not about the bank. Me. Personally. Look, Philip, I ought to tell you—' She broke off, biting her lip.

In the coldest watches of the night, telling Philip what had happened nine years ago had seemed logical. Indeed, it had seemed the only thing to do. As long as she was trying to hide it, Riccardo had the upper hand. He, as he had made perfectly clear, did not care who knew. No, the only sensible thing to do was to tell Philip and trust his discretion.

As she was now finding out, however, it was one thing to reach a reasoned conclusion in the small hours, but quite another to carry it out. She found she was twisting her hands together and straightened her fingers quickly.

'Tell me what?' prompted Philip.

'Oh, this is horrible,' she burst out. 'This is exactly what

they always say women executives do—mess up business
with feelings. And it's so unfair.'

Philip looked at her in the liveliest astonishment. He
even stopped playing with the keyboard.

'My dear Rachel. *Feelings?*' He looked as if he could
not believe his ears. 'Is anything wrong?'

Rachel fought for composure. She smoothed her skirt
with hands that shook slightly.

'I'm sorry,' she said quietly after a pause. 'I didn't mean
to get emotional. I won't again.'

Philip's astonishment was comical. '*Emotional?* About
Rick di Stefano?'

Rachel frowned, not understanding. Then she realised
that Philip was thinking she was much too dull and businesslike to get involved with his demon shareholder. In
spite of the horrors of the previous day, Rachel gave a
choke of laughter.

It made her feel better. She sat up straight and told him
an edited version of the truth. You could see that Philip
found even the expurgated version difficult to believe.

'A—er—flirtation?' he said, torn between honest fascination and the English gentleman's code which regarded
all reference to feeling as a serious breach of good taste.

'I was very young.'

'Yes, of course. You must have been. So that was
why—' He broke off. 'Oh, what's the point? I've never
been any good at hiding things. He was in here last night
demanding to look at the personnel files.'

Rachel felt slightly sick. 'You didn't—?'

'No.' Philip was quietly proud of himself. 'I told him
the bank had a duty of confidentiality to its employees. But
I didn't see any harm in giving him your CV. Damn it,
Rachel, it's practically a public document since you gave
that interview to *Women on the Ladder.*'

Rachel had to admit that was so.

'He was spitting mad,' Philip said thoughtfully. 'I

thought it was because we had employed someone so young to do such a crucial job. But it wasn't, was it?'

Rachel swallowed. 'I don't think so, no.'

'It was personal.'

'I don't see why it should be, but—' She shrugged.

Philip looked uncomfortable. 'Well, if you—er—turned him down... Men don't forget that, you know.'

'Surely he's been turned down often enough since then?' said Rachel, startled into indiscretion. 'It can't be that big a deal.'

'It's always a big deal,' said Philip drily, forgetting the English gentleman's code completely. 'Probably worse if you've got a track record like Rick di Stefano's.'

He thought about it for a moment, his kindly face sober. Then he said, 'I think you need to take care, Rachel. Rick obviously hasn't forgotten and he might want to make you pay. I'd keep out of his way, if I were you.'

She was careful not to let her relief show. 'Do you think I can?'

Philip waved an airy hand. 'Of course. He's only here till Thursday, then he's flying back to New York. All you have to do is keep out of the office. There's the project in Aberdeen. Go up and see how the site evaluation is coming along. Don't come back till Friday.' He gave her a sudden conspiratorial grin which reminded her why she liked working with him so much. 'That will settle him.'

So in the end her strategy worked, even though she had not played her own part quite as she had written it. Rachel walked out of Philip's office not knowing whether to laugh or to be thoroughly ashamed of herself. It was not Philip's ego that had come down on her side; it was his kindness of heart.

The moment she got back to her own office suite, however, she stopped worrying over the ethical point. The place was full of exotic flowers. So full, in fact, that it looked more like a botanical greenhouse than a place of work.

Rachel stopped dead in the doorway and shaded her eyes.

'Mandy, are you in there?'

Her secretary's voice floated out from Rachel's private office. 'Coming.'

She emerged carrying a woven basket of rushes and big waxy flowers. Rachel quailed. 'Do they bite?'

Mandy chuckled. 'Wouldn't be surprised. You should see the instructions that come with them.'

Rachel looked round, feeling helpless. 'What on earth is going on here?'

'Well, he either thinks we should make a bid for Kew Gardens and is starting you off on the acquisition research or he fancies you,' Mandy said calmly.

'He?' echoed Rachel, her heart sinking.

'Riccardo di Stefano.'

'Oh.'

She sank limply onto a chair, found it was occupied by a basket of assorted foliage, and propped herself against the wall instead.

'He's been on the phone too,' Mandy informed her helpfully.

'Oh,' said Rachel again.

She moved the chunky basket to the floor and sat on the chair. Mandy wedged the rushes into the window-sill and turned. She folded her arms across her and considered Rachel.

'Are you going to tell me?' she asked pleasantly. 'Or do you just want me to speculate wildly like everyone else in the building?'

Rachel shook her head helplessly. 'You can't be speculating any more wildly than I am. I don't know what the hell he's playing at. Why all this?' She spread her hands.

'Didn't he say last night?' asked Mandy artlessly.

Rachel stiffened. 'Last night?'

'I know he got your address out of Philip. Joan was worried about it.' Joan was Philip's secretary. 'But by that time there was nothing much she could do. We thought about phoning you.'

'What made you decide against it?' said Rachel bitterly.

Mandy was apologetic. 'It seemed like we were overreacting a bit, when we got to talk it through. I mean he wasn't going to do anything dramatic, was he?' She looked round the exotic plant collection doubtfully. 'At least, we thought he wasn't,' she ended on an uncertain note.

Rachel took pity on her. 'Don't worry. He didn't.' She prodded a yucca plant distastefully. 'At least, not until this morning. What on earth are we going to do with the plant life?'

'Leave it to me,' Mandy said. 'One each to everyone on the Christmas Social committee. That will get rid of them.'

Rachel looked at her with awe. 'You're inspired.'

'All part of the service.'

'They don't have to take them home today. The plants can stay here till the end of the week. I'm going up to Aberdeen. I won't be back in the office until Monday.'

Mandy nodded in comprehension but she did not make any other comment. She reached for her pad and made a note.

'Do you mind which flight you take?'

Rachel grimaced. 'The later the better, I suppose. I don't have much packing but I need to make arrangements for the kids.'

Mandy added the information to her notes. 'Hotel?'

'Whichever the others are staying in.'

'Fine. I'll get onto it.' She peered round a spray of orchids to read her PC screen. 'You're seeing Mr Torrance at ten—did you remember?'

'Yes. Thank you.'

Mandy looked up, her eyes crinkling in amusement. 'And do you want me to get Mr di Stefano for you before or after your meeting?'

Rachel snorted. 'After the next ice age for preference.'

'He'll call again before then,' Mandy said sapiently. 'What do you want me to do about that?'

Rachel was conscious of the beginnings of a headache. She sighed. 'If he calls I'll speak to him. But you'd better warn him that I'm on my way out of town.'

'I'll do that,' promised Mandy. Her expression said that she did not think much of it as an evasion tactic.

In that she was wrong. Colin Torrance came and went and there was no message from di Stefano. Thereafter, Rachel steamed through her in-tray at a rate of knots and heard the telephone ring in the outer office several times. But no call was put through to her.

It was, she thought, half-annoyed, half-amused, oddly frustrating. She did not want to have to talk to him. After last night there was nothing she wanted less. But she was left with the unpleasant feeling that it was inevitable at some point and that she was just marking time while she waited for the axe to fall.

In the end she could bear it no longer. She flung down the pen with which she had been doodling for ten minutes and went out to Mandy's office.

'Er—messages?'

Mandy looked up, unsurprised. She gestured at the screen in front of her. 'They're in the postbox.'

'Ah.'

Rachel still lingered in the doorway. Mandy took pity on her.

'Di Stefano wouldn't leave a message. He said he'd catch you later.'

'Ah,' said Rachel in quite a different tone. She looked at her watch. 'I think I'll take an early lunch. You don't know when I'll be back.'

In the reception hall the security guard opened the door for her.

'Your car's waiting, Mrs Gray.'

Rachel stared. 'My car?'

'Chauffeur came in to say he'd wait on the corner until he was moved on. Been there about twenty minutes.'

Rachel shook her head. 'Not my car, Geoff. Maybe Mr Jensen's?'

Geoff was unconvinced. 'It was you he asked for.'

An explanation occurred to her. 'Maybe Mandy ordered a car to take me to the airport this evening. They must have got the pick-up time wrong. I'll have a word. Thanks, Geoff.'

But when she went to the corner the vehicle was not her usual hired car with a friendly driver she knew but a dark-windowed limousine. The man who got out wore full chauffeur's uniform, including leather gloves. Gloves! Rachel goggled.

The chauffeur showed no emotion. Impassively, he opened the rear nearside door and stood to attention. It was quite clear that he knew who she was.

'Good morning, Mrs Gray.'

'I think there's been some mistake. I didn't order a car.'

No reaction to that either. He simply stood there, like some flunkey waiting to take her to her coronation. Another suspicion presented itself.

'Perhaps you can tell me who did order the car?' she suggested affably.

'I do not have that information, madam.'

'Then let me guess. Di Stefano's private office?'

But the wooden face was not giving anything away.

'All right,' said Rachel. There was something exhilarating in the battle of wills. She was almost beginning to enjoy herself. 'Let's come at this from another angle. Where were you supposed to take me? I mean, you do know where to go, don't you? I don't just get the car and driver to go joyriding all over the Home Counties, wherever I want, do I?'

'My instructions are to drive you to St Thomas' Court.'

She frowned, sifting rapidly through her memory. It was not an address she knew. Briefly she wondered whether it was a hotel and was astonished that Riccardo would stay anywhere but the best hotel in London. Then it clicked into place.

'Chelsea. By the river, right? One of the apartment blocks at the harbour?'

The chauffeur unbent sufficiently to give her a stately nod in response to this.

So Riccardo di Stefano had decided to get her onto his own territory. His own *private* territory. While the harbour development was not exactly off the beaten track, it was hardly central either. Getting away from there could be complicated and time-consuming if she wanted to leave before he chose to let her go. She looked at the chauffeur assessingly.

'Are you also on stand-by to bring me back?'

He did not know. He was only given one instruction at a time. He did not know what his next job might be.

'Which means no,' interpreted Rachel.

She felt suddenly, gloriously angry. She had been spoiling for a fight all morning. Now, it seemed, it was being offered to her. She got into the car.

It took the chauffeur by surprise. It was a good few seconds before he collected himself sufficiently to close the door on her. He got into the driving seat and set the car in motion. They slid into the traffic.

As soon as they were on the Embankment and Rachel was satisfied that she could do so without distracting his attention dangerously, she leaned forward.

'I'd like to make a phone call, please.'

He unhooked the car phone from its stalk and passed it back to her. She dialled Mandy.

'Change of plan,' she told her crisply. 'Di Stefano sent a car. I seem to be lunching at St Thomas' Court in Chelsea.'

In front of her the chauffeur's shoulders stiffened. No doubt he would report back to di Stefano's private office.

Rachel hoped that he would. She hoped he would report verbatim.

To put a bit of ginger into his report, she said, 'No, it's not a kidnap *yet*. I don't intend that it shall turn into one either. If I'm not back by two, send a car out there to pick me up, will you?'

She handed the phone back to the chauffeur.

'Thank you.'

As she expected, the building was a tower. The chauffeur swept into a cordoned stopping-off area and helped Rachel alight. A uniformed attendant opened the security-coded door for her. He did not bother to ask her name. He clearly knew she was coming.

'Mr di Stefano is on the fourteenth floor,' he said kindly. 'Fine view.'

Rachel smiled, not committing herself. She paused, looking round the ultra-modern interior. It was cool and high, with an impressively glassed and domed entrance hall and elevators walled with coloured glass. If big money had a scent, it would smell like this, she thought: high-tech electronics overlaid with the scent of flowers out of their season and out of their natural habitat.

In fact, the entrance hall was full of enough plants to make a botanical-garden director jealous. At one end the source of all this vegetation was clear. It was a shop, small enough to call itself a boutique, large enough to house two very expensively dressed women. Orchids and Friends, it was called, and it lurked behind a dense hedge of jungle leaves. Rachel strolled over, to the confusion of the lift attendant.

'Can I help you?' said one of the women.

'I think you already have. Did you send a shipment to Bentley's Investment Bank this morning?'

'Bentley's? I don't think they're one of our clients. I can check, if you like.'

She did. She came back looking respectful—and a good deal more curious.

'Mrs Gray? Yes, we did. At the request of Mr di Stefano. I'm sorry, did we forget to put in a card?'

'No,' said Rachel. 'Thank you.'

She turned back to the hovering attendant.

'All set for the fourteenth floor, then.'

He did not come up with her. He did not need to. There was only one apartment on the fourteenth floor and the lift did not open without a key. As soon as she arrived, there was a little whirring sound, and the door was flung open.

Expecting yet another uniformed flunkey, Rachel was disconcerted to find herself face to face with the man himself. He stood looking at her for a moment, his eyes dark and unreadable.

'You came,' he said at last.

CHAPTER EIGHT

IT TOOK Rachel several moments to recover from her astonishment. She could not read Riccardo's expression. But, as the world rocked back into balance and became manageable again, she had the distinct impression that he felt he had won a battle. An important battle.

It made her furious. It also made her feel seriously uneasy.

Well, she had built a few defences in the last nine years, to say nothing of acquiring a whole range of social weapons. It had cost her, that armour. There were months when she went out into the world every day expecting to face an enemy. It had taught her self-reliance—and the ability to return fire with fire. What was the point of all that experience, if you did not use it?

So she gathered herself together, ignored the way her heart seemed to be shaking within her ribcage, and prepared to enter battle.

'What else could I do in the face of such a pressing invitation?' she said sweetly.

He laughed then, ushering her into the room with a mock bow. He did not pretend to misunderstand her.

'I know it was kind of dramatic. But what else could I do? You refused all my regular invitations.'

Rachel was feeling more in control than the previous evening. For one thing, she was dressed in her professional camouflage—dark suit, cream blouse, earrings. For another, by calling Mandy from the car, she had held her own against his underhand tactics. At least so far.

So she strolled in and looked around in a leisurely fashion, quite as if she had expected to come here for ages and was not wildly unnerved by the events of yesterday. She even pretended to give his question serious consideration.

'Well, I suppose you could have got yourself a mask and broken into my room at midnight, like something out of a silent movie,' she observed.

'Ouch,' he said, his expression wry.

Her smile got even sweeter, even deadlier.

'Or you could have done what civilised people do and accepted that I do not want to go out with you.'

He flung back his head and laughed aloud at that. 'I'm not that civilised,' he told her.

'So I infer,' she said sharply.

She immediately regretted it. How was she going to steer clear of dangerous subjects if she let him goad her into sniping at him? From his complacent expression, it seemed that Riccardo was thinking along the same lines.

So she did not join in his laughter or let her eyes meet his. She did not get close enough for him to touch her either. She swung sharply on her heel and went to the long windows, well out of his reach. From the amused silence behind her, she was pretty sure he knew exactly what she was doing. For the moment, it seemed he was prepared to go along with it. But for how long?

Rachel shivered, although the windows were closed. They gave onto a balcony with a fine view of the Thames. There was a marina below them. She remembered that nine years ago he had been in the West Indies on a sailing holiday.

She struggled to sound polite, neutral, utterly indifferent. 'Did you buy this place so you could moor your yacht?' She only succeeded in sounding strained.

He looked amused. 'Not guilty.'

She was so startled that she did look at him then. 'What?'

'You've developed a fine curl of the lip since the last time we met,' he explained. He strolled over to her side. 'It comes into play every time you mention me.' He folded his arms across his chest and surveyed her. 'Tell me, Rachel, why do you disapprove of me?'

She had no immediate response to this head-on attack.

'I don't...' she began, floundering.

'Yes, you do. It shows. Even my staff have noticed.'

Rachel raised her eyebrows, returning gratefully to mockery. 'Your *staff*? That's bad.'

'I don't like it.'

The admission almost made her laugh aloud. But she primmed her mouth and tried to look solicitous. 'Image taking a beating, is it?'

'I think my credibility will survive a little longer.'

'Well, of course it will,' she congratulated him. 'It can't make that much difference that one insignificant clerk doesn't like working for you.'

He chuckled. 'Hardly insignificant. You pack quite a punch these days.'

'You flatter me. But I still don't think you or anyone else in your organisation gives a damn whether I'm happy in my work.'

He was still looking as if he was enjoying himself, damn him.

'You're a hard woman, Rachel.' He shook his head mournfully.

She pretended sudden enlightenment. 'Oh, *that's* the trouble. It's because I haven't fallen prostrate at your feet in adoration.'

His brows twitched together. Not enjoying himself quite so much now, thought Rachel. Their eyes clashed. Then he smiled, slowly, outrageously.

'Well, it's certainly got them talking,' he drawled.

Rachel gasped. She recovered at once. She did not like the implications of what he said but she was not going to admit it.

Instead she said with heavy irony, 'That must be a first.'

Riccardo sighed. 'Here we go again. Any minute now you're going to call me a playboy.'

A *playboy*? It did not begin to cover what she thought of him. But she was not going to be tempted into revealing her real feelings. Rachel turned away with a dismissive gesture.

Riccardo was not giving up. He turned her back to face him.

'No? Not a playboy? Or are you more tolerant of playboys these days?'

His hands on her made Rachel tense every muscle. You're in control, she reminded herself. He only sees what you let him. Don't give him a chance to see that he has any effect on you at all.

With an enormous effort of will she stood quiet in his hands. She even shrugged.

He shook her slightly.

'Talk to me, Rachel.'

Some of Rachel's careful indifference slipped.

'Take your hands off me,' she flashed.

His eyebrows rose, but he did not look exactly displeased. He stepped back and raised his hands comically, like a cowboy facing a toy gun.

'OK. OK. No touching. Just talk.'

She turned away, annoyed with herself. 'We have already talked.'

He shook his head slowly. 'I don't think so.' He hesitated. Then he said, as if he was choosing his words carefully, 'You're a key person in the team, Rachel. I can't afford to have you muttering behind my back.'

So that was it. She laughed angrily.

'Don't worry. I don't discuss my private opinions with colleagues,' she said curtly.

'That's not quite what I meant.'

She swung back on him. 'Nor do I lie about them.'

He frowned. 'Have I asked you to?'

Her chin came up. She braced herself for battle. 'If you don't like it—'

'I don't.'

'—then you'll just have to…' Rachel ground to a halt. 'What?'

'I don't like your opinion of me,' he said in his most reasonable voice. 'I want to find out why you feel the way you do about me. And then I want to change it.'

Rachel met his eyes and saw that he meant it. There was a short, shocked silence. Her burgeoning temper disappeared, to be replaced by something a lot more complicated.

She said breathlessly at last, 'You're not going to stay in London. We won't have to work closely. It can't be important.'

He just looked at her steadily, not speaking.

She said in exasperation, 'I don't see why you should give a damn what I think of you.'

'Don't you?'

'Some people just don't get on. It's chemistry or something.'

There was a pause.

Then he said quietly, 'Yes. I remember the chemistry.'

Rachel jumped. Her spine seemed to turn to rubber and go into free fall. She could not think of a thing to say.

'It was—quite something, as I recall.'

Rachel swallowed. 'Really.'

He looked down at her, his face serious. 'Are you saying you don't remember?'

Under that intense inspection, Rachel felt as if she could hardly breathe. She turned her face away. She managed a laugh. It sounded harsh. 'One night? Nine years ago?'

Riccardo's expression darkened. He began to drawl. 'Unlikely, I agree. But the circumstances alone made it memorable.'

'Not to me.'

His brows rose. 'You mean you turned it into a habit? Now, that does surprise me.'

Rachel did not trust herself to speak.

He said reflectively, 'I'd never done anything like that before.'

She snorted.

'You were an unknown quantity. A stranger. I'd always known all my girlfriends through and through. Just like they knew me.'

Rachel gave a nasty smile. 'You mean you both knew the limits of the deal. How convenient.'

To her astonishment, Riccardo's chin went up as if she had hit him. For a moment she thought she had penetrated that armour of his. But then the steep eyelids drooped to hide his expression.

'I couldn't have put it better myself,' he agreed lazily. 'I knew the terms of my deal. So tell me, what were yours?'

'Mine!' She was bitterly scornful. 'You're forgetting: I was too young to know about deals.'

'Yes?'

He was not showing a glimmer of conscience. His eyes were watchful. 'So what happened was purely spontaneous? No calculations? No prior research into the di Stefano millions? Just overwhelming attraction you couldn't run away from?'

Damn, thought Rachel. He had been leading her towards that damaging admission from the moment she'd walked in and she had not had the wit to see it. The silence screamed.

At last she said, 'I don't remember. I keep telling you, it's a long time ago.'

'You remembered enough to time your holidays from Bentley's in order to avoid me,' he pointed out.

There was no answer to that.

She tried to sound cool, logical. 'Well, of course, I remember what *happened*. I'm just not that certain what I felt.'

'No?' He was almost purring. 'Yet you said last night it

was a disaster. An adolescent disaster, if I remember correctly.'

Rachel stared at him, hot-eyed. He was right, of course. Right and clever and utterly without compunction. She could have screamed. But under the anger a slow, horrifying sense of having been cornered by a master huntsman was seeping through her.

She broke away from that mesmerising gaze.

'I also told you last night I don't like post-mortems. What happened between you and me is ancient history and should be forgotten.'

'Have you forgotten?'

'I told you—'

'You told me a number of things,' said Riccardo di Stefano. 'Most of them contradictory. I don't think you know yourself what's true and what isn't any more. Or,' he added, suddenly grim, 'how much you've forgotten. Let's see, shall we?'

Rachel knew he was going to touch her. She knew she ought to move. But her muscles seemed to have locked. All she could do was close her eyes, to shut out that towering figure.

It was a mistake. A terrible mistake. With her eyes closed, she was back nine years in that quiet little room, listening to the old-fashioned fan, the cicadas outside, and their breathing.

This time she was wearing layers of sober cloth and a blouse that buttoned to the neck, not a disastrously tangled sarong. When his practised fingers drifted up her arm in a cruel imitation of love, they no longer encountered bare flesh.

It made no difference. The hurried sounds of their breathing were exactly the same. And she recognised in a flash of insight that Riccardo knew it too. He laughed under his breath.

'Same old instincts, I see.' His voice was not entirely steady.

This time it was not longing which hit Rachel. It was fear, naked and shocking. Her eyes flew open.

'Never again.' She almost screamed it.

The intensity of it shook both of them. He let her go. A blank look invaded his eyes. She stepped back, smoothing the dark sleeve of her jacket with fingers that shook.

'I'm sorry.' She sounded as shaken as she felt. 'I didn't mean to sound like a fishwife. I just meant...'

The blank look disappeared. It was replaced by cold anger. 'It was perfectly clear what you meant,' Riccardo said with bite.

Rachel swallowed. The anger beat at her, making her feel vulnerable and unsure. She shook herself. She might not have chosen to lose her cool and yell at him like that but, now that she had, at least it had made her point, she thought.

'Then perhaps you will accept that I mean what I say,' she said quietly.

He did not answer at once. His eyes flickered. His expression became an unreadable mask.

Eventually he said, 'I accept this is going to be...' he hesitated '...a challenge.'

It was, she could see, another piece of deliberate provocation. He was watching her clinically, like a scientist viewing an experiment, to see how she would respond. Rachel decided to surprise him.

'A short-lived challenge,' she said drily.

Riccardo raised his eyebrows. 'Because you're going to give in gracefully?'

'Because you're going back to New York this Thursday,' she pointed out sweetly.

Suddenly his expression was no longer a mask. His imminent departure must have slipped his mind in the heat of battle, Rachel thought, pleased. For a moment he looked furious.

'That is not—' He caught himself, biting off whatever he was going to say.

As if it had never been, the fury was gone. He lifted one shoulder in a negligent shrug that disclaimed any feeling at all. Rachel's eyes narrowed suspiciously. He saw it. His mouth tilted in appreciation.

He said solemnly, 'So I am. I'm really glad you reminded me.'

It was smoothly spoken but Rachel heard a threat in it. She backed off.

He sighed. 'No need to look like that. You've made your point. I concede.'

She looked at him warily. She did not believe him for a moment. Riccardo di Stefano was not a man to concede a fight unless it was part of a wider battle plan. The same battle. With her defences weakening all the time.

She almost jumped at the thought. Two days ago she would have said it was inconceivable that she could ever be tempted by Riccardo di Stefano again. Today she was honest enough to admit—to herself at least—that the temptation was still there. He looked at her, touched her—and she could feel her defences dissolving.

I must be *mad*, she thought. The sooner he went back to New York the better.

Unguarded, she said so. His lips twitched. She could feel the heat rising in her cheeks. But all he said was, 'Come and eat. The directors' kitchen has sent someone over. The food should be good.'

It was. It was also served by a formally suited waiter. At a stroke it destroyed the atmosphere of dangerous intimacy.

It was a relief. She told herself that it was an enormous relief. Unfortunately, a part of her was also disappointed. Because she had wanted to finish the fight, Rachel told herself. She did not quite believe it—and was furious with herself.

Riccardo adjusted smoothly to the presence of a third party. He seated her, plied her solicitously with wine and set about a social conversation that felt like an inquisition.

'Why banking?'

Rachel was struggling to hide her uneaten pasta under her cutlery. 'Bentley's were the first to offer me a job after my MBA.'

'All right, why a business degree? I know your father was a wheeler-dealer but I don't remember you being interested in business.'

'I don't remember you noticing what I was interested in,' flashed Rachel.

It did not take his satisfied smile to tell her she had made a mistake. She pushed irritatedly at her spaghetti carbonara.

He was too subtle to point it out, however.

She bit her lip and said with constraint, 'My father's company collapsed. I got used to listening.'

'Did you work with your father?'

Rachel found she could not face the spaghetti after all. She put down the forkful.

'No.'

'Why not?'

'Because... It's complicated.'

He leaned back in his chair, one casual arm resting on the table. 'I'm good at unravelling complications.'

Rachel shuddered at the thought of his unravelling this particular one.

'We had some difficulties,' she said briefly.

She saw him store away the information for future use.

'When did you meet Brian Gray?'

'I worked for him.'

He frowned. 'He was at Bentley's?'

Rachel hesitated. Did she want to tell him the truth? Would it lead him into further, more painful deductions? But in the end it seemed easier. She had not had enough practice to go on lying successfully if he asked further questions.

So she shrugged and told him unemotionally, 'No. Before my degree. After his first wife left, I worked for him as an au pair.'

Riccardo was frankly incredulous. 'An au pair?'

'He needed someone to look after the children. I needed a job and somewhere to live while I did my degree. It was ideal for both of us.'

He digested that. 'Was that why you married him? Mutual convenience?'

Rachel almost jumped. She looked round but the waiter had retired to the kitchen with their dirty plates.

She said carefully, 'We grew to know each other very well.'

He brooded.

'So when you married him you must have already known the children.' He looked up suddenly, his eyes like lasers. 'Fond of children, Rachel?'

'Not all children,' she said steadily.

'But these children? Alexandra and whatever-his-name-is? Fond of them, are you?'

'Of course.'

He nodded, as if that was what he'd expected. His voice was almost idle when he said, 'Fond enough to marry a man twenty years older than you so you could look after them?'

Rachel stared at the glass in her hand. Oh, Riccardo di Stefano was too clever. Too clever and too damned determined. He had a battle plan all right. It was going to take all her skill to get out of this one.

She put down her wine. 'Look, I'm sorry. I haven't much of an appetite and I really ought to be going. I need to pack.'

His eyes flickered at the information. Rachel was too perturbed to notice.

He said easily, 'Well, at least have a coffee before you go. Tell me about your delightful stepdaughter. What is wrong with the boyfriend?'

Rachel was relieved at the change of subject. This was one subject at least on which she could afford to tell the truth.

'Well, he's so much older—'

His look mocked her. She flushed but said hotly, 'At that age it's a big deal. He has no job and too much money. He gives her things all the time—'

'Ah,' he said. 'Very suspicious.'

It sounded like an accusation. She was taken aback. 'What?'

'Well, it's not really your style, is it, Rachel? Real women don't accept things from a man.' He gave a soft laugh but he did not really sound amused. 'Does it contaminate their independence irretrievably? You know, I think your stepdaughter has my sympathy.'

She stared. She sought for the reason for this veiled attack. A few moments' reflection gave it to her.

'Is this because I didn't say thank you for all those flowers this morning?' She got up and said without expression, 'Thank you. I was overwhelmed.'

He stood up too. His face was quite unreadable but the force of the movement sent his chair tipping over backwards behind him.

Rachel was suddenly afraid. It infuriated her. 'They weren't a gift. They were a message. You were telling the whole bank that you had the right to send me any damned thing you wanted. Well, now they know and my office looks like a jungle. Happy?'

'You are as original in your gratitude as you are in everything else,' he murmured.

Rachel snorted. 'I saw the florist you use as I was coming up. I suppose I should just be thankful you don't happen to have a chocolatier in your building, or my office would be a candy warehouse by now.'

This time the pause felt dangerous. Then, just as she was bracing herself to turn and run for the lift, Riccardo burst out laughing.

'Oh, Rachel, what a firebrand you are. You can find more reasons to start a fight than any woman I know.' He seized her hand and held it between both of his. 'Yes, I know—you want to go. I won't stop you. This time.'

She felt the warmth of his palm, the strength of his fingers... A little bit more of her defences fizzed and disappeared. Rachel tugged her hand away.

'Goodbye.' She meant to sound decisive and in control. She did not. Even to her own ears she sounded on the edge of panic.

But he let her go easily enough.

He said, 'Not goodbye. You can't expect to have it all your own way.'

Rachel was turning away. She looked back at that. 'I don't know what you mean.'

The smile he gave her was caressing. 'You start the fights, darling. Leave me to finish them.'

CHAPTER NINE

RICCARDO'S words stayed with Rachel all afternoon. She raced through her work and dashed home to pack. She turned the radio up high but it did not drown out that amused, determined voice.

What had he meant? Rachel tried to convince herself that he'd meant nothing, that he had just been trying to worry her. But she could not. She might not have seen Riccardo di Stefano for nine years but in some ways she knew him as well as she knew herself, she thought. She knew he did not make empty threats.

She tried to put it out of her mind. She had to talk to Alexandra and she needed her whole mind on the conversation.

She picked her up from school. Alexandra got into the car. She was evidently torn between satisfaction at getting a lift on a rainy day and wariness.

'Girl talk?' she demanded suspiciously, lobbing her bag into the back seat.

Rachel concentrated on pulling the car out of the double-parked whirlwind outside the crowded school gates.

She chose her words with care. 'Not unless you want to.'

Alexandra shook back her hair defiantly. 'If you think you can talk me out of seeing Theo, you can think again.'

Rachel did not rise to that one.

'I've talked to Mother,' Alexandra announced. 'She says she doesn't see anything wrong with it.'

'Well, that's a body-blow for me,' said Rachel gravely.

Alexandra bit back a snort of laughter. 'She *is* my mother.'

'And she doesn't know Theo.'

The atmosphere chilled perceptibly.

'Nor do you. He's got a lot of potential. It's just that people are prejudiced against him.'

Rachel groaned. 'Don't tell me. The world doesn't understand him.'

'Oh, you're so cynical,' burst out Alexandra. 'Why can't you give people the benefit of the doubt, try being openhearted for once?'

Rachel thought about her interview with Riccardo di Stefano. She had hardly been open-hearted there. On the other hand, that was the legacy of painful personal experience. Were you supposed to chuck out what you had learned and pretend that people were trustworthy when you had serious evidence that they were not?

She said sadly, 'Maybe I am. Maybe your way is better. Perhaps if you trust people to behave well even the worst of them can rise to the occasion.'

She felt Alexandra staring at her. Rachel could feel her astonishment. She drew a deep breath and launched into the speech she had been preparing all day.

She said quietly, 'Lexy, I have no right to give you advice. I haven't run my life well enough to think that I know better than you. But… Well, there was a time when I wasn't cynical enough. You probably won't believe it and I don't want to drag out all the gory details. But, believe me, it changed my whole life. Not for the better. I wouldn't want that to happen you.'

There was silence for a considerable time. Then Alexandra said in a small voice, 'Is that why you work all the time?'

It was Rachel's turn to be astonished. 'Do I?'

'More and more. Hugh says it's because you are so ambitious.' She ended on a faint note of query.

Rachel turned the car carefully onto the dual carriageway.

'And what do you think?'

Alexandra hesitated. Then she said slowly, 'There's a prefect at school. She's very clever. Always in the library. She used to go out with Nick Dorset. He ditched her after the school trip to France. Now she doesn't do anything except pass exams.'

Rachel caught her breath. At fifteen her stepdaughter was more perceptive than she had bargained for.

She said involuntarily, 'You're growing up.'

It was the wrong thing to say, of course. Hopelessly wrong. Alexandra was immediately insulted and said so.

'I *am* grown-up. Why won't you realise it? Does it push you over the hill, or something? Is that a problem for you? You don't respect me. You never have.'

The tirade went on until they reached home.

There were several messages on the answering machine— Mandy with the arrangements for her trip to Aberdeen, Gilly saying she would be delighted to have Alexandra to stay if she wanted, the cleaning lady promising to provide the children's evening meal. Alexandra listened, her face growing tighter and tighter. When the final beep announced the end of the tape she swung round on Rachel.

'You're going away,' she said tragically.

Rachel felt instantly guilty. 'Only until the weekend.'

'*Why?*'

'Work, I'm afraid,' she said, trying to forget that it also conveniently removed her from Riccardo's vicinity until he was safely on the plane back to his country.

'You don't care about us.'

'Of course I care.' Rachel's guilt was swamped by justifiable frustration. 'I'll be back in time to stop you going to the all-night rave with Theo,' she added.

Alexandra was not amused. She stamped. 'You're laughing at me. I *hate* you.'

She fled upstairs. Rachel sighed, shrugged and went to check her packing.

When Hugh came in, her bag was waiting in the hall

and she was going through her briefcase. He stopped, swinging his schoolbag off his shoulders. He raised his eyebrows at the waiting luggage.

Rachel nodded. 'I'm afraid so. Only a couple of days this time. I'm back on Thursday night. Can you cope? Lexy can go to Gilly's if it's too much to ask.'

'She'll do her homework or I'll beat her,' said Hugh, grinding his teeth horribly. 'Of course I can cope. Lexy doesn't have fights with me.'

That was true. Rachel was still worried, though.

'If Theo turns up…'

Hugh's face closed. Suddenly he looked a lot older than his seventeen years.

'I can deal with Theo Judd. He won't try anything.'

'Well, if you have any trouble—'

'I'll lock Lexy in her room and plant a hedge of thorn-bushes,' he said impatiently. 'Don't worry. She's not as big a fool as you think she is.'

There was a swish of tyres, then an impatient honk from outside. The story of my life, thought Rachel.

She called upstairs, 'I'm off now, Lexy. Goodbye.'

There was no answer.

'I'll break it to her that I'm in charge,' Hugh offered.

Rachel hesitated, but she really did not have many options. She gave him a quick hug.

'You're a rock, Hugh.'

He hugged her back. 'Go for it, Killer.'

Rachel picked up her overnight bag and looped it over her shoulder.

'I'll call you from Scotland, let you have my number at the hotel.'

Hugh snapped her briefcase shut and opened the front door. He jerked his head at the door in a gesture of dismissal.

'Fine, if it makes you feel better. But nothing will happen.'

Rachel grimaced. She wished that had not sounded so

much like a challenge to the gods. But she did not have time to discuss it further. Hugh put her briefcase in the car. He even permitted her to plant a brief kiss on his cheek as she got in.

'Don't *worry*.'

It was easy enough to say, thought Rachel as she settled onto her seat on the last shuttle of the day. Not so easy to put into practice. It was not that she did not trust them, she thought, but she saw how young they were, how vulnerable in their youth. How did you get that across without destroying their confidence completely, or else sounding paranoid?

She let her head fall back against the cushioned airline seat and closed her eyes. If only she could forget how it had hurt when her father had rejected her. She turned her head on the cushion restlessly. If only she could forget the even worse hurt: the weeks she'd waited when Riccardo had not come for her, the slow realisation that he was never going to come for her. She thought, What is wrong with me? I have not thought about this for years.

There was not much doubt why it had surfaced now and it was not Alexandra's behaviour. It was just something else to chalk up to Riccardo di Stefano's account.

She remembered his behaviour at lunch and set her jaw. I have made a good life for me and the children, she told herself. That is the thing to remember, not ancient history. No matter what Riccardo di Stefano says, there is no unfinished business between us.

She was still telling herself that when she emerged from the airport into a grey, windy evening. Rain was bouncing up from puddles. Rachel huddled the collar of her suit round her face, thinking bitterly that she would have refused to make this journey but for Riccardo. By the time she got to her hotel she was shivering as much from temper as the drenching.

'Mrs Gray?' said the pleasant uniformed girl at the desk.

'Yes, of course your room has been reserved. Will your husband be joining you?'

Rachel closed her eyes briefly. The girl might be pretty and efficient but she had a lot to learn in the way of tact.

'I doubt it,' she said with restraint. 'Tell Mr Torrance I've arrived when he comes in, will you, please?'

She found she had a huge room which was clearly part of a suite. The door to the adjoining room was locked. She bounced experimentally on the side of the enormous four-poster bed. When she sat on it, her feet did not touch the floor. Rachel stretched luxuriously, then grimaced as her jacket stretched clammily. Her suit was soaked.

The bath was the size of a ship. Fortunately there was more than enough hot water to fill it and the hotel helpfully provided small bottles of heather-scented oils and lotions. Rachel stripped off and sank back into scented steam.

'Thank God I packed a cocktail dress. I wonder how Colin would like to have dinner with a boss in a bathrobe?' she mused.

It was an entertaining thought. She chuckled, giving herself up to relaxation for the first time in what felt like days. Eventually her teeth stopped chattering.

The telephone on the wall rang.

'Hello?'

'Colin Torrance. Had a good journey?'

'I got wet.'

He laughed. 'We have a good bit of weather up here. Wait till you see the views, though. This place is spectacular in a storm.'

'I look forward to it,' said Rachel untruthfully. 'Downstairs in thirty minutes?'

She swirled her hair up in a towel, slid into the thick hotel robe that she was not going to have to wear for dinner and dialled home. Alexandra answered. Questioned, she admitted that she was finishing a history project which had to be given in the next day. Hugh took the phone from her.

'She's got books all over the floor and Susanna and Erica are here. They'll be lucky if they finish before dawn,' he said tolerantly.

'No Theo?'

'No.'

'Thank God,' said Rachel devoutly. She sent them all her love, promised to bring back the biggest box of short-bread she could find and rang off.

Her hair was too damp to pin up. She hesitated over using the hotel drier but she knew that it would only fluff her hair up uncontrollably. In the end she compromised, leaving it loose but pinning it back off her face.

She caught sight of her reflection and stopped, discon-certed. The red-gold waves reflected bronze lights from her smart cocktail dress. It made her look unexpectedly friv-olous. Colin Torrance, she thought, would be astonished.

She went downstairs, pausing by the hotel manager's desk.

'I've left a suit hanging on the back of my door. It needs cleaning and pressing. Could you organise that, please?'

'Of course, madam. What room number, please?'

Rachel checked her keyring. Further down the lobby desk, the teenage enthusiast who'd signed her in was wav-ing excitedly.

'Three-three-one,' Rachel said. 'Yes?' she added, to the receptionist.

'Mrs Gray, your husband called.'

That child needs more than lessons in tact, Rachel thought. She needs a brain transplant. She was about to say so when she saw Colin Torrance across in the bar.

So she contented herself with saying crisply to the girl, 'I don't think so,' before she went over to him.

He had been polite in her office but now he was posi-tively effusive.

'It's a relief you're here,' Colin admitted. 'I can handle the lending but when it comes to the whole package— well—' He flung out his hands. 'They seem to think they've locked in the Far East orders, but I'm not so sure. And as for the currency risk—I don't think it's even occurred to them!'

'Why couldn't you say that in your report?'

He looked wry. 'We may be advising the company but there is a real power battle between father and son on the board. The last thing I want to do is get browbeaten into taking sides before I understand what's going on.'

'And the company is seeing the interim reports before you send them to head office?'

'Well, the board does.' Correctly sensing her annoyance, he added defensively, 'They insisted. It's in the contract.'

Rachel frowned. 'Heaven preserve me from companies who pay for advice they don't want. Presumably they think you're just up here to endorse one side or the other?'

He was philosophical. 'It's happened before. And Philip told me to keep the whole board sweet. We want that account.'

'Someone should tell Philip about logical impossibilities,' muttered Rachel. 'OK, give me a run-down on the personalities.'

Colin looked out of the window. Outside the rain was lashing at the window so hard that it was impossible to see across the road.

'Over dinner? I was thinking of taking you to a very good little Italian place but it might be better to eat here. It's very expensive and a bit—er—formal but we shouldn't have trouble getting a table on a night like this.'

Rachel shuddered at the thought of going out of doors again.

'Definitely here,' she said firmly. 'Bentley's can afford it.'

When they went into the dining room, however, she was taken aback.

'Formal? You have a gift for understatement, Colin.'

The tall Edwardian room had lowered its lights to the faintest of background glows. Illumination of the food was provided by candles in rose-decked candle-holders. The tables were covered with crisp linen and an Aladdin's treasury of glimmering goblets and silver. In one corner a pianist in a smoking jacket played Cole Porter by the light of a candelabra.

'Good grief,' said Rachel with feeling. She touched her bronze skirt as if it were a talisman. 'Do you realise that if my suit had not got soaked at the airport I would be seriously underdressed?'

Colin gave her a faint, uncomprehending smile. They were shown to a discreet corner table. The waiter whispered a welcome and presented them each with an enormous leather-bound menu. Rachel's had no prices. She began to feel an overwhelming urge to giggle.

'This place could give the Tunnel of Love a run for its money,' she said. 'Anyone sees us here and it's the end of your reputation. Probably mine as well. I thought seduction parlours like this went out in the naughty nineties.'

But Colin, a conscientious husband and father, did not see the funny side of it. He kept apologising for the room being too dark for her to read any of the papers he wanted to pass across the table to her.

'Give them to me later,' said Rachel impatiently. 'Just tell me your impressions so far.'

But Colin was worried about client confidentiality. He did not want to name names or say anything which could be overheard and correctly interpreted. As the dining room filled up he became increasingly agitated at the thought of industrial espionage by their fellow diners. In the end he resolved the dilemma by moving his seat to Rachel's right and murmuring about boardroom squabbles in her ear.

By the end of the meal it was not just the ponderously romantic ambience that was making it difficult for Rachel not to laugh. She almost snatched the papers from his hand when they left the dining room. She declined a final coffee in a choking voice and made for her room.

When she got there, she laughed until she cried.

Eventually she sat up, wiped her smudged mascara and blew her nose.

Therapeutic, she decided.

For the first time in days she felt as if she could go to bed with a quiet mind. She undressed, brushed her hair until it jumped with static, and tumbled between deliciously laundered sheets.

'A good hotel,' she said drowsily, 'is halfway to paradise.'

It felt as if her head had hardly touched the pillow when she came out of her dreams with a jerk. She had been dreaming something fast and frightening. Her heart was still pounding as she fought her way back to consciousness. Once her eyes were open, though, she lost all memory of what it was that had frightened her.

She lay there, listening to the strange night sounds of the hotel. It made her feel oddly free. She had thrown back the curtains when she'd come in last night. Now she could see a distant streetlight and the pointed roof of a church, like a woodcut from a children's story book.

Somewhere out there, she thought lazily, there is the big shiny moon. She even toyed with the idea of getting up to look at it. But she was too comfortable. She plumped up her pillows and was beginning to turn over when something stopped her.

It was not a noise. Not a real noise. Not like voices in the corridor or tyres on the wet roads outside. Not even like a creaking door. It was more like a breath, as if some animal had managed to get into her room without her noticing.

Rachel was not afraid. But she was intrigued. She struggled up onto her elbow, listening.

Nothing.

But then her eyes accustomed themselves to the deep shadows in the room. She swivelled, inspecting the room. Door to the corridor. Big landscape on the wall. The picture was indistinguishable in the dark but the moonlight glinted off its protective glass, throwing off strange reflections. For a moment they looked almost like a man's shadow.

Rachel dismissed the fancy, letting her eyes travel on. Bathroom. Door to the adjoining room. Dressing table. Chair. Heavy curtains pulled back to frame the night skyline. And she saw him.

He was standing behind the chair, as still as the unstirring curtains. As still as if he were the real occupant and somebody else the intruder. Now that she looked, Rachel could see that the door to the adjoining room was open behind him.

She stayed there, poised on her elbow, transfixed. She knew she ought to be frightened. She knew she was not.

She also realised that she knew who it was.

Slowly, she sat up. The dark silhouette made no move but she knew he had seen her movement. Her heart began to patter lightly, very fast, somewhere in the region of her throat.

She thought, I don't believe this.

The dark figure came towards her. He was a broad-shouldered outline against the uncurtained window. It was like a dream. A dream she had had many times, Rachel thought now—though she had never admitted it. There was no whirring ceiling fan, no distant hush and lull of the ocean, no cicadas. But everything else was familiar—wholly and heartbreakingly familiar.

He shrugged off his jacket. It fell to the floor. Revealed, his open-necked shirt gleamed white in the moonlight. That, too, was familiar. Rachel said nothing. She sank back among the pillows, watching.

She knew that he was looking at her. He unlinked his cuffs and pulled the shirt over his head, letting it fall unheeded to the floor. A faint fragrance reached her. It spoke of limes and the open air. Rachel swallowed. Suddenly it was suffocatingly difficult to breathe. She put a hand to her throat. He stopped, standing very still for a moment.

'Don't,' he said softly. 'You're not frightened of me.'

His silence commanded an answer. Rachel swallowed again.

'No,' she agreed at last. It was a whisper, no more.

He reached down and took her hand away. She could feel in the darkness that he never took his eyes from her. He bent and set his lips very gently to the vulnerable place at the base of her throat where her pulse raced. A wild sensation swept through her.

It was like fire. Gasping, Rachel fell back. Her throat arched under his touch. Her hands reached for him. She was making small, desperate sounds that shocked some remote part of her brain. It was not the part that was in control.

Her unpractised hands tore at unfamiliar zips and fastenings, fumbling, impatient. He laughed a little and helped her. His breathing was nearly as ragged as her own.

And then he rid her of her nightdress with a speed that was not unpractised at all. It was a small thing—she barely noticed it in the headlong rush to strip away every last covering—but just for a moment she must have hesitated. He stopped as if she had stabbed him.

'No,' he said with deadly softness.

Rachel was bewildered. The sensation of skin against skin was so exquisite that she could hardly bear it. She did not know why he had stilled.

'What is it?' Her voice was slurred, almost unrecognisable.

'No more holding out.'

He was beside her, leaning over her, one hand in her hair. She moved her head restlessly and his hand tightened.

'No more.'

'I'm not holding out.' She sounded frantic, and very young all of a sudden. 'I'm not.'

She was almost faint with the intensity of her need. He must know that, with all that experience of his. Even in her extremity, the distant thought made her wince.

It seemed he did. He bent his head and kissed one lifting nipple slowly. Rachel cried out.

'Maybe not here.' She thought she could feel him smiling against the sensitised skin. His mouth drifted with agonising slowness to her other breast. She moaned. 'Or here.'

He reared up and looked down at her, taking her by surprise. Her eyes flew open. In the room's shadows his eyes were glittering. He touched her temple.

'But in there.' His voice was harsh. 'You're not giving an inch in there, are you?'

'What do you want me to give?' she whispered.

He almost shook her. 'Tell me. *Tell* me.'

So he wanted the complete surrender, in form, spelled out loud so that she could never pretend to forget again. Rachel thought she would die of shame. She shut her eyes tight. 'I want you.'

There, that would do, wouldn't it? That had to be what he wanted. It was the victory he had sought since the first moment he'd realised who she was on Monday.

It seemed it was not enough. He still held off from her.

'Tell me the truth. The whole truth. What happened all those years ago. *Why.*'

There was no escape. Despising herself, Rachel gave him the capitulation she knew he wanted.

'I always wanted you. In the Villa Azul. Afterwards. You said I did and you were right. I—never stopped wanting you.'

'Even when you ran out on me?'

She thought her heart would break. 'Even when I left,' she said steadily.

He bent his head. She thought he was going to kiss her mouth at last, but he was burying his face in her hair. His hands were unsteady.

'God, why did we waste so much time?' he said hoarsely.

He did kiss her then. For a moment she was startled. He

kissed her almost with desperation. But then, twining herself round him, Rachel thought, How could I have held out for so long? She was wrought to fever pitch, responding to his every touch, every murmur, almost every pulse beat.

Just for a moment he paused, cupping her face between his hands. She was breathing hard but he stilled her.

'We're supposed to be responsible adults.' There was that unmistakable note of laughter in his voice. He groped for his jacket and retrieved a small packet. He dropped it into her hand. 'Though you almost make me forget.'

Rachel's heart contracted. Then memory or instinct took over entirely. She stopped thinking at all.

Later they lay quiet, her head on his chest. It rose and fell with his quiet breathing. She thought he was asleep. His hand was curved round her shoulder as if he was saying, She is mine.

She should have resented that, Rachel thought drowsily, but she did not. She was touched to the heart by that small gesture of possession. Moved by something she did not understand, she kissed his chest quickly, shyly. As she drifted into sleep she was happier than she had ever been in her life.

When she woke it was different—altogether different. Riccardo was dressed and looking out of the window. The world beyond the window was grey with morning rain. Inside the atmosphere was almost as chilly.

Rachel struggled to full wakefulness, rubbing her eyes. 'What is it?'

He did not look at her. 'What is Torrance to you?'

'Colin?' Rachel blinked.

'The man you were having dinner with last night.'

'Why?'

He said with apparent irrelevance, 'You wouldn't have dinner with me.'

Rachel stared at his stiff back. 'What?'

'Do you know what you looked like?'

She did not answer. He did not seem to expect her to. He swung round.

'Lovers. That's what you looked like. I thought— But I was obviously wrong. Is he your lover, Rachel?'

She was so taken aback that she could not think of a thing to say. Riccardo seemed to take her silence for agreement. He laughed harshly.

'Has anyone ever known what they were getting in you, I wonder?'

Rachel shook her head, bewildered. 'I don't know what you're talking about.'

'Colin Torrance pushed a message under your door last night. Presumably when you and I were making love.'

Rachel winced. Riccardo was crumpling a piece of paper in his hand. He lobbed it across the room savagely.

'Message?'

'He wants to make sure you'll be discreet,' Riccardo told her. His voice was soft but it sounded like poison.

Rachel gasped.

'Look, you've got this all wrong,' she said, reaching out a pleading hand. 'Last night it was work. He sounded off about our boss. He just wants to make sure that I won't spill the beans when I get back to London.' Her voice rose on a note of desperation. 'He's a colleague, that's all.'

'You mean, just like I am?' Riccardo said. His smile was like a slap in the face.

Rachel's hand fell. She was growing angry.

She said with precision, 'I don't know what you are. Or what you think you're doing here. Are you going to tell me?'

He showed his teeth. 'I told you. Finishing unfinished business. And I'm the man you ran out on.'

'The man I—?' She looked round the room, on an outward puff of disbelief. 'You mean all those years ago? After the Villa Azul? I ran out on *you*?'

He said harshly, 'You knew where to find me. If you wanted to. I didn't know where to start.'

'You could have found out. Anders knew. Well, he could have asked Judy. At least…' Rachel remembered her father's frozen silence, the complete breakdown of communication.

'Judy said you'd moved out. So did your father. I concluded you wouldn't talk to me.'

Rachel was confounded. She had blamed him, *hated* him for not finding her. It had never occurred to her that he could have looked without success.

'I came to London. Then my uncle had his heart attack. The company went into a tail-spin. I had to deal with it. I went back to New York but I hired a detective. Another blank. Your father sent him away too. There were no records of you anywhere—no credit cards, no employment references.' His voice grew bitter suddenly. 'Of course, I didn't realise how young you were. I never thought of telling him to tour the schools.'

Rachel said numbly, 'I'd left school. I was staying with friends all through the summer. I never went to university. I got a live-in job…oh, October some time.'

'The detective just sent me a nil report. He said there was no point in going on. By that time he must have thought I was chasing a woman who didn't want anything to do with me, hounding her against her will.'

'No.' It was a strangled protest. She leaned forward. There was a moment of absolute silence. Now—*now*—it seemed they were telling each other the truth at last.

'So did I,' he said levelly.

It hung in the air, waiting for an answer. Rachel moistened her lips. This had to be the most important answer of her life.

The telephone by her bed rang shrilly. She jumped. Riccardo raised his head. His eyes were hard. The moment of possible understanding had gone as if it had never been.

'If that's Torrance, get rid of him,' he said curtly.

But it was not Colin Torrance. It was Hugh. There had been an all-night party. The neighbours had complained to the police about the noise. And Alexandra had run off with Theo Judd.

CHAPTER TEN

RICCARDO took charge. While Rachel packed and cancelled her meeting he organised their journey. The first flight available was late afternoon.

'Then hire a plane,' he told his assistant curtly.

They flew back on a ten-seater executive jet. Rachel tried to thank him. He shrugged.

'I take it this is the boyfriend who makes you uneasy.'

'How did you know that?'

He gave a wintry smile. 'I listen when you talk to me. It doesn't happen so often.'

Which silenced Rachel.

The chauffeur, whom she recognised, met them at the airport. Riccardo handed her into the car and then went round and got in beside her. Rachel was startled.

'There's no need—' she began.

'Relax. You should know by now I'm not into kidnapping,' he said drily.

'But—'

'You're an independent woman and you can handle anything that hits you,' he supplied. 'I know. But this time you don't need to.'

Rachel stared. As if he could not help himself, he buffed her chin lightly. He was smiling, though it did not warm his eyes.

'Why don't you just lie back and enjoy?'

She had no answer.

When they got there, the house was a shambles. Not a room was unscathed. Rachel looked round the ruined hallway and sat down.

'Some party,' said Riccardo, his brows lifting.

Hugh came out of the kitchen. His face was worried. Rachel looked at him. 'What on earth happened?'

Hugh shuffled uncomfortably. 'The girls were all doing some project for school. It looked all right. I—er—went to a movie.'

'All night?' exclaimed Rachel.

Hugh looked even more uncomfortable. Riccardo touched her shoulder.

'I don't suppose he went alone. Then afterwards they went on somewhere to talk about the movie. Right?' he suggested in a tone of unholy amusement.

'Right.' Hugh nodded, relieved.

'And when he got back the party was in full swing.'

'Well—er—no. It was over. The—er—police...'

Rachel moaned. 'We were raided by the police?'

'It wasn't that bad,' Hugh hastened to assure her. 'Not raided. Just some neighbours complaining about the noise. When the Old Bill turned up, Theo took off.'

'Taking Lexy with him?'

Hugh looked guilty. 'No. That was later. I was pretty wound up when I found out what had been going on. We had a row. She said she was going to Theo and steamed out.'

Rachel stared at him, appalled.

'That was when I called you,' he finished defensively.

'Oh, Lord.' She did not know what to do. She could not think straight. She put her hands to her face. It was cold. 'What exactly did she say?'

Riccardo put both hands on her shoulders. The warmth of his palms felt as if it could put life into her shivering frame. Hardly knowing what she did, she put her head on one side and rubbed her cheek against the back of his hand. Briefly, his fingers tightened so hard that she felt as if he had taken hold of her bones.

But all he said was, 'Do you know where she went?'

Hugh was startled. 'Theo—'

'Bravado,' pointed out Riccardo. 'Never underestimate bravado. Have you actually checked?'

Hugh had not. Rachel got up.

'Gilly,' she said.

But Alexandra was not staying with her friend. Susanna was not at school after the night's excesses, however, and she knew Theo's address. She sounded worried at the thought that Alexandra might be with him there. Rachel wrote down the address, trying not to panic. When she rang off, Riccardo took the paper from her.

'I'll go.'

'But—'

'I bet she isn't there. She's probably sulking in a diner somewhere, writing her entrance speech. You stay here and wait for her. If by some chance she is there, she'll come back with me,' he said with superb arrogance.

Rachel found she did not doubt him.

He went. She shook herself and took charge of her life again. As a first step she sent Hugh to school with a note to excuse his lateness. Then she telephoned her secretary.

'No problem,' Mandy said. 'Colin's been in touch. He said it was a real help to talk things through with you. Even though you weren't there, he took a tough line this morning. The board have agreed. He says you don't need to go back unless you want to.'

'Great,' said Rachel, looking ruefully at the chaos that was her sitting room. 'I'll pass. Give him my congratulations. I won't be in until tomorrow. You can get me at home if you want me.'

She changed into her oldest clothes and set about restoring the house to normal. She was just finishing the stairs when she heard the sound of an engine. She straightened. The doorbell rang imperatively. She almost fell in her eagerness to reach it.

Riccardo was standing there, holding onto a wildly protesting Alexandra. True to his prediction, he had brought her home. Rachel was so thankful that she just flung her arms round her in a bear hug. Her stepdaughter clung.

Riccardo moved them in from the doorstep and closed the door behind them.

'She is unharmed,' he said to Rachel over the top of the weeping girl's head.

'Thank God.' She brushed the lacquered spikes of hair back. 'Oh, Lexy. What a fright you gave us.'

But Alexandra's tears were due to rage and affronted dignity, not guilt. She flung herself out of Rachel's arms and retreated to the wall. Her face was streaked with the remains of last night's make-up. She was in a tearing temper.

'Then it must be for the first time in your life,' she spat. 'You never notice what I'm doing except to spoil things.'

'That's not true—'

'Yes, it is. I talk and talk and talk and you just don't *listen* to me.'

Rachel was strongly moved to shout back in the same vein. She repressed it. Instead she sat down and folded her hands quietly in her lap.

'I'm listening now.'

Alexandra looked disgusted, and very young. 'Don't tell me—the thought police kick in.' She sounded young too. 'A final appeal to my conscience?'

Rachel shook her head. 'No appeal to anything.'

The front door banged and Hugh burst in. He was looking embarrassed and worried. But most of all he was just plain furious.

'You're back are you, you pinhead. Do you know the trouble you've caused?'

Rachel said warningly, 'Hugh—'

'Well, at least I—'

'Lexy—'

'You're no better than a groupie, running after Theo Judd with your tongue hanging out.'

Alexandra gave a scream of outrage and launched herself at Hugh. Riccardo caught her before she hit him.

'That's enough.' His tone was quiet but there was something in it that stopped both of them in their tracks.

He let Alexandra go and stepped back.

'Rachel has put her job on hold to listen to you today,' he told Alexandra crisply. 'So talk.'

She tossed her head, glaring at her brother. 'With the last ninety-year-old A-level entrant taking notes?'

Hugh started forward in protest. Riccardo stopped him. He put just a simple hand on his arm but it was enough. Riccardo was watching Rachel unblinkingly.

Alexandra sneered, 'Go on, say it, Hugh. I'm too young. Too stupid. I'm only a kid. I should listen to the grown-ups—and sensible, responsible people like boring Hugh Gray.'

There was a harsh pause. Rachel thought that, under the sneering expression, Alexandra did not look too far from tears. Her heart contracted with sympathy.

She stood up and went forward.

'Hugh doesn't have to say it, Lexy,' she said quietly. 'I will. I should have done a long time ago. I tried but—' She broke off, shaking her head.

There was no point in excusing herself. She had failed her stepdaughter. She must not fail her any more.

'I know you don't want to believe me, Lexy. But age does make a difference.'

'Yeah. I've noticed.'

'At your age people can think they want things—really want them—which they just don't understand a couple of years later, or sometimes a couple of months later.'

Alexandra snorted. 'I'll grow out of it?'

'If you want to put it like that.'

Even as she said it, Rachel knew it was a mistake. She did not want to let Alexandra down but this was not the way. She was going to have to be more honest than that.

Her stepdaughter smiled nastily. 'You mean I'll grow out of sex? Just like you did?'

Rachel's head went back as if at a blow. Across the room Riccardo went very still. Nobody noticed except Rachel. She was desperately conscious of that silent, watchful presence in the doorway. It made what she knew she had to do a thousand times more difficult.

Alexandra flung her chin up defiantly. 'Well, I don't want to grow out of it. I'd rather take a few risks on people. At least I'll still be *alive*.'

Rachel looked down at her hands. 'Well, at least you know Theo is a risk.'

She looked up quickly and caught Alexandra's involuntary recoil. Hugh drew in an audible breath.

Alexandra said furiously, 'You're trying to trick me into saying I don't trust him.'

'No.'

'Yes, you are. You said—'

'Theo is a risk. He is. We all are. Sex is. Life is.' She gave a little self-mocking laugh. 'My job at the bank is called risk management. It doesn't begin to look at the really big risks. And do you know what the biggest risk is, Lexy?'

'Families,' snarled Alexandra.

Rachel shook her head. 'Love.'

Alexandra cast her eyes to heaven. 'Oh, p-lease.'

Rachel winced. She drew in a careful breath. This was worse than she had imagined.

'I mean it,' she said steadily. 'Anything else, you've got a sporting chance. You can be careful, look at the downside, make a reasoned assessment, guard yourself if necessary. You know that. You know all about safe sex—you told me.' She carefully avoided looking at Riccardo. 'But there's no such thing as safe love. Once you're in love with someone, you're hooked. Vulnerable for ever. If they're hurt, you're hurt. If they cheat you, or let you down or just get bored...'

Rachel's voice cracked. She gave a quick shrug, turning her head away to hide her expression. She prayed that the immense effort that this was costing her did not show.

'There's nothing you can do to protect yourself against any of that. It hurts. It goes on hurting until, if you get really lucky, you fall out of love. Even then—well, you never forget what it was like. To be that badly hurt, I mean. It lasts. It's like a sort of poison you never get out of your system. You think you're cured and then—crash!—something reminds you and it's back, just as bad as ever.'

In the doorway Riccardo was standing like stone. Rachel thought, He knows it all now. It lacerated her. But there was no hope that he would be misled. He was the cleverest man she had ever known and he knew her better than anyone else had ever done. However much she might be able to convince Hugh or Alexandra, or even Gilly, that this was pure neutral observation, she would never get away with it with Riccardo. He knew it was personal. And he knew it was the unadorned truth.

In which case he would also know—or be able to work out all too soon—that she had fallen in love with him at the Villa Azul. That she been in love with him ever since. And that she had been in love with him last night.

Oh, Lexy, she thought, if you knew what I am doing for you.

Alexandra's eyes were fever-bright. 'I can take care of myself.'

Rachel felt the thread by which she was holding onto her temper tighten. How much self-revelation was her stepdaughter going to demand?

She said levelly, 'In most circumstances, I agree with you.'

'Well, then—'

'In *most* circumstances. You're practical. You're intelligent. You're brave. You're just not—' she searched for the right words '—very strong yet.'

Alexandra looked down her nose. 'Tosh.'

Rachel's temper snapped. 'You've got a brain. Use it. You've as good as admitted you know Theo is a risk. He is worse than that. He is a dead-certain disaster and everyone in this room knows it. Including you.'

It was the worst thing she could possibly have said. Alexandra flung herself away, a muscle in her cheek jumping. She picked up her bag defiantly. Hugh shook himself free of Riccardo's restraining hand.

Rachel was the only one in the room who did not move. She said quietly, 'It's not tosh. It's the truth. You're going to give him your heart and all he wants is to score.'

It was a brutal thing to say. They all knew it. Alexandra stopped dead. Rachel could feel everyone in the room staring at her, shocked. But the only expression she saw was Riccardo's. He was looking appalled.

Alexandra turned. Her face was so white that you could see the streaks of make-up where she had applied the false tan unevenly. Her mouth looked pinched suddenly.

'Have you got any proof?' she whispered.

'Oh, Lexy,' Rachel was almost crying herself.

'*Have* you?'

Rachel averted her eyes from Riccardo's expression.

'His whole life, love. You know it in your heart of hearts. He won't tell you anything about himself. Will he?'

Riccardo was very still. Alexandra did not notice but Rachel was so conscious of him that her bones burned. If she ended up without a shred of dignity after today—well, that was what she had been prepared for when she'd started this. There was no point in stopping now.

She said, 'He has his own friends. You don't even know who they are. Or what they do. You're just a—game for him.'

Riccardo drew a sharp breath. Rachel ignored him. Alexandra looked like the child she had been not so long ago, crying out with nightmares, wanting a reassuring story before she went back to sleep.

Rachel's heart twisted. For a moment she almost softened. But this was too important. She could not afford to weaken now, even though she felt as if she was scraping every word up from her deepest hurt.

'When I was young I did something very similar,' she said painfully.

The figure at the door stiffened. Rachel saw it and looked quickly away. Across the room his eyes were as black as coals in a great fire.

She said to Alexandra, 'I was older than you are. There was less excuse. Like you, I thought I knew what I was doing. I thought I was willing to take the consequences, live completely for a burning moment, then pay the price.' She laughed harshly. 'Joan of Arc has a lot to answer for.'

Riccardo did not move. But she could feel him watching her as if he had an arc light trained on her.

'It's not like that. When you're young, sex and love and the imagination are all tied up together. A sort of emotional primeval soup. It's no one's fault. It's just a stage of development. We all go through it. But if you're not careful, if you commit yourself too soon, too deep, you burn up all the oxygen too soon.'

Alexandra was staring. So was everyone else. Rachel felt naked. Riccardo would not be the only one who knew, after this.

She said, with the courage of exhaustion, 'You said you don't think I'm quite alive—not in the way that you are, willing to take a chance on Theo. I can't deny it. So ask yourself why I'm like that. And see if you can avoid going the same way.'

There was a truly horrible silence. Everybody was trying to avoid her eyes. Except for Riccardo. He seemed as if he could not look away. He looked stunned.

Rachel felt as if she had no shred of dignity left, no single defence that Riccardo could not see through as easily as gauze. But she lifted her chin and outfaced him.

As their eyes met, it was like an electric shock. Rachel

could feel it—could feel Riccardo feel it too. It seemed to drive him backwards with its force.

Alexandra gave a shattering sob.

'Oh *Rachel*.'

She flung herself against her stepmother's breast. Rachel's arms closed round the slight figure automatically. Across the dark head her eyes stayed on Riccardo, faintly questioning.

He looked back for what seemed like an eternity. She could not begin to read his expression. Then he made a quick, wholly characteristic gesture, setting himself at a distance from the tableau.

And, as Rachel stroked Alexandra's hair with a hand that shook, Riccardo turned on his heel and walked out of her house.

CHAPTER ELEVEN

IT WAS a bad moment. Rachel watched him go and felt as if the rest of her life had just left. What has happened to me? she thought. She held Alexandra and made soothing noises mechanically while she slowly allowed herself to realise the truth.

Nine years had passed and nothing had changed. She was still in love with Riccardo di Stefano. And she still did not have the faintest idea how he felt.

Except that he's just walked out, she reminded herself. That might just give you a clue.

She kept half an ear open for the telephone for the rest of the day. It rang but it was never Riccardo. And tomorrow he would be flying back to New York. Rachel stayed up till midnight but Riccardo did not come back to the house either. It was a tough day.

Breakfast the next morning felt more like a duel than a meal. Alexandra might have been feeling chastened but that did not change her attitude to her brother. Rachel made toast and refereed until they were both persuaded to go to school. She sank back, exhausted, but there was no respite. She had to go to work and she was already late.

'I know. I know,' she said to Geoff as she slid in through the swing-doors. 'Again. Mr Jensen been asking for me?'

The security guard shifted uncomfortably. 'Not Mr Jensen.'

Rachel raised her eyes to heaven. 'Clients! My stars. How do they find these things out? I was supposed to be in Aberdeen. Some of them must know when I change my toothpaste.'

Geoff grinned and indicated the private lift with a raised eyebrow.

'You're probably right,' agreed Rachel. 'The back stairs it is.'

She slipped round his desk gratefully. She was not so grateful when she reached her own floor. Her imagined client was already there, propping up the wall. He was clearly waiting for her.

Rachel's heart lurched. She felt a rush of warmth so great that it must have shown on her face. And then she remembered that he had walked out. She had no right to feel that gladness at the sight of him. She was only laying up hurt for herself all over again.

She nearly retreated back into the lift. But the doors had closed. So there was no alternative. Rachel stepped forward, her head high.

'Good morning.'

But Riccardo seemed to have lost patience with the courtesies. His jaw was tight. He had every appearance of a man looking for a fight.

'No, it isn't. It's a bloody awful morning. Where the hell have you been?'

Rachel stared. 'Keeping my stepchildren from each other's throats and getting them off to school,' she said literally.

His eyes narrowed. 'I thought nothing came between you and your work?'

She remembered telling him that. She shrugged uneasily. 'Well—'

'Or are children different? Is it only lovers who don't count?'

This was a battle with a vengeance. Rachel's face flamed. 'We are not lovers,' she choked. 'You have no right—'

'I have the right,' Riccardo said softly. His eyes were narrowed to slits of fury. 'I stood there yesterday and had to listen to you telling Lexy things you should have told me nine years ago. Don't talk to me about rights.'

'Oh,' said Rachel.

'And as for us not being lovers—what do you think we have been doing all this week?'

Rachel looked anxiously along the corridor. Fortunately there was no one in sight. Not that it would have deterred Riccardo from his purpose. That was all too evident. Rachel pressed her hands to her cheeks. Her face felt incandescent.

'That was just sex,' she managed.

Riccardo's lips tightened. 'Once. We slept together once.'

She flung her head back and glared at him. 'Quite.'

There was a sizzling silence.

'My God,' he said slowly. 'And I thought I never took anything on trust. I'm an amateur compared to you.'

Rachel sent him a glittering smile. 'Experience.'

She began to turn away. He stopped her by the simple expedient of putting a hand on her arm. Rachel's heart lurched again. The electrical recognition was still there.

In love with him and her body recognising his lightest touch! Heaven help me, she thought.

She shook him off and started off down the corridor. Her breathing was rapid. She hoped that he would ascribe it to the speed of her steps.

Riccardo kept pace with her. 'You can't walk away from me this time,' he told her quietly. 'I'm not letting it happen again.'

Rachel did not look at him. 'You have no choice.'

He gave a soundless laugh. 'Oh, yes, I have. This time I know what I'm dealing with.'

She stopped and swung round, glaring. 'If you're referring to the fact that I work for Bentley's, forget it. I can get another job, like *that*.' She snapped her fingers.

He looked amused for a moment. 'I'm sure you can. I wouldn't dream of using professional blackmail.'

'Then—'

'On the other hand,' he went on smoothly, 'we will be seeing each other all the time. Wouldn't it be better to clear the air?'

Rachel looked at him scornfully. 'Quite unnecessary. The first time we met you didn't know who I was. We can go back to that.'

Riccardo shook his head. 'Unrealistic. And I knew precisely who you were the moment you turned round when we were alone in the boardroom.' He laughed softly. 'Wild red hair all over the place, glaring at me. Of course I knew. I just had not made up my mind what to do about it.'

'And when did you decide?' Rachel said, goaded.

'At the board meeting, of course. Watching you fight for what you believed in. I thought, She hasn't changed.' He smiled down at her. 'I thought—I want her.'

Rachel was shaken. She had a sudden memory, almost physical, of the feeling she had had that first day when she'd seen him in the corridor. The precipice was still there; the mountain was still at her back. If anything it was even more cold and frightening.

Only, this time she knew what it was she was afraid of. It was not Riccardo di Stefano. It was herself. After all this time she was still in love with him. It looked as if she always would be. And all he could say was that he wanted her.

Rachel moistened dry lips. She said, 'Well, it may be a shock to you but you're not the only one involved here. I've taken some decisions too.' She turned and faced him. 'I don't want to see you again, Riccardo. Please respect that. If you don't, I shall leave Bentley's.'

She turned away before she could see his reaction. She could feel him watching her as she walked down the corridor to her own office. But he did not follow her.

In her room she sank bonelessly into her chair. She felt slightly sick. She dropped her head in her hands. What had she done?

I couldn't have taken it again, she told herself. I had to send him away. So Alexandra was right, said another part of her mind. You may not have outgrown normal feelings but you've dealt yourself out of living. Is that what you really want?

She rubbed her eyes. 'What I really want is Riccardo di Stefano. For ever.' She said it out loud. It sounded even worse than it felt. She winced. 'Face it. For ever is not his style. So I can't have him. So get on with your life, Rachel.'

She tried. She really tried for the whole day. By the end of it, her temples were throbbing with the effects of her mighty efforts. It did not seem to make much difference. Every time the door opened she looked up, half in hope, half in dread. It was never Riccardo.

When it was completely dark outside, she stood up, her hands to her aching back. She looked at her watch. Seven o'clock. He must be halfway over the Atlantic by now.

Her computer beeped. Wearily Rachel pushed buttons to retrieve the message. It was from Mandy.

Rachel, Hugh rang. Gas switched off at home. There's no heating and no hot water. So he and Alexandra have gone to Gilly's. I booked you a room at the Langbourne. Have a good weekend.

Great, thought Rachel. Still, thank God for secretaries with the initiative to save her from a freezing house. She rang Gilly.

'Yes, the children are here. Don't worry about a thing. They're actually talking to each other.'

'They must be up to something,' said their fond stepmother. She sent them her love and went off to the discreetly smart hotel that Mandy had organised.

When she arrived the luxury of the suite made her raise her eyebrows. It was a new hotel with a reputation to make but, even so, this was not going to be within her normal price range. There had to be a mistake over the booking. She was picking up the telephone to query it when there was a knock at the door.

Rachel got up and opened it. It was the man who should have just about been watching the end of the last in-flight movie coming into JFK. She fell back.

'Thank you,' he said, taking it as an invitation. He strolled in and closed the door behind him. 'Frankly, I've had enough of slithering round hotel rooms in the dark. It may be your fantasy but it is not comfortable.'

Rachel backed before him. 'My fantasy?' she said, totally bewildered. 'What do you mean?'

He laughed. 'What did you think I was doing, creeping into your room in Aberdeen? Not my usual form. But you said you could imagine your hero breaking into your room at midnight.'

'I didn't,' she gasped.

'Oh, but you did. "Like something out of a silent movie,"' he reminded her helpfully. 'I recall it clearly.'

Rachel had a blinding flash of memory. She had said something very like that, she realised. Now she thought about it, she could even remember when. When his chauffeur had carried her off to lunch, if she was right.

'You didn't take that seriously?'

'I take everything you say to me seriously.' Riccardo paused, then added thoughtfully, 'I drew the line at the mask, though.'

Rachel sat down on the edge of the bed rather suddenly. 'You're crazy.'

That interested him. 'Do you think so? I thought a mask might be difficult to explain if you lost your head and screamed for the management.'

'If *I* lost my head— Oh! You're impossible.'

A half-smile curled the handsome mouth. 'Incidentally,' he said idly, 'why didn't you, do you think?'

Rachel glowered. 'Yell for the hotel manager? I should

have done, the moment you showed up,' she hissed. 'I can't think why I didn't.'

His smile grew. 'You could have been half-asleep,' Riccardo said helpfully.

Rachel was outraged. 'You thought I was half-asleep and you still invaded my privacy?'

He chuckled. He did not need to remind her exactly how thoroughly he had invaded. Rachel began to feel very unsure all of a sudden.

He took pity on her and sat down—on the sofa, not next to her on the bed. 'To be honest, it was not the way I planned it at all,' he admitted. 'I arrived later than I expected. You were already having dinner. With Torrance.'

He sounded grim about that. Rachel remembered his anger over Colin. Had he been jealous? But, if so, why? You were not jealous about people unless you loved them. Were you? She almost demanded an explanation. But her courage failed. It would be so humiliating if she was wrong. She began to tremble, though.

Riccardo went on levelly, 'I decided I'd wait. Then I got a call from London. By the time I'd done with that you seemed to be asleep. I went back to my room.' He paused. 'I would have left you alone but you called out. It might have been a dream but I could not be sure. So I came in to you. And what happened, happened.'

Rachel remembered those dreams. She found she believed him. But she was not going to let him get away with it so easily.

'That still doesn't explain what you were doing in the room next to mine,' she pointed out. 'With the connecting door unlocked.'

Riccardo looked at her for a long moment. He showed no sign of remorse.

'Careful planning. Plus a good eye for an opportunity when it presented itself.' He sounded smug.

Rachel bounced on the spot, revolted. 'I have not,' she told him, 'presented myself to you in any way.'

He laughed again. 'Don't I know it,' he said ruefully. 'I've never cancelled so many meetings in my life. The day before yesterday. Yesterday. Next week's on hold. All thoroughly out of character. And all your fault.'

It shook her. She said, 'I don't believe it.'

He shrugged. 'Believe it or not. It's the truth.'

He leaned forward and smiled straight into her eyes. Rachel felt her senses reel. She could feel herself being drawn off down a path she had never dreamed of, with only Riccardo to show the way.

She brought herself back to the matter in hand with a mental shake. The other road was much too dangerous.

'How the hell did you get yourself installed in the room next to mine anyway?'

'Enterprise and a romantic receptionist.'

'What?'

He stood up and came over to the bed at last. She had discarded her jacket when she'd come in and now he undid the top two buttons of her businesslike blouse. He pushed it off one shoulder. Rachel's mouth went dry but she did not stop him.

Riccardo bent his head and began to kiss her shoulder without urgency. She felt the response in spite of herself.

She said in a high, hurried voice, 'Who told you the receptionist was romantic?'

'She did.'

His mouth barely touching her skin, he travelled along her collar-bone. Rachel could feel herself begin to shake. She could also feel herself tipping backwards dangerously. She swallowed and tried to concentrate on other things.

'When?' It was not much more than a squeak, she thought, disgusted with herself.

He lifted his head to answer her. Her eyes were losing focus. She knew he was smiling from his voice.

'When I arrived. I was annoyed about being late. She thought I was your husband. She said you weren't expecting me.' His eyes gleamed. 'What else could I do but agree?'

Rachel swallowed. 'Clever.'

'Lucky,' he said modestly.

He kissed her throat lingeringly. She felt herself sway back another dangerous ten degrees. 'And all because you *want* me,' she said bitterly. 'It hardly seems worth it, does it?'

There was a short, startled pause. Then Riccardo sat up. It was so far from what Rachel had been expecting that she collapsed in sheer astonishment. He looked down at her but he made no move to touch her.

'I think we may be at cross purposes here,' he said in quite a different tone. 'What exactly do you think is going on between you and me?'

Rachel winced. But she said steadily enough, 'You want to sleep with me. You're an attractive man and you don't see why you shouldn't have what you want.'

He looked as if he could not believe his ears.

Hurting herself more than him, she went on in a hard voice, 'I don't know if that's just because you think it was an untidy ending all those years ago, or whether you want to be the one to walk away this time—'

'Stop it.'

She fell silent. His eyes were blazing. She would not have thought that the cool Riccardo di Stefano could look so wild.

'You insult both of us.'

'Can the truth be an insult?'

'Truth!' He stood up on a surge of contempt. 'Let me show you the truth, Rachel McLaine. Then you tell me if I want to be the one who walks away.'

He strode across to a table under the window and picked up a small box. It looked like a jeweller's box, too big for a ring, too small for a necklace. He almost threw it at Rachel.

'Look.'

She struggled up and opened it. Inside there was something that looked like a pattern of tissue-paper, brown and ginger with a hint of apricot. She looked up, puzzled.

'What is it?'

He took it out of her hands. He handled it very gently. Rachel thought, He's done this a thousand times before.

He turned the thing round, disposing it tenderly over her palm, as if were a small animal. Rachel looked down at it. It began to fold into a familiar shape: a dried trumpet flower.

She said slowly, 'Hibiscus.'

'You were wearing it. Do you remember? When I went to your cabin, that was all that was left. It was tucked down between the pillows.'

Rachel touched one long dried petal with a fingertip.

'It must have fallen out of my hair. You kept it?'

He looked down at her, his mouth wry. 'If it hadn't been for that, I might have started to think you had never existed at all.'

She felt humbled.

Riccardo sat down beside her. He took her hand.

'Why did you disappear like that?' he asked quietly.

She folded her lips together. It hurt to remember. But with that dead flower in her hand she could not tell him anything but the truth.

'My father,' she said honestly. 'You don't know what it was like. He...' Her voice became suspended. She touched the flower, as if it were a talisman, and went on bravely. 'His business was in trouble. He'd married a woman half his age. She wanted to leave him. The easiest thing was to blame me.'

Riccardo stared. 'Blame you? Why? How?'

'I never thought a daughter of mine would behave like a slut,' her father had said, white-lipped. 'Judy can't handle it. You embarrassed her too much. You're old enough to make your own way in the world and that's clearly what you want. Get out of this house now and don't come back.'

For years Rachel had suppressed it. Now she said, 'He was floundering. He felt a failure. If he kicked me out, he felt he had taken control of his life again for a bit. I suppose he thought he would have a better chance of mending things if he and Judy were alone together.'

Riccardo took her chin and turned it to him. 'Kicked you out?' he echoed. 'Are you serious?'

She shrugged.

'Oh, my love.' He sounded remorseful enough now. 'I didn't know. How could he? You were so young.' He paused. 'I didn't know how young until this week. That didn't make me feel any better either.'

Rachel touched his face.

'Not that young. I knew what I was doing.'

'Did you?' He searched her face. All of a sudden he was desperately serious. 'Are you sure?'

'As sure as I am that I know what I'm doing now,' she said.

Rachel put the flower back in its box very carefully. She stood up and restored the box to the table. When she came back to him, she was undoing the remaining buttons of her blouse. She pulled it out of the waistband of her skirt. Riccardo watched her gravely.

She slipped the blouse off her shoulders. It fell to the floor unnoticed. His hands came out to her waist. He tipped his head forward, resting it against her breasts for a moment.

'I love you,' he said against her skin.

Rachel gave a long, sweet shiver. 'Make love to me,' she whispered.

He looked up then. Whatever it was that he read in her face, it seemed to lift a great burden off him. He reached up and pulled her down to him. Rachel went joyfully into his arms.

They lay breast to breast. Riccardo ran his hands over her skin as if he were reminding himself of every curve and texture.

'I never forgot.'

Rachel believed him. She was finding that her own hands knew his body as well as if it were her own.

'Nor me.'

'You were so special. So *real*. You didn't fit in at the Villa Azul. I did. I'd known people like that all my life. Been part of them. Suddenly I didn't want that any more.'

'No one would have guessed,' said Rachel ruefully.

He raised himself up on one elbow and looked down at her.

'I'd been working in Central America. I was running food into hill villages under siege. At the end of a year I was—different. I knew I had to go back to the family business. Apart from anything else, there were too many people dependent on it and no one but me to inherit. But I was kicking against it. When I talked to you, I thought, With her I could have some private happiness as well.'

Rachel smiled up at him. 'Only some?' she murmured.

He slid his hands under her, lifting her comprehensively against him. Her breath caught in her throat at the electric touch. Riccardo smiled, his eyes burning into hers.

'Maybe more than that.'

Rachel stretched against him provocatively.

Riccardo chuckled. 'Only a few hours ago you told me you never wanted to see me again,' he reminded her.

Rachel ran her hands through his hair, wonderingly. She could feel a laugh rising. 'Never underestimate the effects of bravado,' she reminded him solemnly.

She ran a finger up his spine. He gave a little shudder of sensation. She savoured it. He began to kiss her body slowly. It seemed as if he was taking infinite care of her. Rachel basked.

'I thought I meant it,' she murmured. 'At the time. Now you're here, I can't even remember why.' A thought occurred to her. 'How did you get here, by the way? Did you bribe my family or my secretary?'

She could feel him laugh against her skin. 'Does it matter?'

Her hands went round his body convulsively.

'No,' said Rachel on a long sigh. They both knew it was total surrender. 'No, it doesn't matter at all.'

He had reached the silken skin of her stomach. He raised his head and thoughtfully traced the contour of a hip-bone. He looked up, his eyes dancing.

'Then I'll tell you. It was both.'

'*What?*'

'But only on the strict understanding that I made an honest woman of you.'

She was blank. 'You're joking.'

Rachel tried to struggle up. Riccardo held her pinned in place with easy strength. He was laughing.

'On my honour. Marriage or nothing. Lexy was very precise. I think,' he added thoughtfully, 'she feels she's turning the tables a bit.'

'Lexy…?' Rachel was utterly bewildered. 'What are you talking about?'

'Conspiracy. Your nearest and dearest. Hugh turned off the gas. Lexy got the two of them beds for the night. Mandy booked the room I specified.' He leant back on one elbow. 'I organised it but cutting off the gas was Hugh's idea. I think that boy has promising managerial quality.'

Rachel was trying hard not to laugh. 'Really?'

'Really. Also bargaining skills. Same price as Lexy. Legal matrimony. Just what I had in mind, in fact.'

'What about me? What if I had something else in mind?' Rachel demanded, justifiably incensed.

He raised his eyebrows. 'Do you?'

Oh, that smile. It warmed you right through to your bones. It stopped the laughter right there in your throat. Which was not what Rachel wanted at all. She tossed her head, her loosened hair finally tumbling out of its pins, and would not answer.

Riccardo's hands moved, skilfully. Rachel gasped in spite of herself.

'Are you starting another fight, Rachel?' he murmured mischievously.

She moved, arching under his hands, reaching for him.

Her voice was thick with longing but there was answering laughter when she said, 'Only if you finish it.'

He bent his head to her mouth, the laughter dying on their lips.

'We'll finish it together,' he vowed.

Modern Romance™
...seduction and
passion guaranteed

Tender Romance™
...love affairs that
last a lifetime

Sensual Romance™
...sassy, sexy and
seductive

Blaze™
...sultry days and
steamy nights

Medical Romance™
...medical drama on
the pulse

Historical Romance™
...rich, vivid and
passionate

29 new titles every month.

*With all kinds of Romance for
every kind of mood...*

MILLS & BOON®

Makes any time special™

MAT4

MILLS & BOON®

Winner at

2001 IDEA INTERNATIONAL DESIGN EFFECTIVENESS AWARDS

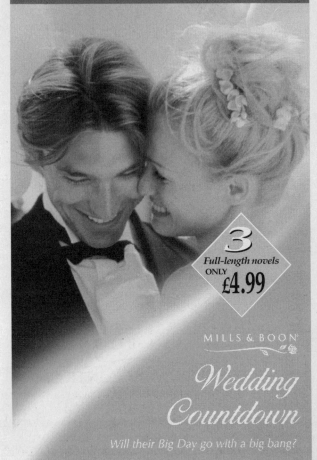

Coming in July

❦

The Ultimate Betty Neels Collection

❦

❋ A stunning 12 book collection beautifully packaged for you to collect each month from bestselling author Betty Neels.

❋ Loved by millions of women around the world, this collection of heartwarming stories will be a joy to treasure forever.

Available at most branches of WH Smith, Tesco, Martins, Borders, Eason, Sainsbury's and most good paperback bookshops.

MILLS & BOON®

heat
of the
night

LORI FOSTER
GINA WILKINS
VICKI LEWIS THOMPSON

3 SIZZLING SUMMER NOVELS

*Available at most branches of WH Smith,
Tesco, Martins, Borders, Eason, Sainsbury's
and most good paperback bookshops.*

SANDRA MARTON

raising the stakes

When passion is a gamble...

Available from 19th April 2002

MILLS & BOON
FOREIGN AFFAIRS
A captivating 12 book collection of sun-kissed seductions.
Enjoy romance around the world.
DON'T MISS BOOK 9
latin liaisons–
Red-hot husband material...
Available from 7th June
Available at most branches of WH Smith, Tesco, Martins, Borders, Eason, Sainsbury's and most good paperback bookshops.
FA/RTL/9